PRAISE F

M000316449

"A magnificent story, skillfu...
experience on the mission field."

—Don Stephens
FOUNDER OF MERCY SHIPS

"In his first book, Maya Hope, Dr. Timothy Browne draws from extensive international experience as an orthopedic surgeon to write a story filled with intrigue and authenticity. The book depicts great acts of evil – contrasted against loving, medical intervention on behalf of the poor and down trodden. In the midst of it all is the story of a doctor…a man who struggles to make sense of loss and grief as he encounters the greatest love of all."

—Jack Minton
CO-FOUNDER AND PRESIDENT OF HOPE FORCE INTERNATIONAL

"Dr. Tim Browne's service in many of the world's greatest areas of need – coupled with his extensive travel and knowledge of geo-political dynamics – create a recipe of adventure and authenticity…culminating in a thriller that is hard to put down until the very last page."

—Cherie Minton
CO-FOUNDER OF HOPE FORCE INTERNATIONAL

"A soul-stirring glimpse into the mercy heart of my friend, Dr. Browne. I was transported to the mission field through the eyes of compassion. Eagerly anticipating the next book in the series."

—Frank Cummings
SENIOR PASTOR OF LIFE FOR THE NATIONS

"Maya Hope has everything I like in a novel—a love story, a thriller that evolves like a movie, international settings and characters whose business deals take place in the shawdowlands between myth with murder, and a stumbling, self-centered man who reluctantly becomes a hero."

—Julia Loren, AUTHOR
THE FUTURE OF US: YOUR GUIDE TO PROPHECY, PRAYER AND THE COMING DAYS

What could be better than a medical thriller written by a physician? Not since COMA by Robin Cook, and The Andromeda Strain by Michael Crichton, have I been this excited about a medical thriller.

—Joni Fisher, AUTHOR
SOUTH OF JUSTICE (COMPASS CRIMES SERIES BOOK 1)

A
MEDICAL
THRILLER

MAYA HOPE

A Dr. Nicklaus Hart Novel

TIMOTHY BROWNE, MD

MAYA HOPE, *a medical thriller*
A Dr. Nicklaus Hart Novel
by Timothy Browne, MD

Second Edition © 2017

ISBN-13:   978-1-947545-00-7 (pb)
           978-1-947545-01-4 (epub)
           978-1-947545-02-1 (hb)

The events, peoples and incidents in this story are the sole product of the author's imagination. The story is fictitious, and any resemblance to individuals, living or dead, is purely coincidental. Historical, geographic, and political issues are based on fact; the stories of the children of Central America are based on truth, however, the names have been changed to protect the innocent.

Every effort has been made to be accurate. The author assumes no responsibility or liability for errors made in this book.

Scriptures quotations used in this book are from the HOLY BIBLE, NEW INTERNATIONAL VERSION. Copyright © 1973, 1978, 1984 International Bible Society. Used by permission of Zondervan Bible Publishers or from the NEW AMERICAN STANDARD BIBLE, Copyright © 1960, 1962, 1963, 1968, 1971, 1972, 1973, 1975, 1977, 1995 by The Lockman Foundation. Used by permission.*

Cover art, *Guatemala Jaguar Temple Tikal* ©Suzanne Parrott
Book layout & design by Suzanne Parrott

Flag of North Korea, ©Gil C / Shutterstock.com
Republic of Guatemala, ©pavalena / Shutterstock.com
Korean peninsula political map with North and South Korea,
   ©Peter Hermes Furian / Shutterstock.com

Printed and bound
in the United States of America.

To Isabella
And all the children around the world
who do not receive medical care.

To my children,
my children's children
and future generations:
May you know

Ephesians 3:16-19

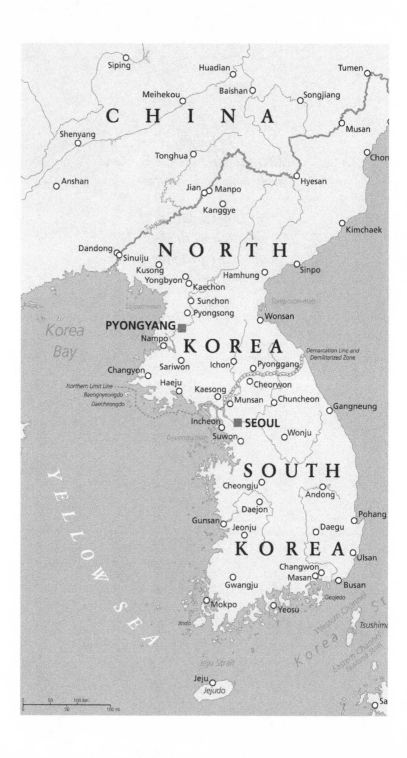

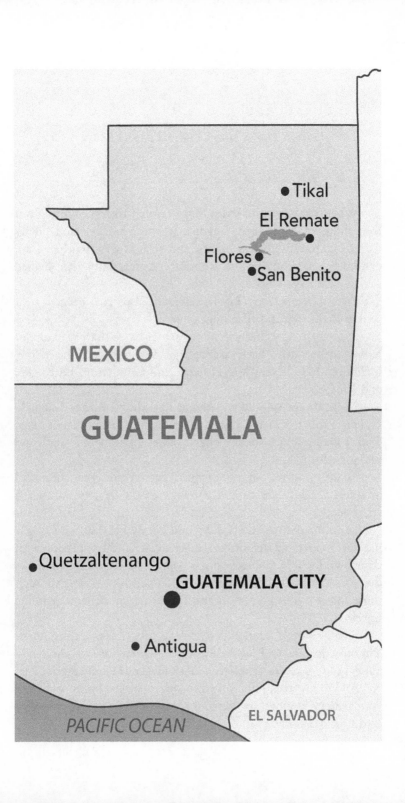

ACKNOWLEDGEMENTS

When I sat down to write *Maya Hope*, I thought writing was something you did alone. But like so much of life, God invites us into communion with others, and so it is with writing. I am extremely thankful for the wonderful community that helped make *Maya Hope* a reality.

First, I thank Katy Joy Richardson. You have been a great source of wisdom and encouragement.

Second, I have been extremely blessed to have a team of fellow authors who have coached, guided, and encouraged me, including: Julia Loren, Joni Fisher, Carol Gunderson, Ed Kugler, and Jeff Gerke.

I would especially like to thank my editor, Burney Garelick. You are a true friend and your skill and tender loving care of *Maya Hope* have made it readable. Thank you for making me laugh and making editing fun!

Thank you to Suzanne Fyhrie Parrott for your beautiful artwork, designs, and patient guidance in publishing—you are a true friend.

I also thank my parents, John and Ginny Browne, who taught me how to love and demonstrated generosity and compassion with their own lives. In the second grade, I could not read because of dyslexia; they had the wisdom to guide and support me through those many challenges. Mom and Dad, can you believe I wrote a novel?

Finally, words cannot convey my love for my three boys, Timothy, Joshua, and Jacob, and my daughters-in-law, Jamie and Sarah. You make life wonderful! With love, our family grows!

And to my wife, Julie: your strength, your love, your faith, and your patient kindness are beyond measure. You deserve the most credit for *Maya Hope*.

CONTENTS

ACKNOWLEDGEMENTS............................8

PROLOGUE - THE EXISTENCE OF EVIL 11

CHAPTER 1 - DR. HART..........................19

CHAPTER 2 - THE MED..........................23

CHAPTER 3 - BAD NEWS.........................30

CHAPTER 4 - REUNION 38

CHAPTER 5 - NORTH KOREA 46

CHAPTER 6 - A TIME TO MOURN...................50

CHAPTER 7 - FOR THE FATHERLAND...............62

CHAPTER 8 - AN INVITATION.....................66

CHAPTER 9 - HUMAN RIGHTS 73

CHAPTER 10 - A WELCOMED HERO 76

CHAPTER 11 - DECISION TIME....................86

CHAPTER 12 - THE TRINITY 91

CHAPTER 13 - CULTURE SHOCK 96

CHAPTER 14 - THE HOPE CENTER 101

CHAPTER 15 - BASKETBALL......................106

CHAPTER 16 - DAY ONE 112

CHAPTER 17 - SCHOOL BEGINS...................120

CHAPTER 18 - FIRST OR DAY....................126

CHAPTER 19 - THE HANDOFF.....................133

CHAPTER 20 - ISABELLA 140

CHAPTER 21 - GOD IS GOOD 147

CHAPTER 22 - THE GOSPEL......................153

CHAPTER 23 - THE VIRUS.......................164

CHAPTER 24 - NORTHEASTERN GUATEMALA.......166

CHAPTER 25 - FREEDOM 170

CHAPTER 26 - HISTORY 177

CHAPTER 27 - THE NEW ORDER 180

CHAPTER 28 - AN EXTENDED STAY................182

CHAPTER 29 - FAITHFULNESS 186

CHAPTER 30 - MUMPS..........................190

CHAPTER 31 - CHURCH 195

CHAPTER 32 - GOOD VERSUS EVIL................197

CHAPTER 33 - THE LORD IS MY REFUGE...........201

CHAPTER 34 - CAMP 22 207
CHAPTER 35 - DEATH TO REJECTION 211
CHAPTER 36 - NOAH INITIATIVE 216
CHAPTER 37 - SEOUL, SOUTH KOREA 219
CHAPTER 38 - THE JOURNAL 221
CHAPTER 39 - PURE EVIL 225
CHAPTER 40 - COMING CLEAN 227
CHAPTER 41 - THE ISLAND OF FLORES 230
CHAPTER 42 - MODERN SLAVERY 234
CHAPTER 43 - TIKAL 236
CHAPTER 44 - CELEBRATION 247
CHAPTER 45 - EL ZAPOTE 253
CHAPTER 46 - THE CROSSROADS 259
CHAPTER 47 - THE SEARCH 266
CHAPTER 48 - WAKING UP 269
CHAPTER 49 - NORTH VERSUS SOUTH 275
CHAPTER 50 - LAST TRIP 279
CHAPTER 51 - TERROR 286
CHAPTER 52 - IN THE BALANCE 292
CHAPTER 53 - SHALOM 297
CHAPTER 54 - BLOOD OF LIFE .301
CHAPTER 55 - IT IS DONE 307
CHAPTER 56 - DARKNESS 309
CHAPTER 57 - REGRET 313
CHAPTER 58 - THE BATTLE 315
CHAPTER 59 - MIRACLE 320
CHAPTER 60 - RECOVERY 322
CHAPTER 61 - REST IN PEACE .326
CHAPTER 62 - YERTLE THE TURTLE 330
CHAPTER 63 - PLEA 334
CHAPTER 64 - FERRETS 336
CHAPTER 65 - THE SPY'S SPY 339
CHAPTER 66 - ON THE TRAIL .341
CHAPTER 67 - TORMENT 345
CHAPTER 68 - GOODBYES 347
CHAPTER 69 - RELEASE – ONE MONTH LATER 350
CHAPTER 70 - THREE MONTHS LATER 353
EPILOGUE - GOOD NEWS 357
POSTSCRIPT - NORTH KOREA .360
THE TREE OF LIFE - 3 CHAPTER PREVIEW 363
AUTHOR'S NOTE - REDEMPTION 383
MINISTRIES 384

PROLOGUE

THE EXISTENCE OF EVIL

Drip.

Drip.

Drip.

Blood pooled in his open chest cavity, overflowed onto his shredded shirt and dripped against the ancient stone altar. His once-tanned ashen face was a stark contrast to the crimson wounds across his lower chin and eyebrow. The flesh around his wrists was torn and raw having been tugged and bound by ropes. His lifeless body lay on its back, stretched over the stone; his face turned upward, as if pleading for mercy. The man's chest, split between the ribs on the left side below the nipple, was flailed open and his heart removed in the traditional Way of the Maya ritual.

The jungle, silenced and confused by this horror not experienced in over 1,200 years, steeped in hushed tension.

When Danilo realized what the men had done, he jerked his head away from the scene and vomited hard. He staggered and glanced back at the dead man as if to verify what he'd seen, only to be confronted by an asylum of terror.

Sacrificial spirits spewed from the dark corners of the temple to merge with sulfuric fumes from hell itself to gorge on the unleashed evil. Wailing and shrieking filled the night as shadowy figures fought for dominance, dancing with fiendish delight and lapping the blood like wolves on a fresh kill. Stench and steam engulfed the demons and formed dark clouds obscuring the full moon that had illuminated the fresh corpse draped over the stone.

A thunderous legion of warring angels, dazzling with light, appeared in a brilliant bolt of lightning just as darkness had all but drained life from the jungle, sending the demons screeching to their hellish destiny and knocking Danilo off his footing. This was the moment Danilo knew that the dead man's spirit left his body because evil had no right to claim a holy man.

* * *

The three killers lagged behind their hired local guide, Danilo Perez, who was being driven forward by the terror of the human heart in his backpack. He couldn't shake the musty smell of wet moss that reeked with a strange sulfuric odor.

Above their heads, a howler monkey bellowed. It echoed the killing screams and encouraged other monkeys, insects and toads to join the chaotic choir, and the jungle cacophony returned.

Suddenly, a booming clap of thunder rattled Danilo, a searing strike of lightning shook the ground, and rain began to fall with a vengeance fiercer than this March rainy season. A torrent gushed from the sky, hitting the flora and fauna with a force that drowned the jungle sounds. Danilo looked through the towering canopy for the sliver of filtered moonlight, but it had vanished, giving way to frightening darkness as the storm devoured the jungle.

Water saturated every leaf, and Danilo wiped his face on his wet sleeve only to obscure his vision further.

While hacking a trail through the jungle with his machete, lead coursed through his veins, and his nostrils stung with the pungent smell of blood not even the rain could vanquish. He moved as fast as he could, hoping to distance himself from the ruthless killers with their strange accents and hardened faces as he led them back to their car. He squinted through the rain at the swaying treetops and tried to make sense of the shadowy figures overhead.

Maybe I'm seeing things.

He tried to quicken his pace, but every slash at the underbrush brought excruciating pain. His legs and arms grew heavy. As he forced his body to move, he remembered feeling this way once before.

As a young boy in Guatemala, during a horrifying vivid nightmare, he had experienced a visitation. He often wondered if it was the devil himself. He remembered feeling pinned to the bed—too heavy to move.

Now, in the impenetrable gloom of the storm he relived the nightmare, but this time it was worse—he couldn't tell if it was rain that dripped down his back or the blood from his backpack that soaked him.

Why had he agree to lead these men? The money, of course. But how could he have known he'd be carrying a human heart in his backpack?

He heard the men behind him utter what sounded like curses.

"Move!" one of them yelled.

Danilo wasn't sure if he had been pushed or if he'd buckled from an explosive clap of thunder, but he found himself on his knees.

Time stood still. His knees sank into the dank jungle mud, and he was simultaneously transported back to his youth, kneeling at the altar railing with Aunt Sandra at the Church of the Holy Mary, La Iglesia de Santa María. He could smell the incense and candle wax that filled the sanctuary. He saw the priest hand out communion and bless the other children. The Father's musky smell brought comfort then and now.

Returning to the jungle mud, Danilo felt his legs sink deeper into the mire, but his wavering psyche sent his mind back through time to the moment the priest held him in his arms and prayed with him. Danilo was only eight when the rebels killed his parents. At their funeral, Aunt Sandra whispered in his ear as they knelt at the altar railing. "Danilo, bow your head and fold your hands together like a good boy. You must pay homage to the Lord." She put her hand on the back of his head and gently pushed it down.

In defiance, Danilo forced his head up.

How could a loving God ever let this happen? I don't know if I even believe in God.

The loss of his parents had been too deep a grief.

Of course Aunt Sandra had loved him. "I believe the Lord has something special for you," she had often told him.

If only she could see me now.

* * *

Danilo had never witnessed anything like what he saw tonight. Growing up in the midst of the war, he had experienced his share of death—unclaimed bodies in the streets, families torn apart by loyalties and conflict. But these men were different. Danilo had really never believed that evil existed. He thought life was unjust and to be survived, but the killing he saw tonight was evil incarnate.

Danilo was accustomed to seeing many different types of people that visited the Tikal ruins. He made his living as a guide to the ancient ruins of the Maya empire and explaining what was known of their culture.

In the last five years, more Asians hired his services. To him, they all looked the same. But these men were different: black clothes, black hair, black eyes, black souls, always looking behind them, always whispering.

"Get up!" was all Danilo heard. The rest was in a foreign language, but spoken in such a way that the meaning was clear.

Danilo willed himself forward and was pushed from behind. He thought he heard the raging river over the pouring rain, but wasn't certain.

* * *

The three men hired him the previous week to tour the ruins. He thought he was doing well, as he showed them a few things off the usual beaten path. For most groups, this favor brought a sense of jungle adventure and, hopefully, a larger tip. These men seemed to care less.

Only when they were shown the large stone at the base of the Temple of The Great Jaguar did they show any interest, whispering eagerly among themselves. Most tourists wanted their picture taken on the stone, like some sort of triumph over death as they stood on the sacrificing altar. These men had no camera.

Loco for Asians.

He thought it strange when they called him again yesterday for another tour. Although this time, they wanted to go at night. Illegal, of course, but in the small town of Tikal, he and all the guides learned how to move in and out of the ruins at any time, day or night. This request was unusual, but not unheard of. His friend had sneaked in a lusty young couple after hours and was paid handsomely to leave them alone so they could enjoy some romance among the ruins.

Gringos, Danilo shrugged.

When the men picked him up in town, they handed him a large wad of money. He didn't have to count it to know he had really scored.

"You may see some things that you will not speak of," the taller Asian said to him as he climbed into the Jeep Cherokee, with its heavily tinted windows. He thought it odd that the man spoke with a near-perfect British accent. The other two men never said a word to him, and the three only spoke when he was out of earshot and then in Asian gibberish.

* * *

Danilo stumbled over a tree root, and his mind focused on the present. The mud was difficult to move through, but he knew from instinct that they headed in the right direction.

"Yes, I know I can hear the river now," he said to no one.

This will all be over soon.

They had less than a quarter of a mile to go before they hit the road where they had parked the Jeep.

I'll make a run for it when I get to the road.

* * *

On the trip out, Danilo sat in the front passenger seat to guide them to the secluded parking spot. It wasn't until they stopped that he realized that they were not alone in the Jeep: a man was bound and gagged in the very back. He wanted to protest, but by then, it was too late. The wad of money swelled in his pocket.

Probably more money than he'd made all last year. He would lead them in and look the other way. A quick night's work and then a cold cerveza.

He could buy his wife, Maria, and their son, Danilo junior, something extra special this Christmas. The most rewarding part was that little Danilo could finally have his surgery.

He was born with a clubfoot, something so easily treated as a newborn, but because they could not afford the treatment, Danilo junior went without. Now that he was turning one, the toddler walked on the side of his foot as it continued to turn inward more and more.

Soon, my son won't have to suffer the humiliation.

His mind tried to make sense of the killing, to justify his unwilling participation in the murder, yet the images continued to flood his mind as the trauma tossed his thoughts from present to past.

Another push from behind.

He wondered about the dead man.

What had he done to deserve such an execution?

Guatemala could be a brutal place, but killings were usually over money or drugs. This was different. This was done to send a message.

Of what, I have no clue.

The man was white, American or European maybe. He must have been unconscious during the drive, but when they dragged him out of the Jeep, it was like someone shot him with adrenaline—every muscle in his body fought for freedom. Danilo saw the ropes that bound his wrists and feet slice unmercifully into his flesh and the gag tear the corners of his mouth. The short, stout Asian with a severely pockmarked face struck the man's chin, opening a bloody gash that sent him into submission.

They dragged the man to the altar and threw him across the stone with such force, Danilo heard his forearm snap. The larger Asian ripped the man's shirt open with one hand. From a sheath strapped to his back, he pulled a large hunting knife. With a quick strike of the blade, he cut the man's gag from his face, flaying a large slice of his lower lip.

But the man wasn't dead.

Danilo shook his head, trying to banish the words of the dying man who pleaded, gargling words through blood spurting from his lip, pleading not for himself, but for his wife.

"My God, why are you doing this?" the man screamed.

"You, American pig, you should not have involved yourself with our affairs." The Asian put the knife to his throat.

"What do you mean your affairs? I've cared for people in these villages for years!" the man gasped.

"Do you think we are stupid?" the Asian growled. "We know you ordered blood work at the lab, that you have been asking about us!"

The sharp blade pressed into the victim's skin, opening a fresh wound. "You and the world will know soon enough what is happening," the Asian declared. "By then, it will be too late!"

Danilo watched as understanding came to the prisoner. "It's you...you are responsible!" the wounded man cried. "The villages...the children...My God!"

Even though it had been many years since Danilo had set foot in the church, he knew the hostage was a man of God.

The executioner grabbed his victim by the hair, pulled him up and stared into his eyes. "Where is your God now?" he sneered.

* * *

Danilo's arms grew so heavy that he dropped the machete. Sharp, shooting pain gripped his chest.

My God, what have I done? That man has a family. Had a family.

Tears streamed down his face. *Why did he stand there and do nothing?*

* * *

It all happened so quickly. They stretched the man over the

stone and cut between the ribs. The man screamed and fought for his life, but the executioners pinned him down. Standing too close, Danilo was sprayed with blood from the cut arteries. He saw the spongy pink lung bulge out of the wound.

As the dying man gasped for breath, he caught Danilo's eyes. Danilo froze in awe. It was nothing he expected.

No hate, no fear…how could that be?

Instead, Danilo saw compassion that made his head swirl in confusion. But there was no misunderstanding the man's last words: "Forgive them, Father."

One of the killers shouted, and Danilo looked up. He saw the taller Asian holding the heart of the victim. Without emotion, the man threw the heart to Danilo who caught it by instinct.

"Put it in your pack," the Asian ordered.

Without thinking, Danilo did as he was told.

* * *

Danilo staggered on.

This nightmare has to stop!

Yes, I think that is the Jeep up ahead.

Even so, he could go no farther. Every last bit of strength was gone, and he found himself on his knees again.

I'll walk home and leave all this behind me.

Then he did something for the first time in his life. He prayed out loud.

"Oh, God, save me."

He tried to cry out again and again to the Heavenly Father, but it was too late.

The man standing over him had slit his throat.

CHAPTER 1

DR. HART

The coolness of the windowpane against his forehead soothed his aching brain. Dr. Nicklaus Hart stood alone on the fourth floor of the hospital, one of the few dark and quiet corners of the medical complex. As he stretched his aching hands across the glass, he caught the scent of his scrubs and winced. They smelled of a hard day laboring in the Operating Room. He sighed deeply, and his breath fogged the window.

Lights from the softball field next to the hospital gave a translucent glow through the fogged glass and evening mist. He heard the players better than he saw them. His breath, the mist, and large oaks swayed by the wind made the field lights dance like flames from a campfire.

Suddenly, a bat cracking a ball into right field pierced the rumble of the game, and laughter and cheering burst from the crowd. Nick wiped the window with the edge of his hand and saw the runner round the bases for another score as the team's bench erupted in celebration. He knew everyone on the hospital team—nurses and techs of one kind or another and one doctor, a dermatologist who worked nine-to-four, four days a week.

Lucky son-of-a-gun. But who wants to look at nasty skin all day?

He made ten times more than any one of the players, except for the dermatologist. His heart longed for the fun and fellowship they enjoyed, and he wondered what it would be like to put in your shift and then leave.

Freedom. He bounced his head against the pane.

He noticed his Rolex tied to the cord of his scrub pants and remembered he hadn't eaten dinner. It was already quarter past eight. He'd barely seen the light of day in the last three weeks, and his call shift that evening made for a long forty-eight hours. He bounced his head gently against the glass again, trying to remember why he'd gone into medicine, especially into a surgical field.

It wasn't as if he didn't know what he was in for. After all, he'd watched his surgeon father struggle through the rigors of medicine. He was reluctant to go there, but his angst was overcome by his desire to please his father by following in his footsteps to become a fourth-generation physician. How could he have imagined doing anything different? Secretly, he had always wanted to be a forest ranger.

The final nail in his decision to pursue medicine came when his best friend, John, set his sights on medical school. Always competitive, Nick could never let John one-up him.

Nick heard another round of laughter from the group below as the game appeared to wind down.

He'd followed his destiny, life had been good, and here he was. But then there was the ever deepening whisper of his heart—a call that told him that there was something more—something more meaningful in life. He closed his eyes and remembered the last time he'd heard that call. He was standing at the base of the towering Mission Mountains in Montana.

He looked at the softball field again and saw the players high-five and hug. A wave of loneliness swept over him.

Nick saw his tired reflection in the window and rubbed his eyes. His sleep cycles were askew and he was sleep deprived. He'd been grateful to one of his nurse buddies for slipping him some weed. It had worked like a charm, and he'd been reinvigorated by a restful night's sleep. But he knew such dependence was a dangerous, slippery slope.

Is this what depression feels like?

His stomach growled, and his tired brain asked his aching feet to find something to eat when a vaguely familiar perfume filled his nostrils and a pair of warm hands encircled his waist. He dropped his arms to his sides and stood up straight.

"I hoped I would find you up here," a young woman's voice murmured. "I looked for you down in Emergency and the OR, and when you weren't there, I thought I'd find you here."

Nick tried to turn, but the woman tightened her grip.

"Oh, no you don't. You have to guess first," she said and pressed her body into his.

He looked at her hands.

White. That narrows it down a bit.

He thought for a moment and made up names. "Shakala? Henrietta? Brunhilda?"

"Funny." She head-butted his back.

The woman loosened her grip enough to let Nick turn to face her. She pursed her lips and pressed her chest into his stomach. Her bleach-blond hair was highlighted with a band of pink that matched the color of her scrubs and her streak of naughtiness.

"Hey, Melody. You need something?" he teased. She was one of the nurses from the orthopedic ward.

"So glad you asked, Dr. Hart." She stopped, mid-sentence. "Wow, your eyes are blue." She pulled him close and tucked her face into his chest. She held him for a moment and then playfully pushed him away. "Phew. I need to get you out of these scrubs. You stink."

He sighed. "You know I'm on call?"

She pretended not to hear. "When I saw you on the ward earlier, I couldn't get you off my mind," she said, rubbing against him.

"Shouldn't you be down playing softball?"

"That silly ol' game," she drawled. "I'd rather play hard ball." She laughed at her own joke. "Anyway, it seems like a month since we've been together."

Nick's head spun. He knew what she wanted, but he was tired and hungry. He longed for intimacy and love, but the closest he seemed to get was a quickie in the call room. He also knew sex was the best anti-stress drug around, and despite himself, he felt his brain succumbing to its allure.

Melody untucked Nick's scrub shirt from his pants and ran her fingers over his toned stomach. "Let's me and you step into the call room, and I'll help you relax."

The spell was cast. Nick looked up and down the empty hallway, pulled her into his call room, and slammed the door. Warning sirens rang in his head, but they were soon deafened by pounding desire. Only heroin was slightly more addicting.

Melody shed her scrubs, revealing skimpy lingerie. She held Nick at arm's length, then jerked him to her and ripped off his scrub top, mussing up his thick blond hair. Admiring her prize, she sighed, "Lordy, you're gorgeous!"

He was about to return the compliment when his beeper went off. He looked at the message, and then at her. His shoulders drooped.

"Noooo," she whined.

"I'm sorry, gotta get downstairs." He pulled on his shirt and reached for the door.

Melody watched him pull himself together, rolled her eyes, and shook her head, "You sure know how to show a girl a good time."

"Sorry," was all Nick thought to say as he took one last glance at her and left the room.

Geez, what am I doing?

A sense of relief washed over him as he shook his head and headed to the Emergency Department.

CHAPTER 2

THE MED

"Dr. Hart...Earth to Dr. Hart."

Elizabeth Jackson, one of Nick's favorite operating room techs, called to him and patiently held out the screwdriver he needed to insert a screw into the bone of the ankle exposed on the operating table.

As if awaking from a dream, Nick looked up and back. Elizabeth popped the screwdriver into his hand which accepted it by instinct. He shook his head to clear the fog of physical and emotional exhaustion. He glanced up at the clock—2:02 a.m.—and felt even more tired. He listened to the hypnotic, rhythmic beeps of the anesthesia monitors in his operating room and was comforted. He saw the OR nurse quietly sifting through a mountain of paperwork in the corner and the anesthesiologist adjusting a dial on his machine.

Dr. Hart filled his lungs with the cold air of the operating room hoping to jumpstart his brain. He was relieved to be away from the chaos of the trauma room and the emergency department.

"Thanks, Lizzy."

Nick was one of the few that got away with calling her by her nickname.

Her dark, graceful eyes smiled back across her surgical mask.

Because of her seniority, Lizzy rarely took night call, but he was thankful to have her by his side tonight. He would never ask her how old she was, and it was hard to judge her age with her beautiful brown complexion, but she had worked in this same OR for over forty years. She had trained more Residents than most of the Attendings. Some of the young doctors fresh out of medical school starting their five years of orthopedic residency training came with an attitude. If that was never adjusted, they became insufferable staff Attendings once they became board certified.

When a junior Resident was confused during a procedure, Lizzy—if she liked them—silently handed over the proper instrument to keep them on track. She enjoyed watching the arrogant get flustered. All the Residents tried to stay on her good side, and she liked it that way. Nick was one of her favorites.

"Dr. Hart, I remember when you first arrived at the MED eight years ago," she teased. "Lordy me, how you made the nurses swoon. I never seen such a sight when you strolled in with your full head of hair and swagger, you was this hot new surgeon from Montana with tight blue jeans and cowboy boots. I thought I was going to have to resuscitate a few of the nurses."

"Oh, Lizzy." He tightened the screw into the bone. "Was I really that handsome?"

"Oh yeah, ruggedly handsome, I'd say." She cackled and fanned her face. "Just glad we got them rough edges knocked off you."

"Ouch." He glanced at her. "I wasn't that bad, was I?"

Without saying a word, she handed him a bulb syringe full of saline to moisten the wound.

He thought of the first time they met. Ms. Elizabeth Jackson had been the scrub tech on his first surgery, a difficult pelvic fracture. Without introducing himself, he prepared for the case, rapidly listing all the instruments and fixation devices he needed. Finally, she stopped him and with no disrespect in her voice put a hand on his arm, looked him straight in the eyes, and said, "Cowboy, this ain't my first rodeo." Nick had looked at her with alarm and then broke into a belly laugh. They had been friends ever since.

"Lizzy, you could fix this ankle better than I can. Why don't you finish this up so I can take a nap?" He smiled through his mask, knowing it would be illegal for her to complete the surgery and knowing she'd never let him get away with it.

"Oh, Dr. Hart," she half-sighed and for the umpteenth time she said, "What you need is a good woman to take care of you. In fact, if I was a few years younger and had six less kids, I'd make you a fine wife."

"I bet you would. I just don't know I could keep such a fine woman like you happy."

Lizzy playfully bumped him with her shoulder and handed him another screw.

Nick understood her advice and felt her concern. "I'm looking, I'm looking," he said, but they both knew he was lying.

It was good to stay in life's comfort zone. His own biological clock was ticking, but fixing a bone was way easier than resolving his personal life. He wished he wasn't so exhausted all the time. He looked back at the wall clock and stretched his back.

Two-o-five. Time moved slowly, and this was just the beginning of the night at the MED.

The MED—Regional Medical Center at Memphis—was the trauma and burn center for six states as well as a world-renowned teaching institution. It was also the only hospital in those six states where the sick and injured got care without the consideration of insurance or ability to pay; it was the place of last resort for tens of thousands each year.

Chronically underfunded, the neon sign outside the main entrance once read "REGIONAL MEDICAL CENTER". Over the years, all the letters except MED had burnt out, and the administrators had left it that way. Even the inside of the hospital was falling apart. Most nights the ER looked like a war zone.

One of the Residents should have fixed this patient's ankle, but they were all swamped in the ER, so Nick had volunteered to give the resident staff a hand. He was known as one of the few attending staff who cared about the Residents and the hectic demands put upon them.

The Orthopedic Department was staffed by the forty-some surgeons from the Memphis Clinic. Many were uninterested in the Residents or the patients at the MED. Trauma call was challenging. Most of the work was charity care, which meant that in addition to long hours and low pay, staff had a greater chance of getting sued and risked higher exposure to AIDS and hepatitis.

Nick understood that the community doctors looked at the MED as the dumping ground of humanity. It was easier, cleaner, and, of course, much more profitable to stay within the confines of their multi-million dollar clinics with paying patients.

On nights like tonight, that view of doctoring sounded better to him, but he felt a real calling to both the patients and the Residents. It was his parents who had instilled in him the importance of service to those who lived without. Also, he thrived on the camaraderie of the Residents.

As far as the patients were concerned, Nick felt it was important to treat everyone as if they were a member of his family. He certainly wouldn't want a Second-year Resident fixing his mother's broken hip all by himself. The Chief Residents, in their fifth year of training, were good, but even they got in over their heads from time to time.

"Okay, let's get a picture," he announced, motioning to the x-ray technician to bring the fluoroscopy unit in before he placed the last screw through the plate that held the fracture in place.

The ankle was both broken and dislocated. When the young patient, for whatever reason, ran from the cops, his ankle rolled over a curb, snapped out of joint and forced the bone through the skin. In the ER, the foot laid at a right angle to the leg. Not a pretty sight.

He studied the x-ray image revealing his handiwork and nodded approval. "Not too bad, if I must say so myself—"

"And I *must* say so myself," Lizzy finished.

They chuckled.

"Let me close this thing up," he said and addressed the heavy Filipino nurse who was filling out paperwork. "Betty, can you call down to the guys and see what's happening in the ER and what's next on the plate?"

Lizzy handed him some suture without needing to be asked. "You have given this young man a good leg to stand on when he appears before the judge."

He appreciated her judgment and hoped that now he'd be able to get some sleep, a hope that was quickly dashed.

"The boys need you in Trauma 2," Betty announced. "A sixteen-year-old with one to the chest and one through the hip and femoral artery."

The *one* she was referring to was probably a high-powered rifle bullet. The gun of choice these days was an M-15 assault rifle.

A person did not want to end up a patient in Trauma 2. At this time of night, it had a near fifty-percent mortality rate. Many of the older and faith-filled nurses prayed daily over that room and anointed the door with oil. They claimed it kept the spirit of death at bay. It was a constant and herculean-sized battle. Nick thought they were wasting their time and was mostly annoyed when a few of them told him they prayed for him as well.

The MED was the MASH unit of the Memphis battleground. People in Memphis settled most arguments with guns. Nick even wore combat boots. Some of the Residents preferred knee-high rubber boots to keep their socks from getting soaked through with blood.

Nick heard the more religious nurses state that violence was a spiritual stronghold over the city. They said their churches knew to pray, but the foul spirit had not yet been broken.

He tried to reduce the tension as he quickly sewed up the wound. "Lizzy, did you hear about the guy we took care of last week?"

She said nothing and let him ramble.

"This guy came in who had been shot in both legs with a shotgun," he continued. "I asked him, 'Wesley, who shot you in the legs?' 'My uncle, my uncle,' " Nick imitated the man's voice writhing in pain. " 'He kept telling me he would.' So I asked him, 'What do you mean?' And he said, 'My uncle kept telling me if I didn't get my 'filthy' feet off his coffee table, he would shoot them off. I didn't believe that slime ball would actually do it.' "

Lizzy and Nick laughed, but at the same time shook their heads.

"I don't know what this world is coming to, Dr. Hart," Lizzy said. "Lord, save us all."

* * *

Nick ripped off his surgical gown, entrusting Lizzy to close the skin with staples and apply the dressing. He hurried from his operating room to the large trauma OR down the hall. He barely stopped to spray sterilizing foam in his hands.

He was met at the door by one of the five scrub technicians holding an unfolded and opened gown. He thrust his arms into it and entered the room where the atmosphere was electric and the adrenaline palpable. It looked like chaos, but it was tightly orchestrated. Everyone knew their job and was good at it. Two surgical teams, one for the chest and one for the leg, called out orders. REO Speedwagon's *Time for Me to Fly* blared from the stereo in the corner.

A young, naked black man was stretched crucifix-style on the OR table. Blood pooled on the floor. The pungent, earthy smell of blood mixed with alcohol hit Nick's nostrils. The young man had been drinking.

Two anesthesiologists and their technician tended to the boy, one squeezed a bag of blood and instructed the tech to get more. The other anxiously scanned the various monitors that chattered with different chimes and alarms reminding them that they were losing the battle.

The chest surgeon barked out orders above the rest of the bedlam. A nurse poured sticky brown, betadine antiseptic over the chest as the surgeon used the scalpel to slice between the ribs and insert spreaders. He wore gloves but no gown. There was no time. If this boy was to be saved, the bleeding had to stop. Blood gushed to the floor when the surgeon put his hand into the chest to pinch off the bleeding vessel. It was a lucky grab. The high velocity bullet transected a branch of the pulmonary artery. It was this boy's lucky day.

The chest surgeon beamed at Nick as he approached the table. "Am I good or am I good?"

Nick smiled at him and shook his head. *Just don't ask his first three wives or his sons—one in rehab and the other in jail.*

He was an arrogant son-of-a-gun, but also one of the best surgeons.

Nick looked at his sweating Chief Resident whose hand was thrust into the boy's thigh.

"My young Thomas, what d'ya have?"

"The femoral artery between my fingers, sir." He looked relieved to be addressed. "The bullet shattered the proximal femur after it tore through the artery."

"And your plan?" Nick asked, expecting the right answer.

"I was about to cross clamp the artery to see if we can repair it or graft it. I was waiting to see if the chest surgeon would make it necessary."

Nick frowned. "Time's a-wasting," he said. "Never wait. Focus on what you need to do and do it."

They explored the wound together, extending it where necessary to examine the damage, and found the artery could be repaired.

"What do you want to do with the bone?" He asked.

"Wash it out and put on an external fixator," Thomas said with as much confidence as he could.

There were a few ways to repair it and he wanted a spectrum of correct answers. "What does the literature say?"

Everything was a teaching moment, even at three o'clock in the morning.

* * *

Two hours later, a portion of lung was resected, the femoral artery repaired, a set of external pins and rods held the leg together, and fifteen units of blood were infused, twice replacing the normal amount, the young man was still alive. He had a long road to recovery, but he would live to fight another day.

CHAPTER 3

BAD NEWS

Nick heard the gentle knock on the door behind him, but chose to ignore it.

Gladys, an elderly woman dressed in a modest plaid dress that smelled of Dove soap, sat on the exam table fidgeting with a tissue as she told him about her sore knee.

"I live in a second-floor apartment, and I'm struggling getting up the stairs, especially when—" she paused and looked past Nick at the door that opened.

He turned and saw his nurse poking her head in. He scowled. Nurse Emily smiled apologetically at the patient, but did not make eye contact with him. He had been up all night, his temper was short, and he didn't like to be disturbed. She seemed hesitant to deliver the message, but it must be important. She swallowed hard and said, "Dr. Hart, your father is here and waiting in your office."

She disappeared, quickly closing the door.

Nick hated to be interrupted when he was examining a patient. It wasn't so much for himself as it was for the patient.

He stared at the door. He had changed out of his blood-stained scrubs from the night before, but he still wore an unshaven face and baggy eyes. The message puzzled him. Absorbing it, he turned back to Gladys and her sore knee.

"I'm sorry, Gladys, you were telling me your knee hurts going upstairs?" he asked, trying not to look distracted.

Nevertheless, his heart sank, and his mind raced. His father was retired but still consulted for a medical company, often traveling from their home in Montana, so Nick wasn't surprised he was in Memphis. But why was he here at the MED? Why didn't he call?

Dad has never come to visit him at the office. Is it Mom?

Gladys examined him tenderly. In her aged wisdom, she said, "Dr. Hart, you should go talk with your father. My knee will be here when you get back. Now you go on."

"Thank you, Gladys. I'll be right back."

As he walked down the hall toward his office, he felt like a schoolboy sent to the principal's office. When he stopped at the door to his office, he was met by a sense of dread mingled with fear.

He loved his father, but his father cast a large shadow over his life. Nick was never sure if he lived up to unspoken expectations of the man and the surgeon.

He opened the door.

His father stood slightly stooped, staring through watery eyes at a photo on the wall behind Nick's desk. The photo featured Nick and his friend, John, sitting on a mound of rocks that marked the summit of McDonald Peak in the Mission Mountains. They were young men with sunburned faces and grinning smiles that said it was good to be alive.

When his father heard Nick push the door closed, he stood up straight and turned to his son.

Nick could count on three fingers the times he had seen this stoic man cry. He was stunned by the sight and paused to brace himself for whatever his father was about to say.

Even though retired from a general surgery practice, his father still carried that confident, surgeon's air about him. It was a strength he had always been able to summon—except now. His confidence crumbled as he faced his son.

"Johnny's dead. He's...he's been killed," the elder Dr. Hart said through tears. He reached out to embrace Nick.

Nothing prepared Nick for the wave of shock and grief that crashed over him. His jaw dropped. He shook his head, and when he could utter a sound, he said, "What? No! John Russell? No!"

Then, in an effort to distance himself from his emotions, young Dr. Hart went into overdrive. It was as if he'd been called to the ER. He pushed his father away and peppered him with questions. There was not a moment to waste. Time saves lives. He needed to save John's life.

"Where is he? What are his vitals? What are his injuries?" Nick asked. The questions tripped off his tongue.

His father grabbed him by the arms and pleaded with his eyes.

Nick knew it was true. John was gone.

"Oh, Nicklaus, I'm so, so sorry."

His father hugged him, and Nick came back to the moment. He still needed to do something. He tried to pull away, but his father's still strong arms held him firm. "He's gone, son. There's nothing you can do."

Nick went slack against his father, and he let his tears fall. The two surgeons, no longer able to distance themselves from life's trauma, commingled their pain for a moment of rare intimacy.

Nick broke the embrace first. He went to his desk chair, changed his mind, and sat on the edge of the desk. His face was wet, and he was still in shock. His father stayed where he was, wiping his eyes with the back of his hand.

Then, as if they'd remembered Harts don't cry, father and son stood tall and breathed deeply. They were surgeons and had long ago buried their hearts; it was part of the job.

Nick spoke first. He asked exactly what had happened to John and steeled himself to accept the answer.

His father knew few details. He'd received the call two days ago from John's family that John had been found dead in Guatemala, and his wife, Maggie, was unharmed. She was escorting John's body back to their hometown of Seattle.

"Two days ago?" Nick's pain turned to anger. "Why didn't you call me?"

"Nick—" His father's face flushed. He took a deep breath and his expression softened. "Nick, I'm so sorry about John. We did try to call you, son, but we—" he let the rest go.

Nick slumped his shoulders and looked down at his beeper attached to his belt, remembering the pages he got from the answering service to call his parents. He sat in silent guilt.

John was his best friend—they were closer than brothers—

and his own father thought of John as another son. Their families had little in common with John's folks working in the local wood mill, but one thing they shared was the love of their children. An extra chair always sat at the dinner tables at each home. Some nights the friends would eat at both tables, their adolescent metabolisms yearning for more food than usual after the afternoon soccer games.

His father squeezed his shoulder. "You going to be okay." It was a statement more than a question.

Nick sighed through his nose and nodded.

"Well, call your mother. She'll want to know how you're doing."

He watched his dad walk to the door, limping slightly on an arthritic hip. His father seemed to have aged in the last few minutes; his shoulders hunched, and his spine curved to the right.

The elder Dr. Hart paused at the door and turned to look at his son. He almost spoke but closed his mouth and gave Nick a tight-lipped, half-smile. He nodded slightly, looked at the floor, and left without saying another word.

* * *

Nick pulled himself together. He told the office staff to cancel the rest of the day. He went to the exam room to apologize to Gladys and got an uncomfortably long hug from her. It seemed that people around him understood how to grieve better than he did; after all, it was *his* best friend who had died.

He sat in his midnight blue Porsche Boxster in the parking garage, feeling the perfectly supple leather on the steering wheel. He was not an emotional man; he couldn't succumb to emotions in his line of work. He had cried all the tears he could for one day. He was numb.

No, he was furious. His stomach filled with surging acid of helplessness, anger and anxiety. He hated those feelings and sat very still to keep them from erupting.

God, my back is sore.

He pushed against the steering wheel trying to get his back to pop.

His mind spurned his physical discomfort and returned to the death of his friend. He didn't know what to do next, another strange sensation for him. He could try to call Maggie, but he wasn't sure he was ready yet.

"Go home!" he said out loud.

What can I do? What must I do?

He glanced at the sign painted on the cement wall of the parking garage: RESERVED FOR N. HEART, MD. They had spelled his name wrong, but he'd always figured it was close enough for government work. He shook his head in disgust. *Is this all I've worked for: a nice car and a parking spot?*

A rap on the car window startled him.

The impatient intruder rapped again.

Nick looked through the window. "Oh geez," he said, not so silently under his breath.

Outside his car stood the devil herself: Anita Roe. Most referred to her as Cruella de Vil, from the movie, *One Hundred and One Dalmatians*. Nick let his head fall back and closed his eyes, hoping she would go away.

Anita Roe was chief administrator of the MED. She had been in the position for three years and had managed to alienate the entire medical staff. Her every decision was based on money, not what was best for the patients or the doctors or the nurses or the rest of the staff, but how it affected the bottom line.

She did her job with no shame—lowering wages where she could, increasing staff workloads, leaving patients without a nurse for hours at a time, and overhauling the system into a shamble of a work place.

She tapped on the glass again. Nick felt the bile in his belly readying for eruption. Without opening his window, he glared at her. She was stooped over and peered at him through the glass. A strand of gray ran through her close-cropped hair. Her frame was tall and bony thin, but somewhere along the way had gone under the knife, giving her disproportionately large breast implants and a small nose. She wore a pink knit suit and diamond earrings that he guessed cost more than a nurse's monthly pay.

"Dr. Hart, I need to talk with you." She looked perturbed.

He realized she was not going away. He relented and powered

his window down. He could smell her. He thought it was strange that such an immaculately dressed woman would have such a vile odor, worse than bad breath.

She took a step back from the car and put her hands on her hips.

He gave her a bewildered look. *"Yes?"*

"My assistant called me at lunch and told me the news of your friend…and I'm…" she began in her overripe Georgia peach accent and then uncharacteristically stumbled over her words. She even blushed slightly.

He was surprised. *Am I seeing some humanity in this woman?*

"I wanted to make sure you are going to be okay?" she asked. "I noticed you have a full day in the OR tomorrow, and I wanted to make sure you would be there."

Nick rolled his eyes. *I guess not. I'll bet she doesn't even have a heart.*

"Look," Roe continued, "I am sorry for your friend and all, and I have been meaning to talk with you anyway." She took another step back, sensing his growing anger. She was not about to back off. "I heard you cancelled your clinic today, and I have to tell you I'm concerned about your numbers. Your elective cases are down fifteen percent the last two months."

Nick had not spoken a word. He gripped the steering wheel so hard that his knuckles turned white. He wanted to jump out of the car and snap her in two. At the very least, he wanted to rip her apart with his words. *How dare you?*

"You are under contract, Dr. Hart," the chief administrator said. "Because of what we are paying you, we expect that you do ten elective cases a week in addition to trauma call."

He couldn't hold his tongue another second. "I operate on those patients that need it. Period," he shouted. By the way she looked at him, he knew his face was turning bright red. "Do you want me to make up cases? Operate on people that don't need it, just to make your quota?"

"Well…" she seemed to stop herself from actually saying yes. "…or see more patients in your clinic to get those cases," she said, flustered by his irate stare.

Nick put the Boxster in reverse, and the tires squealed. His anger had reached the breaking point. He jammed it in drive, and this time the tires smoked. Anita Roe jumped two steps back.

"Ten cases, Dr. Hart," she yelled as he sped away, no longer sounding so much like a southern belle.

* * *

The alarm continued to buzz. Nick wasn't sure which was worse, moving and making his head throb or listening to the buzzing alarm. He had a hangover larger than the six-pack of beer that had been in his fridge for months. He rarely drank that much at one time, but last night there seemed to have been more than enough reasons.

Am I too hung over to operate today?

He glanced at the clock on the nightstand: 5:30 a.m. He squeezed his throbbing head. The pain lingered, and he wondered if he could handle the cases scheduled that day.

He'd done them a hundred times. Sick or not, I can do it. A shower and a few cups of coffee, he'd be fine.

The throbbing increased as he became more conscious. He struggled to remember what he had done after leaving the MED.

His mind flickered like an old black-and-white movie, and he groaned. His groan elicited movement beside him, and he turned to a mass of black hair partially covered by the pillow which was held in place by two hands highlighted with bright red nail polish.

"Not again!" he moaned.

The young woman grabbed another pillow in a further attempt to drown out the alarm.

Nick's head fell hard on his pillow as it all came back. Last night in the middle of his third beer and Monday night football, Jasmine had appeared at his door with a smile and a bottle of whiskey. She, too, had heard about Dr. Hart's friend and thought that she could help ease his pain. Jasmine worked with him in the OR, and she was one of many women who wanted to snag him for a husband.

He shook his head and sat up. He needed a change in his life. He didn't know how, but he needed to start now. For the first time in eight years, he reached for the phone and called the MED. He told the scheduler he was coming in but he would need to take a few days off. He put the phone back in its cradle, got out of bed, stood up, and stretched. He looked at the sleeping Jasmine.

She can look after herself.

He had things to do. He had to see to John's funeral. He had to check on Maggie. He went to the bathroom to scrub the hangover out of his head.

CHAPTER 4

REUNION

Three days later, stepping off the plane into a dreary, rainy day in Seattle, Nick caught a glimpse of himself in the steel pole of the airport gift shop outside the arrival gate. He looked like one of his strung-out meth patients.

He made a feeble attempt to push his blond waves back and rub the bags from under his eyes.

The last few days had been a blur of bitter emotions as he realized he would never see his best friend again. The nurses at the hospital had sensed a change and cut a wide circle around the uncharacteristically edgy Dr. Hart.

He stretched his shoulders back. He regretted he hadn't seen John and Maggie for five years. They had invited him many times to join them in Guatemala, but with his busy schedule, it never seemed possible. But he knew that was not to blame.

Why hadn't I made it a priority?

Trying to get away from a busy hospital was like trying to stop a boulder from rolling downhill—patients had to be rescheduled, surgeries cancelled, and call schedules rearranged.

He was grateful his partners in the Trauma Service at the MED had been more than willing to pick up the slack that allowed him to attend the funeral.

He sighed and headed down the long, busy corridor. Maggie had asked him if he would say a few words at the memorial service. Of course, he had accepted. But he wasn't sure that he would make it through without breaking down. Besides, he hated public speaking. There was so much to say about his remarkable friend. His head was muddled, and he had so many questions about what had happened to John.

His was grief so heavy it felt like somebody had kidney-punched him and he wondered if he was walking crooked.

Poor Maggie. He didn't even know what to say to her.

He tried to remember exactly how many years that she and John had been married.

Grieving as he was, he smiled to recall the first time he met Maggie. John had told him that he was headed into the Mission Mountains for a few days of camping. Nick was in Seattle in his third year of medical school, and he was hurt that he hadn't been invited on the adventure.

Then he got a brilliant idea. If he skipped physiology that Friday afternoon and drove most of the night, he could surprise John by late Saturday afternoon in time for dinner. John had told him he would be camping by Mollman Lake, one of their favorite spots. The lake was filled with huge trout, and they could catch a fabulous dinner.

By the time Nick made his way up the steep trail to Mollman, the Missions were falling into dusk. Sneaking up to the tent, he couldn't wait to scare the daylights out of John when he kicked over a pile of wood by the fire and growled like a grizzly bear. But the surprise was on Nick when a beautiful young woman wearing a tank top and pink panties jumped out of the tent with a .44-Magnum pistol pointed at his chest.

She stood her ground, tossing her long, black hair. "What do you want?"

He put up his hands and stuttered an apology. "I'm sorry. I must be in the wrong place. I'm looking for my friend's camp. My friend John Russell," he said nervously, looking at the large-bore end of the 44.

She looked him over. "Are you John's friend, Nick?"

He nodded eagerly, wondering how she knew.

She read his mind and lowered her weapon. "I know a lot about you. John told me not to be surprised if you showed up."

Nick lowered his arms. He was baffled. "What? Where's John?"

"John is fishing. He'll be back soon. Come sit by the fire and have some cider. I'm Maggie." She transferred the large revolver to her left hand and stuck out her right.

As they shook hands it dawned on Nick. *So, this is why John hadn't asked me to come. John found himself a woman.*

And a good one she turned out to be—strong and beautiful with a real sense of identity Nick rarely saw in a woman. It was her Native American heritage that gave her both her looks and her strong spirit.

Back in the airport, Nick sighed. *I wonder how she's surviving this?*

As he looked for the exit sign, memories of that camping trip continued to flood his mind.

Nick joined Maggie beside the fire after she'd dressed, and it wasn't long before they saw John walking along the lakeshore carrying a string of large trout and smiling. John was gangly with long, skinny legs and equally long arms. He carried an unmistakable bounce in his walk and a smile that seemed to penetrate all darkness. Nick had never met another man like John—smart, funny, caring, with an uncanny sense of life around him. Even with all his kindness, he was as strong-willed as they came and took no crap from anyone.

When John saw them, he waved, and out of the corner of his eye, Nick caught the huge reciprocating smile from Maggie, and he knew right then that he had lost his best friend to another.

* * *

Nick didn't expect Maggie to pick him up at the airport; after all, she had returned from Guatemala with John's casket a few days ago. But when he looked up from the drab airport carpet near the exit, he saw her waiting. Nick sensed her sadness from a distance. She was accompanied by her older sister, lending support with a hand on her back. Nick quickened his pace. Maggie's skin was paler than he had ever seen, but she still looked beautiful.

"Maggie, you didn't need to—"

She silenced him by throwing her arms around his neck. They stood oblivious to everyone around them and wept.

* * *

As they pulled up to the house in Maggie's Subaru, Nick felt another twinge of guilt that it had been so long since he last visited.

Medicine is an unkind mistress, one that robbed me of my time.

John and Maggie's house in Ballard, a suburb of Seattle, was ridiculously small for a talented general surgeon, yet perfectly appropriate for the couple. Stepping from the car, Nick saw how beautifully kept it was. The old-fashioned wooden screen door on the front gave it a hint of Montana. As with many houses in Seattle, an abundance of colorful flowers filled the lush gardens encircling the house. Spring rains had painted the lawn an emerald green, crisp and sparkling in the cool, clear air. John's eye for order was reflected in his exquisite landscaping, as it was in his surgical expertise. The house and the lot were perfect.

"We don't need anything bigger," John had told him. "It's just a waste of money. To the rest of the world, we live like kings anyway."

John and Maggie ran the Hope Center in Quetzaltenango, Guatemala, and they were only home a few months out of the year.

Their families sat in the crowded tiny living room and stood when Nick, Maggie and her sister entered the room.

John's dad was first to hug him. "Hey, Nick. We're so glad you're here." It was an extra-long hug.

"Hey, Pops," he said, using his nickname for his second father. John's dad was a bear of a man, generous with hugs and affection. John was a clear reflection of his parents: his mother's thinness and strength and his father's height and compassion.

John's mother, Joan, gasped with grief and hugged Nick even longer, as if to let him know how unimaginable it was to lose her son and only child.

"I'm so sorry, Joan." Nick hugged her.

Not the natural order of life, when parents bury their children. He tried to keep his grief distant yet be there for her. He felt her legs almost give way and held her tight to support her tiny frame.

"Oh, Nick, it's just too much," she cried into his chest. "I just don't know who would do this to our John."

Pops put his hand on her back and gave her a tissue. She loosened her grip from Nick and blew her nose into the tissue.

"I thought I had stopped crying," she said, "but when you walked in…you were such good boys." She patted Nick's heart and turned to sit down.

The handshakes, hugs, and kisses continued around the room as each family member greeted him. Maggie's parents, Cliff and Mary, also hugged Nick, as did her two brothers.

Nick had met Maggie's brothers at John and Maggie's wedding. Both were handsome, tall, muscular and dark-skinned, reflecting the family's heritage from the Blackfeet tribe of eastern Montana. Maggie's older brother was always serious, but the younger had a quick wit and immediately reminded Nick of the prank they had pulled on John and Maggie the night of their wedding. They had removed the bed from the honeymoon suite at the local hotel.

Maggie thumped her brother in the chest, hard enough to make him take a step backwards. "I'm still mad about that."

The story and the rebuke provoked laughter and relieved the sadness in the room.

Nick blinked his eyes and looked around. The air was fragrant, and flowers were everywhere, like a florist shop with a holiday sale. Every shelf and counter space burst with beautiful blooms.

Maggie watched him. "My folks have already shared bouquets with the neighbors. Everybody loved him."

Nick nodded and put his arm around Maggie, giving her a strong, sideways hug.

"You okay?" he asked.

Maggie exhaled. "I'm just glad my family is here. That you're here. I don't know, Nick, without my faith in heaven and knowing I will be with him again…I don't know…I'm just not sure about getting through tomorrow." She stumbled over her words, thinking about the funeral. "It seems like it will be so final."

"I'm so sorry." It was all Nick could think to say. "I'm so sorry."

Two of Maggie's nieces scampered past them chasing a frightened little dachshund.

Maggie pulled herself together. "Come on out to the back yard," she said. "You're probably starving after your trip. The rest of the family is out here cooking burgers and dogs." She led him through the kitchen to the back door.

Just like Maggie to think of everyone else when she's in such pain.

* * *

Maggie was tough. Growing up in Browning, Montana, did that to a young woman. With an unemployment rate nearly matching the divorce rate of sixty percent, alcoholism the number one killer, and a poverty level that matched any inner city, Browning was tough. Sitting on the eastern slope of the Rocky Mountains, it was the government seat of the Blackfeet Nation and at the heart of the reservation—a meager slice of what was once the vast Blackfeet Territory.

Maggie's family had seen their share of grief, but they were a remarkable family. Her parents, Cliff and Mary Black Elk, grew up in Browning and raised their four children on a small farm outside the city limits where sadness and grief often overtook families. Last winter, three middle school boys were found frozen in a field; they had skipped school, guzzled a fifth of vodka, and passed out in the subzero weather. A month later, Cliff's brother was killed on an icy road. That was just last year.

Cliff and Mary were the first to say it was only by God's grace that all of their four children were alive and doing well. Their witty younger son had survived a stint in prison and a rehab program, but was now four years sober and helping on the farm. Three of their kids, including Maggie, finished college, something that Cliff was especially proud of.

The Black Elks grew up in the Catholic faith, but when one of their own tribal members returned from a school of ministry in Pennsylvania with a message of hope and healing, they quickly became a part of the new church plant. The blending of their Indian culture and Christian faith made for rich worship and faith-filled children.

Maggie received a full-ride scholarship to three schools—Stanford, Harvard and Brown. She claimed it was because of her Indian blood and the schools needed to fill their quotas, but everyone knew she was brilliant.

She was younger than her sister by three years, and her brothers bookended them both. At five-foot-one, Maggie was dwarfed by her six-foot-two and six-foot-seven brothers and five-foot-eight sister. Her brothers teased her unmercifully, telling her she was an orphan baby they found in a shoebox on a long, empty road. Maggie's mother laughed it off, but with the amount of teenage pregnancies in Browning, Maggie had to admit that the thought occasionally crossed her mind.

What Maggie lacked in height, she made up for in determination. She excelled at everything she put her mind to, whether it was the winning lamb at 4-H competitions or her straight-A grades. But what made her stand out was her compassion for people in need.

Her parents saw that compassion with the farm animals. Maggie was the one to sit up through the night nursing a sick lamb or a foundering colt.

Maggie's dad would laugh and say, "If it was up to Maggie, we would have the oldest living cattle in the world. None of them would make it to market."

They saw Maggie's compassion for people when she brought wildflowers to the elders of the Tribe. Maggie always made time for her friends. One night she scared her parents to death when she didn't come home. Later, when they found out she had sat up all night with a friend who was raped, it was hard to be angry at her.

It was no wonder Stanford, Harvard and Brown wanted her. She chose Stanford because it was closest to home, but after a pretty rocky first year and a heavy dose of homesickness, she returned to Montana to finish her degree in social work at the University of Montana. That's where she met John.

* * *

With John next to her, Maggie liked to tell people that there were four things that had impacted her life the most—"My faith in God, my parents, my college trip to Guatemala and—what was the other one? Oh yeah," she'd grin at his worried eyes, "meeting John." She loved to tease him, and he loved being teased.

On a whim, a college friend had talked her into going on a mission trip to Guatemala between her junior and senior years. It was two weeks in a small village, San Pedro la Laguna in the Lake Atitlan basin, where they were to minister to the indigenous Maya Indians. The group was going to help rebuild and paint a small school that had been damaged in an earthquake.

When the two weeks were over, most of the college kids were overjoyed to spend a few days relaxing in Antigua and loading up on souvenirs to bring back to family and friends. But Maggie was different; saying goodbye to the villagers was heart-breaking. She would have liked to say goodbye to her life back in the States and stay in Guatemala forever.

"I've never met a group of people like the Indians of San Pedro," Maggie explained. "Even though they lived in severe poverty and hardship, they were some of the most loving and kind people I have ever met. One family gave everyone in our twenty-member team a Coke as we stepped off the bus. We later found out that the father had saved for two months to be able to buy the Cokes and proudly carried the case on his back three miles up the steep trails to the village."

Maggie also loved it when the village women dressed her in the colorful Maya weave clothing that fit perfectly. With her long, straight black hair and dark complexion, she could have easily passed as a villager, something the women giggled about with great joy. Maggie pledged that one day she would be back. She would become a missionary.

CHAPTER 5

NORTH KOREA

It had been an unusually bitter winter, and March was no different as Pak Song-ju peered through the frost out the side window of his Mercedes. The streets of Pyongyang, North Korea, were mostly clear of cars, except for his chauffeur-driven vehicle. It was still early in the morning and his faithful countrymen were lined up in a perfectly straight line at the bus stop, staring straight ahead. A light snow fell over them.

Stupid people.

He shook his head and let out a sigh. It was probably the reason he was on the outs with his father. Even in this regimented society, where one did not show emotion, it was hard to mask his disdain for this place. It was the reason he longed to travel. Ever since he was expelled from Greece, he was forbidden to leave North Korea. And unless he wanted to run with the dissidents into China, there was no way out. Even then, if he was caught, he would be shot on sight.

After the disgrace of the expulsion, Father would delight in it.

Other countrymen walked briskly to their menial jobs. Each was dressed alike in drab brown, looking like an army of United Parcel Service drivers. Pak smirked, reminded of the UPS drivers he'd seen in Greece. He watched his countrymen marching to work. No one spoke or even acknowledged one another. His country was based on uniformity and control. If anyone was cold or uncomfortable, no one dared complain. They were the lucky ones, the privileged who were allowed to live in Pyongyang in relative luxury, compared to the rest of the country. While people outside the city died of starvation, these people received a meager ration of rice. They occasionally had electricity. They were the chosen ones, picked for their intelligence or special skills. It was the ultimate in race selection. To live outside of Pyongyang meant an early death.

"Turn up the heat," Pak Song-ju ordered his driver.

His acquaintances outside North Korea had heard reports from the World Health Organization (WHO) that millions had died from starvation. They assumed that all of North Korea was a slurry of slums or, at best, grass huts. But Pyongyang was beautiful with amazing architecture, museums, massive buildings that housed institutes of art, culture and sports. The city boasted of a multitude of monuments to the late Great Leader Kim Il-sung.

Great leader, Pak Song-ju scoffed. *Look at the mess we are in.*

His car was driven past the Ryugyong Hotel, a monstrosity of a building, a 105-story pyramid, the seventeenth tallest skyscraper in the world. It sat as a ghost, an empty shell, and a failed attempt of national pride. Construction began in 1987 and was halted in 1992 when the funding ran out.

It's a disgrace—it dwarfs the rest of the skyline.

He wondered how long the people would believe the propaganda—that, as North Korea regained global domination, the city would be transformed into the world's political center, and everyone would bow to the dead Great Leader, Kim Il-sung.

Kim Il-sung's son, Kim Jong-il, referred to as the Dear Leader, ruled for eighteen years and perpetuated the lie. Now dead, he had run the country further into the dark ages and closer to the brink of destruction.

The kingdom was now in the hands of the third generation, Kim Jong-un.

Pak shook his head. *How could the leadership pass over the older two brothers and other great leaders in his country? Hereditary succession does not breed success.*

His thoughts were interrupted when a group of school children started to cross the street in front of his speeding car. His driver accelerated and leaned on the horn. The grade-schoolers leaped back or were yanked back by their teachers who bowed low in apology and disgrace. They had learned from an early age their place in the world.

How dare they interfere with the important.

His driver glanced at him in the rearview mirror, but he stared straight ahead without a fleck of change in his steely eyes.

Pak Song-ju knew he looked the part of the oldest son of the Vice-Chairman of the National Defense Commission, Pak Song-nam, one of the most powerful men who controlled North Korea's vast army. At thirty-eight, Pak Song-ju's chiseled features and good looks came from his mother, Song Hye-suk. He kept his coal-black hair trimmed close to the scalp and wore a tailored suit, in drastic contrast to the drab clothes worn by most officials, including his father. His sense of style was acquired in France where he studied in Paris, and it was yet another personal trait that irritated his father.

Pak tightened his jaw as he thought about his father ordering him to change his appearance when he returned from Paris. "Homosexuality is punishable by death. You look like a woman with that long hair." Pak was not gay. In fact, he prided himself on his virility with the girls.

If he only knew how prolific I am.

Finally, he and his father had come to a compromise. Pak was allowed to wear his suits, but not to any official functions, lest he stand out.

Pak reached for a crystal glass from the middle console, took a sip of water, and replaced the glass.

North Korea has to catch up to the rest of the world.

Most people were not allowed to own a television or even a radio. Only if they were one of the upper most echelon in society could they own either, and then they were restricted to the State's broadcast and nothing more. A typical North Korean had never heard of the Internet nor seen a computer. North Koreans were totally isolated from the rest of the world.

Lest their eyes and minds were opened.

Pak wondered how the people would handle freedom.

Would they embrace it? Or, like a caged animal, be afraid to leave the safety of their shelter? It was only a matter of time until they found out.

"Should I pull to the back of the building?" the driver asked, although he already knew the answer.

The building was a drab, two-story building with no windows. The Korean writing on the front indicated that it was a medical research facility. Pak exited the car and quickly entered through the back door. He was there to make a deposit.

CHAPTER 6

A TIME TO MOURN

Nick had never been very good at socializing. He avoided cocktail parties and hospital fund-raisers. He'd rather watch a ball game alone than make idle chatter with strangers and acquaintances. Public speaking frightened him, and he shied away from serious discussion. He was particularly anxious about speaking at John's funeral the next day. That, combined with the grief of losing his friend, made him exhausted, and he fell back on the hotel bed.

He stared at the ceiling, letting his thoughts drift. Even though he had devoted so much of his life trying to keep people alive, he had spent little time thinking about death. He had experienced the deaths of some of his elder family members—a grandmother and two uncles—and he had witnessed the death of patients, but these events had rarely impacted him. John's death hit him hard.

Was that it? Was that all there was of John's life?

Nick pulled a blanket around his neck. The last time they had talked on the phone was over a year ago, and he remembered his frustration. All John wanted to talk about was his faith and the miracles he and Maggie had witnessed in Guatemala. It was like he and they lived on separate planets and spoke different languages.

Nick had hung up with a strange sense of jealousy. John had married an incredible woman, and now he had this amazing, adventurous and fulfilling life.

They always competed, but how could he compete against that? And now he's gone.

Nick wiped a tear from the corner of his eye and cursed aloud.

It had been many years since his shadow fell anywhere near a church. Growing up, he and his family had attended the Episcopal Church where he was an altar boy. His years of education and focus on science-based work had led him to agree with those who thought religion was for the weak, but he was learning that it was a thin and permeable membrane that separated science from faith.

In his exhausted delirium, the words of an ancient creed filtered through his veil of rational science—*We believe in one God, the Father, the Almighty, Maker of heaven and earth* Something, something. *Came down from heaven, by the power of the Holy Spirit, became incarnate from the Virgin Mary.* Whatever that means. *We look for the resurrection of the dead and the life of the world to come.*

Then it occurred to Nick. It was the Nicene Creed the church recited every Sunday. It stirred something within him. Maybe it was just a longing for simpler times when God was in His heaven and all was right with the world, as they had told him in Sunday School.

But was there really a heaven?

Maggie and John seemed to think so. Nick decided he probably believed in some sort of after-life, but heaven, he wasn't sure of.

Most surgeons compartmentalize pretty well, he concluded. They had to, to be able to do the work. Four days ago, he had accompanied the general surgeon to the surgical waiting room to deliver the news to a waiting family that their son had not made it through surgery. The motorcycle wreck had broken both legs, but the lethal blow was to his chest and had transected his pulmonary artery.

That had been emotionally difficult, but this was physically painful. Nick pushed on his sternum. He couldn't decide if he was having chest pain or a sour stomach. Waves of anxiety washed over him. How was he going to stand up in front of people and talk about his friend?

He sat up and walked into the bathroom, pulling off his

shirt. He turned the faucet to warm and ran the water into the sink, then splashed some over his face. He grabbed the hand towel and dried off. Then he paused, resting both hands on the counter. He looked in the mirror and felt old. His forty-two-year-old body was still in fairly good shape despite call nights, day-old tuna fish sandwiches, and diet Cokes from the fridge in the surgeons' lounge. He was getting a few crow's feet in the corners of his eyes and patches of gray at his temples. But those weren't so much age as badges of experience to give his patients confidence that he had been around the block a few times. Still, he felt old and used up.

Nick pulled off the rest of his clothes, dropped them on the floor, and fell on the bed, pulling the blanket over him. He needed sleep badly, and was almost past the point of exhaustion, but he couldn't turn off the memories of John.

* * *

John and Nick grew up together in Whitefish, Montana. "A stone's throw from where Maggie grew up," as John liked to say. Nick reminded him it was a really, really long stone's throw over the vast Rocky Mountain range and Glacier National Park, but John believed distance was relative.

Even though he and John were best friends, they competed at everything—starting with marbles, on through track and grades, and finally as physicians. John claimed Nick had wimped out by taking the path of least resistance, going into orthopedic surgery to deal with bones. Nick, in turn, told John that there is something wrong with a guy that likes to play in someone's bowels and other orifices with foul-smelling secretions. But they both were excellent at what they did; some had said they were the best.

Whitefish was, at that time, a blue-collar town where logging and the railroad were the main industries. Only half of the high school graduates ever went on to college and only half of those finished. So, when John and Nick were both accepted to medical school from the same class, it was big news.

Once the local ski area was discovered, old Stumptown, as it was called from its logging days, turned into a resort town. The same slopes on which Nick and John had raced began producing Olympic champions like Tommy Moe.

With memories of winter skiing and summer camping, Nick fell into a restless sleep.

* * *

Maggie lay in bed, curled in the fetal position on a pillowcase twice-soaked by her tears. She, too, was exhausted and restless. She'd fall asleep, only to waken with panic and loneliness known only those who have lost a spouse. She felt as though the darkness would swallow her up and spit her into a bottomless pit over and over again. Her body ached as much as her heart. She felt the warmth of her sister, Julie, laying close to her, still supporting her, lightly touching her back, sometimes praying, other times gently singing to her, and, at times, weeping with her.

Since John's death, nighttime was the worst: lonely, cold, and empty. Her family forced her to go to bed; they'd even asked the family doctor for sleeping pills. Of course Maggie refused to take them; she'd dealt with strife, and she'd do it again. She'd remember the nights with John. Like all marriages, theirs had had its ups and downs, but nighttime had always been their solace. It was their time to put the anxieties and pressures of the day behind them and lay naked, spooning as one, their hearts in perfect harmony.

Maggie shuddered in pain. They would never again beat in harmony in this world. John's heart had been ripped out, and her heart was ravaged in agony. Maggie didn't think she could survive. She wasn't sure she wanted to.

"Oh my God, help me," she cried, sobbing so hard she gagged. "I love you so much, John. I love you so much," she repeated over and over, lost in grief and oblivious to her sister's nearness.

Julie turned. "It's going to be okay," she whispered.

"I have never been this afraid in my life," Maggie cried. "Who could have ever done this to him? I keep having visions of John being so alone out there. When they…" Once again she was overcome by sobs.

* * *

In the morning, Julie and her mother helped Maggie to the shower. They then twisted her long hair into a bun, put on a thin camouflage of make-up, and dressed her.

"There, darling. You are so beautiful." Maggie's mother cupped her daughter's cheeks with both her hands.

Maggie wore a simple black skirt and jacket with a purple silk blouse. John had always said she looked beautiful in purple.

The memorial service started at 11:00 a.m., but Maggie was in no hurry. She hoped that the longer she put it off, the more this would all be a bad dream and John would come back to her.

Her mother understood and consoled her. "This will be the worst of it. I know John is with you. Try to feel him with your heart." She wiped a tear from Maggie's eye. "We are here to help you through this, my dear child. Your Heavenly Father is here, too. I know you know that." She wiped a tear from her own eye and looked up. "Lord, give your dear child strength."

Maggie's older brother entered the room and without saying a word wrapped his strong arms around his baby sister.

Maggie took a deep breath, stifled her grief, and straightened up. She found the strength to face their friends. "We better go."

* * *

The service was held in the Christian Life Center in downtown Seattle, a mega-church best suited to fit the expected crowd of well-wishers. When they were home, John and Maggie had attended a small, intimate Bible church in North Ballard, but Pastor Evans of the Christian Life Center graciously opened the doors for this service. John and Maggie's good works were well known around the city after being featured twice in the *Seattle Times*. Even Channel Eight once came to Guatemala to do a piece on the hospital and orphanage. John hated the spotlight, but he knew it would help the kids.

When they pulled up to the church, Maggie watched the people pour in.

"The Pastor told us to take you to the side door so you

wouldn't have to face everyone beforehand," her older brother said, pulling the black suburban the funeral home had loaned to them around the corner.

He would have hated this, Maggie thought. *All the fuss that people are making over him.*

Both Pastor Evans and their own pastor, Chris O'Reilly, met them at the door.

"Hi, Maggie," Pastor Chris said giving her a big bear hug. A rotund man, he smelled of pipe tobacco and exuded the love of the Father. He had been with Maggie and her family all week and was a great source of strength, comfort and even joy.

"Thank you for being here for John," Maggie said, hugging him back.

Pastor Evans stepped up and gave Maggie a hug. "I'm so sorry, Maggie." He had a kind smile. "John was so loved. Our church holds 6000 people. I'm not sure there are many open seats. He has touched many lives in ways I'm sure we can only imagine."

Maggie nodded and patted his arm in thanks.

"We will escort your family up to the front. We are all here for you. If you need anything." He motioned to the ushers. "Okay, let's go in."

Maggie wanted to scream. Her legs would not move. Her head was swimming, and for the first time in her life, she felt like running away. It seemed like forever since she had to do anything without John at her side.

Sensing her difficulty, her brothers came to her aid, grasping her arms, and practically lifting her for the walk down the aisle. Her younger brother kissed her cheek, and she and her family filed in.

As they entered the sanctuary, Maggie saw the floral display on the slightly elevated stage at the front and froze at the sight of the huge screen projecting pictures of her life with John. It was meant as a celebration of their life together, but she was too numb to celebrate. Their life together was over, in spite of the pictures. Still, she looked at them as she moved slowly on the arms of her escorts. There was a photo of their wedding, one of John trying to dance at their reception, one of John standing with Nick on a mountain top, another of John standing by a stream with that goofy hat that he loved and his favorite fishing pole, and still another of the two of them painting the inside of the hospital. So many pictures, so many memories. She wanted to shut her eyes and make them stop. She wanted the service to be over. She wanted to curl up alone in bed and fly away to heaven to be with him. She didn't want to be here. She didn't want to be in this place.

As they drew near to their seats in the front of the church, the slideshow mercifully stopped on a black and white photo of John. It was one that Maggie had taken. It was her very favorite.

There was John squatting on his heels in the middle of a slum in Nicaragua. The people were living in some of the worst conditions Maggie and John had ever seen, each family barely surviving in huts made of palm branches, tin and anything else they could find. Hurricane Andrew had destroyed their homes. Death and sickness swirled thickly in the air. There was John, wearing his Nike hat turned backward and his signature Hawaiian shirt, putting the end of his stethoscope on the belly of a naked five-year-old child, a belly that was huge and probably full of parasites. The wide-eyed child was mesmerized by this tall, thin white person, full of life and at the center of his godly destiny. John smiled gently at the boy.

Pastor Chris stepped to the pulpit. He stood silently for a moment, then turned slightly, extending a hand toward the screen behind him. "I picture Jesus that way," he began, his voice breaking as he drew a handkerchief from his pocket and wiped his eyes.

Pastor Chris briefly introduced John and Maggie's families and read a portion from an article in the *Seattle Post*. Then he invited Maggie's sister to sing one of John's favorite songs, *Holy, Holy, Holy.*

Maggie's father and older brother shared some thoughts. Her father spoke in his native Blackfeet tongue, and her brother translated. He said it was the only true way he could express his feelings about John. Even then, no English words could do justice to the tenderness with which he spoke. He said that he could never have picked out a better husband for his little Maggie. He spoke of the Blackfeet's definition of a man: strong, honorable, and courageous. John was a true warrior at heart.

Nick was next to share. When Maggie's father called him to the front, Nick stumbled to the pulpit and shuffled his papers, inadvertently dropping them. He opened his hands and looked up to heaven. Then he half-smiled at the congregation. "I'm sure John loves to see me looking clumsy," he said, releasing the tension as the crowd chuckled.

"I could tell some real stories on my best friend John," he began, glancing up again. "No worries, mate. I won't destroy your sainthood." He tried to smile through his anxiety.

Nick's faced flushed as he clearly struggled with emotion. He cleared his throat a few times. "John and I sure had some times together," he said, unable to choke back tears. He dug in his pocket for a handkerchief and blotted his eyes.

He looked over at John's folks. John's mother sobbed, her head pinned to Pops's shoulder.

Nick blinked and cleared his throat. "Mom and Pops, I was always thankful for your family. Pops, I was always thankful that you forgave John and me for sinking your boat in Flathead Lake."

Nick seemed to relax as he told the tale about taking Pops's boat out on a sunny Montana afternoon.

"The boat was a beautifully restored wooden motorboat. Pops had spent many years restoring it and only reluctantly gave us permission to take it out by ourselves. After we got the boat in the water, we were cruising along on a beautiful day on Flathead Lake. We hadn't been out but a few minutes when the boat began to act funny and become more and more sluggish. John and I looked at each other with a sense of panic as we realized that in our exuberance to get the boat out, we had forgotten to put the plugs in the back of the boat. We were sinking."

The congregation chuckled.

"Our only hope was to try to get back to shore, which we almost did." Nick shook his head and smiled. "Twenty feet from shore, the boat slipped underwater. It was slow motion: John and I staring at Pops on the dock, Pops staring back at us, the boat sinking lower and lower, and Pops's face getting redder and redder."

From the pulpit, Nick watched Pops shake his head and manage a smile as the crowd laughed.

"After the rescue by a barge with a crane and a long summer of sanding and varnishing, the boat was back as good as new. Right, Pops?"

Pops held out his hand and gave the so-so tilt, and the church crowd laughed again.

Nick paused to regain his thoughts. "John is my best friend." His face flushed as he grew serious. "I, too, have so many questions about this senseless, random act of violence. I find myself asking the *why* in all this. I am really struggling with it. But I do know this: there is no one better than John to teach us about love. He gave up fame and fortune. He gave up the big house and the fancy cars to minister to the poorest of the poor—freely giving of himself. He felt more comfortable in the slums or in the back of a Central American chicken bus than anywhere else. Looking around at all of you today, John is the richest man I know."

Nick choked back more tears. "Love you, John. Save a place by the campfire for me, bud."

Maggie smiled at Nick as he left the podium. An inner sense of peace slowly pushed at the gloom and darkness filling her soul.

He's right. It will only be a short time in the scheme of eternity that I will be with him again. She touched the ring still on her finger. She knew *Forever Yours* was engraved inside.

Pastor Chris returned to the pulpit and adjusted the microphone. "You know, John would have loved this laughter. His wonderful spirit toward life is what makes us miss him so much."

He paused, gazing over the guests. "Last night I didn't sleep well. A scripture kept waking me up. It was John 15:13: '*Greater love has no one than this, that he lay down his life for his friends.*' We know John and Maggie truly demonstrated God's love by laying their lives down for the people in Quetzaltenango, Guatemala. We just never expected something so tragic to happen to such a godly man."

Pastor Chris fidgeted with the large wooden cross hung around his neck. His voice deepened. "I am reminded today that Easter is only a few days away. Like that day 2000 years ago, today…today is the worst of days and the best of days." He paused. "John has been taken from our lives here on earth, but he now walks with Jesus in Heaven, his body, mind, and spirit fully restored, fully resurrected. For those of us who believe in the Lord Jesus Christ, this is our hope. This is the promise that has been made to us. There will be that time when we are all there, together, with all the saints, rejoicing. No more pain, no more sorrow, no more tears. Truly, it is the worst of days and the best of days."

The pastor nodded to Maggie's sister.

On cue, she stood, took the microphone, and sang, *Because He Lives*, the song that Maggie and John had learned while visiting a church in California.

Her sister's song filled the church with joyous lyrics of belief and faith—of Jesus's triumph over death.

Maggie closed her eyes, listened to the words, and held her hands in prayer. In her mind's eye, she saw John standing next to her as they worshipped their God together. She could see his smile and the look of peace that came over him as he entered into the Lord's presence. A great warmth flooded her, and she stood and raised her hands over her head, creating a ripple throughout the church as the congregation rose to stand with her.

When the song ended, Maggie slowly opened her eyes, surprised she was on her feet and blushed with embarrassment. Then, when she realized everyone was standing with her, she felt a wave of strength enter her.

She gestured to her sister to give her the microphone. Maggie's legs would not carry her up to the pulpit, but she knew she had to speak.

But when she opened her mouth, nothing came out. She had a terrible urge to sit down when her father, standing beside her, supported her with his hand on her back.

Maggie wiped a large tear. "Um…John and I…um…I wanted to thank you all for showing so much love to us." She looked at Nick. "I, like you Nick, have so many questions as to how something like this could happen. Everyone here knows that John would do anything for anybody in need. He often would say that his favorite people were the poor."

Maggie's mother handed her a tissue, and she wiped her eyes. "But John loved what he did. He loved the mission. He loved the families. He loved the children." She dabbed her eyes. "Even though…" Her lower lip quivered. "Even though I miss him…" She cleared her throat. "I know that I know I will see him again in heaven. One of John's favorite verses from scripture is in Psalm 23: *'Surely goodness and loving kindness will follow me all the days of my life. And I will dwell in the house of the Lord forever.'*"

Her body heaved with sobs, betraying her spiritual courage, and her father wrapped his arm around her.

Maggie persevered. "I want you all to know. God is good. This evil did not come from God. But God will be faithful to make good things come from this." With increasing strength and resolve, she smiled. Speaking to herself as much as to everyone else, she said, "Evil does not win."

She gave the microphone to her father, and he helped her sit down. The congregation sat. Her father turned to a group of elders from their Tribe standing against the wall at the back and waved them to come forward. The elders marched solemnly to the front of the church where Maggie's father and brothers waited. The tribesmen positioned themselves around a large ceremonial drum placed at the center of the stage. In front of the drum and facing the crowd was an empty chair on which a drumstick had been placed.

Maggie's father spoke. "With my Native People, we celebrate Jesus with our song and dance. This song talks about the love that our Heavenly Father has for each one of us and how He longs to be reunited with each one of His children and the promise of heaven."

He began the rhythmic drumming and was joined by Maggie's brothers and the elders. A beautifully haunting Blackfeet song filled the church. Only a select few understood the words, but everyone understood the meaning. It was a transcendent moment. The song reached a crescendo as the drummers beat the taut, elk-skin drum. The song grew louder and louder, then suddenly stopped. The congregation sat in total silence.

Then, silently and in single file, the tribesmen left the stage, with the exception of Maggie's father who remained standing beside the empty chair. When the elders had returned to the back of the church, Maggie's father held up the drumstick. An eagle feather dangled from its ornate, beaded end. With both hands, Maggie's father raised the stick to the ceiling and then gently placed it on the drum. A single beam of light streamed from above and bathed the drumstick in a rapturous glow.

CHAPTER 7

FOR THE FATHERLAND

Dr. Chul came around the corner, sweat-soaked, frightened, just in time to see Pak. While he was called "doctor," the closest medical training he had had was as a medic during the Korean War. When the North invaded South Korea in what the North calls the *Joguk Haebang Jeonjaeng* or the "Fatherland Liberation War," Chul was in the first wave of infantry. He knew horror. Four million people died in the conflict that left a divided peninsula, devastating the economies in both countries and separating families. Now, at age seventy-five, the memories of his fallen comrades lodged deep in his soul.

Gowned in a blood-stained, white butcher's apron and surgical gloves, he wiped dripping sweat from his forehead with the back of his wrist. It was not heat that made him sweat, it was fear.

Chul watched Pak pluck an apple off the table and put it in his pocket. Chul had saved it for the girl upstairs, but he did not stop Pak.

"Chairman Pak," he said, bowing low at the waist. "Your arrival is unexpectedly early."

Chul called him "chairman" only out of respect for Pak's father, Vice-Chairman of the National Defense Commission. Pak Song-nam had appointed his son begrudgingly to Minister of Cabinet General Intelligence Bureau of the Korean Worker's Party Central Committee, North Korea's equivalent to the CIA. To his father's surprise, Pak had blossomed, performing his duties well and surpassing expectations when his team recently executed a successful cyber-attack on American and South Korean government computers.

Pak barely acknowledged Chul's presence, even though Chul was the director of the medical research facility, but Chul's blood-stained gown caught his eye as he passed the doctor, anxious to get to the business at hand.

Pak gripped the handrail to pull himself up the stairs to the second floor. He had gone only a few steps when Chul spoke.

"Excuse me, Mr. Chairman, Sir?"

Pak whirled around with anger at his subordinate. He didn't have to say a word; his expression said it all.

Chul knew to speak out was a life-altering decision. He bowed so low that his knees gave way, and he fell to the cold, grey tile.

"Forgive me, Chairman, I wanted to ask—"

"Can this not wait?"

Chul had anxiously pondered this moment for weeks, but in a society based on fear, nothing could have prepared him for it. Standing up for righteousness was unheard of. After all, what was the definition of right in a country that dictated what was right and what was wrong? Someone like Chul was not to have an opinion. He'd known for a while what Pak was doing was wrong, but he had put it out of his mind and enjoyed most of the work. It was a privilege to be a part of this secret new order.

But Chul couldn't overlook it any longer. The girls had gotten younger and younger, and the risks greater and greater. He saw his bloody handprints on the tile. This was the fourth girl in two weeks who died. It was time to say something.

"Forgive me, *Suseung-nim*," he said, using the ultimate term for master.

He could feel Pak's eyes burning holes in the back of his neck.

"We just lost another young girl," Chul said. "I tried the best that I could, but she was too small and the baby…I could not get the baby out. She bled. I could not stop it." Chul knew what would happen for speaking out because no one ever questioned authority.

Even so, he found courage in his mind and body and lifted himself off the floor. Pictures of his wife and son flashed in his mind. He saw his own twelve-year old granddaughter in the faces of the girls at the clinic. This was a defining moment in his life; he sensed a presence that gave him courage. Chul didn't know about a god. He knew about the dead Great Leader Kim Il-sung. Maybe that was the presence that gave him courage to abandon the discouragement and hopelessness that filled his days in exchange for this new, inexplicable peace.

A frail, aged man, Chul stood as tall as his arthritic spine would allow. He looked Pak in the eyes. What he saw was darkness, rage and hate that sent a shiver down his spine. But Chul continued. He had to.

"Mr. Pak," he announced, addressing him as an equal. It was the first time he had done so, and it would be the last. "We must not use girls so young. They are too frail, their bodies too immature. There are plenty of older girls that are of age."

Pak stared through Chul without emotion. "Yes, like your granddaughter," and turned to continue up the stairs.

Chul knew his family might never see him again.

* * *

Pak regarded Chul's voice an unwelcome intrusion in the excitement of his daily visit. But he was glad when the antiseptic smell of the facility erased the sound of Chul.

There were no windows on the second-floor, and the hallway was dimly lit. One of the few lights illuminated pictures of Kim Il-sung, Kim Jong-il, and the newest dictator Kim Jong-un. Every building and almost every room in the country was plastered with portraits of the leaders. Pak had almost stopped noticing them. He hated them.

Pak entered the room without knocking. He paused for a moment to let the sweet perfume fill his nostrils. It was the same as it had been every day for years—the same lighting, the same décor, the same fragrance, but a different girl.

The perfume was ordered from Paris. It was rumored to be his mother's favorite, but no one but Pak knew for sure. The room was set up like the room he loved—his mother's.

The girl had been told on how to lie on the bed and what

expression to hold on her face. As Pak appeared in the doorway, this girl emitted a small, nearly inaudible whimper. Her attendees had covered her small budding breasts and waist with silk and painted her face with heavy makeup. She shifted slightly as she fought the urge to cover herself.

Seeing her fear, Pak's excitement rose. He had never been able to distinguish between fear and sexual excitement. The child's pupils were dilated with terror. Pak noticed her lack of pubic hair and judged her to be about eleven years old.

Pak thought of his mother. If she'd still been alive, she would have delighted in this scene. Pak imagined a whole cloud of generational witnesses rejoicing in this ritual. Many times in history, Japan had invaded Korea. Even up to World War II, the Japanese used millions of Koreans in forced labor camps. Pak and his maternal lineage were born out of this, a secret hidden from his father but revealed to him by his dying mother. His mother was the only one in generations not forced into sexual slavery. But the evil ran deep in her psyche, and she was a slave to her own sexuality and the foul spirits that controlled her compulsions.

Pak began to undress, making a pageant of shedding his garments. He had learned to linger in the moment. It was a pleasure to do his duty. Thanks to him and a few chosen associates, the country was experiencing a baby boom. Under his direction, baby factories operated throughout North Korea. The plan was to produce a superior race, and the method was artificial insemination. While Pak was in charge and delegated his directives, he believed there was something sacred in performing the act himself.

He loved when the girl was a virgin. His perennially cold stare warmed with sentimentality as he sat on the edge of the bed and stroked the girl's hair.

"It is all right, my little one," he whispered, "this is your destiny. Today you become a mother for the Fatherland."

CHAPTER 8

AN INVITATION

Maggie and Nick stood beside the car at the airport, neither wanting to say goodbye. Nick was sorry he had to leave the morning after the service. He pulled Maggie's rain jacket closed around her neck to shield her against the Seattle mist.

"You going to be all right?"

She nodded, looking at her feet. "My family will stay as long as I need them."

Nick experienced a twinge of guilt. "Maggie, I'm so sorry I have to leave today. I'm on call tonight, and I just couldn't find anyone to cover for me."

"I understand," she smiled, looking into his eyes. "Really, I do."

Nick knew that she did, but that didn't help to ease his guilt. He asked, "What can I do that would help you the most?"

She hesitated. "Nick, I know you're busy. I don't even know if I should ask this of you." She paused. "Would you consider coming down to Guatemala to help me? I really need to return to the Hope Center and our staff."

It was his turn to look at his feet.

"You don't have to give me an answer right now," she said. "But would you at least think about it?"

He looked into her deep, dark eyes. "Let me see what I can do."

* * *

Back home in his apartment, Nick had barely put his keys down when his beeper went off. He glanced at its message: *STAT. Dr. Hart, please report to the ER immediately.*

Living five minutes away from the MED was a huge bonus for Nick as his Porsche sped down Dr. Martin Luther King Jr. Ave. He was on his Bluetooth phone in the car. "What do you have?" he asked the chief resident.

"Dr. Hart, we have a ten-year-old that was playing by train tracks. He slipped under one of the train cars. It got both his legs. It's bad, probably need amputations, but thought we better get your thoughts before we proceed."

"His parents there yet?"

"They're on their way. Not sure we can wait."

"You get pictures?" Nick asked, thinking of the legal implications. "I'm there in two."

"We're headed to the OR. He's lost tons of blood, but I think we are getting caught up."

"See you there."

Nick squealed into his parking spot and saw the tire marks that he left behind after his talk with Anita Roe a few days earlier. Residual anger rose inside him.

"What a bitch," he muttered. He really could not say he was happy to be back.

* * *

Nick burst through the OR doors to Trauma One. The room buzzed with activity. James Taylor's *Fire and Rain* came through the stereo in the corner.

The young boy looked ghostly from the blood loss. A red puddle stained the blue surgical drop cloth underneath him.

What a contrast.

Nick looked at the boy with tangled blond hair and a healthy dose of freckles on an angelic face, a skinny preadolescent body, and gruesome and grotesque leg injuries.

The loss of innocence.

Nick put his hand on the boy's arm. At least he was warm and alive. Dr. Andrews, a female anesthesiologist, looked up from her monitors at the head of the OR table. She wore her mask pulled down under her nose. The whites of her eyes were red as they met Nick's.

"You okay?" Nick asked.

"My son just turned ten. Sometimes it gets to me." Her face flushed as she turned her attention to the patient. "I mean, yeah, I think we've pretty well transfused him. He may need more depending on what you guys do."

"This is a bad one," Nick said as he looked down at the mangled legs. "Never easy."

"Yeah, it really keeps you on your knees for your kids," she replied.

Nick thought about asking what she meant. He had heard a lot about prayer the last twenty-four hours, but he was interrupted by the OR nurse handing him a pack of sterile gloves. It was Jasmine. He smiled at her through his mask, remembering their encounter a few nights ago.

But this time Jasmine was all business. "Dr. Hart," she nodded. "The guys are out scrubbing. They told me to tell you they have already taken pictures but wanted your final word."

With all the tables around him filled with sterile instruments and supplies, Nick found a flat surface on the boy's chest for the pack of sterile gloves. He removed the pair, carefully unfolded the wrapping, and slipped them on.

He gently lifted the boy's right leg at the thigh, where a mangled mess of muscle and tissue, connected by frayed tendons, hung from above the knee, or where the knee used to be. He could see the jagged end of the femur stained with grease from the train.

"Geez," he said, shaking his head.

The mess continued down to mid-calf. There lay the dilemma. A perfect ten-year-old foot and lower leg lay at ninety degrees to the leg, hooked on by the grizzly mess. Nick picked up the other leg to see mirrored injuries.

"What a mess." Instinctively, he felt for pulses in the feet. He was almost relieved that there were none. He had no idea how to reconstruct all the damage to the tissue and muscle, never mind the huge loss of bone. He hated amputations. They felt like such a defeat.

Nick's head spun, and he realized his heart was racing. He leaned against the table to steady himself and wiped sweat from his brow with the back of his wrist.

"Turn the frickin' heat down," he ordered the nurse by the door. "It must be ninety degrees in here."

The nurse looked at Nick and shrugged at the anesthesiologist. Dr. Andrews stood up. "I'm sorry for the sauna, Nick, but we have got to keep the little guy's temp up."

Maybe I'm coming down with something, Nick told himself, not wanting to admit his anxiety with the gruesomeness of the situation.

Two Residents, led by the Senior Trauma Fellow, interrupted Nick's assessment as they backed through the OR door with their scrubbed hands held up in front of them.

"Terrible, huh?" Pete, the trauma fellow said, almost reading Nick's mind. Pete was doing an extra year in trauma training and would join the team as staff in five months. "I thought even about a femoral turn down," he said, describing a very rare surgery that was mostly used in limb salvage from malignant tumors around the knee. In this surgery, the knee is resected and the lower leg brought up and coupled with the femur, and the foot is intentionally put on backward so the ankle becomes the knee, essentially resulting in an above-the-knee amputation to function as a below-the-knee amputation, speeding up the patient's recovery.

Nick stared at the boy's legs.

Pete is going to make a great surgeon. He's a good, critical thinker.

"That's good thinking, Pete." Nick rubbed the end of the bones with his gloved finger. Grease and dirt had been ground into them.

A nurse slipped Pete's surgical gown over his arms. Again, as if reading Nick's mind, he said, "But I've made the call to amputate. The wounds are too dirty. Besides, the femoral turn down takes an hour surgery and turns the whole thing into an all-nighter. I'm just not sure the little guy would survive it. Even with the amputations there is no way we will close the wounds today with them being so contaminated. It will probably be at least a week before we can even attempt to close the wounds if he doesn't pus 'em out too bad."

Nick was aware of the possibility of infection. "That's the right call," he sighed. "I'll go scrub."

* * *

Nick was in no hurry to talk with the boy's family, but he understood how anxiously they waited an answer. He leaned against his locker as he put on fresh scrubs. No one wants to see their own child's blood.

Blood. Maggie's pastor talked about Christ shedding His blood for all of us. Just not sure I get it.

It felt like his life was unraveling, and he wanted to run away. Instead, he sat on the bench. He thought about calling his parents, but he didn't want to worry them. Would they even understand? The Hart family dealt with pain by not talking about it. *Pull yourself up by the bootstraps and get on with it.* Anxiety was becoming Nick's constant companion. Even in the OR, typically his place of solace, he found fear and self-doubt creeping in.

He willed himself up from the bench and his thoughts.

Hope Maggie is doing okay. I don't know what I'm going to tell her. I can't imagine trying to take a week or two off to go to Guatemala.

Nick went to the waiting area. He realized he didn't even know the boy's name. Guilt washed over him.

Am I getting too calloused by all this?

Fortunately, staffing the waiting room desk was a volunteer who knew Dr. Hart. He had fixed her broken hip two years earlier.

"Dr. Hart, Jeremiah's folks are over there in the corner." She looked him with tenderness, knowing what he had to do.

"Thanks, Rose."

"Jeremiah," he said repeating the boy's name.

The family stood when they saw the volunteer pointing to them and a surgeon looking their way. The woman held her hand cupped over her mouth, and the man wrapped his arm around her. A teenage boy and older teenage girl stood on either side of them. They were dressed plainly, the bearded man in a plaid shirt and jeans and the woman in a cotton dress and cardigan.

Nick shook the man's heavily-calloused, dirt-stained hand, redolent with a mixture of chainsaw oil and sawdust.

"You are Jeremiah's parents?"

The woman nodded.

"How's our Jeremiah?" the father asked, still holding Dr. Hart's hand.

"The tremendously good news is that it appears that your son is going to survive."

Jeremiah's mother gasped with relief, and his father hugged her with his free arm.

"Here, please sit down." Nick gestured to their chairs and pulled another directly in front of them. "I'm sorry that we could not have talked before going into surgery, but your son's life was in the balance, and we had to proceed quickly to save his life. I'm Nicklaus Hart, and I am his orthopedic surgeon. What have you been told about Jeremiah's condition?"

"The police told us that he had been hit by a train. We have been expecting the worst," the father relayed. "One of the nurses came and sat with us and told us that he was in surgery."

"Can we see him?" the mother cried.

"We will get you back to see him as soon as they have him well-stabilized in the recovery area."

"But he's going to live?" the mother asked.

"Jeremiah is still very sick from the trauma he has gone through. We have him in a medically-induced coma, and machines are breathing for him so his body can rest, but yes, I expect him to live."

Jeremiah's parents hugged each other again.

"Thank you, Lord Jesus," his father proclaimed.

"Thank you, Father," his mother said, choking back tears. "Thank you, Dr. Hart, for saving our little boy." She touched his arm.

Nick felt guilty. It wasn't even him they should be thanking. It was the EMTs who provided first care to the boy at the scene and the trauma team in the Emergency Department who really saved his life. He wanted to explain, but they needed to know the bad news. Nausea swept over him.

"Jeremiah has a long road ahead of him," Nick began.

How do I tell his parents that I took off their son's legs?

"Did the police or the nurse tell you about the damage the train did to Jeremiah's legs?"

The parents stared at him without saying a word, so Nick pressed forward.

"You see, the train either went right over his legs or his legs somehow got tied up in the wheel mechanism. It was really severe." Nick flashed back, seeing the mangled legs for the first time. "I want you to know that if there had been absolutely anyway we could have saved his legs, we would have."

Nick could see the tears welling in their eyes and feel tears in his own. He could not imagine what it was like to be a parent absorbing this news.

"I am so sorry, but we had to amputate your son's legs above the knees." Nick reached out to both parents and put his hands on their shoulders. "I am so sorry."

CHAPTER 9

HUMAN RIGHTS

Sitting in the grandstand, Pak scanned the sea of soldiers and citizens—63,453 all together—that filled Kim Il-sung Square. Knowing the exact number and the names of each one was the business of his office.

He winced when a stiff wind blasted his face and the faces of the leaders sitting adjacent to him. There was nothing he could do about the weather, but he was satisfied with the sun warming their backs and the bright light gave them the best view of the crowd.

He glanced down and to his left and saw his father sitting three chairs from Kim Jong-un. Pak would be glad to see both of them dead. The entire crowd and leadership, including Pak, wore drab green uniforms; only Kim Jong-un wore his trademark black overcoat and leather gloves.

Between the massive crowd and the grandstand, a military band performed the North Korean national anthem. Kim Jong-un stood, attentive to the massive red and blue flag. The single-starred flag appeared to genuflect in his presence.

The anthem rose to a deafening crescendo, and Kim turned and waved to the crowd. As if on command, the crowd erupted in loud applause and praise for their Supreme Leader. The military band followed with a rousing march. Kim clapped his hands to the music's rhythm, and everyone followed his lead.

The wind blew the bowl-cut tuft of hair on the leader's head, and many other leaders reached to secure their own oversized, soviet-style dress uniform headgear. Across the center of the crowd a large banner whipped in the wind, its words dancing like a dervish: "LET'S DEFEND WITH OUR LIVES." Pak secured his own hat and caught a residue of perfume from the latest girl that morning. He could barely suppress a smile of pleasure. Earlier, when he was told he would not accompany Kim to the Sinchon Museum that morning with his father, Pak didn't protest. He preferred another appointment at the same time at the maternity clinic.

The rally and the museum visit had been set in motion when a U.S. delegation led the United Nations General Assembly in drafting a resolution to indict Kim on human rights abuses.

The Sinchon Museum commemorated the alleged mass killing of over 35,000 North Korean civilians by the U.S. military in 1950. It housed rooms full of anti-American propaganda and hatred, including hundreds of paintings depicting U.S. soldiers tearing babies from their mother's arms, cutting the hearts out of their countrymen, shooting women and children in the back of their heads, and other atrocities.

Pak knew the museum well, both from the annual visits he had made with his school class and now as the leader of North Korean spy organization. Many of the accusations were unproven, but the museum served its purpose well to feed the masses with hatred of the U.S. pigs.

He had watched from the clinic the televised and closely orchestrated visit. Kim Jung-un posed in front of a large painting of an American soldier holding a bayonet with a baby speared on the end while the child's mother clawed at his feet.

"The massacres committed by the U.S. imperialist aggressors in Sinchon showed that they are cannibals and homicides seeking pleasure in slaughter," Kim shouted into the microphone of the North Korean Broadcast.

After the Supreme Leader spoke, a top general was interviewed by the news agency. He stated, "The U.S. imperialists should bear in mind that we have the option to launch a pre-emptive nuclear strike."

Pak smiled to himself. The pre-emptive strike was in the works—something that neither the Supreme Leader nor the general knew. He wondered how his team in Guatemala was doing.

His thoughts were interrupted when Kim Jong-un pumped his fist into the air, and the crowd did likewise followed by a thunderous cheer, "Long live the Kim dynasty."

CHAPTER 10

A WELCOMED HERO

The amputation of Jeremiah's legs catapulted Nick back to the frenzy of the MED, keeping him occupied with more surgeries, procedures, and appointments, busy enough to be distracted from the pain and emotion of the previous week. He did try to call Maggie, but was interrupted by his beeper in mid-dial. He planned to call her back, but hadn't yet. *Maybe it was just as well.* He still hadn't made a decision about going to Guatemala. He hoped time would pass and everyone would forget.

Nick still wasn't getting enough sleep. What rest he got was interrupted by dreams, hideous dreams from which he'd wake up, drenching in sweat, narrowly escaping being strangled by a large snake curling itself around his neck. And he was drinking more than usual, including the hard stuff. He knew better; addiction traps of alcohol, drugs and sex run deep for surgeons. But he needed relief from stress.

Nick was pacing outside the main entrance to the MED, waiting. He glanced at his watch. He was supposed to meet Jeremiah's family at ten, and it was already quarter past. Jeremiah was recovering nicely, at least physically. They had removed his breathing tube, but it was necessary to take him back to the OR daily to wash his wounds and change the Wound-Vacs. Dirty wounds like Jeremiah's couldn't be closed after surgery. They had to be left open to mature and closed only when the infection risk passed. Even with daily anesthesia, it would have been too cruel to pull bandages off the raw flesh. The Wound-Vac was a wonderful addition to a doctor's toolbox. The Wound-Vac consisted of sponges with a vacuum that sucked fluid and infection from the wound and pulled together the edges of the skin. Jeremiah's wounds looked so good that Nick hoped to be able close them this afternoon.

Kids are so resilient.

But Nick worried about Jeremiah's mental state because the boy was withdrawing more each day. At Nick's request, the hospital psychologist visited the boy. The visit occurred on the day Jeremiah looked under the sheets where his legs used to be and was devastated. The psychologist assured him everything would be all right, but Jeremiah only stared out the window saying nothing.

When that proved fruitless, Nick had another idea, and he was about to put it into action. He glanced at his watch again. *Come on.*

He was distracted when a man nearby chuckled, precipitating a coughing spasm. Nick figured the man was one of the many homeless that hung around the MED, and, instinctively, he took a few steps sideways to escape the phlegm from the cough.

"Your watch broken?" the man said, catching his breath.

Nick flashed a half smile to appease him.

The man sat on a bench, bundled in three coats on this warm day; next to him was a bag stuffed with what looked like his worldly belongings.

"What time is it?" the man croaked.

"Uh," Nick glanced at his watch again.

The man broke into a fit that was more laughter than cough. Nick flinched. "It's quarter past ten. Ten sixteen, to be exact."

The man snorted with laughter.

Nick looked at him and scowled.

Bug off, old man.

"You know what time it really is, son?"

Nick crossed his arms and squared his body. He did not like being ridiculed, especially by this dirty, old bum.

The man hobbled to his feet. Nick held firm; he could give a sharp right cross if the man came any closer. But just for good measure, he took a step back.

When he stood upright, the man's face softened. He smiled and spoke clearly. "Nicklaus, it's time for a change."

Nick was surprised and wary. "Do I know you?"

"No. No, I suppose you don't." He reached for his bag, mumbled something, and nodded at Nick.

Nick didn't know what to say or what the man expected. On guard, he watched the man pick up his bag, steady himself for mobility, and walk away. After a few steps, the man turned and winked at Nick. Then he turned away and ambled down the sidewalk.

That was weird. And how did he know my name?

Nick pondered this for a moment. *Of course.* He was wearing his white doctor coat. His name embroidered in blue above the chest pocket. He tried to make sense of the encounter when he was interrupted.

"Hey, Nick. Sorry I'm late, man."

Nick whirled around to face a familiar face in a Service "C" Marine Uniform, looking every part a soldier—leathery face, square jaw, tremendous build.

"Buck. It's so good to see you." Nick stuck out his hand.

Sergeant Blake "Buck" Hanson pushed his hand away and embraced him. Buck's big bear hug almost lifted him off the ground. They laughed at Nick's embarrassment. Nick wasn't accustomed to this show of affection at work, but Buck was famous for hugs. He was a man who loved life and was not afraid to show it.

"Who's your friend?" Buck asked, looking after the old man tottering down the walk.

"Just one of my many fans, I guess," Nick shrugged. *Who was that man?*

"Well, let's head 'em up and move 'em out," Buck said in his deep, husky John Wayne voice. He put his arm around Nick's shoulders and steered him toward the entrance.

Nick noted Buck's chest full of ribbons. "Geez, you get some more of those?"

"Yeah, only two bits apiece at the commissary. Just picked a few more up today," Buck ribbed back.

Nick knew Buck had earned each one. The pink scar across his lower jaw was a footnote in his story.

Nick and Buck made their way to the elevator and walked in. The door was halted by a hand from outside. It belonged to a young woman, accompanied by another. Both wore white scrub uniforms with nametags hanging from lanyards identifying them as student nurses.

"Sorry," the first student apologized as they joined the men and turned to face the closing door. They nudged each other. The shorter student blushed and they giggled.

The blushing student nurse fanned herself with her hand. "Eww, it's hot in here!" They laughed again.

Nick noticed the taller student's white scrub pants revealed bright pink, cheeky panties. She might as well have worn a sign that said, "CALL ME." He elbowed Buck and tilted his head.

Buck frowned and raised his fist at Nick.

Is he going to beat me to a pulp if I don't stop or is he showing me his wide, gold wedding band?

Nick held up hands in surrender.

The elevator stopped, and the girls walked out. As the door closed, the taller student turned and smiled at the men.

"See how hard my job is?" Nick grinned.

"Stand down, soldier," Sergeant Hanson ordered.

"Whoa, Buck, I bet you're a tough drill sergeant."

"You have no idea."

He sounded gruff, but Nick admired Buck for being a man of principle, and he was embarrassed for his elevator antics.

What's wrong with me?

"Don't be so hard on yourself," Buck said, reading Nick's body language and putting a hand on his shoulder. "You've had a tough go of it yourself. Come on, let's go see this boy."

The elevator door opened to the orthopedic ward.

"Jeremiah is in that room," Nick said, pointing to a room a few doors down.

When they walked through the door, Jeremiah's father got up from the chair next to the bed. His mother, sitting in a chair in the corner, looked up, marking a page in a book with a soft, well-worn leather cover. She smiled brightly at Dr. Hart and the uniformed soldier. Jeremiah sat in bed with a heavy affect, scowling as usual and staring blankly out the window.

Jeremiah refused to look Nick in the face, and Nick understood. He was the bearer of bad news—more tests, more shots, more surgery, more pain.

Jeremiah's father met them halfway into the room.

"This is the special guest I told you about," Nick said. "This is Sergeant Blake Hanson. These are the Berglunds."

Mr. Berglund shook Buck's hand. "Sergeant Hanson, thank you so much for coming to see our son. It means so much to us that you would take the time."

Nick saw Jeremiah steal an admiring glance at the tall, muscular soldier with a chest full of colorful ribbons. Then, as if he knew Nick was watching, Jeremiah turned back to the window.

"Sir, the honor is mine," Buck said, returning the handshake.

The sergeant ducked under the overhead bar attached to the bed that suspended the trapeze patients use to pull themselves up. "Ma'am," he extended his hand to Mrs. Berglund.

She stood, dwarfed by the soldier, and shook his hand. "Thank you." She smiled broadly. "My father was a Marine. Thank you for serving our country."

"You're welcome, ma'am. Good book you're reading." Nodding at the book in her hand. She smiled back in agreement.

Buck stood at the end of the bed and looked at Jeremiah, not saying a word. If it had been Batman himself standing at the foot of his bed, the boy would have probably ignored him as well.

Buck and Jeremiah were locked in a silent battle.

Nick glanced from one to the other, not sure what to do. Then he saw a tear roll down Buck's massive cheek.

Mr. Berglund broke the silence and went to Jeremiah's bedside. "Son, this is Sergeant Hanson, a friend of Dr. Hart's. He's come to see you. You know your manners."

"Yes, sir," the boy answered without conviction.

Nick sensed that Jeremiah was trying hard to conceal his surprise. Like many boys, Jeremiah probably played with GI

Joes, and he must have been surprised to find a real one standing in front of him—flat top haircut, radiant green eyes, and a large jagged scar down the left side of his face.

A male nurse poked his head in the door. "What do you need?"

After exchanging puzzled looks, they realized Jeremiah had accidentally pushed the nurse's call button.

"Give us a minute," Nick snapped at the unwelcome intrusion. He guessed he probably overreacted, but the nurse was one of his least favorites.

"Whatever," the nurse sneered, turned on his heels, and slammed the door behind him.

Nick fumed.

Jeremiah took it all in.

"Doc Hart always grouchy like that?" Buck winked at the boy.

Jeremiah stared at the sergeant without blinking, sizing him up.

Poor kid. There were probably not many people in this place that he trusted. Nick watched the encounter. *Probably the last thing he remembers is having fun around the trains and then waking up here in incredible pain. And having no legs.*

"You want me to smack him one?" Buck said lifting his fist toward Nick.

Jeremiah almost smiled. It was the first near smile they had seen for days. Then he turned swiftly back to the window, fighting a full smirk with little success, the corners of his mouth twitching with a concealed grin.

Buck took the opportunity to sit in the chair next to the bed. "What do your friends call you?" Buck offered his hand to shake.

Jeremiah turned to him, his eyes widening at the massive hand, and pulled himself up slightly with the overhead trapeze. "JJ. They call me JJ."

"My friends call me Buck. You can call me Buck."

"Yes, sir," Jeremiah pulled himself higher and put his little hand in the man's huge grip.

"I hear you've had a pretty tough go of it, my friend."

Nick sensed that Jeremiah was tempted to pull away, far away, out the window, but he could tell something about this man gave the boy comfort.

"I hear you've been one tough soldier."

Jeremiah grinned and refocused on the man with the military ribbons in brilliant colors.

"You know what a lot of those mean, don't you, son?" Jeremiah's father said. "He loves to pore over his grandfather's ribbons," he told Buck. "I've watched him spend hours running his fingers over the awards. He bugged us to death to tell him stories of the man."

Buck watched the boy admire his ribbons. "Would you like to touch them, JJ?"

"Oh no," the mother stood and moved toward the bed. "He shouldn't…"

Buck softly motioned her to stop. "I really don't mind, ma'am." He moved closer so Jeremiah could touch the ribbons.

Jeremiah reached out but stopped. He glanced at both of his parents to make sure he wouldn't be in trouble. They nodded slowly.

"It's okay, JJ," Buck said. "I would be honored."

Jeremiah ran his finger over the ribbons, mesmerized. He stopped at the purple ribbon.

"You know that one?" Buck asked.

Jeremiah hesitated. "That's a purple heart. My granddad had one. Ma tells me that's when he was shot," he said turning back to the window, "and when he died."

"I've had many friends who have laid down their lives for this country, just like your granddad," Buck reassured him. "He must have been an honorable man."

Jeremiah looked back at Buck.

Nick saw trust build.

"Hey, I have something for you." Buck announced. He stood and dug into the front pocket of his uniform shirt. He pulled something out and held his closed fist to Jeremiah.

The boy didn't know how to respond.

"Hold out your hand," Buck said.

Jeremiah held his tiny hand under Buck's fist. Buck opened his hand and dropped a heavy, metallic coin into the boy's palm and closed the boy's fingers around it. Jeremiah lifted his fist to his face and opened his hand.

The coin was the size of a super-sized silver dollar. Jeremiah's eyes got wider and wider. He saw the image on the front of the coin; it was the Purple Heart medal coin.

"Turn it over, son."

Jeremiah turned it over and read the engraving: JEREMIAH BERGLUND.

Jeremiah's parents began to cry, and tears formed in Nick's eyes. *What a guy. A replica coin with a Purple Heart image engraved with the kid's name. Above and beyond the call.*

Buck stood, snapped to attention, and smartly saluted the boy. Jeremiah sat up straight. He looked like he'd grown a foot taller.

"Ooh Rah," Buck grunted the marine call. "You're a good soldier, son."

Jeremiah's parents rushed to thank the Sergeant.

"I can't tell you how much this means to all of us," Mr. Berglund said and Mrs. Berglund nodded enthusiastically.

Then a small voice said, "Sergeant Buck, can you tell me how you got your Purple Heart? I mean, I can see the scar on your face and all."

It was Jeremiah. His parents were surprised to hear his voice, as he had not uttered many words all week.

"Well, you see…" Buck stumbled over his words, as he didn't much care to remember the day he was nearly killed. "That'll be a story for another day, but just two years ago I was in a bed just like this. Dr. Hart here was one of my doctors. He took real good care of me, like he's doing for you. He's a good guy."

Nick was embarrassed with the focus on him, but he saw Jeremiah's look soften toward him.

"Do as he says, and he'll fix you up as good as new. Just like me."

Jeremiah's face was doubtful.

Buck leaned toward him. "Can I show you something, JJ?"

Jeremiah had to lean over the bed to follow Buck's hands down to the bottom of his pant legs. He admired Buck's highly-polished black shoes, but he wasn't sure that was what he was supposed to see. Then Buck lifted his pant legs. Jeremiah couldn't believe it. His eyes filled with wonder as he beheld Buck's metallic prosthetic legs. Not just one leg but two.

"You see, son, we have a lot in common, you and I."

Jeremiah saw truth in his eyes.

"JJ, you do as Dr. Hart says, and you will get a pair of these babies, and you will do everything you ever dreamed of doing."

Tears streamed down the boy's cheeks. "I really like baseball...I just thought...Do you really think?"

"I don't think, son, I know. I see your mama reading the Good Book there." He indicated the Bible in her lap. "I'm a Christian, too, and I'll be praying for you. *'You can do ALL things through Christ who strengthens you,'*" Buck added, quoting from the book of Philippians.

* * *

Buck and Nick said their goodbyes at the front of the hospital.

"Oh here, give Jeremiah this card with my phone number and let him know he can call me anytime. It will give you some brownie points when he starts to forget that you're the good guy."

Both chuckled. "Buck, you're the good guy. Thank you so much for coming over."

"Well, thank the Wounded Warrior Project. Besides you, they are the ones that really helped me get back on my feet."

Buck gave Nick a sharp slap on the back. "I'll be praying for you."

Nick considered letting it go and returning to sanctum of the hospital, but turned back toward Buck. "You really believe that stuff?"

"In Christ, you mean?"

"Yeah, and what you said to Jeremiah and about prayer?"

"Brother, when you've been to hell, you're glad when someone has been there before you to conquer it. It's not a place you want to linger." Buck looked into Nick's eyes. "You okay?"

Nick sighed loudly.

"When's the last time you had a vacation?" Buck asked. "Nick, man, I've known you as a doctor and a friend. You're looking ragged around the edges. You know that 'physician heal thyself' thing?"

Nick looked down to hide the anger and hurt inside him. "Hmmm," he uttered, trying to find words to respond.

Buck was probably right. He had not only fought for his country, he had fought for his life.

Buck was the only other man beside John that Nick would truly ever want next to him in battle. He would trust him with his life.

"Look, man, you are the best surgeon I know," Buck continued, "and a true friend. Believe you me, I know how hard it is to be vulnerable, to be mortal. It's time to take off the cape, Superman, and take a rest."

Buck gave Nick one of his famous bear hugs wrapped in a belly laugh. "It's going to be okay, my friend. I WILL be praying for you."

Somehow, Nick knew there was truth in both statements.

CHAPTER 11

DECISION TIME

Nick hit the button on the wall that gave him access to the operating room. The automatic doors swung open.

"Oh, Dr. Hart," Anita Roe called out from behind him in her southern drawl.

He took two steps forward.

"Dr. Hart," she clipped the drawl. "I do need to talk with you."

Nick turned to see the woman walking quickly down the hallway, her large breast implants bouncing with every step. She wore a bright turquoise jumpsuit with a gaudy necklace of large colored beads and a matching, jangling bracelet.

"Ms. Roe," he said pleasantly. He was in a relatively good mood after time spent with Buck and the possibility that they could finally close Jeremiah's wounds. He hadn't felt this good for a while. Not even she could ruin his mood.

He was wrong.

"I've come from the Value Analysis Committee meeting and want to tell you the good news myself."

Nick frowned. This was the committee responsible for approving new equipment for the OR and evaluating new techniques. It was a rubber stamp group of Roe's bidding that said a big *NO* to anything new or innovative. He had requested a new OR table six months ago because the table in Room 2 was being stabilized with wooden blocks from someone's garage.

That could be good news.

"Two months ago, I brought in a consultant to review the orthopedic service."

"Did I meet him?"

She ignored his question. "He reviewed the procedures we do, insurance coverage, how long ya'll take to do a procedure, hospital stay, those sorts of things."

"I don't remember him. Did any of the other staff talk with him?"

She continued to ignore his questions and pressed on. "One of the metrics that he analyzed was the orthopedic implants ya'll use. All your expensive little toys. He has helped many other hospital systems around the country save millions of dollars doing this sort of thing. So I had him look at the implants we use here."

Nick crossed his arms. *Now what?*

"He noted that ya'll use the Zenith brand of implants. All your screws and plates and iron rods and such. Isn't that right, Dr. Hart?"

"Well, titanium and stainless steel would be more accurate," he said, knowing she knew nothing about what they really do.

"Well, the good news is this. We are going to switch to use Plymouth products. And that, my dear Dr. Hart, will save us two and a half million dollars a year," she said, turning on her fake charm.

Nick stared at her, his good mood fading fast.

"Isn't that good news, Dr. Hart?" She raised her eyebrows and nodded, trying to will him to agree.

"They break."

"But isn't that why ya'll use those things—to fix those broken bones?"

"The plates, the nails, the screws. Plymouth imports all their implants from a developing country. The implants break."

"Well, I'm sure they don't break all the time. Besides, other places don't have the quality surgeons that we pride ourselves on, now do they, Dr. Hart?"

"They break about ten percent of the time."

"I can live with that."

"So, you are going to condemn every tenth patient to a disaster and more surgery so you can save money?" His face flushed. He was getting angry.

"With this whole Affordable Health Care Act thing, we have no idea what it's going to do to us." She raised her voice. "We have to look at ways to cut back, and this is my decision."

"Let me get this straight. You brought in some hired gun to whom you probably paid a bundle to tell you to use cheap implants so you could prepare for something you don't know will affect us or not? Is that right?"

"You have my decision."

"You know, Ms. Roe, when we choose an implant, we base our decisions on what is best for our patients. We prescribe that implant for that patient. Like a medication type and dose tailored for that patient. We go through four years of medical school and five years of residency to make these kinds of decisions." He felt his blood pressure rising. "Are you telling me you are now prescribing these implants?"

She looked away from him and smiled at two surgeons passing by. "Dr. Hart, that's not exactly true."

"Ms. Roe, that is exactly what you are doing." He turned toward the OR. He didn't know if he could hold his temper much longer. "This is unbelievable."

She took a step toward him and lowered her voice. "Dr. Hart, when you signed your contract, you came to work for us. Not the other way around. We hired you, we can fire you. It's that simple." She leaned into him and stared him down.

He could smell her sour breath. "Yeah, you hired me. But not to commit malpractice."

Nick stepped into the doorway.

"I am not done with you."

Nick glowered at her. "There's more good news?"

"I know that you are going into the OR to close the wounds on that boy that got hit by the train," she announced and pressed her case. "With all the OR time, his stay in ICU for a couple days and the rest, that family owes us well over a hundred-thousand dollars. They have no insurance. We aren't going to see a dime out of this. His dad is a logger, and the mom is a stay-at-home type, wouldn't you know? You need to get him out of here tomorrow."

Nick had had it with this woman. "Are you kidding me?" He took a step toward her. "Don't you dare tell me how to treat my patients. He has just started turning the corner. There is way more to do, work on his stumps to mature them, get him up on temporary prosthesis, get him some permanent ones."

"At $30,000 apiece, there is no way on earth that I'm getting that boy legs." She had lost any semblance of charm. "He can go to the Shriners or somewhere else, for all I care."

"You know we are called to serve the poor of this community," Nick raged, loud enough that the crew at the OR desk inside the door heard and craned their necks to see what was happening.

"Oh, Dr. Hart, spare me the sermon. I know what kind of car you drive. You think we can pay your salary by giving all our care away? Wake up."

Nick's fists tightened at his sides. He was overwhelmed with a mixture of anger and embarrassment. "I've got to go."

The electronic doors shut between them. Through the glass, he could see her mouth still moving.

I have to go.

* * *

Nick leaned against his locker in the quiet of the changing room, stabbing his fingers into his chest hoping the Tums would kick in. He felt like Roe would be the death of him, if he didn't strangle her first. He wondered how people like her got into the medical system. The old nuns who use to run hospitals would be turning over in their graves.

He pulled his cell phone from his pocket. Three-forty-five. The crew should be bringing Jeremiah down from the floor any minute. He noticed that the dressing room smelled rank and saw an overflowing basket of sweat- and blood-stained scrubs and nasty OR shoes lined up at the door, thanks to another cost-savings move by Roe that cut back on housekeeping.

He needed a break from this place. But the thought of visiting a tropical resort alone depressed him. Of course he could head to Montana to see his folks, but he wasn't sure he could handle his mother doting on him. The only place he knew to go was Guatemala to see Maggie.

Geez. Mom. He remembered. *I promised Dad I'd call her. That was ages ago.*

He looked at his phone and decided there was no better time. Maybe they would be at one of their many doctor's appointments, and he could leave a message.

His mother picked up on the first ring as if she had been sitting by the phone waiting for his call.

"Nicklaus."

He heard the concern in her voice and regretted making the call. "Hi, Mom."

"Let me get your Dad on the line. We have been so worried about you."

"Mom—" but it was too late. He could hear her calling in the background for his father. He sighed and waited for them to come on the line.

"Hi, son," his father said.

"We have been so worried," his mother said again. "Where are you? Are you back in Memphis? How was John's service? How is Maggie doing? How are you doing?"

Nick held the phone away from his ear, but he could still hear her firing off questions, hardly taking a breath.

"Nancy, let the boy speak." His father chastised his mother. "Son, we are so sorry we missed John's funeral. Your mom was not up for travelling."

There was a long pause before Nick took his turn to speak. "Uh, yeah, sorry I haven't called until now, but Dad, you know how it goes. The hospital keeps me busy. I had to get right back after the service. I think Maggie is doing as well as expected." He paused, trying to remember the questions his mother had fired at him. "Look, I'm in the OR waiting for my next case, and I just wanted to call and say hi." He tried to end the call.

"And how are YOU doing?" his mother persisted.

"I'm thinking about taking some time off." Nick cringed and waited for his father to tell him what a bad idea that was, that he should keep his nose to the grindstone.

"Like a sabbatical?" his mother said with concern.

"No," Nick laughed. "I'm thinking about going to Guatemala to see Maggie."

That statement even surprised himself, it sounded so certain.

There was another long pause.

"Son, I think that sounds like a wonderful idea," his father finally said.

Nick looked at his phone in shock.

CHAPTER 12

THE TRINITY

"*Ah buh ji, Ah buh ji*! Daddy, Daddy!" the two young girls shouted and bounced up and down when their father walked through the apartment door in northern Pyongyang.

Mr. Pak slipped off his shoes as the girls hugged his legs. "*Ddal, Ddal*, please be patient," he told his daughters.

He felt the warmth of the heated floor, and the aroma of *Kimchi-chigae*, spicy cabbage soup, wafted from the kitchen. He knew his wife was working hard to please him.

Even though they lived in a cramped apartment with two rooms, a living space and a kitchen, he lived like a king, compared to the rest of the country. He traveled throughout the country with his work. Most of his countrymen lived in abject poverty with little to eat, barely surviving in shacks with no electricity or running water. Many ate only boiled tree bark and grains of oats they stole from the fields they worked for the government.

Pak's family had both water and power—at least when the government turned it on. It surprised him that the State still had the hot water turned on. It had been a bitterly cold winter and spring. Of course the luxury of the hot water would not last; a few more nights above freezing, and the central city hot water would be terminated. They would have to suffer with cold houses and colder showers until the weather warmed. In this country where individuals have zero control, Pak learned to appreciate the slightest amount of comfort.

"Father, is that something for us?" Pak's younger daughter asked, eyeing the sack he carried.

"Wouldn't you like to know," he teased them, holding the sack above his head. His oldest daughter was eight, and her sister was six. They would be his only children, and while he was disappointed they were girls, he loved them deeply.

"Father, pleeeease show us," the older girl begged.

"Okay. I'll show you at dinner. Go sit at the table."

The girls leaped and jumped with joy; at the same time, they were quick to obey and took their places at the table in the middle of the sparse room. There were bright-colored, embroidered cushions on the floor in front of the table. Unlike most of the furnishings, the cushions added color to the room. The faded walls had been painted a pale yellow. Pictures of the Great Leader and the Dear Leader hung on one wall with a photo of Pak's parents on one side and his wife's parents on the other. A small hutch sat against another wall with bedrolls neatly folded on each side. The only view was the cinderblock wall of the apartment complex next door.

Pak set the sack in the middle of the table and watched the girls stare at it, trying to will it open. Out of the corner of his eye, he saw his wife pause at the kitchen door with a stone bowl in her hands. She knelt gracefully at the threshold, set the bowl in front of her and bowed deeply. Without a word, she rose with the bowl, walked quickly to the table, and set the bowl on top of a hotplate. She turned up the temperature and backed out of the room, paused to drop to her knees, bowed again, and left the room. She would eat in the kitchen.

Pak's wife meant nothing to him. She had served her purpose and given him two precious daughters. She had become more of an annoyance than anything. He'd contemplated sending her away to a labor camp, but thought that might be too hard on his daughters.

But maybe the loss would make them stronger.

"Father?" The younger girl tried to interrupt his thoughts.

He took off his suit jacket, laid it next to his cushion, and sat down at the head of the table. The kimchi soup simmered with a pungent aroma. There would be no rice again tonight. The drought last year had depleted the food supply. Even though it was not his wife's fault, Pak boiled with anger at her.

If I could just leave this place.

"Father," his daughter interrupted again. "May I thank the Great Leader tonight?"

He looked sternly at her. She lowered her face and looked at her crossed legs. No god was worshiped in North Korea, only Kim Il-sung, Kim Jong-il, and Kim Jong-un. The trinity. It was Kim Il-sung's spirit that provided for them and was their source of strength. No one quite knew what to do with the new young dictator, except maybe to fear him. Even at four years of age, Pak's daughter was indoctrinated to believe in the Kim dynasty.

If I could take you away, you would know the truth.

Pak softened his expression. "Yes, my dear daughter, you may thank the Great Leader."

After she recited a well-scripted eulogy that she learned at pre-school, Pak slowly reached into the paper bag. The girls could hardly hold their excitement. He pulled an object out of the bag and set it gently in the middle of the table. As soon as the girls saw the beautiful present, they clapped and giggled. It was something they hadn't seen in six months.

"Now, if you eat your dinner, we will have this for dessert."

The precious object was the apple he had taken from the maternity clinic hours before.

* * *

Pak answered the vintage black phone on the second ring. The antiquated phone, a museum piece in the States, was the only kind of telephone available in North Korea. Most homes didn't have a phone, but as the Minister of the Cabinet General Intelligence Bureau (GIB), Pak's home did.

"*Ye seon-saeng-nim,*" he used the formal affirmative to the Vice-Marshal of the National Defense Commission. It was out of respect for his father, since the Vice Marshal worked directly under his father.

Pak cupped his hand over his mouth and spoke softly into the phone so as to not disturb his daughters' sleep.

"*Ye, ye.*"

"Yes, I will be at the airport in the morning to meet the plane."

"Six players and twelve staff."

"Skiing. No, I was not told about that."

"*Ye, ye.*"

"Give me the report in the morning."

* * *

Pak's wife lay motionless on the bedroll with her back to her husband. She listened to Pak speak into the phone, but it made no sense because she couldn't hear what the caller said. She heard her husband set the receiver in its cradle.

She heard him move across the room, stop, continue through the kitchen into the bathroom, and close the door. Moments later, he returned to the floor bedroll. She thought he smelt strange, like a burnt match. His nocturnal movements and his smell were odd, and she decided she would report them to her handler.

She wondered if the master of the North Korean spy world knew he was being spied upon. She decided he must know because everyone in the country was watched and monitored. It was a matter of checks and balances.

* * *

As Pak sat down, he glanced at his wife's back for any movement. *No. Just deep, rhythmic breathing.* He lay on his back and wondered if she would ever betray him. He thought she was too afraid, but he couldn't be sure. No one in this country was to be trusted.

But how else will this revolution happen?

There could only be one of two outcomes, death or an overthrow, the most likely being death. Pak almost welcomed death as a relief from the stress. In this country where everyone spied on each other, not reporting illicit activity was punishable by death or life in a reeducation camp if not done with full diligence. The chance of keeping his secrets would be minuscule, but he had to try or lose his sanity altogether.

The phone call worried him; it concerned his job, but it was the note slipped under the door after the phone call that captured his thoughts. He knew even his phone line was monitored and the phone call, which had been listened to, would be reported as a typical call from a superior. He hoped that only a select few would know anything about the note under the door. It read "Charles Hall." Pak had burned the note in the bathroom and flushed it down the toilet.

CHAPTER 13

CULTURE SHOCK

Miraculously, it took Nick only a few days to make the arrangements to Guatemala. His partners were happy to cover his call and practice for the two weeks he planned to be away. His patients were in good hands, including Jeremiah. His colleagues promised to continue the boy's rehab and begin the process of procuring temporary prosthetic legs.

He didn't even speak to Cruella de Vil. He wondered if she'd fire him, but he believed her bark was much worse than her bite. He knew it was a challenge to find a trauma surgeon who would put up with the conditions of the MED and the long hours of call required.

Nick looked out the window of the plane as it bumped through the clouds toward Guatemala City. He could not believe how close the mountains were as the plane made its descent. The landscape was emerald green. Suddenly, the plane shuddered, and he gripped the armrests. It seemed like an unusually steep descent. He felt and heard the landing gear snap into place. Buildings appeared on both sides of the plane.

I hope these guys know where they are going.

It looked like the plane was landing in the middle of downtown. Nick glanced around to see if anyone else was alarmed, but most of the passengers read calmly or snoozed.

The plane leveled off and almost simultaneously its wheels touched down. High-rise buildings practically lined the runway, as the plane reversed thrusters. Reflexively, Nick put his hand against the seat in front as the plane quickly slowed to its taxi speed.

He sighed with relief and wiped his brow. He didn't realize he was sweating. He didn't like to fly, and this was the reason why. G*eeez*. He knew that he, like most surgeons, was too much of a control freak.

What have I gotten myself into? Maggie didn't warn me about flying into Guatemala City.

Then he smiled, recalling Maggie's response to his call.

"I've decided to come see you in Guatemala," he had said. When the phone went silent, he thought they had a bad connection.

"Maggie, are you there?" He checked his phone to see if he was still connected. "Maggie?" In frustration, he was about to hang up when he heard a shout of glee from his phone.

"I'm sorry, Nick, did you say something?"

He didn't realize she was teasing him. "Yes." He put the phone close to his mouth and spoke louder, carefully enunciating each word. "I am coming to Guatemala."

"Yes, everything is fine in Guatemala." Still teasing, she mimicked his voice.

"No, I am coming to Guatemala."

"Yes, I'm already in Guatemala," she played him.

Nick was becoming exacerbated and considered calling back for a better connection, until Maggie giggled, and he got it. "You are so bad," he said.

There was a long pause before she responded without jest. "Nicklaus, I am so happy. Thank you so much. John would be so happy." Her voice was breaking with grief and joy.

* * *

Nick stood by the baggage carousel, his shirt already soaked through in the humid air. He had entered a different world. The smells of damp earth, body odor, and barbecue drifting from a nearby café mixed in a brackish stew.

Nick was one of the few gringos to arrive that day. The baggage area was filled with a carnival atmosphere with laughter and chatter as people pulled off their bags and boxes, some wrapped with twine and others newly packaged containing TVs and small appliances. He could feel the excitement, even though he couldn't understand the words. He wished he had studied Spanish instead of German in high school.

Then he noticed large cockroaches scurrying across the ceiling, or what was left of the ceiling. Many of the acoustic ceiling tiles were either gone or dissolving from what looked like water damage. There were hundreds of the bugs. One of them took flight, and Nick ducked as it dive-bombed him.

"I guess I'm not in Kansas anymore," he said to no one.

Nick glanced to his right to see a small man in a large cowboy hat canvassing his six-foot-two frame. Nick smiled, and the weathered-faced man said something in Spanish. Seeing that Nick didn't understand, he buzzed his lips, waved his hand like a flying bug, and laughed.

Nick laughed with him, keeping a wary eye out for other kamikaze bugs.

"*Cucaracha.*" The man repeated.

"*Cucaracha,*" Nick said, recognizing the word from the song.

Great, my first new Spanish word. Yes, definitely not in Kansas anymore.

Nick walked to the customs counter and set down his passport. "Welcome to Guatemala, Dr. Hart," declared the uniformed officer as he stamped Nick's passport.

Nick pulled his bag behind him through an automatic door into chaos. A throng of humanity lined the waiting area, shouting at friends and relatives as they exited. Hugs and kisses were liberally exchanged, as shouts of joy mixed with traffic sounds and taxi horns.

Two boys ran up to Nick and pulled at his bags.

"Sir, sir, let me help you," one said.

"Where are you going?" the other asked eagerly. "I know English very well. Do you need a translator?"

"A guide?" the other added. "What is your name?"

"Where are you from?"

Nick felt like the ball in a ping-pong game, batted between the players.

He saw an unkempt, unclean, urchin girl no more than six years old, standing on the walkway. She bit her lip, shyly held out her hand to him and said something.

Nick barely heard her over the ruckus. She had no shoes and wore an ill-fitting, dirty dress. Tangled black hair covered her delicately featured, dark-skinned face.

"Please," she pleaded, raising her voice.

One of his would-be escorts spoke sharply to the girl, and while possessively holding onto Nick's arm, he used his other hand to move her out of their way.

Nick was about to rebuke him when he saw a man lying on the ground behind the girl as she stepped back. The man lay on a piece of cardboard. His leg was grotesquely disfigured with a large, draining, open sore above his shin. Flies gorged on the wound. His other leg was altogether missing.

People stepped over the man's outstretched leg, oblivious to his plight.

Nick's would-be escorts continued to pull at him to keep his attention.

Nick wasn't sure if it was the heat or the chaos, but he was suddenly dizzy and short of breath. Then he felt a hand touch his back. He turned, not knowing what to expect.

"Hey, stranger. Need a lift?"

"Maggie!" He had never been so happy to see anyone, especially her.

She looked radiant with her long black hair flowing down her back. She wore a beautiful red blouse with brightly embroidered flowers around the collar. She gave him a long, stout hug with both arms around his neck.

"Nicklaus, it is so good to have you here. I can't tell you what this means to me."

Nick could not explain it, but he felt that all darkness that he was feeling had lifted. There was no explanation, but felt like he was home.

The would-be escorts still clamored for Nick's attention.

Maggie squatted to eye level with the boys and said something in Spanish. They looked at their feet. Maggie lifted their chins to meet her eyes and spoke to them.

She put her hand on one boy's shoulder and asked a question. The boy nodded shyly.

After a moment, he dug in the pocket of his shorts and pulled out a wallet.

Nick thought it looked like his wallet, and instinctively dug into his own pocket. It was empty.

Maggie said something to the boy.

The boy handed Nick the wallet. "I'm sorry, mister." The boy looked at his feet again.

Nick was shocked as he accepted his wallet. "Uh, thanks," was all he could think to say.

Maggie stood and opened a small purse slung around her shoulder. She handed each boy a coin and patted their heads.

Nick was still in shock. "How did you know? What did you say to them?"

"I told them that the Heavenly Father knows them by name and sees everything they do. And that He loves them very much."

She watched the boys walk away. One of them turned to wave at her and smile.

"It's amazing what love does," she smiled and waved back.

She looked into the sky at the setting sun. "Well, we better get going back to the Hope Center. There have been many incidences recently with bandits on the road back to Quetzaltenango."

She said it so matter-of-factly that Nick looked down at her five-foot frame and smiled. "Uh...Bandits?"

"But they usually only come out after dark so it's important that we get up over the pass before sundown," she said with all seriousness.

"Usually?" he said, all of a sudden not feeling very confident.

CHAPTER 14

THE HOPE CENTER

Nick lay on his back in the small twin bed with his heels hung over the end of the mattress. He felt disoriented. The ceiling fan circled above him clicking in rhythm, and a delicious aroma made his stomach growl.

It was the best sleep he had experienced in weeks. He stretched his arms over his head and surveyed the room. It appeared he was alone, as all the other beds and bunks were empty in what appeared to be a dormitory.

Nick heard a brood of squawking hens and the bleating of a sheep. Not since his youth in Montana had he awakened to an animal sound, in that case, the crow of the rooster.

It had been dark when they arrived at the Hope Center on the outskirts of Quetzaltenango. Nick had been relieved when they pulled up to the gate.

No bandits.

Maggie had shooed him directly to bed and told him to sleep as long as he wanted. He hardly remembered climbing into the small bed, and now he wasn't sure he had moved at all during the night.

He let his feet drop off the side of the bed and sat up. He ran his fingers through his hair and remembered the warm kiss Maggie gave him on his cheek as they parted for the night. He wasn't sure what he had gotten himself into, but for some reason it felt good to be here.

John, wish you were here, my friend.

Nick pulled on a pair of jogging shorts, a T-shirt, and running shoes and opened the door to the outside. He had no idea what time it was, but the sun filtered through the scattered clouds at the mountaintops, painting them in pink.

The compound of the Hope Center appeared to be a couple acres in size, surrounded by a high, cinder-block fence with razor wire coiled on top. It was immaculately clean with gravel pathways leading from one building to another, lined with flowers, palm and banana trees, and various shrubs.

It had John's fingerprints written all over it.

Nick could hear the soft voices of children coming from a building to his left. He saw a large metal gate on his right, which he assumed they had come through last night.

He walked toward the gate. A Latino man in a tan uniform rose from his chair next to the gate. Nick was surprised to see a sawed-off shotgun strapped to his back.

"*Buenos dias*, Dr. Nick," the man smiled at him. "Can I help you?"

"I was going to go for a short run."

"Aw, like our Dr. John," the man nodded. Then he realized what he had said. He looked down and shuffled his feet in the dirt.

Nick saw the pain on his face. "Yeah, I miss him too."

The man shook his head and looked at Nick. "*Mi nombre es* Joseph," he said, sticking his hand out to shake.

Nick offered his name and shook Joseph's hand.

"Be careful out there," Joseph warned. "Maybe go toward town." He smiled broadly and pointed to the left out the gate.

As Nick started out the gate, he saw a large group of people waiting in line outside the fence.

Wonder who they are?

* * *

It didn't take Nick long to realize he was in a different world as he made his way down a rutted dirt road and tried not to sprain an ankle. The air was surprisingly cool, and he wondered if he should have worn a jacket. The sun was peeking over the mountains, and he hoped it would warm up. The area was surrounded by mountains and reminded him of his hometown.

Most of the mountains were covered in lush jungle and a couple of them looked like sleeping volcanoes.

An old man that looked to be about ninety smiled at Nick as he trotted by. The man carried a large bundle of sticks wrapped in cloth and slung behind his back, supported by a sling around his forehead. Nick estimated fifty pounds of wood and was amazed the old man's neck could support such a load.

The rural road was dotted with shack-like structures, presumably houses, built from whatever was available—sticks, logs, bricks, tin, or thatch. A small boy in a dirty red Air Jordan shirt and tousled hair stood on the other side of a barbwire fence in front of his house and waved to Nick. A pig rooted through rotting trash that was piled to one side of the structure. An old woman sat on a rickety stool in the shade, waving a towel to shoo away flies.

At another house, rusted oil barrels sat under the tin roof, providing a make-shift water collection system.

Memphis had its poor sections, but this was poverty Nick had never seen before.

Mongrel dogs with raw looking mange and prominent ribs barked from houses or trotted down the road. They didn't bother Nick, for which he was relieved, as he doubted they were vaccinated for rabies.

As he approached the town, the impoverished houses gave way to more permanent looking homes of cinder block. A short man in a cowboy hat and a stained, button-down shirt guided an ox pulling a load of firewood, similar to what the old man carried on his back. The ox pulled against a large wooden yoke, but it looked healthy.

The firewood business must do okay.

As Nick entered the town of Quetzaltenango, the dirt road yielded to brick, and retail businesses appeared. A small group of children, three boys and two girls, walked down the road dressed in matching school uniforms, white shirts and black pants or skirts. When they saw Nick, they chattered in Spanish and pointed at him.

One brave boy waved at Nick. "Hello," he said with a heavy Spanish accent.

That caused them all to giggle and inspired further bravery.

"Hi," the smallest boy said.

"Hey, mister." A bigger boy said with macho confidence, checking the girls to gauge their reaction, which turned into a shoving match among the boys.

I guess nothing changes between boys and girls, no matter where you are.

It wasn't long before Nick entered the city square with a large park in the middle and a central gazebo. At one end of the park was a large, official government building. A small group of vendors operated a farmer's market at the other end.

He walked into the park and, eyed by the market-goers, he felt like an alien. He gave himself a once-over and realized he was the only one in shorts and bright blue and green tennis shoes. *I must look pretty odd to them.*

A woman sitting in front of a variety of fruit and vegetables smiled and waved him over.

"*Señor*," she said. "*Señor*, come buy from me."

Nick patted his pockets and gave the universal shrug of no money.

"Hope Center?" she asked.

"*Si*," Nick replied back with one of the few Spanish words he knew.

She jumped to her feet and grabbed a banana. Nick tried to protest, but before he knew it, she had it peeled and held it out to him. He tried to protest again.

"Please," she said offering it to him. "Present for you."

"Thank you," Nick said, realizing that he was hungry. He took a large bite. It was the sweetest banana he had ever tasted. "Thank you," he said between bites.

* * *

As Nick made his way back, the roads filled with people—school children headed to classes and adults headed to work. Nick noted that even in the midst of poverty, the people, for the most part, dressed nicely, women in beautiful, colorful dresses and men in long pants, collared shirts, and often cowboy hats.

As he got closer to the Hope Center, Nick realized that most of the people were headed in the same direction. At two blocks away, he realized that a line had formed down the side of the road leading to the Hope Center.

I wonder what event Maggie is holding?

Nick saw Maggie with a clipboard about half way down the line talking with the people. She hugged some of the women and patted the children's heads. She wore a bright purple skirt and white linen blouse and looked radiant, probably more at ease and relaxed than he had seen her in years.

Maggie handed the clipboard to a woman holding a baby and took the child from her arms and gave it a big squeeze. She put her face to the baby's belly and gave it a raspberry, which made the baby giggle and squeal with delight.

Nick made his way to Maggie, and everyone looked at him. Many of the women eyed him up and down, staring bashfully at his bare, hairy legs. Self-conscious, he blushed.

"*El Doctor,*" Maggie smiled and used the baby's hand to wave at Nick. The baby shyly turned away.

Maggie said something to the crowd in Spanish. He could tell it was about him.

The crowd responded in unison: "*Buenos dias, El Doctor* Nick.*"

Nick thought it was funny how they said his name, like Neek.

"*Buenos dias,*" he said slowly, in not very good Spanish, which made the crowd crack up.

He spoke to Maggie. "Are you having a fair or a party? Everyone is so dressed up and happy. What's up?"

"Why, *El Doctor*…they are here to see you."

CHAPTER 15

BASKETBALL

Pak Song-ju was not often intimidated, but as he watched the old Russian-built jetliner roll to a stop, he was filled with anxiety. His only relief was the memory of his last encounter with the girl at the clinic. He imagined the sweet smell of her perfume and the feel of her tender skin.

But this was not the time to show any weakness. Pak slowed his breathing and pulse, something he learned long ago in order to beat a polygraph test, if ever he had to.

He stood with a delegation of top leaders of North Korea. Typically, they would not lower themselves to meet an airplane, but the order had come from Kim Jong-un himself. Pak sensed a similar annoyance from his counterparts. He stood next to the Vice-Marshal of the National Defense Commission who had called him the night before. On his other side was a ranking member of the Korean Workers Party Committee, and next to him was a member of the Cabinet, and behind him, multiple generals and department chiefs. All were in their required military uniforms, including Pak, to his displeasure. He would have preferred one of his tailored suits, an overcoat and a fedora, the dress appropriate for the head of the country's top spy organization.

All this for a group of stupid basketball players.

Eighteen Americans altogether were met by twenty highly-decorated and uniformed North Korean officials. The higher number of Koreans was deliberate, a show of power, the upper hand. The North Korean government-sponsored media outlet was present to record the ceremony. The government loved the fact that this trip caused a stir in the U.S. and hoped to add to the fire between the nations.

Although it was humiliating to stand in the cold, waiting for the Americans to deplane, it worked in Pak's favor. He had a mission. He knew when and how the hand-off with his contact was supposed to go, but in his line of work, he realized nothing was ever as easy as it seemed on paper.

The jet engines wound down, and the ground crew wheeled a set of deplaning stairway to the side of the aircraft. A military band, ordered by Kim Jong-un, started up the DPRK's national anthem.

The tension rose as the Americans exited the plane. Pak instantly recognized the third player. Karl Oakland, sporting neon blue hair, facial piercings, and dark sunglasses, ducked out the aircraft door, threw both arms up in triumph and smiled broadly, waving and flashing peace signs.

As Pak thought of his mission, his jaw tightened and his brow furrowed, but he didn't think his comrades were aware of his changing physiognomy. They stood frozen at attention, eyes straight ahead, united in hatred for evil America, as they had been taught as children.

The great evil had landed.

The rest of the players left the plane, each having to duck as they came out the door. As the group descended the stairs, they were met at the bottom by two young women dressed in *Chosŏn-ot*, the traditional Korean ceremony dress—flowing, vibrant pink gowns with white *jeogori* tops trimmed with a bright red ribbons. The women looked like dolls next to the American giants as they handed each player a bouquet of flowers.

Pak had seen black people in Paris during his schooling years, but never in his life had he seen men this tall. As the team approached, he was relieved that someone had the forethought to place the welcoming committee on an elevated platform that would require the players to reach up to the North Koreans to shake their hands.

With disdain, Pak shook their hands and smelled a combination of body odor, alcohol, and tobacco. The Americans talked loudly and walked at random down the receiving line. They slapped each other on the back and gave hi-fives.

What an uncivilized group of pigs.

The players were escorted to a nearby bus. It was the beginning of a highly-choreographed event that would showcase the very best of North Korea. Nothing was left to chance. The bus would drive only on certain streets; the team would see only what the officials wanted them to see and nothing more.

* * *

Charles Hall sat near the back of the bus and looked out the window as the large coach wound its way through downtown Pyongyang. He was surprised. He had heard of the poverty and starvation in North Korea on CNN, but the city was beautiful and clean, with large granite buildings everywhere that equaled the size and grandeur of Washington, D.C.

He thought it was strange that none of the North Korean officials had joined them on the bus. Only two young Korean men in suits sat silently at the front and another stood at the front facing them. His arms were crossed, and there was a permanent glower on his face.

A Korean girl dressed in a green uniform and garrison cap with a red star medallion and holding a microphone stood and faced the team. She couldn't have been more than sixteen. She spoke with a slight British accent and her English was perfect. Peering over the seats at the girl, Charles thought it was unnatural for such perfect dictation to come from an Asian woman.

"You have entered the eternal city of Pyongyang," the girl began, "the greatest city in the world because of the sovereignty of the Great Leader, Kim Il-sung, whose spirit leads us to victory today to defeat the fascist pigs, and the Dear Leader, Kim Jong-il, who, by his great intelligence, developed nuclear weapons that will be used to destroy our enemies."

She almost shouted, even though the volume on the microphone was at its maximum. It made his ears hurt.

Man, I need some Advil.

"No enemy has been able to harm us with their corruptible

power and evil ways," the girl continued. "The great satan of America was turned back by the heroic efforts of the Great Leader, Kim Il-sung."

Did she just say that?

Charles pushed himself up in his seat to get a better look at the girl. If he didn't know better, he'd have thought Oakland had put her up to this, but the tone of her voice and her determined face told him her ranting was serious.

"Now, as the spirit of Kim Il-sung lives eternally in his grandson, our Supreme Leader, Kim Jong-un, the people of the Democratic People's Republic of Korea will destroy all remaining enemies and conquer the fascist pigs."

Huh?

Without hesitation, she went on. "Over to your left you will see the Kim Il-sung Stadium which is the world's largest stage for the largest games." She gestured out the left side of the bus. "Next to the Stadium, you will see the newly built Institute of Basketball, built personally by our Supreme Leader Kim Jong-un who designed it and personally attended to its building."

Charles looked at the white granite building that appeared to take up two square blocks. There was a large fountain in front with a picture of Kim in a hard hat pouring concrete.

"You kidding me? That's just for basketball?" one of his teammates said.

Another whistled, and another exclaimed, "Amazing!"

"You can see by the superior intellect and resourcefulness of our great country. No other people can match our superior race."

I wonder when she is going to talk about the twenty million people who have starved to death the last few years in this superior country?

Charles remembered the nerdy dude from the State Department that lectured them before they left. The man showed nauseating pictures smuggled out through China of starving women and children.

"Our first stop is to the glorious Mansudae Grand Monument of our Great Leader, Kim Il-sung, and the Dear Leader, Kim Jong-il," the guide continued. "I would respectfully ask that you remain in an orderly and quiet group as we approach the monument. You will each be given a bouquet of flowers to present to our leaders as you bow and give them their due respect."

Charles got the feeling that this was a required part of their visit when the sullen man behind the girl deepened his glare. Charles was tired. He was not interested in gigantic statues of dead guys. Not only was he jet-lagged, he was extremely hung over from the party on the plane.

Man, what I would do for a score of snort.

He had cut a line in Beijing before they left for North Korea, but had been warned countless times about misbehaving in North Korea and ending up in one of the rumored gulag camps and tortured. The State Department guy was dead serious. Charles had left the remainder of the coke behind.

Man, what a headache.

But he needed this trip. He was a quarter million dollars behind on his taxes, with no relief in sight. Oakland told the press the players and staff were doing this for goodwill, but no one in this group did anything for free. It was how they rolled. The 50,000 dollars he was promised was not much, but better than a kick in the shorts. It was the 100,000-dollar bonus that had gotten his attention.

Charles patted the front pocket of his suit to make sure the envelope and small metal box were there. He thought back to how he got to this place.

* * *

It had started when he was at the gym getting into reasonable shape for these games and a man approached him. Dressed in a casual jogging suit, the small, oriental man confronted him as he sat alone at the bench press.

"Charles Hall?"

"Yeah, what about it?"

This man did not look like a cop.

"I have a business proposal for you that I think you will like."

"Oh really? You a fag or something?"

The man was neither intimidated nor deterred. "Mr. Hall, let me be brief. I know of your many problems." He paused to let

Charles catch up. "I have a very simple request that could put a dent in your debt."

He paused again to let the big man comprehend. "Something so simple, even you, Mr. Hall, could do." He glared into Charles's eyes to let him know who was in control.

Charles nodded.

"In the next few days, before you go to North Korea, I will give you an envelope and a small package that—"

"Hey, dude, how do you know I'm going to North Korea? I haven't even decided for sure myself."

"I think once you hear my offer, you will not have a difficult time with your decision."

* * *

Charles returned to the present when the woman guide ordered the men in the bus to stand and prepare to unload.

Man, oh man! She'll make someone a good wife someday. Nasty little Nazi woman!

He stood with the rest of the rag-tag team. He knew he was on his way to becoming a has-been, and the parties and coke didn't help. At least the organizers told them the games would be a joke, and they were expected, no, required to lose. The whole saving-face thing.

But for him, relief was in sight. He patted the package in his pocket.

CHAPTER 16

DAY ONE

Nick was already sweating, and it was only his first hour in the Guatemalan clinic. He hadn't thought much beyond seeing Maggie on this visit, but this was the furthest thing from his mind. He couldn't resist Maggie's plea to see a few patients.

We have different ideas of a few. He sweated even more thinking of the long line of people waiting to see him.

A wrinkled old woman sitting across from him beamed a toothless grin. She alternated between clapping her hands and holding Nick's arm, all the while chattering in Spanish.

"Dios te bendiga, Dios te bendiga."

Nick looked at Anna from Alabama—his new shadow and translator sitting next to him. She had been in Guatemala for five weeks with a group of young adults from a church in northern California.

"She is saying, 'God bless you.' " Anna smiled at him as the woman continued to jabber.

"She wants me to tell you that you are a good man, and God will richly bless you and your family."

Anna leaned closer to the woman, trying to catch all her words. The woman kept raising one hand to the heavens and patting Nick's arm with the other.

"She wants to know where your wife is and how many children you have and she says 'God bless you. Thank you for coming to Guatemala.' "

Using the universal sign language, Anna finally told the woman to slow down, but she continued to chatter in Spanish, then leaned over and kissed Nick's hands over and over again.

"Thank you, thank you," Nick said reassuringly, trying to squelch her enthusiasm by gently pulling his hands away.

"Ask her how I can help her," he pleaded with Anna. This was awkward; Nick had never worked through a translator.

"*Abuelita, Abuelita,*" Anna said, still trying to slow the little grandmother. She leaned toward her and patted her arm affectionately to get her to focus.

The woman began a highly animated story, talking with her hands as much as with her mouth. The story went on and on. Nick was getting anxious; he looked through the doorway of the small clinic room. He could see the long line of patients snaking through the courtyard and out the gate.

Yikes, this might be a long day.

Nick watched Anna talk with the woman. She caught his glance and smiled at him. He liked her already. She had bright blue, clear eyes and golden blond hair. Her royal blue scrubs complemented her eyes and fit snuggly around her shapely body. Judging from her translations, he thought she spoke incredibly good Spanish.

He and Anna sat in old plastic deck chairs that were already uncomfortable. The woman continued her story. She clasped her shoulder and tried lifting her arm above her head, but could only raise it to shoulder level.

Nick understood a few words here and there that were similar in English, and he nodded.

"How long has her shoulder bothered her?" he asked Anna.

Anna was surprised at his question, knowing he didn't speak Spanish.

"I've been doing this a few years," he said.

She smiled at him.

"Ask her how she hurt her shoulder."

Anna asked, prompting a brand new, dramatic story from the woman—a very long story.

Anna related the tale about a bus and the market and going to get fruit for her grandchildren. She had seven children and twenty-two grandchildren and eight great-grandchildren.

Nick sighed, ran his fingers through his hair, and pushed it back.

Anna saw Nick's impatience and mouthed *sorry* to him.

"It's okay, let's try another way. Ask her what she can't do and what she would like to do."

Anna looked him in the eyes. "I tell you what, Dr. Hart. Let's do this." She hesitated, hoping not to step out of bounds because she realized they were in for a long day. "Just think of me as the Google translator on your phone. Talk to the patient like you normally would, and I'll automatically translate for you."

He smiled at Anna, leaned toward the grandmother, and spoke directly to her. "What can you not do because of your shoulder?"

Anna translated almost simultaneously.

The woman responded with a calm, measured explanation.

"Smart girl," Nick whispered to Anna.

She put up her hand to silence Nick and leaned closer to the woman to catch all her words, smiling gently.

Love the spunk. And nice to look at, he thought, admiring how Anna's form filled out her scrubs.

"I have a hard time with firewood," Anna translated. The woman's demeanor changed rapidly as she held her shoulder and looked pained and discouraged.

Nick leaned back in his chair to consider the problem. The grandmother was dressed in a clean, respectable, church-going dress and a colorful apron with large pockets. She smelled strongly of smoke.

"They cook with wood," Anna said, as she studied him, seeming to read his mind.

Nick smiled at Anna again. "You ever watch 'MASH'?"

"You mean the old TV show? No, but my papa did all the time. Why?"

"I'm going to call you Radar." He suddenly realized that he could be her father's age. That sobered him up and turned his mind on task.

Anna raised her eyebrows in question.

"I'll explain later," he said turning back to the old woman.

"You can't carry the wood here in front of you?" Nick asked

holding both arms in front of him like he was carrying a small bundle of wood. He couldn't imagine why this eighty-seven-year-old would carry any wood with all those children and grandchildren to help.

Anna continued to translate: "I can't gather the wood any more and it is my job."

"I guess I don't understand. She obviously has a rotator cuff tear, but people can usually carry things in front of them." He held out his arms again.

Anna continued to question. A large tear ran down the woman's face.

It was Anna's turn to sit back in her chair. "She can no longer gather firewood because she cannot climb the trees to gather it." She turned to Nick. "You see, Dr. Hart, the country is so deforested that if you live close to the city, you are forced to climb tall trees to cut branches." She shook her head. "These are very poor people."

Nick saw Anna's compassion. He nodded. The old woman looked inquisitively at Nick, pleading for an answer.

"You have a tear of one of the main tendons in your shoulder," he told her and patted her hand.

"She is asking what you can do for her?"

He suddenly realized that everything was happening so fast, he hadn't asked Maggie what to do if he wanted to operate on someone or even if he could.

Geez, what about x-rays?

"I suppose you didn't bring an MRI scanner from Alabama, did you?" Nick quipped. That was the first thing he would do back home to evaluate the size of the rotator cuff tear. He couldn't believe he actually missed the MED.

Anna frowned.

"Well, tell her that I am going to talk with the Director of the Hope Center and see what we can do."

When Anna told her, it was as if the old woman had won the lottery. She began praising God and kissing Nick's hands.

"Okay, okay," Nick stood up and held out his hands to help the woman up. "Tell her there are no guarantees. I still have to look into it."

As he walked her to the door, he noticed how short she was, how old age had reduced her height well below five feet. She tenderly patted Nick, reaching out to him with her good arm.

"*Dios te bendiga. Dios te bendiga,*" she said and left the clinic room.

* * *

After seeing a number of people with low back pain, an old machete wound to the forearm, and a woman with bad rheumatoid arthritis, Nick and Anna settled into a comfortable flow. There was not much he was able to do for many of the patients, except to suggest a few exercises and to provide some reassurance.

He looked up and smiled as Maggie walked through the door. Behind her was a young woman in a colorful embroidered skirt and top.

"El Doctor. How's it going?" Maggie smiled at Nick. "You tired yet?"

"Just another day at the ol' office." He rolled his eyes around the sparsely appointed room.

"You get paid in any chickens yet?" she teased.

"Hey, I need to ask you about what to do about any surgical cases."

"Aha! I wondered when you'd ask. I can't wait to show you John's operating room. I know you probably feel like you have fallen off the edge of the world, but I think you will be pleasantly surprised at our abilities. You know John," she smiled.

Nick nodded at the girl standing silently behind Maggie. She carried a small bundle of what appeared to be blankets, and kept her gaze locked on the floor.

"Who's your friend?" Nick asked.

Maggie turned and put her arm around the girl, encouraging her to move closer to Nick and Anna. She gently swept the girl's black hair out of her face and whispered to her. The girl shook her head and tightened her grip on the bundle.

"This is precious Elena, and she has something she wants to show you."

Maggie kept her arm around Elena's waist to keep her from bolting. She talked with the girl and tugged at the bundle.

Anna went to the girl and put a hand on her shoulder. She spoke to her in Spanish; she said something about Nick. Elena looked at Anna and then shyly at Nick. With a sigh of resignation, she unwrapped her bundle. One blanket, then two, then a third, until a tiny little face appeared and whimpered.

Elena stared at the newborn.

"One of the ladies from the local Catholic church found them on the side of the road last night," Maggie explained. "She had recently given birth and was lying in the ditch. The baby was found naked a few steps away. Thank God that it was not very cold last night. Elena will not tell us what happened to her. I can only imagine. It has taken us most of the morning to get her name and convince her to let us clean them up and feed the baby."

Anna spoke with Elena who responded to her, perhaps because Anna was only a few years older. Anna asked if she could touch the baby, and the girl held the baby toward her.

Anna gently touched the baby's cheek, ran her finger over its eyebrows, and felt its fine black hair. "She's beautiful. *¡Qué milagro que es!*," she told Elena and translated for Nick: *"What a miracle she is."*

Anna stroked Elena's hair, and the small Guatemalan girl wept. Maggie still had her arm around Elena and gently kissed her forehead. By now, all three women were crying. Nick swallowed hard. He almost said something and then held his tongue.

Maggie finally looked at Nick. "We'll probably get the full story over time. Obviously, an unexpected pregnancy; probably rape or incest or some terrible injustice is what we usually find in these cases," She knew the girl spoke no English.

"You mean there are others?"

Maggie sighed. "Welcome to the jungle, Dr. Hart."

Nick shook his head, but wondered why they were showing him this heartache.

"Can you look at the baby's hands?" Maggie asked, moving the blankets enough to show the tiny arms and hands.

Nick looked at the young mother and held out his hands toward the baby as if to say, *Is it all right if I touch your baby?*

Elena understood and held the baby toward Nick. The baby really was beautiful. Thick, jet-black hair, and tiny features. She still had white vernix at the corners of her nose and in the folds of her ears. They missed cleaning a bit of the waxy material that covers most babies when they are born. This one looked remarkably healthy for being born prematurely and found naked in a ditch.

Then the baby started to fuss at being uncovered and handled.

Nick held one tiny hand and then the other. They were doll hands, dwarfed in his. Nick counted four fingers and a thumb on each hand.

Beautiful.

But as he tried to separate the fingers, he saw the problem. Syndactyly. Each finger was joined to the next by thin sheets of skin.

"Hmmm," he said and looked at the mother's face. A large tear rolled down her cheek.

Nick studied the baby's fingers. There were many different types of syndactyly, some with webbing between the fingers and others much more complicated that involved the bones. He was glad to see that the baby had the simplest form.

"Well, the good news is," Nick started, "the syndactyly is fairly simple, and I think we could separate the fingers relatively easily, in a month or so. We need to put a little weight on this nipper before we give her an anesthetic." He smiled at Elena.

Maggie translated Nick's words for Elena. "You have a beautiful baby, and you are a beautiful girl. The doctor will fix your baby's hands, and they will be a good as new. You will stay here at the Hope Center with us."

Nick could tell that Maggie was embellishing his words to encourage Elena.

Maggie stroked the girl's hair like a loving mother. "Oh my dear, I am so sorry this happened to you, but God has given you a great gift."

The girl wept and spoke for the first time. "But God is mad at me for having this baby. See? Look at her fingers."

Anna continued to translate the conversation for Nick.

"Oh, Elena, God is not like that. He loves you and brought

you here to us," Maggie assured her.

Anna added, "You will see. You will know that God loves you. We love you already, and we hardly know you. God knows every hair on your precious head. He loves every part of you, and He loves your baby."

Maggie held Elena's cheeks. "Oh my dear child. I am so glad you are here!" She wrapped her arms around both mother and child as the girl sobbed.

Nick watched them all wipe tears from their eyes and, growing uncomfortable, he pushed on his sternum.

CHAPTER 17

SCHOOL BEGINS

Nick couldn't explain the feeling except that it felt like freedom. Something similar to what he remembered at the start of college spring break. Maybe it was the young men tossing the football in front of him or the group of young men and women sitting around him that filled the atmosphere with chatter and laughter, creating an almost festive atmosphere.

Nick and Anna sat on a picnic table outside the clinic in an area of randomly grouped picnic tables shaded by palm and banana trees. The day was warm with a fair amount of humidity, stirred by tropical breezes. Birds with a multitude of shapes, sizes and colors darted in and out of the trees, serenading their lunch break.

He should feel anxious about the significant amount of trauma and heartache he had already seen in one short morning. It was an overwhelming amount of orthopedic pathology. Untreated broken arms and legs had left patients with deformed and disabling injuries. *Maybe they brought all the really hard cases first?*

In spite of the difficult procedures, he felt a curious peace deep inside.

Nick was accustomed to witnessing acute trauma, but what he'd already seen was altogether different. Back at the MED, he patched people up and sent them on their way. Once their fractures and wounds healed, he rarely saw them again. Here, he'd been dropped into a reality where suffering people could not afford to pay for treatment, and in some cases, treatment was not available. These were terrible odds; nevertheless, Nick connected to the simple and joyous rhythm of life.

"What are you thinking?" Anna asked.

Nick looked into her kind eyes and hesitated. He did not readily go to his heart. "What a day so far." He bailed and took a bite of his sandwich.

"I guess you're used to this stuff?"

"Well…I…uh. How about you?"

"I have to admit, that last guy with the nasty wound on his shin almost got to me. Maybe it was the smell and the fact you could see the bone."

"Yeah, that was pretty nasty."

The man with the wound was middle-aged and had been hit by a car two years earlier. He had lived with an open, draining wound and a floppy, lower leg ever since.

"Are you going to be able to help him?"

"Well, even back home that would be a really tough one," Nick said thinking out loud. "It would involve multiple surgeries with some pretty specialized equipment. Specialized and expensive. I bet in the States, that treatment would cost upwards of a quarter million."

"Dollars?"

"Yeah. Unbelievable, huh?"

Anna got very quiet. Then it was her turn to think out loud. "That's bad."

"So the other option is to amputate the leg. It would instantly get rid of the bad infection and the deformity. But I have no idea how we would ever get him a prosthetic leg."

Nick took another bite from his sandwich. "You sure you still want to be a doctor?"

Earlier, she had shared with Nick that she had applied to medical school.

"Oh my gosh, yes, Dr. Hart. To be able to help people like this. I think this is what God made me for." She smiled broadly at him.

A football landed between them, and Nick grabbed for his soda before it tipped over. A fit young man ran up to retrieve the ball.

"Hey, sorry about that."

Nick flipped the ball into his hands. "No worries."

The young man smiled at Anna and backed away flexing his arm as he threw the ball.

Nick smiled at Anna. "Looks like you have a fan."

"Yeah, whatever."

"Tell me about your band of friends here."

"There are twenty-two of us, all from the School of Ministry at Living Waters. Ever heard of it?"

"Can't say as I have," Nick shook his head. "What's Living Waters?"

"Living Waters is a church in northern California. It has a great school that trains people in the ways of God."

"You mean like a seminary?"

"Well, sort of. We go for at least one year, and then at the end of the year, most of the students go on some sort of outreach. Kind of like, to share what we have learned for the past year."

"So, all these kids were in your class?"

Anna laughed, "Yeah, these and almost a thousand more like them."

"A thousand? You kidding me?"

"Well, that's just the first year."

"There's more?"

"Many go on to do a second or even a third year."

Nick looked at the young people around him. They looked like very normal twenty-somethings.

"What have you all been doing since you got here?"

"Oh, all sorts of things. It's been so great. Helping here at the Hope Center—painting, cleaning, playing with the kids. Things like that. Anywhere we can help. We have gone to a number of the villages. We actually helped another church team from Denver drill fresh water wells for a couple of them. It was so awesome." Anna's enthusiasm was palpable. "In fact, a lot of the patients you are seeing today are people that we met in the villages and brought here." Anna smiled proudly.

"Thanks a lot," Nick teased, thinking of the complex cases he had seen that morning.

"Anything for the good doctor."

They sat in silence for a couple of minutes as Nick pondered this group of young do-gooders.

What was I doing at twenty-two? School, I guess. And chasing girls.

"You go to church?" Anna interrupted his thoughts.

"Well, I grew up in the Episcopal Church, but I..." Nick said, feeling self-conscious. "It's been a while since I've been. I'm afraid I know more Dr. Seuss than I do the Bible."

Nick saw Maggie coming toward them and felt relieved that he didn't need to say more.

Maggie gave him a hug. "How did your first morning go?"

"I'm hoping you had me see the hard ones first."

Maggie looked at Anna and smiled like they had a secret. "I bet you're doing great," she reassured him. "You ready for a quick tour before we put you back to work?"

"That would be great," he said, jumping off the table.

"You want to go with?" he asked Anna.

"You go ahead, Dr. Hart. I want to hang with my friends for a minute."

* * *

The operating room was beautiful, just as Maggie implied, state-of-the-art. John had done an amazing job of fundraising, and it showed in the operating room equipment. Maggie reassured Nick that it had not always been this way. For many years, they had coped with the basics until a wealthy donor from Seattle came to serve with his church and saw their struggles. Scraping by ended that day. At the end of the year, they had a new fluoroscopy machine, anesthetic machine, laparoscopic equipment, and new surgical tools.

On the other hand, the need was never-ending. Maggie and Nick strolled through the back half of the Hope Center to the orphanage, which currently housed seventy-three children. It was recess, and many of the children ran around the playground.

They entered a modest building filled row upon row with bunk beds, all neatly made up.

"You run a tight ship."

She smiled at him. "Yeah, kind of like controlled chaos. We

only have room for around fifty kids, but we never turn anyone away, not ever. It's the kids with disabilities that really strain the system. But Jesus says, *'whatever you do for the least of these, you do for me.'*" She looked at Nick to see if he understood.

Nick started to speak, but his voice broke. He attempted to start again, and it broke again. "Maggie. I had no idea what you and John were up to down here. I would have…"

Maggie put her hand through his arm. "Really, Nick, it's okay. I'm just glad you're here now."

"I am so sorry, Maggie. I don't know how you are doing it. I mean, I miss John so much right now."

Nick looked at Maggie and regretted his words. The dam broke, and her emotions poured out. He pulled her close. She dissolved in his arms, her body quaking with grief. Her tears soaked his shirt. He paid it no mind and stroked her hair.

"I am so sorry, Maggie. I am so sorry."

Even though he was uncomfortable, Nick let her grieve. She felt good in his arms, but it wasn't supposed to be like this. He missed John fiercely.

As her grief subsided, she pulled away from him. He was reluctant to let her go.

She wiped her nose with one hand and her eyes with the other. "Oh my Lord." She patted him on the chest where she'd left tearstains. She wiped at her face again and dried her hands on her pants.

"I try to be so strong for everyone here." Her tears flowed again.

Nick tried to pull her close, but she resisted, so he held her by her shoulders instead. Maggie wiped her nose with the back of her hand.

"I feel like my heart is going to burst open." Her tears continued to fall. "I guess I needed a good cry." She nodded to the wet spot on his shirt, and her tears turned to deep sighs. "I'm so glad you're here. John would be so happy to be here with you right now. You know, you were his best friend."

Nick was speechless. He could never replace John, but he wanted to wrap her in his protection. *Maybe this is what love feels like.*

They stood in silence with their own thoughts.

Finally, Nick broke the silence. "I just don't understand how someone could have taken John's life. It doesn't make any sense to me. What in the hell is that all about?"

"Exactly."

Nick was confused.

"Hell. That sort of evil only comes from hell."

Nick was still confused.

Maggie straightened up and wiped tears from her eyes. Something was coming. He could tell she was choosing her words carefully.

"You see, Nick, there's a battle raging around us. You may not understand. I don't know, but I pray that the Lord opens your eyes."

"I guess I don't understand, Maggie."

"Oh my dear, Nick," Maggie patted him on the chest again. "We have a lot to talk about, and you better hold on to your socks. You just might have your world rocked. Have you ever seen an angel or a demon before?" She looked at him seriously. Before he could answer, she went on. "Most people have no clue of the spiritual world around them, but you see enough miracles or ancient curses over peoples' lives, and it will quickly make you a believer of the unseen."

CHAPTER 18

FIRST OR DAY

Nick stood at the threshold of the operating room. The sign above the door read: "Peace To All Who Enter Here."

He smiled, thinking of John up on a ladder nailing it in place.

Nick had had a restless night, tossing and turning. He knew it was, in part, because of the busyness of the full clinic the day before, the amount of pathology he had seen, and the anxiety of operating in an unfamiliar OR, but the main reason was the dream that he had about John.

Nick only remembered part of it, the part where they were standing near the summit of very high mountains in the middle of a blizzard. It was a strong storm and they were in danger. John kept encouraging him to take shelter amongst the boulders, but Nick wanted to keep pressing forward. To what, he had no idea. That's when he woke up with sweat rolling down his neck.

Maybe the most unsettling part of the dream was that it was so real. It was as if John was alive. Nick had sat in the dark on the side of his bunk with his head in his hands and wrestled with the issue of heaven. He realized that if John existed in some cosmic realm, it meant one thing—his own love for Maggie had to remain platonic.

But could he love her without wanting to love her physically?

Nick looked at the sign above the OR. "You left big shoes to fill, my friend."

* * *

It was mid-morning and Nick had already enjoyed a hearty breakfast of eggs, beans, homemade tortillas, and two cups of delicious, strong Guatemalan coffee. The coffee was the best part; he loved the way it infused life into his foggy brain.

He had met the local surgical team that would help him today. They worked at the government hospital in Quetzaltenango, but they had promised Maggie to take a few days off to help Nick with any surgical cases.

They were a friendly bunch—a middle-aged female nurse, a younger male scrub technician, and an attractive female anesthesiologist who was not more than five feet tall. Nick wondered about their capabilities, but with Maggie's reassurance, he decided to proceed.

The day started slowly with only a few scheduled cases. Nick realized that even though John had put together a fully functional operating room, it lacked orthopedic implants. Nick recognized that he would have to figure out a way to get implants from the States if he wanted to do significant cases.

He looked over his shoulder at Anna. He had spent the last fifteen minutes showing her how to do a surgical scrub.

"You ready?"

He thought Anna looked cute in her surgical cap and mask that highlighted her bright blue eyes.

"Uh, I don't know. You sure this is okay?" she said holding her hands and arms in front of her. Her mask had crept up on her nose and pushed under her eyes, and she tried to move her chin to force it down.

"Hard when you can't touch anything, huh?"

"That's for sure."

"You'll be great. I'll get you all set, and you'll have the best seat in the house. You've been in the OR before with your pre-med preceptorship, right?"

"Yeah, but never scrubbed in before. I'm pretty nervous," she said, still trying to move her mask down.

"Do exactly what I do, and you'll be fine."

"Yeah, right."

"Remember, don't lock your knees, and if you do start feeling faint, just sit down or step out into the hallway."

"Oh great."

"Come on, Dr. Anna, you've got this. And I need you. Our team here doesn't speak a word of English, and you know how excellent my Spanish is."

His humor made Anna relax. She took a deep breath, and they backed through the OR door.

The well-equipped operating room was small, compared to U.S. standards, but it was brightly lit. Nick could hear the anesthesiologist talking with the patient. Whatever she said, the old woman practically sat up. It was the woman with the torn rotator cuff.

"*Dios te bendiga, Dios te bendiga.*" The woman started chattering where she left off from the day before. The anesthesiologist encouraged the patient to lie back down on the OR table with her hand on her chest, but the woman continued to chatter.

Nick had met with her and her family early that morning and talked to them about fixing the torn rotator cuff in her shoulder and what to expect. He had hardly gotten a word in edgewise. He laughed to think of the twelve family members all crammed into the waiting room and more waiting outside. Obviously, there was a lot of love in this family.

Nick smiled at Carmen, the anesthesiologist, and gave a sleepy head nod, like 'okay, time for her to take a nap.'

Carmen raised a finger in agreement and gladly pushed the plunger on a syringe, injecting narcotics through the IV. Nick was impressed. Carmen had given the old woman a technically difficult shoulder block to avoid the danger of a deep anesthetic. The woman's entire shoulder area was numb; she would have just enough drugs to slow the chatter and give her a wonderful nap.

Nick watched the woman's eyelids flutter closed as the narcotics hit her brain.

With the help of the scrub technician and the nurse, Nick helped Anna gown and glove. He motioned to the nurse to pull Anna's mask down out of her eyes. He told Anna how to hold her hands, to fold them in front of her. After the nurse had finished the prep, Nick placed the surgical drapes on the woman's shoulder.

He guided Anna up to the table and placed her gloved hands on the drapes.

"Rest your hands here."

Juan Carlos, the scrub technician, was already busy putting the suction and cautery in place.

Just like back home. Man, it feels good to be back in the OR.

Nick used a surgical marking pen to show the anatomic landmarks and trace a line on the skin where he would make his incision.

"Scalpel."

Juan Carlos looked at him blankly.

"Uh, scalpel." Nick looked at Anna.

She looked stricken. "I don't know that word in Spanish."

Nick thought for a moment. He had seen a number of machete wounds the day before. He put out his hand. "Machete?"

That made the whole crew crack up.

"Ah, *bisturi*." Juan Carlos said and grabbed the surgical knife.

Nick held his hand out waiting for the scalpel. Juan Carlos and Carmen talked back and forth.

Nick looked at Anna. "Have I forgotten something?"

There was an exchange between Anna and the staff.

She turned to Nick. "They want you to pray. Dr. John always prayed. They don't feel right unless you pray."

Panic rose in Nick's chest.

Except for the chirp of the heart monitor, a thundering silence stilled the room.

"Well, the only prayer I can remember right now is grace."

Anna translated for the room.

"What do you mean grace?" Anna translated for Juan Carlos.

"You know, what you say before a meal," Nick said sheepishly.

Anna spoke to the staff. There was a long silence.

Then everyone burst out laughing. Juan Carlos spoke, and Anna translated. "Okay, grace it is. Thank you for this food."

Juan Carlos handed Nick the scalpel.

* * *

Maggie joined the team for lunch. They sat in their scrubs on the same picnic table as the day before. The young adults from

California were nowhere to be seen. Nick assumed they were off on a project or tracking down more patients for him to see.

"How did it go?" Maggie asked Nick.

"It was great. Just like back home." Nick paused, thinking through what he had said. "Well, except I like your OR lounge better." He lifted his face to the afternoon sun. "And your staff is nicer." He smiled at the surgical team as Anna translated.

"Wish my assistant was better," he joked poking Anna's arm, making her blush.

"Hey, I think I did pretty well," she retorted. "At least I never keeled over."

Anna translated for the team, and they laughed.

Nick put up his hands. "Okay. You did great."

Maggie turned to Anna, "What'd you think?"

"It was awesome. I mean, I was really nervous when I saw that scalpel go across the skin. But I kept reminding myself that *I can do all things through Christ who strengthens me.* I could really feel His peace."

Maggie watched Nick study Anna's face and interrupted his concentration. "You have what you needed?"

"Oh yeah." Nick returned to the moment. "Maggie, I honestly can't believe how well you have your little hospital decked out. I'll need to figure out a way to get some ortho implants down for the bone cases, but otherwise, it was great."

"Well, it's all John. He worked tirelessly to equip the place, and it wasn't always easy. When we first started here, people would call us and tell us they had a donation. Sometimes we would fly or drive somewhere to pick it up, and, honestly, more often than not, it would turn out to be a worthless pile of leftover junk, stuff you wouldn't even treat a dog with. We would have to find the nearest dump and put it where it belonged. We tried not to be ungrateful, but sometimes we wondered what people were thinking."

Maggie put her hands on her head and sighed. "I remember a wealthy woman from our community called John and was all excited about a donation she had collected for us. She was a well-known philanthropist in our area, so John went to her home filled with expectation."

Maggie tossed a bread crumb to a colorful bird at their feet.

"Of course, I don't do the story justice like John does. But he walked into this beautiful mansion overlooking Lake Washington. Her late husband had recently passed away and suffered with terrible sores on his legs that needed to be wrapped every day. She saved all the elastic wrap bandages they had used. It was this huge plastic bag of stained, worn-out bandages." Maggie stood for emphasis and stretched out her arms as far as they would go, making a funny face as she did.

"I can still see John standing there with this huge bag of trash trying to be grateful," she continued. "He said it was one of the first times he felt speechless, all the while holding this huge bag of bandages, trying to not let it touch him."

She stretched her arms out further and spread her legs, illustrating the image. "He told the lady that her bandages were really going to help some people, all the while wondering how fast he could get the mess to the dump and wishing he didn't have to put it in our car."

"But you know John. He went out the next day and bought a bunch of boxes of bandages with whatever little money we happened to have then. The next time we got back here to Guatemala, every time he used one of those bandages, he took a picture and sent it to that woman to thank her for her support and told her what a great memorial it was for her husband. That was so John. No malice in his heart, always grateful. Even for the little things."

Anna translated Maggie's words, and the team nodded.

Nick noticed Carmen blink back a tear.

"You know," Maggie said, "that woman ended up becoming a great friend to us. In fact, she donated the new X-ray unit and suite just last year." She shook her head. "Amazing how God works."

"Amen," Carmen agreed.

"Of course it wasn't always this nice," Maggie said, looking around the compound, "but in John's heart it always was. He believed you give your very best to the poor, not your leftovers."

Everyone sat in silence, missing him terribly.

Nick finally broke the silence. "You guys have been here—"

"This is going on to our sixteenth year," Maggie finished his sentence. "Hard to believe."

"I remember you telling me about your mission trip in college. Was that here?"

"Well, Guatemala, yes. But I was in San Pedro la Laguna in the Lake Atitlan basin about two hours away." She pointed to the east. "When John and I made the decision to become missionaries, we knew it would be Guatemala, but we decided on Quetzaltenango because it was a bigger town, but not too big."

Nick looked at Maggie and then at Carmen, the anesthesiologist, and then back at Maggie. "I just noticed something. You two could be sisters."

Maggie put her arm around Carmen and laid her head on her shoulder. "*Mi hermana pequeña*, my little sister."

Carmen gave her a kiss on the forehead.

Maggie smiled. "The Maya, or maybe I should say the descendants of the Maya, are amazing people."

Anna spoke up. "The Mayas were supposed to be one of the most advanced civilizations on the planet. We studied them in our anthropology class. They had amazing architecture, art, and science. It's fascinating, because around 900 AD their culture vanished, and nobody really knows why."

Nick stretched his leg and brought his foot down hard, squashing a huge cockroach scuttling across the dirt. "Maybe the *la cucaracha* ate them."

The team laughed, mostly at his Spanish.

"*La cucaracha. Machete. Hola. Dolor*," Juan Carlos said counting on his fingers the Spanish words Nick knew. Holding the fours fingers up to Nick proudly with a huge smile.

"Okay, okay. I'm trying."

CHAPTER 19

THE HANDOFF

After the basketball team's required homage to the late leaders, their bus headed toward downtown Pyongyang. Charles Hall could not get over the beauty of the city. Everywhere he looked there was some monument or impressive building: The Institute of Music, The Institute of Art, even an Institute of Taekwondo. All stunning, granite monuments dedicated to the past and present leaders of the country.

At their stop at the Mansudae Grand Monument, Charles noticed how clean and fresh the air was, and he suddenly realized why. He could have counted on one hand the number of cars he had seen on their ride through the city.

The bus made a sharp right, causing the young tour guide to grab the railing above her head. Charles tried to shut out her rambling about how every building was practically built, brick by brick, by their great leaders.

Maybe they are the only ones who live here, he thought, looking at the nearly empty streets.

"This is the main shopping district of the great city of Pyongyang, where ladies can find the very latest fashions from around the world."

Charles looked at the stores as the bus passed slowly, each store window perfectly arranged in faultless order. Every dress, suit, and luxury item, including the canned goods at what appeared to be a grocery store, was displayed with precision. Eerily, there was not a single shopper.

It seemed to Charles as if they were in a Los Angeles movie

set with wonderfully decorated store fronts, all for show.

The bus rounded another corner and drove down a major thoroughfare lined with high-rise apartment buildings and a smattering of people walking in the neighborhood. Then Charles saw one of the largest gatherings he had seen since leaving the airport, approximately twenty people standing along the road, lined up in a perfectly straight line. He watched a bus pull up to the group and stop. The people filed into the bus as orderly as robots.

Well, at least a few people actually live here.

Their last stop before the hotel was an orphanage. Oakland wanted to display the appearance of goodwill on this trip, and the North Korean diplomat had suggested a visit to a children's home, as he called the orphanage.

The State Department told the team that visiting the orphanage was simply a stunt by the DPRK in response to a CNN report of a damning plight of the orphans in North Korea with horrific stories of starvation and cruelty. An older orphan had miraculously escaped into China and told stories of indescribable abuse. To counter this, Kim Jong-un was recently filmed visiting an orphanage in Pyongyang, surrounded by happy children. Charles wondered if this was the orphanage where they were headed.

The bus slowed to a stop in front of a one-story gray building with no markings.

"Please follow me into the children's home," the tour guide ordered as the bus door opened.

"Thanks a lot, Oakland," one of his teammates quipped, throwing a children's bouncy ball at the back of Oakland's head.

The rest of the team grabbed duffel bags full of toys that they brought to give to the children.

Charles was one of the last off the bus to be greeted by a line of ten women in dresses covered with white aprons or medical lab coats and odd-looking chef hats. All the women bowed to the players as they passed, but they never made eye contact.

The orphanage lobby was filled with large portraits of Kim Il-sung, Kim Jong-il, and Kim Jong-un holding children, dancing with children, and playing with children. The woman with the largest hat escorted them into an adjacent room, indicating that they were to leave their bags of toys in the entryway.

Wonder if she's a doctor or something. She looks more like the head chef.

The tour guide helped herd the group into the room. Even though she was dwarfed by the tall men, she did not appear intimidated. There were chairs in the room, and she ordered them to sit.

"We are honored to be in this great children's home that was built by the Great Leader, Kim Il-sung, as a testimony of the great perseverance of our children despite the horrific atrocities the great satan, America, has affected upon our people. These children represent the victory over that fascist government."

Charles clenched his fist. *Man, if she was a guy, I'd…*

After her speech, a door opened at the far side of the room, and ten children marched in, boys in blue shorts and white shirts, girls in tiny Korean ceremony dresses, like the *Chosŏn-ot* worn by the women who met their plane. Each child wore lipstick, and red rouge had been painted on their cheeks.

Charles expected the children to be shocked by the huge black men seated before them, but each child stood at attention and stared past them. Charles estimated that they were only four or five years old, and he could not believe their discipline.

The headmaster said one word to them. In unison, they said something in Korean, probably more propaganda, Charles surmised, and then the children began singing and dancing, each step, each note highly choreographed.

Charles watched in fascination as the children moved like puppets on strings. They sang two songs, and as abruptly as they had entered, they left. The door shut tightly behind them.

Charles looked around, thinking that maybe they could give the children the toys they brought, but the staff did not move to retrieve the bags.

"Follow me." The guide ordered the men to follow the headmistress of the orphanage. They entered a separate but similar room. Laid out on the floor were ten babies wrapped tightly in blankets. They looked to be about a year old. The babies rested their heads on pink pillows. They were covered by yellow blankets with bright red flowers.

The headmistress spoke to the tour guide.

"Mrs. Gae wants me to tell you the babies names," the tour guide told the men. She walked down the line of babies and spoke each name.

"Bullet, Bomb, Gun, Sword," she continued down the row.

"For Pete's sake, where is Little Brass Knuckles?" Charles's teammate whispered to him. Charles could hardly contain his laughter and covered his mouth.

The tour guide caught him and shot him a nasty look. "The babies will grow up to finally defeat the imperial pigs once and for all."

Charles turned away from her stare.

The headmistress spoke to the guide again. The men were escorted to the next room. This room was the nursery, filled with cribs, and each holding a baby. Charles counted thirty-three.

As they walked through the room, they heard not a peep from within the cribs. Charles worried that the babies were dead. He peeked into the cribs and was relieved to see the babies sleeping.

"Hey, Charles, smell that?" his teammate whispered. Charles took a big breath.

"What the—? Is that what I think it is?"

"Dude, is that weed I smell?"

"Yeah, I could sure use a hit of that right now."

"You think they smoked these kids to keep 'em quiet?"

"Dude, from what I've seen so far, I don't doubt it."

The men walked from the nursery through a back door into a hallway, and before they realized it, they were escorted out the back exit and directly to the awaiting bus.

Charles heard Oakland begin to protest. "Hey, we need some pictures with the kids. What about the toys?"

"I'm sorry, Mr. Oakland. It is time to get you to your hotel." The tour guide herded them onto the bus without flinching.

"Whatever."

Charles heard the resignation in Oakland's voice.

* * *

Pak and two of his subordinates were waiting in the lobby of the Yanggakdo International Hotel when the team arrived. They watched and listened as the unruly crew admired the ornate lobby, their voices echoing off the granite walls. Pak had already shed his uniform for his suit and overcoat.

He doubted that any of these buffoons would know or care about State secrets, but he had no doubt that the mongrel Americans would have planted a CIA agent in the group. That's why their every movement would be closely monitored. Every room was bugged with the latest eavesdropping equipment. The country may not have adequate medical care, but when it came to the military and spy organizations, little was lacking. Every conversation at their tables in the dining room would be monitored. A handler was assigned to each team member. Nothing would be missed.

Even if the men visited the massage club in the basement with an exclusively female staff, their visits would be recorded and analyzed. As much as they hated the Americans, they were fascinated by them, like scientists studying animals. The more they knew about them, the more they could control them.

Charles Hall was told to ask for and to use the bathroom in the lobby of the hotel. He hoped Hall was smart enough to remember. Then, on cue, he heard Hall ask the tour guide for the restroom. She pointed to a room across the lobby.

Pak nodded to one of his men who understood and followed Hall. Passing a small package seemed like such an archaic way to pass information, but it was the safest. Every tiny bit of electronic information in and out of the country was monitored, and even he, the Director, could not escape the fact that the wrong people could intercept an electronic message.

Pak scanned the lobby and watched his man. No one was the wiser. His spy agency was doing its job monitoring every movement of the basketball team, and following one of them into the bathroom would not be suspicious. Pak's man followed Hall inside. In short order, Hall exited. After a moment, Pak's man exited. Pak did not flinch or speak when his man returned to his side.

* * *

Pak's car phone rang as his Mercedes pulled away from the hotel.

"Yes."

"Jang Song-thaek has been arrested," the caller stated.

"Excellent." Pak hung up. A surge of electricity flew through his body. It was one of the first times in his life that he wanted to laugh out loud. But he refrained so his driver would not see a change in his countenance. Nevertheless, he was ecstatic.

The framing of Kim Jong-un's famous uncle was a crowning moment in Pak's career. Jang, who was married to Kim Jong-il's sister, was the true leader of the country, and Kim Jong-un simply a figurehead. Jang controlled both the military and the head of the Korean Worker's Party and was the most powerful man in North Korea. He was also old school and had to be eliminated if the new order of Korea would succeed.

How easy it was to manipulate that boy.

It had taken two years to lay down the groundwork for Kim to believe that his uncle was undermining him and about to stage a coup.

Pak smiled to himself. The whole Kim family line had to be exterminated from the earth. Soon, even the famous aunt would be collected and executed, along with every possible descendant. They would not have the luxury of being sent to the work camp to die of starvation. Their death would be swift and thorough.

But Pak wondered if he should have Jang tortured and die a slow, humiliating death.

Feeding him to dogs would be appropriate. Dogs eating dogs. He picked up the phone to relay the message.

After hanging up, Pak pulled the envelope and the small metal box from the inside pocket of his suit coat. It had taken all his will power to wait, but the delayed gratification was his hallmark and delight.

Pak felt blood surging into his loins; once again he thought could smell his mother's perfume. He wondered if his mother would be proud of her son if she knew what he was accomplishing.

As he opened the envelope from his three-man team in

Guatemala, he noticed that his hands were shaking. This was uncharacteristic; Pak was always steady as a rock. He shook it off and read the typed note: **Phase 1 completed. 100% successful. Final formula included. Phase 2 begun and going well. Threat eliminated as requested.**

Yes, indeed, it was a very good day. Pak barked an order to his driver. *I cannot wait to show this to Professor Kwon.*

CHAPTER 20

ISABELLA

Nick sat alone on a bench in a far corner of the compound shaded from the noonday sun by a large mango tree, heavy-laden with ripening fruit. He had found this secluded spot one night while strolling around the Hope Center. He was glad to have a place to go to gather himself. Two green and yellow parakeets chattered overhead. His sack lunch sat next to him, but he didn't feel much like eating.

The kids from California were fantastic, but he had a hard time keeping up with their energy. They worked as hard as he did everyday, but instead of collapsing into bed, they either played volleyball or soccer or headed into town to go on treasure hunts. They tried to explain it to him, but he was still not sure he understood. Something about praying together and hearing from God and then finding the people that God had shown them to talk to.

Their faith both inspired him and confused him. He had never in his life seen such enthusiasm for God. As the week went on, he learned not to fear the long lines of people that would queue up in the morning because they were not all there to see the gringo doctor. Many came for prayer with these passionate young Christians.

Nick had overheard the kids talking about the miracles that had happened. He decided one of these days he needed to check it out. But he wasn't sure how he felt about it. God seemed like such a distant thought.

A surgical case yesterday with an elderly man still had him

a bit unnerved. The man came to the clinic with a dislocated shoulder. The problem was that it had been out of the socket for three months. The other problem was that the man was ancient.

Carmen, wisely, did not want to give him a general anesthetic or even a block, for that matter. But she and Nick, and the others decided it was worth giving him some narcotics and try to put the shoulder back into place; otherwise, the man would be in considerable pain. Resetting it would be a long shot, as the tissues would have scarred down by now.

Going into the case, he was nervous that he would break the fragile bone and make matters worse.

Once they got the old man comfortable on the OR table, Nick put a sheet around his chest. Juan Carlos pulled from the opposite direction for counter traction, as Nick manipulated the arm. They pulled and twisted and tugged and pulled—it looked like they were going to pull the man in two—but to no avail. The x-ray images taken with the C-arm showed that only with the most extreme effort would they *almost* get the shoulder relocated.

In his head, Nick heard his father's voice: "*Almost* counts in horseshoes, hand grenades, and skunks." He hated the saying because it meant he wasn't trying hard enough.

"Stink," he said in defeat.

If they pulled any harder they could break ribs or the arm itself. Discouraged, with sweat dripping down his face and back, he told the team they better stop.

Anna stepped up and asked if she could give it a try.

"Seriously?" Nick snapped at her in frustration and was immediately sorry for his insensitivity.

Not letting it phase her, Anna responded gently, "Can I pray for you and this man?"

Nick stared at her, not knowing what to say. Sarcastic words came to mind, but he held his tongue.

She put her hand on Nick's and said a prayer for Nick and the patient. The Guatemalan team also prayed with her out loud in Spanish.

When they finished, Nick wanted to ask them if they felt better, but he said nothing. Instead, he gently pulled the man's arm up to remove the sheet out from around him. He heard a pop. Heartbroken, he thought he had broken the shoulder and asked for another x-ray with the C-arm.

There, in perfect position, sat the shoulder in the socket.

What in the world is that about?

He pushed the thoughts from his head. There was no way he was going to be able to reconcile this experience with his medical training.

From under the mango tree, Nick watched a Monarch butterfly flutter and float around the flowers planted in the garden surrounding the bench. It finally settled on the outstretched hand of a small statue of Saint Francis of Assisi.

Nick leaned back and stretched his arms across the top of the bench and wondered if he should head back to the clinic. He was enjoying the momentary solitude.

A wayward ball rolled to Nick's feet. He kicked it back to the young crowd without leaving the bench.

It was already Friday. He could not believe how fast his first week had gone and that his team had fallen into a pretty good rhythm of clinic one day and surgery the next. But he had a growing sense of uneasiness, with the expanding list of patients that needed surgery.

Nick was still trying to figure out how to get the supplies down for next week. He had talked with his favorite orthopedic implant rep in Memphis who had agreed to put together sets to send him. The problem was, they would practically need a truck to bring down the different instrument sets and boxes of implants, as well as, plates, screws, nails, and other implants to be used to fix bones and replace joints. He would have to prioritize somehow, and that didn't make him feel any better because there would be people who'd go without.

How do I make that decision?

That thought and the amount of pathology he saw overwhelmed him. Each story from the patients and their families was heartbreaking. Patients with broken arms and legs so easily fixed in the States had received no treatment here, leaving them with devastating deformities and chronic pain. He had already shed more tears here than at any other time of his life, except when he heard the news that John had been killed. He was embarrassed by his tears, but no one seemed to care or even notice. What a different world this was than the hardcore grind of the MED.

The Monarch butterfly flitted from its perch on Saint Francis and landed on Nick's hand stretched across the top of the bench. It sat on his finger and flapped its wings. Its weight was light like a warm breeze. He admired its beautiful, integral pattern of black and yellow.

"What do you think about this, little guy?"

Anna rounded the corner and interrupted his thoughts. He hoped she hadn't seen him talking to the butterfly.

"I thought I might find you here. I'm so sorry to bug you, but we have people waiting." She saw the butterfly. "I see you have a new friend."

"Cool, huh?" He lifted his finger, and the Monarch drifted away.

"Here," she said, handing him a glass of iced tea. "You might need this."

* * *

The exam room fell silent as two of the California students escorted a girl inside. With the young men at her sides, she shuffled into the room. A Maya man and woman followed behind. The man held a cowboy hat to his chest. Nick assumed they were her parents.

Never in his life had Nick seen such a pitiful child. When she entered, it was as if a shadow of gloom filled the room. Nick surveyed the girl and estimated she was around ten years old. She was neatly dressed in a yellow skirt and clean white shirt, but her face was drained of color and life. Nick couldn't get over her look of sadness, shame, and unfathomable defeat.

But it was not her face that everyone else stared at; it was her bare feet. Nick could tell the child was aware of their stares. He had an instant thought that if he had to take his biggest regrets and deepest, darkest secrets and wear them around his neck, this is how it might feel.

He looked at her feet. Compassion overwhelmed him. The girl's feet were so badly deformed, they looked as though they had been put on backwards and upside down. In order to walk, she had to walk on the tops of her feet. How painful that must be?

He noticed Anna watching him with her cheeks wet with tears, and he swallowed hard.

The young men helped the girl stand in front of Nick. "Dr. Hart, this is Isabella."

One of them put Isabella's hand in Nick's. Her eyes fixed on the floor.

Nick took her hand. It was limp and lifeless. "Isabella, my name is Dr. Hart. You can call me Nick."

Anna translated.

"I'm going to put you in a chair, if that's okay."

She nodded slightly, and Nick lifted her under the arms and set her down on the chair. He sat in his own chair and looked at her. Despite her feet, she was beautiful—perfect, delicate facial features, and thick black hair. But he remained unsettled by her defeated expression and wondered how often she had to endure public humiliation.

"Would you like some water?" he asked.

She shook her head.

"How old are you?"

Isabella did not reply, her eyes locked on the floor.

"Do you go to school?"

Still no reply.

Nick looked at her mother, who came forward to put a hand on Isabella's shoulder.

"*Ella es de doce,*" she said looking at Anna to translate.

"She is twelve."

"Can you tell me about Isabella?" Nick asked the girl's mother.

Anna translated a sentence at a time as the woman answered.

"Isabella was born very normally. Except that both her feet turned in." Anna demonstrated with her hands, imitating the mother.

"She is actually a twin, and her sister is without problems. We live far into the jungle and we thought that her feet would straighten themselves, but they kept getting worse and worse. We took her to the local *hueseros,* and he wrapped her feet and sprinkled medicine over them. The *huesero* said there was a curse on this child."

Nick watched Isabella's face as her mother spoke, blinking back tears.

Nick patted the child's thigh and looked at Anna. "Sorry, what is the *huesero*?"

"They call them bonesetters here."

"You mean an orthopedic surgeon?"

Anna shook her head, "Oh no. More like a witch doctor. It's something that is usually passed down through the generations. They have *sacred objects*," Anna made quotation marks with her fingers, "pieces of bone and stones that they use with chants to break curses."

Nick raised eyebrows and turned back to Isabella. "Have you ever been to a real doctor?" he asked without thinking.

Anna looked at Nick without translating. She paused, carefully picking her words. Finally, she said, "Things are different here, Dr. Hart, in lots of ways. It might take them a day or so to walk out of the jungle and then two days on buses to get anywhere with medical care. Not to mention the fact that it might take three or four months of wages to pay for the trip, not counting the cost of medical care."

Nick was chastened. To cover, he smiled at Isabella's escorts. "You boys must have had quite an adventure."

"Yes, sir," they said proudly.

"This one of your treasures?"

They beamed.

Nick looked at Isabella. "Can I look at your feet?"

She didn't reply. Nick took that as an affirmative.

He picked up one leg and then the other. Her feet hung from her shinbones like useless appendages. It was disorienting. It was as if her feet really had been put on backwards. For a second, Nick wondered about those curses.

He moved her feet back and forth. Both had five toes and significant calluses on the tops of her feet on which she walked. The tops of her feet were now her soles.

"Unbelievable."

All of a sudden, it occurred to Nick. "Oh my God. These are untreated clubfeet," he said inadvertently.

"Really?" Anna joined his enthusiasm, having no idea what he was talking about.

"About one out of a thousand kids are born with this. Way more common than what you would think."

"Do they all look like this?" Anna asked.

"Oh gosh, no. They are treated as babies, and most the time, you can never tell they had clubfeet."

One of Isabella's escorts spoke up. "I had a clubfoot as a baby." He lifted one of his Nike-covered size-eleven feet.

Everyone looked at his perfect feet, even Isabella who had no idea of what had been said.

The young man didn't realize the implication until after he had said it and looked down at the ground, "I'm sorry you all. I feel terrible."

Nick interceded. "Well, you can't help where you were born. Just be grateful your parents could get you the right care."

He turned his attention back to Isabella and gently stretched her feet the way they were supposed to go. Her feet went barely a fraction of the way.

"Well, that's great. Right? If you know what's wrong, then you can fix it." Anna looked at Nick waiting for answers. "What can you do to fix her feet?"

Nick was silent for a long time; he moved Isabella's feet back and forth. His eyes were moist with tears. "I have no idea."

CHAPTER 21

GOD IS GOOD

"Maggie, I can't do it. I don't know where to start." Nick's anxiety pumped his heart and he wiped sweat from his upper lip.

Maggie rose from the bench to refill Nick's lemonade glass. A full moon illuminated the Hope Center. It was a relatively warm night. Insects chirped in the trees and the toads croaked in the grass.

Maggie returned to the bench and put her hand on his arm. Nick was glad to have her close.

They sat in silence for a long time, and an indescribable peace enveloped them.

Maggie felt Nick's muscles relax as he slumped down on the bench. She continued to let him vent.

"I'm not sure I've ever been this..." he searched for the words. "I think I'm in over my head. Besides Isabella, we saw three other kids with clubfeet. During residency, I maybe saw one clubfoot surgery. It's just not done anymore. Those babies are treated with stretching and casting so fast that not even the pediatric orthopods do the surgery much anymore."

His pulse pounded and his muscles tightened.

"And that's on a one or two-year-old, let alone a twelve-year-old. There is no way." He shook his head. "Even if I knew what I was doing, that surgery is fraught with landmines. My God, you could so easily cut those tiny nerves or blood vessels. Then you would have to cut her foot off." He made a slashing move against his leg. "I'm sure that would go over good with her parents!"

She patted his arm and smiled at him.

"Maggie, say something. Help me out here."

Nick was at a loss. It was as if dark clouds smothered his soul and filled his brain with self-doubt and incompetence, echoes of messages he told himself growing up.

How would Maggie see me if I told her I am too afraid to do it?

He steeled himself against her stare. "What are you thinking?" he ventured.

"I'm just sitting here praying for you, Nick."

"Geez and that's another thing. This whole God thing. I don't get it." He stopped before he said something that would hurt her feelings.

Again, there was silence.

Maggie cleared her throat. "You know I believe in you."

"Yeah, but clubfeet?" He covered his face with his hands.

"Nick, I believe in you," she began again, "and I trust you to make the right decision."

He grabbed for a solution. "How about sending these kids to the States? I'm sure we could find someone who would be brave enough to tackle this."

Maggie sipped her lemonade. "Well, I wish it were that simple. We have been successful in sending exactly one person to the States for care and that was seven years ago. It was a young man with the worst scoliosis that John had ever seen. It was going to kill this kid. His heart and lungs were being compressed. A friend of John's is a spine surgeon in Texas, and he helped arrange it all. John went to assist and did the initial approach through the chest and abdomen. They opened him up from his throat to his pubis."

She stood for effect, drawing the incision line down her front.

"John had to move everything out of the way—heart, lungs, intestines—everything. John swore he had never sweated so much in his life. They had to go to every level of the spine and cut all the ligaments. Even then, they had to remove some ribs to release the deformity. After a week in ICU on a respirator, they took him back to surgery and opened his back all the way from the base of his skull to his sacrum and put in screws and rods to stretch his spine." She illustrated, turning her back, stretching one hand to the base of her skull and the other to her lower back.

"John said he had never seen anything like it in his life. But that young man survived all that and walked away six inches taller, his dignity restored."

"Wow."

"Yeah, right?" she sat back down.

"Can't we do something like that?" Nick asked.

"At the end of it all, the bill was close to a million dollars. It was so remarkable that the hospital and surgeons wrote the bill off."

"Try to get that done these days," Nick said.

"Exactly. Hospitals don't have that kind of expendable money anymore. Even the Shriners are having a hard time taking care of the kids in the States."

Nick stood. He needed to move. "So what happens to Isabella?"

"Well, we tell them that there is nothing we can do for her except to pray, and we send them home."

"You're kidding me. I feel like I'm in an impossible situation."

Maggie smiled and searched his eyes. "Nick, honestly, sometimes when we get to the end of the rope, when nothing seems possible, that's when we find God. I've seen Him do the impossible. That's the God we serve. If there is anything I learned growing up on the Rez and living here, it's that."

"What kind of God would let a child be born like this and not give her a way out?" His voice was angrier than he'd intended.

"Oh, my dear Nick. This sort of thing does not come from God. God doesn't give what he doesn't have. The God we serve is a loving, kind God. Our heavenly Father is a good daddy."

"How do you explain something like this then?" Still frustrated, he returned to the bench.

"Nick, it is terribly difficult to understand how an all-seeing, all-knowing, all-powerful God could let this happen. I know you are going to hate this answer, but sometimes you have to embrace the mystery of it all. I do know this—there is a battle that rages between good and evil. Look what happened to John." She stopped and began to cry.

Nick's head swirled, not knowing what to say or do.

Then she pierced his eyes with a gaze that was kind and full of such conviction that moved his heart and soul.

"Maggie, I am so sorry." He wiped a tear from her cheek, and quickly lowered his hand, reluctant in the intimacy.

But Maggie took his hand and held it against her cheek. Then she kissed his palm and said, "You're a good friend, Nicklaus."

Suddenly, their moment was shattered by shouts and screams outside the compound—the sounds of an angry mob, yelling men and women, and a woman screaming for her life.

Maggie squeezed Nick's leg and bounded from the bench. "Oh my God, what is happening?" They took off running, Maggie three steps ahead of Nick. The gate was swung open and they were confronted by a howling, frantic mob. The guard was nowhere in sight.

The ruckus had awakened the entire campus, and some of the California men, shirtless and in sleeping shorts, had raced to the fracas.

Car lights shed some light on more than thirty people huddled in a circle, shouting. Nick couldn't understand what they said, but he knew they were angry.

As danger bells rang loudly in his head, everything inside of him told him to slow down. He watched Maggie dive into the melee, and he couldn't let her go alone.

Despite her tiny frame, Maggie was a scrapper. She pushed through the crowd into the center. Nick followed. He heard Maggie screech at the top of her lungs: "Joseph, no! Stop! Joseph! For God sake, Joseph, remember who you are."

Nick caught up to her to see Joseph, the Hope Center's guard, looming over a crouching, screaming woman, holding his gun above his head and aiming its butt at his victim's head.

Maggie blasted past him and threw herself over the woman, raising an arm with fingers splayed and pleading, "No, Joseph, no."

Standing beside Joseph, Nick was afraid of his wild eyes and clenched jaw. Miraculously, Maggie's pleas stopped his rage, and Joseph lowered his weapon and he froze in place. The mob went silent. Then, in slow motion, Joseph lowered his gun. He tore off his hat and looked to the sky, asking God what he had done. "*Dios, ¿qué he hecho?*" Joseph wailed.

The woman continued to sob. Nick wondered if she was afraid or in pain or both. Maggie wrapped her in her arms.

Half-dazed, Joseph wandered off, and the mob parted to let him through.

"Go after him," Maggie yelled at one of the Californians.

"Give me some light," Maggie ordered as she assessed the woman. People stepped away from the car lights so she could see.

The woman bawled relentlessly, but the mob hushed enough for Nick to hear a whimpering. He looked around and saw a tiny child wrapped in a bundle between Maggie and the wailing woman.

Maggie begged Nick. "Please help me."

Nick bent to assist Maggie and pull the woman to her feet, but the woman was strong and refused to budge. She said something Nick didn't understand. "*Lo siento, lo siento, lo siento.*"

Nick was relieved to see Anna push into the crowd.

"She is saying that she is sorry," Anna translated.

Maggie quizzed the crowd in Spanish.

It was as if everyone was hesitant to speak.

Maggie pleaded with the woman to stop crying. She checked her head for damage and found it damp from tears or blood, Maggie guessed both.

Finally, an old man from the town stepped forward. He spoke in broken English with a heavy Spanish accent. "Missus John. This one untouchable. You not want to be here with her."

The mob burst into obscenities. A woman from the town spat at the scorned woman and kicked dirt at her.

Maggie hollered at her to stop and threw protective arms over the woman and child. The mob kept yelling obscenities.

The old man raised his arms to silence the mob and said to Maggie. "Missus John. Please go back inside. I beg you."

Maggie was indignant. "I will not go inside, and I will not let you harm this woman and this child. What do you think you are doing? Someone, tell me who this woman is."

The mob went stone cold silent.

Maggie wiped her brow with the back of her arm. "Well?" She stared at the old man. "What's going on?"

"Missus John…" he began.

"Tell me," she demanded.

The old man shrugged in resignation and pushed the words out. "She…she is wife of man who kill Dr. John."

They had all heard the story of the man who was found with John's heart in his bag.

The wailing woman cried for mercy. "*Lo siento, lo siento, lo siento.*"

Maggie was stunned. Pain stabbed her heart. She grasped her chest with one hand, the other still holding the woman. She gasped for breath. Nick grabbed her and tried to pull her up and away, but Maggie resisted. Then she began to choke and gag. Nick tried harder to pick her up, but she pushed him away with incredible strength and collapsed around the woman and child.

Catching her breath, Maggie leaned over the woman and held her shoulders. "Is this true?"

"*Lo siento, lo siento, lo siento. Por favor, perdóname…*please forgive me," she cried.

Maggie let go of the woman and slumped back in the dirt. She pulled her hands over her face, leaving blood streaks from the wailing woman's wounds.

The mob's noisy rabble rose again.

"Stop," Maggie finally demanded, pushing herself to her knees. The mob quieted, and the woman whimpered, catching her breath and waiting.

Maggie stretched as high as she could without rising. She scanned the crowd, and declared not only to them but to herself, "This is not John's killer. This woman is not John's killer. This child is not John's killer." She paused and appealed to heaven. "Jesus, help us." Then she collapsed on top of the woman and child.

CHAPTER 22

THE GOSPEL

Blood dripped down the woman's face as Nick helped the team get her onto the exam table in the clinic. One of the California men held pressure on her scalp wound. They finally learned her name—it was Maria.

She clutched her one-year-old boy to her chest; any attempt to separate them had failed. She was still in shock, but at least she had stopped wailing. Now the baby screamed, either from the assault, the surrounding gringos, or, judging from his smell, a dirty diaper.

"Get me some gloves." Nick directed a young man to the cabinet in the corner.

Anna came running into the clinic with an armful of supplies from the OR—gauze, saline, suture, instruments, and a large basin. "Here you go Dr. H. I grabbed everything I thought you would need and then some."

"That a girl."

Nick slipped on a pair of gloves and did a cursory exam of Maria. There were no obvious signs of trauma, except for the large gash on her forehead at her hairline.

The baby continued to scream.

"Oh my gosh, we're going to have to do something with this kid," Nick said.

Anna came to the rescue and spoke to Maria. "Momma, let me hold your baby so the doctor can look him over and fix you up. I'll stand right here with him. I promise."

Gently, but assertively, she pulled the baby away, encouraging

Maria to hold her son's hand.

Nick examined the child. Although very dirty, he didn't seem to be injured. Nick turned his attention back to Maria when the boy's kicking feet caught his eye.

"Here, turn him around toward me," he said to Anna.

He held a tiny foot. "Oh great, another one."

"What's that?"

Nick lifted the child's leg so Anna could see the foot. "Another damn clubfoot."

"Looks like you're going to be the local expert."

It was Maggie's voice. She came up behind them with a bottle of milk for Anna to give to the baby.

After the ordeal outside the gate, everyone was surprised to see her. She had washed the blood and dirt off her face, but she still wore the dirty, bloody shirt.

Paying them no mind and without hesitation, she went to Maria and put a gentle hand over her heart. "It is all right now, Momma. You are safe. We will not let anyone hurt you or your baby."

The woman wept and barely able to get the words out, she said, "I am so sorry, I know I have no right to come here. When I heard there was someone here that could help my baby, I decided to come. I didn't think people would recognize me. Please believe me. I can't believe that my Danilo would have anything to do with your husband's…" She couldn't say the word. "He was a kind man, a good husband, and he loved our little Danilo greatly. Please believe me." She covered her face with her hands and sobbed. "Please forgive me."

Maggie held Maria's hands. "It is okay. I know that God has brought you here for a reason. Now please stop apologizing, and let us take care of you and your baby."

Anna translated for Nick, but all he knew was that right now he had a patient to attend to.

* * *

"You okay?" Nick asked Maggie, as the Land Rover bounced

along a rutted dirt road toward San José Ojetenam on the way to Isabella's village. Nick watched Maggie fight the Rover's wheel. "You sure you don't want me to drive?"

"I'm good," she said, her eyes intent on the road.

"Okay," he said, but he was still worried. They already had a mishap on this road. One of the many colorful buses packed with passengers had blown past them with its air horn blasting. When the bus forced them into the ditch, he was glad they were on the inside of the mountain road; otherwise, the near collision would have been sent them flying hundreds of yards down the steep mountainside.

Nick glanced back at Isabella and her parents as they jostled in the back. Her sad and solemn face never changed.

And why would it? God, I feel terrible.

* * *

Nick thought back to the long night before. After they got Maria sutured up and settled with Danilo Jr. in a room at the Center, everyone had gone to bed, except Nick and Maggie who sat and talked well into the night.

After talking it through, they had decided that it would be best to get Isabella and her parents' home over the weekend to the rest of the family until Nick could decide what to do. He still had no idea.

Having Maria and her baby in the complex had been unsettling to everyone, including Maggie who had been the one to insist. Nick was amazed at Maggie's courage when, after they got mother and child to bed, she told her team, "God has given us an opportunity to show love and mercy to someone that we might prefer not to. But isn't this the very core of our faith?" She looked at her staff and the missionaries from California.

Nick saw fear and anxiety on their faces.

"You guys remember the story of Jesus teaching his disciples? I think it's the one right after the Beatitudes, *'Blessed are you that...'*" She checked for their acknowledgment, and they nodded.

155

"Jesus said that we have to treat others the same way we want them to treat us. That if we love only those that love us, what credit is that to us? For even sinners love those who love them. He also said, *'Do not judge, and you will not be judged; and do not condemn and you will not be condemned; pardon, and you will be pardoned.'*"

Maggie wasn't finished. "Look, you guys, moments like this define us. Do we really believe that Jesus died for everyone? Do we really believe that we are meant to forgive the unforgivable? Can we really love the unlovable?"

The young man who had carried Maria and her baby to the clinic raised his hand. Maggie smiled at him, waiting for him to speak.

His large, muscular shoulders trembled, and tears filled his eyes. He struggled to begin. "I…we…we have to watch over her. As I was carrying her, I felt the Lord speak to me. In my heart, I felt Him tell me that I was supposed to protect her…and the child." He wiped his eyes and nose on his shirt. "I don't know, ya'll. Maybe this sounds weird. But as I was carrying them, I felt like Jesus was carrying me. Of all the stupid stuff I've done in my life…" He paused to sob. His friend put an arm around his shoulders.

"Like Jesus was telling me that I was forgiven for all the stupid stuff I've done," the young man wiped his eyes and continued. "I've never felt like that before. I really don't know how to describe it. I just feel free."

Spontaneously, everyone cheered, and their fear and anxiety left the room.

"That mother risked everything for her baby. That kind of love triumphs over everything. That is the love our Heavenly Father has for us," Maggie declared.

Somewhat to his surprise, Nick found himself agreeing.

* * *

As they pulled into the small village near the Guatemala-Mexico border, Nick's stomach was unsettled from the bumpy ride. Anna had been right in describing their destination as

National Geographic territory. The pavement had ended hours ago.

The high mountain village consisted of twenty or so shack-like houses scattered on ten acres surrounded by dense jungle. Maggie parked at what appeared to be the central area. A few children and mongrel dogs greeted them. In the center of a worn, dirt-packed area was an old-fashioned, hand-dug well.

Nick helped Isabella and her parents out of the Land Rover. Isabella's father, not much bigger than Isabella, picked her up and carried her over his shoulder. He turned to Nick and thrust out his hand. "Thank you, Dr. Hart, for all that you are doing for my daughter," Maggie translated for Nick who, given his guilt for not doing anything, didn't know what to say.

Maggie smiled and answered for him. "We know God will make a way."

"Amen," Isabella's mother replied.

Nick watched Isabella's father carry his daughter up a path to their house.

"They want us to come to their home," Maggie told Nick.

An old man with a large, toothless smile greeted them. By now, a small crowd had gathered, including some goats and chickens. Maggie shook the man's hand and then translated for Nick.

"This is the village elder. He wants to welcome you. He says that it is a great honor to them for us to visit."

The elder spoke, and Maggie translated. "He wants to thank you for all you are doing for his people."

Nick started to say that he had done nothing, but Maggie interrupted. "He wants you to pray for them. There has been much sickness in the village, and some of the children have died. And, of course, you have seen Isabella."

The elder spoke again, and Maggie translated. "He says he knows you have been sent by God and asks you to please pray."

Maggie saw Nick's anxiety and reassured him. "I think he sees you for who you really are, my friend, not how you feel." She clapped her hands and winked at Nick. "You start, and I'll help."

"Maggie, I don't think..." Nick began. Then he saw the men take off their cowboy hats and the women bow their heads.

Many of them made the sign of the cross.

"Oh Geez."

"That's a good start," Maggie grinned. "*Jesús*," she translated for the villagers.

"*Jesús,*" they repeated.

There was an uncomfortable silence as Nick searched for words. Then, almost involuntarily, the prayer emerged. "Help me God. Help us God. Help us to understand this sickness and what we can do about it. Break the sickness. Bring health to this village and to these people. Bless these people, God."

Maggie added, "In Jesus' name, Amen."

"Amen," the villagers echoed and rushed to shake Nick's hand, hug Maggie, and thank them both.

Thank you, Nick mouthed to Maggie.

She squeezed his arm. "You did great."

The elder told them about their village and how they survived by farming and raising animals. Many of their family members had died during the war.

Maggie translated and added some history so Nick would understand. "The internal conflict lasted about thirty years, 1966-1996, and over 200,000 people died. I have heard that most of the people who died were Maya—most of them very poor. It was a terrible, terrible time in Guatemalan history."

Nick listened to stories of the brutality, with much of the tragedy affecting women and children.

While they conversed, Nick watched a teenage girl lead a burro to the well. She reached the frame over the well that supported an old wooden pulley and grabbed the end of a rope. She tied the end of the rope to the burro and led the animal away from the well. After they had walked a hundred feet or so, Nick saw a bucket come out of the well. It was full of water.

Not sure I've ever seen a real water well.

The burro faithfully stayed in place as the girl came back to the well and unhooked the bucket. She poured the water into two large plastic containers. Then she attached the bucket back to the rope and returned to the burro to untie the rope.

Nick watched as the rope snaked along the ground, retracting into the well as the bucket plunged into the water. Something occurred to him. "Uh, Maggie—I think I just figured out why everyone is sick," he said, interrupting the war stories.

Maggie turned in time to see the pulley finish swinging back and forth.

"That rope from the well got pulled through the dirt—and all the goat and chicken poop—and fell back down into the well. That can't be good."

* * *

Isabella's mother set bread on the table, and her father poured warm Coca Cola into a glass in front of Nick, Maggie, and the village elder.

I'm glad we are not drinking the water.

Nick had no idea that people still lived like this, or at least he never wanted to think they did. The single room was dark, except for what light came through the door. When his eyes adjusted to the dimness, he realized that the floor was dirt, and the walls were made of clay bricks.

A row of hammocks hung on one side of the room. On the other side was what Nick assumed was the kitchen. He saw an open fire under a chimney. He wondered how they kept their clothes so clean living in these conditions.

He realized that Isabella was watching him look around the room, and he smiled at her. Instantly, she avoided eye contact and looked at the floor.

He was shaken as he realized how awful it must be for her to have to get around on her deformed feet, not only on the dirt floor in the house, but in the surrounding jungle.

Maggie smiled at Isabella. "What do you dream about, *mija*?"

To Nick's great surprise, Isabella spoke. She answered Maggie's question as though she had been waiting all her life for the opportunity. "I want to wear shoes." She paused. "And I would like to go to school with the other kids in my village."

When Maggie told him what she'd said, he felt a knife stab his heart. *There has got to be something we can do.*

Isabella sat next to her twin sister, who hugged her sibling. Their older brother popped in and out; like most boys, he was not much for socializing. A baby cried, and Isabella's mother went to the crib in the corner and brought the little one to the visitors.

Nick couldn't believe what he saw. "Are you kidding me?" He looked at Maggie. "Did you know her sister has clubfeet, too?"

"I had no idea." Maggie held the child and cooed to her. She glanced at Nick, "Welcome to clubfoot haven."

"More like clubfoot hell."

* * *

As evening fell, Nick was relieved to be safely out of the mountains and closer to Quetzaltenango. It didn't help matters that they'd heard a car had been pulled over by bandits near Isabella's village. The passengers had been robbed, and fortunately, no one was killed.

"I feel like the Grinch. You know, *How the Grinch Stole Christmas*," Nick informed Maggie. "I've puzzled and puzzled till my puzzler is sore. I just can't figure out what to do."

Maggie laughed. "You know, Nick, I'm actually starting to feel bad. I had no idea how many kids around here had clubfeet. It's like they've come out of the shadows."

She pulled the Land Rover to the side of the road and turned to Nick. "You mind if I pray for you?"

"I guess it would be okay," he said reluctantly.

She put a hand on his shoulder. "Father. My good Father, thank you for Nick. Thank you for his heart of compassion, because I know it is your heart toward these children. Thank you that you have arranged for this time. Now, Papa, speak to us. Amen."

They sat in silence for a long time. Nick wondered if he should be waiting for a lightning bolt or something. He glanced at Maggie. She sat still with her eyes closed.

Suddenly she straightened up, reached into the glove compartment in front of Nick, and pulled out a small Bible. "I'm hearing Hebrews 12."

She opened the book and read: " *'Therefore, since we have so great a cloud of witnesses surrounding us, let us also lay aside every encumbrance and the sin which so easily entangles us, and let us run with endurance the race that is set before us.' "*

She then paraphrased a section on discipline. Nick watched her finger trace down the page. "Yes, this is it. This is what I think God wants to say to us—to you. Hebrews 12:12 and 13. *'Therefore, strengthen the hands that are weak and the knees that are feeble, and make straight paths for your feet, so that the limb, which is lame, may not be put out of joint, but rather be healed.'* Sounds like Isabella, doesn't it?"

"Yeah, but I'm not sure I understand."

They sat in silence. Nick slumped in his seat, not sure what was expected.

He then laughed. "Sorry, I'm still feeling very Grinchy and I just *thought of something* I *hadn't before.*"

"Huh?"

"Sorry, I'm not trying to be sacrilegious, but I've had this idea pop into my head." He pulled his cell phone from his pants pocket. "You think I could get cell service here?"

"Yeah, probably. Why?"

"One of my classmates did a pediatric ortho fellowship. I think he's at Seattle Children's."

He did a quick search and sure enough, there he was. Tod Goodman, Department of Orthopedic Surgery, Seattle Children's Hospital. Nick looked at his watch.

"I doubt that I'll catch him on the weekend," he said, dialing the phone. "Hi, this is Dr. Hart from, uh, Memphis." He almost said Guatemala. "I'm looking for Dr. Goodman."

There was a long pause.

"They are connecting me to the floor," Nick told Maggie. He was excited.

Nick took a while to explain to the floor nurse who he was and tried to patiently break through her defenses. He pleaded with her to put him through to his friend. Nick looked at his phone a few times to make sure he hadn't been disconnected during an excruciating long hold.

Maggie teased him, "Now you know how the rest of us feel."

Nick started to make a playful comeback when his friend came on the line.

"Nick Hart, how in the heck are you?"

"Hey, Tod, good to hear your voice. Thanks for taking my call. I hope I'm not catching you in the middle of something."

"Oh, you know how it goes. I'm on call this weekend—never a dull moment."

"Look, I know you're in the middle of it, so we'll catch up later, but I really need your advice."

"Sure, Nick. Anything for my chief." Nick had been chief resident when Tod started his training. Nick was glad he had been nice, for the most part, to the guys under him.

"It's a long story, Tod, but I'm actually calling you from Guatemala."

"Really? Guatemala? You in jail?" He laughed loudly.

"Man, I miss that infectious laugh of yours."

Nick covered the phone with his hand. "He thinks I'm in jail."

She laughed. "He must know you well."

"No, I'm changing my ways, but I do have a situation. I'm down here to help a friend at a mission hospital."

"A mission hospital? Is this really Nick Hart? The guy who doesn't take vacations and doesn't believe in God?"

"Okay, okay. But really, I am—and I need your advice."

"What's up?"

"I'm at the Hope Center, and I have seen six kids with clubfeet."

"Six? Wow. All babies?"

"No—and that's the hard part. All of them are past the age of stretching and casting. The oldest one is twelve."

"Twelve? Man, that's a tough one."

There was a long pause. Nick looked at his phone. "Tod, you there?"

"Yeah, just thinking. I wish I could tell you that we could bring them here and operate on them. But there's no way. Ten years ago maybe, but now, no way."

Nick nodded at Maggie, hoping she could hear the conversation. She nodded.

"You thinking of fixing them there?"

"Yeah, for about two seconds, until reality struck. Tod, I wouldn't even know where to start."

"What if we did them together?"

"What do you mean?"

"I don't know, Nick—just thinking. Kim and I have always wanted to do a mission trip, and our kids are getting old enough where we would feel comfortable traveling with them. When are you thinking?"

"Uh…Monday?"

Tod executed one of his flamboyant laughs. "Now that's the Dr. Hart I remember."

There was another long pause.

"I'm just thinking out loud here," Tod began, "so please don't get your hopes up. My kids are on spring break next week, and we are headed to Disneyland for the week. So I have no idea. I'll have to talk with Kim and the kids. Could we even bring our kids down?"

Maggie nodded enthusiastically.

"Yeah, sure. Of course," Nick told Tod.

"Well, I better get back to my patients. Can I call you back on this number? You're going to owe me big time," Tod laughed again.

"Man, I will personally buy your plane tickets down here."

"Nick Hart flying me to Guatemala. Now I know that God is really in this."

Oh no, not you too.

CHAPTER 23

THE VIRUS

Pak Song-ju handed Professor Kwon the box. He was one of the few men in North Korea that Pak respected, both for his intelligence and for his passion for what they were accomplishing.

He could easily overlook his appearance. Kwon's wardrobe was pretty much the same from day to day—a threadbare, wool sweater over a white shirt with one or both collars turned up or out, and his unkempt, black hair shot out of his head as though he were standing next to a Tesla coil.

Kwon adjusted his glasses, the lens heavily spotted with grime, and stared at the box.

"This is from Professor Suk and his men in Guatemala?"

He sat forward in his squeaky desk chair and set the box down in front of him. Savoring the moment, with his eyes fixed on the box, he stretched both hands on his desk and sighed loudly. "I can't believe this is finally it, Song-ju."

Kwon was the only other person in the world besides Pak's parents who would dare address him by his first name. Not even his wife was allowed to do that.

Pak put a firm hand on the professor's shoulder. "This is your hard work, my friend. You are to be congratulated. They tell me it is 100 percent effective now. You will be richly rewarded."

"100 percent?" He looked at Pak in surprise.

"Yes."

"That is more than we hoped for." He looked back at the metal box. He picked it up and carefully inserted a magnetic key into the tiny lock. His hands shook.

"Careful, Professor, you don't want to break the tube. This is the crown of your life's work."

"Yes, indeed." Kwon opened the box carefully. He saw that the dense gel inside the box was still frozen. "Good." With trembling fingers, he pulled out the vial and held it up to the light. There was a slight phase separation of the blood and plasma, but the specimen was frozen solid. "Excellent."

CHAPTER 24

NORTHEASTERN GUATEMALA

"I'm tired of those filthy things and their smell," Hwang snorted at Suk as he sat at the table, sharpening a knife. He inspected the large blade. The missionary's blood had long been washed off. "Let me skin them and put them out of my misery," he sneered, testing the edge of the sharp knife.

"All in due time." Suk stood in front of the row of cages against the wall. He petted one of the ferrets he had removed from its cage. "You served your purpose well, my little friend." With affection, he held the creature in front of his face.

"All I know is they stink," Hwang frowned. He stood and holstered the large hunting knife into its sheath strapped to his back.

Suk put the ferret back in its cage. The wall of caged ferrets erupted in a choir of chortling and clucking sounds, anticipating their breakfast.

"Shut those things up while you're at it," Hwang groused. "I'm going to find Cho." He left the room, slamming the door.

Suk looked around the room. He was going to feel sad to leave this place. He had more freedom and autonomy here than ever in his life. In this place, he was the decision maker. The hard part had been keeping Cho and Hwang in check.

Suk trained in microbiology in London, but he liked Guatemala, especially its Gallo beer. He had rented a house in San Benito on Lake Petén Itzá four years earlier because of its proximity to the old Maya ruins in Tikal and the villages in northeastern Guatemala. It was the perfect location because it held the only other international airport in the country, aside from Guatemala City.

He had not been back to North Korea for eleven years—not long enough to forget how difficult life was there. He shuddered to think of going back.

Maybe I'll be reassigned somewhere else.

As he walked down the row of cages, pouring food into the dispensers, the ferrets settled.

"I guess I'll release you guys before we go," he said to the small weasels.

They had been perfect hosts. Hosts for the virus.

He wondered about his longtime mentor, Professor Kwon, the one person he missed from North Korea. He had no idea if Kwon had received the vial of ferret blood or his note.

I hope the Professor is pleased.

Professor Kwon was a decorated national hero, developer of all of the biological warfare for the country. He had overseen the development of thirteen different biological agents that could be weaponized, including anthrax and the plague. Kim Il-sung personally awarded him the country's highest civilian honor for his work with smallpox.

Suk poured a little extra food for one of the large male ferrets.

Regrettably, six months after Kwon received the award, his uncle was caught with a counterfeit U.S. twenty-dollar bill he had lifted from the government-sanctioned counterfeit presses where he worked. The punishment was swift and firm. The entire family was rounded up and sent to the northernmost prison— Hoeryong Political Prison Camp. Kwon's wife and three-year-old son had been included in the incarceration.

Suk vividly remembered that day. He was working alongside Kwon when the government police came into the lab to inform him of the arrests. Kwon was told that because of his status, he was allowed to remain in his position, but his wife and son were gone.

Kwon showed no emotion at the news, but shortly after they left, he collapsed. With over 50,000 prisoners and close to a fifty-percent mortality rate due to malnutrition, he doubted the family would survive. Suk had pledged to the professor that he would do anything he could to help exact revenge.

Suk opened one of the top cages and pulled out his favorite ferret. It purred as Suk nestled it against his neck.

Kwon's genius had brought them to Guatemala as an NGO. The non-governmental organization was registered in Seoul, quite a coup in itself. It was called The Friends of Children Organization; FOCO was its acronym. It was well funded, ironically, with profits from counterfeiting.

Because Suk was not only a world-class microbiologist, but also a student of world history and war, it did not escape his attention that the *foco* theory details rebellion by way of guerrilla warfare—revolution accomplished using small, nimble rebel groups that provide a focus—*foco*, in Spanish—for popular discontent against a sitting regime.

I wonder which came first, the acronym or the name?

Suk replaced the ferret gently in its cage and filled its food dispenser.

Their NGO status gave them easy access to the villages of Guatemala. They had one of the most advanced well-drilling rigs in the country, and the communities welcomed them with open arms.

Hwang and Cho came through the door, interrupting Suk's thoughts. Cho was shirtless and sweating. He had been working out on the heavy bag, and he began to unwind the wraps that protected his knuckles. He was a short, stocky man with a shaved head. His face and chest were covered with terrible acne, a condition made worse by Guatemala's humidity.

With an abundance of food and beer. Cho had gained fifty pounds in Guatemala. He saw Suk staring at his big beer belly. He slapped his abdomen with both fists. "All muscle, you geeky scientist."

Suk watched Cho flex his biceps in the mirror hanging in the entryway. They would betray him in a heartbeat, and he was constantly on guard.

Hopefully, I won't have to put up with these two much longer.

"We should be going," Suk addressed them both. "We still have work to do. Do you have the spraying equipment ready?" he asked Hwang.

"Where are we headed today?"

"We will be going south, to the village of La Libertad."

"How much longer until we leave Guatemala?" Cho asked, pulling on a shirt.

"I suspect three months, if they received the vial."

CHAPTER 25

FREEDOM

Nick dabbed Maria's head wound with gauze soaked in hydrogen peroxide. She pulled away in pain.

"I'm sorry. I know it's pretty sore."

He was trying to remove a large clot of blood around the sutures.

Nick looked at Anna. "This thing was so dirty, I'm afraid it's going to get infected if I'm not pretty aggressive with keeping it clean."

"Try to hold still while the doctor looks at your wound," Anna told her. "We don't want it to get infected." She held Maria's shoulders and translated for Nick.

"Thank you for taking care of me, doctor, but do you think you will be able to do anything for my son?" Maria asked through Anna.

Nick searched her eyes. There was such a sincere depth to her request that it made it difficult for him not to empathize with her.

"Well, there is a chance. I usually don't do that kind of surgery, but I talked with a friend in Seattle, and he may come down to help. I can't guarantee anything yet."

Anna continued to translate as Maria took Nick's arm. "Thank you for trying, doctor. I cannot repay you for your kindness."

"You certainly have a lot of courage," Nick said as he snapped off his exam gloves and tossed them into the trash can near the exam table.

"I took little Danilo to the government hospital, but they

told me that I would have to pay for the supplies for the surgery and for the hospital stay. His father and I tried and tried to save enough money. There was never enough. I think my husband was hoping he would get paid well for his last job."

"What was his job?"

"He was a tour guide for the ruins in Tikal. His father was the same, so he grew up doing that. He knew so much about the Mayas and the ancient ruins."

She continued to wring her hands, and Nick could tell the discussion was difficult. But he encouraged her because he was anxious to get more information about John's death. Maggie had not told him very much. After a brief investigation, Maria told him, the police had closed the case. They believed Dr. John was in the wrong place at the wrong time, apparently something that happened all too frequently in the country. They did think it was odd *how* the doctor had been killed, but because the presumed murderer was found dead himself, they had nothing to go on. The rain had washed away all traces and clues. Therefore, the case was closed.

Maria seemed to read Nick's thoughts. "Danilo was an honest man. You have to believe me. He was a kind man. I never saw him cheat anyone. He was not a violent man."

Nick sat back in his chair, glanced at Anna, and pressed on. "Where do you live?" he asked Maria.

"We live in El Remate, south of the ruins."

"How far away is that from here?"

"It is very far, maybe two days on the bus."

"Did you ever see Dr. John there?"

"The police asked me the same thing. They showed me his picture, and I had never seen him before. We get lots of tourists there, I don't pay them much attention."

"Why do you think Dr. John and your husband were out there together?"

She looked him straight in the eyes without blinking. "I don't know, doctor. I wish I did. Maybe he was giving him a tour? Maybe they ran into the drug cartel? I just don't know. None of it makes sense to me. All I know is, Danilo could never kill anyone."

Sweat formed on her upper lip and forehead, and she trembled. "Really, that is all I know. I have been very afraid that, whoever they are, they would come for little Danilo and myself."

Anna wiped Maria's brow with a cloth.

Nick rubbed his eyes and crossed his arms.

Had he really lost his best friend from some senseless act of violence? What was John doing in that part of Guatemala anyway?

He stood, as if to conclude the interview and told Maria, "I know this is hard for you, I am sorry for your loss."

"You were friends with Dr. John?"

Nick nodded. "Yes, he was my friend, my best friend." He decided he couldn't talk about it anymore and headed to the door. Holding the doorknob, he turned back to Maria and Anna. "Did you say that your husband told you he was being paid well for his last job?"

"Yes, but I thought it was with the men from FOCO."

"Foco?" Nick asked.

"Foco,"Anna repeated. "It's spelled f-o-c-o. I don't understand how she's using it, but the word means *focus* in Spanish."

Anna asked Maria what she meant.

"It is a group that has been helping villages in our area," Maria said. "They drilled a new water well for our village. I must have been confused."

"Did you tell the police about that?"

"No, I thought I was mistaken."

"Well, if you think of anything else, let me know," Nick said. "I'd really appreciate hearing about it." He turned back to the door.

"Dr. Hart, I am so sorry," Maria said.

* * *

Maggie and Nick sat in tranquility on the bench under the mango tree; it was a respite they looked forward to at the end of a busy day. They watched in companionable silence as the moon rose over the mountains. Only the hushed voices of children at the orphanage whispered in the night.

"I talked with Maria today when I changed her dressing," Nick said, breaking the stillness.

"She doing okay?"

"Yeah. I've been pretty worried about her wound."

But her wound wasn't all he wanted to talk about. Nick wasn't sure where to start. He had so many questions. "Do you know what John was doing up in that area of Guatemala?"

Maggie sighed. She'd known he was bound to ask, but didn't want to talk about it. "I don't know, Nick, I guess checking on some of the villagers that we see. He would often travel all around Guatemala. Honestly, I thought he wanted to get away from here every once in a while," she smiled at Nick, "for a fresh perspective."

"Was there anything different about this trip? Did he say anything?"

"I don't know. I've racked my brain about that. He was just going to be gone a few days. The only thing that I have been able to remember is he told me that some of the villages in the north were having fertility problems. John thought it was the pesticides they use so heavily in their agriculture that was causing the problem. What's weird is that I can't even remember that much about the day he left. You know happy-go-lucky John—he gave me a big kiss and a smile and was gone." Tears welled up in her eyes.

"I'm really sorry, Maggie. I'm sure it is hard to talk about."

"It's okay, Nick. Maybe it's just my Blackfeet blood. We don't like to talk about the bad things. My God, if we did, that is all there would be to talk about."

Nick saw Maggie's discomfort and his brain raced for a positive subject. "I can't believe how all this is working out. My instrument rep in Memphis gathered all the implants and supplies together, but I couldn't figure out how to get them here until I thought of my friend Buck. I called him yesterday and thought he was going to jump on a plane that moment, he was so excited. He flies in tomorrow with eleven boxes of implants. Unbelievable."

She finally smiled. "Goes to show that nothing is impossible with God."

"Well, I guess I have to admit, it sure appears that way."

Nick drank some iced tea. "You're really going to like Buck.

He is a gem of a guy and women always swoon over his good looks."

"Nick, how come you never got married?" It was Maggie's turn to change the subject. "Weren't you pretty serious with that one girl in med school?"

"Michelle? Yeah, I guess, but it didn't work out. I don't know, maybe I'm too picky or too busy or just too handsome."

"Certainly not too humble," Maggie retorted.

"I guess the real reason is that the best one was already taken." He rolled his eyes at Maggie.

"Oh, stop it," she said, punching his arm.

"John was very lucky. That's all I can say." He wasn't kidding around.

Their moment was broken when Nick's cell phone rang. He answered immediately. "Hey Tod, let me put you on speakerphone. I'm sitting here with Maggie Russell who runs the Hope Center."

"Hi, Maggie," Tod's voice came through the speaker. "You want the good news or the bad news?"

Nick grimaced. "I guess you better start with the bad." He had prepared himself all day for this. *What am I going to tell those kids and their parents?*

"Well, the bad news is that you are going to owe me big time," Tod roared with laughter. "The good news is that you are going to have to put up with me and my family for a few days."

Nick wanted to stand up and shout, and Maggie did.

"Oh, that is so great, Tod. Thank you so very much. I can't tell you how much this means to me."

"Kim, the girls, and I prayed about it, and we really felt like we were supposed to do this. Honestly, I wasn't so sure. You know the whole money thing. We were sitting at the table eating, and my youngest girl looked up and asked, 'You know what we learned in school today?' 'What?' I asked. And she said, 'We were reading out of First Samuel. We learned that for God, obedience is better than sacrifice.' I told her she was getting too smart for her own britches," Tod guffawed.

"The real clincher for the deal was when I called my friend, the travel agent," he continued. "I forgot we had taken out trip insurance. Turns out we could change our plans without losing a dime. Then she got us some screaming deals on the flight to Guatemala. Goes to show nothing is impossible for the Lord."

Nick laughed. "Seems like I just heard that."

Maggie was still dancing. *See, I told you so*, she mouthed to Nick.

"We get in on Tuesday. I figured that would give us Wednesday, Thursday and Friday to get all the kiddos done. That okay with you?"

"Oh man, I don't know how I am ever going to pay you back for this one, my friend. Honestly, I'm speechless."

"Well, that's payment enough," Tod hooted. "See you Tuesday!"

Nick hung up. "I don't know what to say."

"Well, a good place to start is, thank you, Jesus." Maggie sat down again, jiggling her knees with joy. "God is so good. Don't you think?"

"I don't know, Maggie, I've never thought of God that way. I don't know. I guess I thought of Him as out there somewhere. The great observer."

Maggie put her hand on his. "And now?"

"I guess some would say it's all coincidence."

Maggie tilted her head, *"Really?* Is it that hard for you to see God's fingerprints all over this?"

"Well, honestly, no."

"Then what is it?"

Nick turned away and thought for a long time. "I don't know. I guess it's easier for you to think of God like that. Most of my time is either not thinking about God or thinking that he's mad at me." He turned back, his face crossed with pain. "I haven't been the best person in the story of my life."

Maggie squeezed his hand. "Then you've been reading the wrong story."

"What do you mean?"

"Oh, Nick, God loves you so very much."

"I don't know about me, but I can see why he loves you," he said.

Maggie leaned back and crossed her arms.

"Maggie, I am so sorry. I didn't mean—"

"Did you ever wonder why John and I never had kids?"

"Well, yes. I guess I did."

"You know I grew up in Browning on the Rez—not the easiest of places for a kid. Our parents were pretty darn strict, but we got into our share of trouble."

Maggie searched for words. "Nick, I haven't told anybody about this except my parents and my best friend growing up. And, of course, John. I got pregnant. Twice. One ended with an abortion and the other an ectopic pregnancy. The second one just about killed me. They flew me to Great Falls for emergency surgery."

"Oh, Maggie," Nick hugged her shoulder.

"That was the end of my baby days. It caused me a lot of shame for a long time. When I met John, I didn't tell him right away. I was so afraid to lose him."

Maggie shifted in her seat.

"When I finally told him, he just held me, and we both cried buckets. But he didn't cry out of hurt or anger or anything like that. He cried because he felt God's heart break for me. He said God's heart broke for the pain and shame that I carried."

Tears fell from Maggie's eyes as she looked at Nick to see if he understood.

"I know God loves me," she said. "He sent his only Son to redeem me. He has become so real to me. John would tell me that God takes ALL things and turns them for good. Talk about good," she smiled. "Look at me now—I have seventy-three children." She wiped her tears and laughed.

Nick smiled briefly and looked up at the stars. "Maggie, I'm trying to understand. It's like my brain hears, but my heart can't translate."

Maggie put her hand on his. "You see, Nick, we all have our stinky stuff. That is why we need a Savior. People have it so very wrong so much of the time when they turn away from God. They think He's a killjoy, a party pooper. They couldn't be more wrong. If they only knew the joy Jesus brings. If they only understood what is available to them from heaven. I pray that you will come to understand what I'm saying."

CHAPTER 26

HISTORY

Professor Kwon stared at the picture as it came off the printer connected to the electron microscope. As the paper spooled out and dropped onto the tray, he paused to savor the reality of his discovery.

Even though he had been up all night preparing the specimen, he was not tired. He was excited like a boy on his birthday. He took the picture from the tray. The greyscale image was indistinct, an array of spheres arranged in a random pattern. But to Kwon, it was magnificent, a Michelangelo, a Leonardo. It was not just a virus that would change the world, although it would certainly do that! It was magnificent because it confirmed his discovery and validated his reason for living. It had been a winding road to this truth, and Kwon had enjoyed every moment. He loved reliving those moments on the way to creating his masterwork.

A preeminent microbiologist, Kwon realized that it would be a microbe—one of the tiniest of earthly elements—that would shape history more than any war or nuclear device. Many of his friends had chosen to pursue careers in nuclear physics; they considered him irrelevant for his minor role in science. *The fools will now know where the real power lies.*

It all started that day in grammar school when he'd studied the great epidemics of the world. He asked the instructor for a copy of the list of epidemics the teacher presented to the class. No one else in his class seemed to care, but Kwon was fascinated.

Like his classmates, except for the Great Leader, he had no thought of a supreme being or beings. His instructor provided a brief history of the Greeks, the ancient civilizations, and world religions, but he taught the class that any belief outside of North Korean culture was for the weak and should not to be taken seriously. Kwon wasn't much interested in anything except epidemics. Wiping out huge swaths of populations fascinated him to his very core like nothing else ever had.

Was there something in the cosmos that held the power of life and death?

The only evil he was taught was the evil that came from countries like the U.S. and Europe, but the more he studied epidemics, the more he believed there was even greater evil.

The great Bubonic Plagues of the fourth and twelfth centuries wiped out half of Europe's population. Smallpox, measles, and influenza epidemics single handedly eradicated entire cultures in the fourteenth, fifteenth, and sixteenth centuries. It was these microbes that Kwon spent his life studying. Over his career, he had created stockpiles of them for his country's biological warfare programs.

In the early 1900s, seventy-five million people worldwide died from an influenza epidemic. He knew that whoever controlled the microbe kingdom controlled the world.

There was so much that puzzled him.

Why had the great epidemics not wiped out the entire population? Why had they stopped?

No one ever truly controlled microbes. Extreme caution had to be observed when producing super-bugs for warfare against another nation; if anything went wrong the microbes could just as easily wipe out his own country.

Five years ago, one of his Kwon's assistants had contracted the swine flu H1N1 virus that typically only infected pigs. His assistants had manipulated the virus which allowed for human transference. Fortunately, quarantine in North Korea was simple—infected people and those in close contact were quickly eliminated by fire. Only fifty people died from the virus, but nearly a thousand died from quarantine.

* * *

Kwon held the image of the virus to his eye level and turned it ninety degrees, then another ninety. The image reminded him of a blurred picture of a butterfly feeding on a flower.

Strange, something so beautiful, yet so noxious.

His epidemic would be entirely different. There would be no deaths, and he would not see the ultimate results in his lifetime. He created the virus for his children's children and generations beyond.

Since his family had been thrown in prison, he assumed his biological son had not survived, but his own gene pool would live on, thanks to his friend Pak and his baby factories.

Kwon held the image to his chest.

His epidemic would be different by its stealth. The virus had been engineered to be less virulent and less deadly but extremely effective. As rapidly as biological warfare programs developed an infectious disease, other world scientists would manufacture vaccinations or treatments, making the warfare less threatening and less effective. As death tolls mounted for the bird flu or swine flu, worldwide resources produced vaccines that were quickly distributed.

Kwon's virus would cause only a small blip on the World Health Organization's epidemic and pandemic monitors; its cold-like symptoms would be mild when released at the height of cold and flu season. But, it was not symptoms Kwon was after. It was the side effects.

CHAPTER 27

THE NEW ORDER

Pak knew he did not have to hurry. Like Professor Kwon, he was a cog in the wheel of change for the destiny of the New Order of North Korea.

He sat at the desk in his sparsely appointed government office and reviewed the numbers. The population growth rate in North Korea was a measly 0.8 percent. He doubted they would ever get it up to two percent, like most developed nations, and even if they did, their economy could not support it. At least it was up from 0.6 percent—reflecting an additional 38,000 babies born this year. But it wasn't so much the quantity that mattered, but the quality, and the quality was first rate because hundreds of those children were his.

Sperm had been donated by many of the top scientists, creative artists, and leaders of the country, including Kim Jong-un, himself. But Pak controlled the program. When he had returned from his studies in Paris, the government had finished a survey of the population and realized that its growth was too small in relation to that of South Korea. The government called for an accelerated population growth plan. Although large families were encouraged, the population did not grow fast enough for the government's liking. That's when Pak's suggestion of baby factories garnered instant favor.

Access to the labs allowed him to switch out Kim's sperm for his own.

I will not allow that weak family line to continue.

Pak glanced at his framed diploma hanging in front of the

desk. His degree from the University of Paris was in History. His father had sent him to study, hoping that he would learn lessons from the great civilizations of the world and bring the best of what he learned back to his homeland. All North Koreans knew their destiny was to dominate the world. Theirs was the superior race, and all others should be eliminated. As a superior people, their birthright was to dominate society by purging inferior elements.

Pak's studies brought him to the realization that domination could never be achieved by raw power. Even with the development of their nuclear weapons program, they had little ability to attack other nations, not even the South, and any outright aggression would mean certain death and destruction of their people.

Pak stared at the photograph next to his diploma. It showed him standing in front of the Coliseum in Rome with a fellow student from the university. During their visit, he and his colleague went to the Sistine Chapel. Pak was fascinated with Michelangelo's *The Creation of Adam* and wondered about this "God" that could create life and take it away. Pak even went to the university library on his return to Paris and read the book of Genesis. It was the first time he had touched a Bible. Bibles were restricted in North Korea, and the possession of one was punishable by death. Pak was riveted by the story of Noah and how his God destroyed the entire population of the earth.

Because Pak rejected the notion of a god, any destruction of mankind would be at the hands of man. That was the reason he was such a staunch supporter of Professor Kwon and his profound knowledge. Pak ensured that the professor had the most sophisticated microbiology lab in the world. Pak marveled at the fact that he and Kwon shared the same belief in ethnic purity. He vividly remembered the day that he and the professor stood and talked beside his limousine parked at a farmer's field as they watched the farmer till the soil. Kwon pointed out how the earth had to be worked, the old crop had to be removed or tilled under, and the new crop planted.

CHAPTER 28

AN EXTENDED STAY

"Look, Ms. Roe, I am not asking for a leave of absence. I just need another week here."

Nick's face flushed. He and Maggie sat on the picnic table outside the clinic. A line of patients had returned at the start of his second week, and Nick realized he needed more time.

Buck was bringing the equipment, and Tod was bringing the expertise, and they would arrive tomorrow evening. He would have only three days to operate, and most of that time would be spent on the kids with clubfeet. He was responsible for the children's post-operative care, but he also wanted to operate on others before he left.

Nick held the phone away from his ear so Maggie could hear the woman bark.

"You didn't even have the decency to talk to me before you left," Anita Roe yapped, "and now you want me to approve another week. Dr. Hart, you are so far out of your contract you have no idea what kind of field day our lawyers will have with you."

The California mission students having lunch with them became quiet. Nick felt everyone staring at him as he tried to control his temper. He hated this woman, and everything she represented was what he detested most about modern-day medicine.

He had not realized how unhappy he was in his practice at the MED until this week in Guatemala.

Medicine ran in Nick's blood. As a fourth-generation

physician, his destiny was set when he started school. He really never thought about another career. He loved the stories of his great-grandfather riding a horse-drawn buggy to make house calls. Legend had it that his faithful horse, Smoke, would find the way home with the good doctor asleep in the buggy after being up all night with a laboring mother.

That kind of romanticized practice of medicine had given way to production charts, procedure coding, battles with insurance companies, fending off lawyers with frivolous lawsuits, and overall greed. Nick heard the sucking sound trying to pull him back to the treadmill in Memphis.

"I don't give a flip about the poor people in Guatemala; we have plenty of poor people here in Memphis, and this is where you belong," Anita Roe barked. "This is where your contract is."

Nick could see her cold, merciless expression. "Well, Ms. Roe, I'm not exactly asking for your permission. I've already talked with my colleagues, and they're fine with it. They're going to pick up my call." A long silence followed. "Look, Anita, you called me. I just want to let you know what I'm doing and that things at home are covered. I don't know what to tell you except that I'm really needed here."

Nick thought she had hung up. He had never used her first name before and thought he had offended her. He looked at the phone to see if he was still connected and put it back to his ear.

"Okay fine." She was still there, and her voice had softened. "But come see me in my office when you get back."

As he hung up the phone, Nick realized that the team around him was praying.

* * *

The next day, Maggie and Nick stood outside the exit of the airport in Guatemala City, watching the people file out with suitcases and fall into the arms of waiting loved ones. They waited anxiously for Buck and for Tod and his family to make their way through immigration and customs.

What a difference a week makes.

Last week Nick had felt like a fish out of water when he faced long lines of people seeking medical help and jabbering in Spanish. This week he was at ease with the Hope Center's chaos; it was as though he belonged here. Even though he hated the drive over the pass with the possibility of being held up, robbed, or worse, he was comfortable with the sights, sounds, and smells of the jungle. Just the same, he was glad Joseph had come with them and brought his shotgun.

After his assault on Maria, Maggie had seen to it that Joseph was reinstated to his post. She had spoken with them both and told them that God is a God of reconciliation and encouraged them to forgive each other. In truth, Maria and Joseph were relieved of the heavy burden of guilt and shame. Nick observed the amity between them and noticed Joseph checking on Maria and the baby the night before.

* * *

"I hope they get through customs okay," Maggie said, interrupting his thoughts. "I've got the team praying, but you just never know."

"Yeah, anything can happen. Buck's bringing a bunch of supplies for us. I don't know what we'd do if he got delayed in customs."

"Lord, we ask for your favor and the favor of the custom agents as our friends come through," Maggie prayed.

"I say Amen to that."

Maggie smiled at Nick.

Watching the exiting crowd, Nick saw the young hucksters that had accosted him on arrival in Guatemala. They were plying their trade on an elderly couple.

"Hope those folks are holding tight to their wallets."

Then he saw the man with the badly infected leg wound lying on the ground in the same spot.

"His name is José," she said, following his gaze

Nick wasn't surprised she knew him. "Why doesn't he do something about his leg?"

"I know. It's heartbreaking, isn't it? John stopped every time and talked with him, prayed for him, and gave him a little money.

He offered many times to pack up José right then and there and take him to the Hope Center for treatment. His leg is so bad; it really needs to be amputated."

"And the guy never wanted to go?"

"He told John that he didn't know what he would do besides beg. That's all he knew for the past twenty years. You remember the story of Jesus going into Jerusalem when He saw a crippled man lying by the side of the pool of Bethesda?"

"Does it have anything to do with Thing 1 and Thing 2?" Nick grinned and deflected the biblical lesson with an allusion to his mentor, Dr. Seuss.

Maggie gave him a dirty look. "You're impossible."

Nick sighed, knowing he had to take the medicine. "I'm afraid I don't know that story."

"The man had been an invalid for thirty-eight years, and Jesus asked him this crazy question: *Do you want to get well?* It sounds absurd, right? Who doesn't want to get well? But I think about it every time I see José. John and I asked him the same question, and his answer was always no. He didn't want freedom. It's so sad, I can hardly stand it."

"It is sad."

"But honestly Nick, we all tend to have a bit of that in us. Jesus is asking us all the same question. Whatever our wounds are, Jesus is asking: Do you want freedom from that bitterness, that anger, that addiction? Whatever it is, He is offering freedom."

Before she could amplify her story, Nick waved his arm at the exiting passengers. He'd spotted Buck's square jaw as he walked out the doors. Wearing a huge smile, Buck was pushing a large cart stacked full of plastic containers.

"Thank you, Jesus," Maggie whispered and gave Nick's friend the once-over. "You're right. Buck *is* handsome."

Nick rolled his eyes at her.

Maggie shrugged. "Just saying."

But Nick's attention had moved on. He pushed through the crowd to greet Buck when he saw Tod and his family behind his friend.

CHAPTER 29

FAITHFULNESS

The room buzzed with exhaustion and anticipation as the entire team gathered in the Hope Center's dining room long after the orphans were asleep. Everyone was tired, but no one was in any hurry to go to bed. Besides, there wasn't much night left for sleep, after the drive from the airport and two hours spent examining the children. It seemed like the perfect time to worship.

One of the young Californians strummed his guitar, and the team sang *Great is Thy Faithfulness*. They were all suffused with God's faithfulness for their own lives, for the team the Lord had put together, but mainly for the six young lives that would forever be transformed as they grew from shame to wholeness, from lame to healed.

A cool, refreshing breeze drifted through the room, making the candles flicker.

Collectively, they decided tonight was the ideal time to take communion. It had been Buck's idea, and Maggie loved it. Of everyone, Buck was the most undone when they examined each of the children; the big man was a puddle of tears by the end of the evening. Nick asked Buck to sit with him and Tod when they had a chance to reexamine the children's feet and give them an overall medical assessment to make sure they were healthy and ready for anesthesia. Buck had to leave the room several times to regain his composure, especially when Isabella shuffled in. Buck understood perhaps more than anyone what it meant to get your life back.

The adventurous young Californians were happy to make the mountainous trek to retrieve Isabella and her family, and her parents were pleasantly surprised to see them return so soon.

Isabella's father bonded instantly with Buck when he learned the big man was a soldier who gave his legs and almost his life for his country. Isabella's father fought in the Guatemalan conflict as a young man and lost countless friends; he understood the cost of war.

That night in the dining room, Maggie held a small loaf of bread. "Just like on that night before Jesus gave His life for us, He sat with his disciples and took bread and broke it, saying '*This is my body that is given for you. Take it in remembrance of me.*' " She split the loaf in two and passed the halves around the room; everyone broke off a small piece and ate it.

Then Maggie held a carafe of wine and said, "Then He took a cup of wine and said, '*Drink this. This is my blood which is shed for you for the forgiveness of sin.*' " She poured the wine into small Dixie cups and passed them around.

Holding her cup in front of her, she prayed, "Blessed are you that show mercy, for mercy will be given to you. Thank you, Lord Jesus, for giving your life for us. For giving your life for the children, that they would find redemption. Now Lord, I pray your protection over them. I pray that you guide everyone's hands and thoughts and minds tomorrow as you, Lord, bring healing to these children. Give everyone here the rest they so desperately need tonight. Thank you Lord for covering us with your blood of mercy and grace over these next three days, as you do every day of our lives. Amen."

A resounding "Amen" issued from the team, and everyone drank from their communion cups.

Nick realized it had been almost twenty years since he had taken communion and then only when he was home visiting his parents at Christmas. He had to admit this was different. He even found himself praying. "God, help me," he'd said and believed he meant it.

Tod put his arm around Nick's shoulders. "Man, thank you so much for asking me down here. Kim and the girls may never want to leave." He pointed over his shoulder to where his girls were huddled close to Carmen, the local anesthesiologist, already practicing their Spanish.

Nick shook his head with wonder. "Tod, I just don't know what I would have done. You have no idea how grateful I am for you. When all these kids started coming in with clubfeet, it was like I lost confidence in myself as a surgeon. I'm not sure I've ever experienced that in my life."

"I'm not going to lie to you," Tod laughed, "my knees are shaking. I work on kiddos day in and day out, but we hardly see clubfeet like this any more. I've been reading like crazy the last few days to figure out how to do this. I thought before we go to bed, me and you could review the anatomy and our exposure for tomorrow."

"That would be great."

"I'm still awful nervous about Isabella," Tod said. "We know we're going to have to be real careful not to overstretch her vessels or nerves. Her feet won't survive an insult like that."

"Agreed."

"This is what I'm thinking. Let's start with that three-year-old boy with the one side clubfoot. We can do that one together. I'll show you the approach and how to isolate out the neurovascular bundle, what ligaments to cut, the tendons to lengthen, and then how to pin it in place. It's too easy to either undercorrect or overcorrect these darn little feet."

"That sounds great."

"Then we'll do the other three-year-old with the bilateral clubfeet. I'll do one side, and you do the other."

Nick grimaced.

Tod hooted. "You know, the ol' see one, do one, teach one. You'll be the local expert when we're done."

Nick wasn't sure.

"We'll do one step at a time. Together. I figure we could get two kids done tomorrow and three on Thursday, and when we're really feeling confident, we can tackle Isabella on Friday."

"That sounds good," Nick nodded. "I'm just not sure I'm ever going to feel confident."

"You know, that's when God meets us the most, when we are at the end of ourselves." Tod squeezed Nick's shoulder. "Oh yeah,

I almost forgot, I brought you something." He reached for his backpack, pulled out a wooden box just right for holding small pencils, and gave it to Nick. "I figured you didn't have a pair of these with you."

Nick opened the box. Inside was a pair of brand new loupes, surgical magnifying glasses. "Oh my gosh, Tod," he exclaimed.

"You have a pair of these?"

"I don't. In my world of fixing big bones, all we need is a splash shield. We don't fix anything small enough to use them."

Tod slapped him on the back. "Welcome to the microscopic world. The nerves and vessels are going to be tiny. These should help you stay out of trouble."

"I'm not sure what to say." Nick knew the special glasses cost a couple thousand dollars.

Tod slapped his thigh. "There you go. I've made famous trauma surgeon Nick Hart speechless twice in one week. Payment enough."

CHAPTER 30

MUMPS

Hwang swerved the SUV into the oncoming lane, hit a howling mongrel dog, and caused the small trailer attached to the FOCO vehicle to careen wildly. Hwang and his seatmate Cho laughed.

"I don't care about the dog, but I sure the devil care about the equipment!" Suk snarled from the back seat. He looked back to see the severely injured dog collapsing beside the road.

Suk was glad that CA13 from Santa Benito to Dolores had little traffic and that no one saw Hwang's reckless escapades. Hwang liked to kill things, a trait that had been useful when the *miguk*, that American doctor, snooped into their business. Still, Suk had been surprised at how much Hwang enjoyed killing. As a microbiologist, Suk was fascinated by life; Hwang, on the other hand, was fascinated by death.

"How much farther?" Cho asked Suk.

Suk checked his GPS unit. "Just under an hour."

"Pull over," Cho snorted, "I gotta piss again."

"For a fat man, you certainly have a small bladder," Hwang snorted, "just like the size of some of your other body parts."

Cho shoved Hwang who nearly lost control of the vehicle.

"Okay, okay. Pull over so he can urinate," Suk shouted. He could hardly stand another day with these clowns. He often wondered who would win if they ever got into a fight. They'd tear each other apart like two rabid dogs. He shuddered to think about it.

Hwang eased the SUV and the trailer off the road onto a

turnout, Cho jumped out.

"Should we leave him?" Hwang grinned, gunning the engine.

Suk ignored him and surveyed the surrounding fields of agriculture. This area in the northeastern corner of Guatemala was considerably flatter than the rest of the country and covered with large fields of maíze.

Cho climbed back in the SUV. "What's the plan today?"

"I talked with the town's mayor so they know we are coming," Suk replied. "They're welcoming us with open arms."

"I suppose drilling a few wells helped," Hwang said.

"Now that we are satisfied with the virus," Suk explained, "we move into Phase 2—The Miasma Theory. At the other small villages, it was easy to infect everyone when we told them we were vaccinating them for the flu. They never knew we actually gave them nasal doses of the virus."

"Sure didn't help much with the flu," Cho laughed.

"What's miasma?" Hwang asked.

Suk was surprised he had grasped the word. "It means bad air. It was an ancient Greek theory that disease was caused by bad air. It was before we understood about microbes."

"Huh?" It was Greek to Hwang.

"The people think we're doing them a favor by spraying for mosquitos," Suk explained. "In eight days, they will all have a very mild cold. We need to evaluate the effectiveness of aerosolization of the virus. That's the plan."

* * *

Professor Kwon worked under the isolation hood. The thick gloves of his hazmat suit made it difficult to work the pipette. He pried off the top of the blood vial as best he could, inserted the tip of the pipette into the blood, and withdrew one cubic centimeter of fluid.

Now that he understood the effectiveness the virus, there were two immediate goals—mass production of the virus and development of an effective vaccine.

He watched the blood droplets fall from the pipette into a

small tube. Finding the virus had been no easy task. Kwon's faith was in his own intelligence, but he had admitted to Pak how surprised he was by the discovery.

Kwon loved riddles and read extensively about the Maya civilization. He was fascinated by their gods. In their time, the Maya were one of the most advanced cultures on the planet, and Kwon admired their development of a written language and their mathematical and astronomical achievements.

As he watched the blood drip from the pipette, he thought about the difference between the Maya and the Aztecs, the other great civilization of the time. The Aztecs practiced human sacrifice, while the Maya believed in blood offerings. The Maya were equally acquainted with the spiritual world, both the divine and the demonic.

So why would such an advanced culture pass into oblivion?

Kwon aspirated another cubic centimeter of blood into the pipette.

Theories abound as to the reason for their demise—meteorites, infectious diseases, war, over-population, and drought. But Kwon found it strange that such an advanced civilization that recorded every detail of its history had nothing to say of its downfall.

From what he understood of microbiology, his theory of extinction centered on an infectious disease. But his studies of the great epidemics told him populations did not simply disappear in one fell swoop. It took time—enough time for the great Maya to have recorded the devastation.

He knew that the Maya should have produced drawings and writings about a great sickness—pictographs of dead and dying people. But only one such image had ever been found.

In his many books about the Maya—books Pak had given him for his exemplary service—Kwon remembered when the inspiration struck him. He had been flipping through pages of logo-symbolic pictures and actual photographs of pictograph panels rescued from Maya temples. It was as if she jumped off the page—her presence was that palpable. He had been studying the gods and demons worshipped in the culture when he read about *tzitzimimeh*, a female deity, related to infertility and considered to be a demon. She was feared by midwives and pregnant women.

The demon deity was portrayed as a skeletal female figure with claw-like hands and feet, a snake-like object slithering between her legs, and an animal figure on her shoulder. She was Kwon's inspiration. Surrounding her were heartbroken women and their babies—drawn head downward—indicating they were dead. The text in the book explained that *tzitzimimeh* was the demon that embodied the souls of barren women. It was the animal figure on her shoulder that fascinated Kwon the most—the animal looked like a ferret.

Could the Maya have died off by attrition, so the impact had never been depicted?

Kwon shrugged, finished inserting the blood and fastened a cap securely on the vial. Then he put the vial in a separate tray.

The ferret was key, and no one else would have understood.

Only a microbiologist would know that the ferret was the best animal model scientists had for carrying the influenza virus. But the influenza virus was not known to be associated with infertility or stillborn babies. The only virus that Kwon knew of that had any association with sterility was mumps. Kwon understood that both the mumps virus and the influenza virus were single-stranded RNA viruses that come from closely related orthomyxoviruses and paramyxoviruses.

There was one fact about the mumps virus he had forgotten until he happened to be reading one of his textbooks. A paramyxovirus follows the rule of six; that is, the total length of the genome is always a multiple of six. Kwon knew very little about the Bible, but had read parts of Revelation in his search for understanding epidemics and the end of the world. He nearly fell out of his chair when he realized that the mumps virus was 666 nanometers in length.

It was then the big revelation hit him. Maybe the Maya did not die all at once from an infectious disease, maybe they just died off. *If a virus could cause sterility, how long would a civilization survive? Not long.*

If a virus was the cause of the Maya demise, Kwon had to find the original virus. It wasn't going to be easy. His own stores of biologic elements were full of the mumps virus, but the current mumps virus caused sterility in humans in about five percent of cases. The original virus must have mutated in order to survive and still keep its human host alive.

The only way Kwon could find the non-mutated virus was to search for it in Guatemala. Ancient blood was not easy to find, but if a remnant could be found anywhere, it would be in Tikal, the heart of the Maya kingdom. If he could find an animal that carried the virus, recovering it was possible. After all, the HIV virus was discovered in monkeys in Africa.

Kwon and his protégé Suk surmised the non-mutant mumps virus might be found in local ferrets. The HIV monkeys didn't develop disease from that virus, and they thought it was possible that ferrets would not show ill effects from the non-mutant mumps virus.

As it turned out, Tikal was exactly where the virus was found. It was very much dormant and very much present. Its only mutation was that it was no longer contagious to humans. But that was easy to overcome; Kwon and his team supercharged its infectious nature.

A former student of Kwon's, who had defected to the Netherlands, had recently mutated H5N1, the avian flu virus. He had combined it with the highly contagious H1N1 flu virus to create a doomsday virus. Kwon admired his student's courage to publish the results in the journal *Science*, in an article titled "Airborne Transmission of Influenza A/H5N1 Virus Between Ferrets."

CHAPTER 31

CHURCH

Pak was irritated. He sat in the back seat of his limousine and waited for the bus to arrive at the church. The only good thing about this was that it signaled the end of a very long week with these baboons from the United States. The fake basketball game had been a disaster. The Americans were supposed to lose, but they were so much better at pretending to lose than the home team was at pretending to win. And Pak could have done without the singing. When star player Karl Oakland sang "Happy Birthday" to Kim Jong-un, the boy blushed like a school girl. *What an embarrassment.* The whole week was a joke. The person responsible for the visit would take the fall. *A bullet more likely.*

After the game, Kim Jong-un insisted the players be taken to the new Masik Pass ski resort, recently built at a cost of slightly over $300 million dollars. The lavish resort had infuriated Pak when he thought of his daughters going without rice day after day so that stupid man could have his own ski hill. The ski trip had been a nightmare even though some girls were provided to entertain the players.

Pak glanced at his watch for the tenth time. At least the week hadn't been a total waste. He had received the vial and the note, and confirmation the plan was on schedule. Professor Kwon was busy working on manufacturing mass quantities of the virus and a vaccine. *I wonder when I will be vaccinated?*

The bus pulled into the church parking lot. It wasn't Sunday, the customary day of worship in the U.S.; the team was here because one of its members had asked about freedom of religion in North Korea. It became incumbent upon the authorities to demonstrate that freedom, no matter that it was irrelevant. So, before the players boarded the plane, they were taken to the church.

The building was designed to look like the Presbyterian churches in South Korea; it was such an odd sight in the North. Kim Il-sung had built it as a monument to his mother who was a devout Christian, when North Korea worshipped one God. That was before the Kim dynasty and the cult of personality requiring the worship of the false trinity. Pak knew that it was rumored that Stalin himself commanded Kim Il-sung to remove Christianity from North Korea.

The church was a sham, like the basketball game. It was a propaganda tool to show religious tolerance to visitors. Kim Il-sung and his son were the only ones who were worshipped in this place. He wondered how that affected Kim Jong-un's personality. *Probably why he was so brutal—if you can't be worshipped, you should at least be feared.*

He was glad he didn't have to go into the church. Just being in the vicinity of this place made him uneasy. He was there to observe and to make sure the plan was on track.

The basketball players were ushered to the front pews in the church. His agency had handpicked faux parishioners to sit through the short service. A so-called priest gave a sermon on the deity of Kim Il-sung, and the players were ushered out. That was that—mission accomplished: a demonstration of religious freedom.

While the Americans were in the church, one of Pak's trusted agents entered the team bus with an order to search for anything suspicious. He was actually there to insert an envelope into Charles Hall's pack. When Hall returned to the U.S., another of Pak's agents would intercept him and take the envelope. Other agents would see that the message got to Guatemala. Pak recalled with satisfaction the note inside the envelope. It read: **Excellent work. Great rewards await you. The Professor states that it is everything you have said. Will await aerosolization testing to move to Noah Initiative.**

CHAPTER 32

GOOD VERSUS EVIL

Maggie arranged to bunk Buck and Tod in Nick's room. The Hope Center did not have housing for couples or families, but Tod's wife, Kim, and their daughters were happy to bunk with the women from California. With their constant chattering, Nick wondered if the girls got any sleep that night.

He certainly didn't. It was because he was worried about the difficult surgeries ahead, but Buck's snoring didn't help, and neither did his dream.

It was the third time since he arrived that Nick dreamed of John. All the dreams were similar. This time, he and John were in their beloved Mission Mountains. Nick remembered how peaceful it was, sitting next to each other beside the campfire on the shore of the high mountain lake. Until a powerful storm kicked up—a wilderness storm with death on its breath—thick, dark thunder clouds crackling with lightning. The tempest began so suddenly and with such force that Nick panicked trying to escape. He got separated from John and was terrorized by the isolation. As he stumbled through the raging storm, he heard John calling him. He followed the sound of his voice to safety and shelter behind a huge boulder.

Buck's alarm jangled, and Nick startled awake. He heard Buck stretch and pray, "Thank you, Jesus, for a great sleep."

"That makes one of us," Nick yawned.

"I didn't snore, did I?"

"Heck no," Tod broke in. "But there may not be any paint left above your bunk."

"Man, I should have warned you guys. I'm sorry."

"Yeah and handed out ear plugs." Nick threw his pillow at his bunkmate.

"Let's go get that breakfast Maggie promised us."

"And coffee."

* * *

The three-year-old's foot looked tiny once they got it prepped and covered with surgical drapes. Nick was thankful they were going to sit down for the case. It made it easier to rest his arms on the table to help soften tremors in his hands intensified by the magnification of the surgical loupes.

With a surgical marking pen, Tod mapped out and explained the landmarks on the child's foot. "You have to know that the anatomy is always a bit off in these kids."

"What causes it?" Anna asked. She sat next to Nick.

"No one is quite sure what causes these darn things, but all the structures tighten up on the inside of the foot and ankle and they pull the foot over, eventually making it look like a club. As they grow, it gets worse and worse. It's idiopathic."

"What's that?" Anna asked again.

"It means us idiots don't know what causes it," Nick said, making everyone laugh. Anna translated for the Spanish speakers.

Tod wrapped the tiny foot and leg with a tight rubber strap that exsanguinated all the blood from the leg. He asked Carmen to inflate the tourniquet. Because the neurovascular bundle was small, they needed a bloodless field to see clearly.

Tod sighed. "Let's do this thing." He held his hand to Juan Carlos. "Scalpel."

"Thank you for this food," Juan Carlos said, handing the knife to Tod.

Tod looked at Juan Carlos and then at Nick. "Huh?"

"It's a long story. I'll tell you after this case. Just asking for a little holy guidance."

"That's a great idea. Jesus, guide my hands," Tod said as he made the incision into the side of the tiny foot.

* * *

The hour-and-a-half surgery went well. Nick was reminded how good Tod's hands were when he was a resident; as an experienced surgeon, they were even better.

"Man, that was great! You did an excellent job!" Nick said, slapping him on the back.

"Well, great help can make you look good," Tod shrugged, not one to toot his own horn.

"His foot looks perfect. Really glad to see those toes so nice and pink."

"Obviously," Tod said, "what we do today is important, but honestly, the follow-up care is super critical. We probably need to talk about that. You can do it or I will need to return in six weeks and remove the casts we put on, pull the pins holding everything in place, and fit them with a removable splint to help keep the foot in place. These things are like teeth. You can't simply put braces on for a short time and then expect them to stay in place."

"Yeah, I thought that might be the case. I'm happy to do it, but you're always welcome."

"Thanks. Who knows? I'd love to see the results of our handiwork."

"You ready for a Coke?"

"Am I ever! You ready for the next patient?"

"I'm just glad you're here, my friend!"

* * *

In the town of Dolores, the three Koreans loaded the virus into the sprayer. The mosquito fogger was the perfect vehicle to deliver the mumps virus to the small town. They knew from their experience in the other villages that it took an extremely small dose to infect a person, and because it was highly contagious, whoever did not catch the virus from the spraying would catch it from a friend or relative who had caught it.

It took an hour to drive up and down the streets of Dolores, the mist from the fogger wafting through the houses, businesses, and school. The Koreans took no precautions because, thanks to

Hwang's clumsiness when he dropped a vial of the virus in their rented house, they had already been exposed. Exactly eight days later, they had come down with colds. A week later, Suk's testicles were a little sore, and the others reported similar sensations. He was surprised; he had expected worse from chemical castration. It was good thing none of them planned on producing children.

* * *

At the hospital, the second surgery had gone equally well. Tod led Nick step-by-step through the procedure. It took longer, but they finished both sides in less than two hours.

"We're going to make a pedi-pod out of you yet," Tod teased Nick.

"I thought I was going to be sick when we took off the tourniquet, and the toes didn't pink right up."

"But they did. The vessels sometimes spasm for a bit."

"Yeah…just long enough to give a guy a heart attack."

"Always something to keep you humble in this game, right?"

"That's for sure. Hey, before we finish for the day, can I show you a little baby with syndactyly and see what you think?"

CHAPTER 33

THE LORD IS MY REFUGE

Nick, Tod, and Buck could hear a buzz of conversation as they approached the small hospital ward of the Hope Center. Seven children and their families occupied almost every inch of the room, and Maggie and Anna chatted with all of them. Carmen and the local nurse focused on Isabella's family. Isabella's sister, Elsa, was due for surgery that morning. The air was charged with hope.

Maggie had squeezed cribs for the smaller children between the hospital beds so their mothers could stay with them. Maria sat in a rocking chair, rocking little Danilo back and forth. He was scheduled for surgery that afternoon.

Nick was glad to see Elena sitting next to them, nursing her baby with the syndactylized hands. Maggie had told him how the other mothers and their children had helped Elena bond with her infant, how they had put a blanket of love around them both. Last night, when Nick brought Tod to see the baby's hand, he barely recognized Elena. Her whole countenance had changed, and light had returned to her eyes. Her baby girl had already gained two pounds. She would be christened Anna Elena—something that Anna from Alabama could not stop smiling about.

Tod and Nick decided they would spend some time that evening researching the standard of care in hopes they could separate her tiny fingers on Friday. The baby was still very small, but they weren't sure when they would ever have another chance to correct her deformity.

When Nick, Tod, and Buck came into the crowded room,

the chattering stopped.

"How are the *tres amigos* today?" Maggie smiled.

"Thanks to the ear plugs you gave us, well rested," Nick poked Buck's arm.

Buck put his hands together beside his tilted head and pretended to snore loudly. The room erupted in laughter. Even Isabella smiled. Buck spent the previous day entertaining the troops. He showed off his prosthetic legs and amazed them with his soccer skills. He was a huge hit with the families and the orphans of the Hope Center.

The men stopped at the first bed where a mother held her toddler with a bright blue cast. The child eyed the crowd and retreated shyly into his mother's arms.

Nick noticed that everyone was watching them and waiting. "I guess we're doing group rounds today," he said sotto voce to Tod.

"So much for HIPPA regulations," Tod laughed, referring to the strict U.S. regulations for patient confidentiality.

"I could excuse everyone," Maggie whispered.

"That's okay. I think we're all in this together," Nick reassured.

Tod picked up the bright blue cast attached to the shy child. He pushed back the cotton wrap from the boy's foot and revealed five pink toes that wiggled as he touched them. He looked at Anna and motioned to the mother and asked, "Your son do okay through the night?"

Anna translated, and the mother smiled and nodded. "*Si. Gracias doctor. Que Dios bendiga ricamente te.*"

"Thank you, doctor. May God richly bless you," Anna repeated.

Tod smiled. "I think He already has."

The doctors moved down the crowded row. A mother stood next to a crib, stroking her sleeping daughter's black hair. She uncovered the girl's lower body to show hot pink casts on both legs.

"Nice touch with the color," Maggie admired.

"You think she'll be able to keep them clean for the next six weeks?" Nick asked her.

"Oh yes. You'll be amazed. Even with dirt floors."

Nick touched the girl's toes, and she opened her eyes and

smiled at him as her toes wiggled. "Kids are so resilient," he said to Tod. "I can see why you like working on them. The first thing my patients usually ask is when they can smoke and then go through alcohol or drug withdrawal."

"You can always stay here." Maggie said, blushing when everyone looked at her.

* * *

The three amigos sat in John's office as evening fell. The surgeries on the three children that day had gone perfectly with no complications, except when Nick drove one of the pins too far through Danilo's foot and into the palm of his own hand. He pulled his glove off, inspected and cleansed the hole in his palm with alcohol, but didn't think he needed to worry about exposure to HIV or hepatitis. At the MED, a whole battery of tests were initiated on both patient and doctor to assess the risk after a stick. The only risk Nick now faced was teasing from Tod.

They used John's office computer to check the web on syndactyly and to discuss Isabella's surgery for the next day. So far, all the repairs had gone smoothly, but this was not the time to be overconfident; Isabella's surgery was in a league of its own.

Sitting at John's desk was unsettling for Nick; Tod and Buck, aware that Nick and John had been best friends, understood how difficult it was but had insisted. Buck had been unafraid to wade into the heart of the matter when he expressed sorrow upon seeing the photo of the two on top of McDonald Peak. It was the identical picture that hung in Nick's office back at the MED.

"Thanks, Buck. This is the first time I've come in here. It's been too hard."

Maggie came through the door with a tray of glasses and a pitcher of lemonade. She set the tray on the desk. Nick saw her look at him and then at the floor. Her face went sad, and her bottom lip quivered.

Nick jumped out of John's chair. "Maggie, I'm so sorry."

Buck put his arm around Maggie's shoulders, and she leaned into his massive embrace, wiping a tear from her eye. She smiled at Nick. "Oh, sit down." She waved him back into the seat. "I was just thinking that John would have loved to be here with you all. As much as he loved this place, I think he missed doctor camaraderie. He dreamt the Hope Center would be like this, with lots of friends coming in and out."

There was a long pause as the men absorbed her words. Finally, she broke the silence. "You guys help yourself to the lemonade and to anything else in here. John would have wanted it that way. I'm going to have myself some girl time." She patted Buck on the chest and pulled away. "Kim and your girls are lovely," she said to Tod. "We're painting nails tonight." She wiggled her fingers at them and left.

When Maggie was gone, Buck was first to speak. "She's something." He smiled at Nick and raised an eyebrow.

"Yeah," Nick said, embarrassed by the topic.

"And?" Buck egged him on.

"And I don't want to talk about it. I can't even go there."

"Okay, okay." Buck backed off.

Tod rescued the conversation. "Look at this." He turned the laptop toward Nick.

"It's a pretty good article in the *Journal of Pediatric Orthopedic Surgery* on early syndactyly repair. It divides the patients in the different types of syndactyly and says that the type that Anna Elena has does fine with early surgery. I think it really comes down to how comfortable Carmen is with putting an infant to sleep. What I've seen of her work, I'm pretty darned impressed. I think we should get it done while I'm here. What do you think?"

"Agreed," Nick replied. "It might make for a long day tomorrow, but let's start with her. I wouldn't want the baby to go all day without food."

"Perfect."

"I've been thinking about Isabella's surgery a lot," Tod was on to another case. "Her anatomy is going to be so weird. All the bones will be misshapen because her feet have been deformed for so long. I like your idea, Nick, of doing one at a time together. We'll see how it goes, but we may be only able to partly correct them and have to do more surgery down the road. We'll have to see how the tissues stretch."

"I'll sure be praying for you guys," Buck put in. "I've never seen anything like that in my life. Yesterday, Maggie told me what life was like for Isabella. She told me Isabella would never marry because no one would want a deformed wife that couldn't work. Poor little thing. It breaks my heart."

"Thanks, Buck," Tod said. "We need all the divine guidance we can get."

Nick pulled an anatomy book from John's bookshelf.

* * *

Nick and Tod went over each step for more than an hour, meticulously writing them down, when Buck interrupted their concentration. Crouched over at the side of the room, he was looking at the back of the office door. "Hey," he said, "where was John murdered?"

Nick and Tod did not look up, and it took a minute for Nick to focus away from Isabella's surgery.

"Uh, it's a place called Tikal. It's up north where some of the old Maya ruins are."

"I asked Maggie about John yesterday," Buck said. "No one really seems to know what happened." He was still staring at the back of the door.

Nick was tired and not sure he wanted to talk about this right now. "I don't know, Buck. Wrong place, wrong time." Nick recited what he had heard over and over again.

"You ever think about going up there to see for yourself?" Buck turned toward him.

"Well, uh…sometimes. Maybe. I guess so. I just wouldn't want to go alone."

"That's probably smart," Buck agreed.

Nick was fully in the moment now. He straightened his back. "Why you asking, Buck?"

"I'm not sure, but look at this." He shut the door so Nick and Tod could see what he was examining. It was a large map of Guatemala. Near the northern part of the map were a number of red and yellow stick-on dots. Some of the dots were nearly on top of each other. There were some yellow dots by themselves, but wherever there was a red one, a yellow accompanied it.

"Do you know where Tikal is?" Buck asked.

"Not sure."

Buck thumped his finger smack dab in the middle of the dots. "Tikal. It's right here." He stabbed his finger on the spot a couple of time to reinforce the location. Then he pointed to the yellow dots and traced his finger down to a yellow key at the edge of the map and read the text John had written.

"It says 'FOCO wells.' Mean anything to you?"

When Nick said nothing, Buck turned toward his friend. "Nick?"

All of Nick's attention was on the framed calligraphy above the door. He hadn't noticed it until Buck showed them the map. His head swirled, thinking about his recurring dream of John. The calligraphy read:

> *'The Lord is my rock and my fortress and my deliverer;*
> *The God of my strength, in whom I will trust;*
> *My shield and the horn of my salvation,*
> *My stronghold and my refuge;*
> *My Savior, You save me from violence.*
> *I will call upon the Lord, who is worthy to be praised;*
> *So shall I be saved from my enemies.' 2 Samuel 22: 2-4.*

CHAPTER 34

CAMP 22

Professor Kwon knew that he didn't need to go to Hoeryong Political Prison Camp 22. He could have given the vials to one of his lab workers to take to the infamous camp. Convincing Pak that it was a good idea for him to personally oversee the experiments did not prove difficult. Pak even offered his car and driver to take him to the northernmost prison.

Kwon wondered if Pak suspected him, but had to take the chance, even if there was the slightest possibility of success. For all he knew, Pak was responsible for the arrest of his family.

As Pak's car passed through the town of Hoeryong, Kwon saw the prison against the mountainside. At that distance, it was impossible to see the entire boundary of the eighty-seven-square-mile prison. He could make out the massive wall of the southernmost entrance rising like an impenetrable castle from the surrounding rocks. Reports showed what separated freedom from the horrors of the prison was an inner wall, electrified with a 3300-volt electric fence and an outer razor-wire fence, with landmines and traps between the two.

As the car approached the entrance, Kwon remembered the day he heard where his wife and son had been sent. He never asked what happened to them for fear his fate would be the same. It took all his strength not to react when Pak told him the news. He wasn't sure if Pak had made a mistake in telling him, or if it was a well-calculated seed of manipulation. Even though Kwon thought of Pak as a friend, he knew what a dangerous man he was and never to be underestimated for shrewdness.

It would be a fatal mistake to ask to see his wife and son. In a prison of 50,000, the odds of catching an accidental glimpse of his family were nil, but it was worth the risk. Any glimmer of hope was better than none.

He cringed to think his wife and son might be part of this testing, but human experimentation at Camp 22 was well known. It was the perfect place to further test the virus.

Although the virus was a mutation of modern-day mumps, he needed to be certain that people inoculated with the current mumps vaccine would not be immune to his new strain, the one he called M2H1. The abbreviation would be accepted in the scientific world, as it was a mutated mumps virus, (M2), combined with the influenza virus, (H1N1).

Five months earlier, Kwon had asked that 200 people at the prison be vaccinated with the mumps vaccine, long enough for their bodies to produce immunity. Now they would be exposed to the M2H1 virus. They would be quarantined so as to not infect the whole prison colony and the guards. He should receive his own vaccine soon, but there was no reason to risk a premature release of the virus. He did not want to think about the fact that all the patients would be quickly eliminated once its effectiveness was established.

Kwon had not expected the M2H1 virus would cause sterility in both men and women, but the discovery that it did was a pleasing bonus. It would result in an even faster halting of any population propagation.

He adjusted the case on his lap that contained the virus and took a handkerchief from his pocket to wipe his upper lip as they pulled up to the first of a series of guard stations.

Everyone in North Korea knew what these camps were like. It was one more measure of control for the government to remind its people what could happen if anyone so much as hinted at stepping out of line. Occasionally, the government revealed photos of skeletal prisoners working in coal mines surrounding the prison. The pictures showed prisoners with missing ears, broken noses, and smashed eye sockets from repeated beatings and torture.

Camp 22 was the worst of the worst, reserved for anyone who

criticized the government, anyone who had attempted to escape to China, South Korean prisoners, and, of course, Christians.

* * *

Pak was furious. Whoever had interrupted his time at the medical clinic would be reprimanded. New, young girls had been brought to the clinic, including Dr. Chul's granddaughter.

Chul had been sent to the Hoeryong Political Prison Camp for his insolence. Pak had been incensed. *How dare that man question my decisions?* That's why he had sent him to be *re-educated* at Camp 22. Chul was better off dead and being in that camp was as good as dead.

To interrupt Pak's clinic time made him angry, even though he understood the reason why. Kim Jung-wook, a South Korean Baptist missionary captured and imprisoned the previous year, was about to be paraded on North Korean TV to confess his crimes against the government. One of Pak's subordinates thought he would want to attend. He was right, of course, but the interruption came at an inopportune time.

Last week Pak's agency had arrested thirty-three people who appeared to be associated with the missionary. Pak knew Kim was trying to start underground churches in North Korea, but he'd told his agents to torture the prisoner enough to get him to tell them he was a South Korean spy. Pak's agents were to convince Kim the lives of the thirty-three other prisoners would be spared if he confessed.

They will all be sent to Camp 22 anyway, so they are dead, one way or the other.

Pak knew how necessary it was to tighten security at the northern border with China. Except for the Amrok River, there were no fences or barriers that separated the countries, and there had been a five-fold increase in defections the past five years. Fortunately, North Korea had an extradition agreement with China, and many of these traitors were returned and sent to Camp 22.

Just because they were trying to escape starvation was no excuse.

The Christians were a problem. Not only did they help on

the Chinese side by providing shelter and food for the defectors, but many of them slipped back into the country and brought their propaganda and literature. Pak's government had decreed that anyone caught with a Bible would be tortured and shot.

CHAPTER 35

DEATH TO REJECTION

The children at the Hope Center were curious about the girl with deformed feet. Many of them were playing in the courtyard when the team from California brought Isabella and her family back for the pre-op day. They couldn't help but stare at the girl as she shuffled into the clinic. News of visitors or anomalies traveled at the speed of light throughout the orphanage.

Maggie had anticipated their reaction, and before Isabella's arrival at the compound, she had gathered the children in the cafeteria and told them about the girl with the deformed feet. If anyone understood rejection, it was an orphan. Many of the children had been abandoned by their own mothers and fathers at the doorstep of the Hope Center; their families had run out of money and hope. It took a long time to break the children of the orphan spirit, but when it was done, the children flourished.

Maggie also knew what prayer warriors these little saints were, and Isabella needed all the prayer she could get. Maggie realized that the prayers of children were often answered. She thought it was their innocence or their insight, something many adults grew out of, but whatever it was, their simple prayers seemed to have a direct line to the Father.

These children would help Isabella. She had been amazed by their ability to respond to visitors in distress. She had once seen the children gathered around one of the visiting young women from California who had been a victim of sexual assault by an uncle. Guilt and shame had convinced her to keep the secret from her team. But the children had seen right through it. For them, it was like it was a sticky note posted on the girl's forehead. Maggie had watched in awe as the children prayed for the woman and dissolved her heartache.

In that spirit of hope, Maggie asked the children to pray for Isabella. The children knew Isabella was not allowed to eat on the morning before surgery, so they decided to fast that day and skipped breakfast in solidarity with her. They had also spent the last few days in school making banners and flags to celebrate Isabella.

While Isabella was being prepared for surgery, the children gathered in anticipation along the covered walkway between the ward and the operating room. Maggie had kept their celebratory surprise a secret from the surgical team.

When Nick and Tod, still wearing scrubs, came through the ward doors to the walkway, a loud shout surprised them. A louder shout greeted Buck who, carrying Isabella, backed through the door and turned to face the crowd of well-wishers. Isabella looked tiny wrapped in a surgical blanket in Buck's massive arms. The children shouted encouragement and waved their flags and banners. The banners read: *The Lord is my Strength* and *Be Strong and Courageous*. At the Hope Center school, in addition to reading and writing, the children were taught the ways of God, and they learned their lessons well. Isabella couldn't stop smiling. She waved to the children with her little hand held out like a triumphant queen, even though it was attached to an IV line. Healing had begun.

As Nick and Tod paused at the door to the OR they heard the group of children outside break into a chorus of song in Spanish, *¡Grande es tu fidelidad! Great is Thy Faithfulness.*

Tod patted Nick on the back, speechless, but they also understood the difficult task at hand. "Come on. We've got work to do," he said.

* * *

The first foot took over two hours to correct. As expected, the anatomy was anything but normal. The talus—the bone that sits under the ankle connecting the tibia to the foot and the cornerstone for correction—was oddly shaped from the years of deformity. There was, however, one hope. Although Isabella was chronologically twelve, she was physiologically much younger and had not yet had her first menses. That meant that her bones were still growing, and there was a possibility that her bones would remodel. Otherwise, her joints would not be congruous, making them more painful and in need of fusing down the road.

Nick and Tod were surprised that once all the tissues were released, the foot could be stationed in a relatively normal position. But because of the severe stretch of the skin and neurovascular bundle on the inside of the foot and ankle, they could not possibly keep the foot in that position. They splinted the foot halfway corrected. Nick would need to do serial castings to bring the foot more and more into position over the next few weeks. He decided that, even though he hated to fly, he would gladly come down every weekend if he had to over the next few weeks.

Spending time with Maggie would be the bonus.

* * *

Buck stood between Nick and Tod with his arms around their shoulders as they stood in the ward at the end of three days of work.

"You guys have done a good thing," he said, squeezing their necks and wrinkling his nose. "But man, you stink. You both need a shower."

Tod held his scrub top to his nose and laughed. "Yeah, I guess we better shower before the party."

"I'm not sure I have ever sweated so hard standing still," Nick said, "but what a day."

* * *

Isabella's other foot took under two hours and went smoother than the first, but concluded with the same problem. Nick and Tod explained the situation carefully to Isabella's family, as they were disappointed that her feet were not perfectly straight like all the other children who came back from surgery. Satisfied with the treatment plan, Nick and Tod received hugs from the family.

The doctors also received hug after hug from the grateful families whose children lay in cribs and hospital beds, wearing bright pink and blue casts.

The doctors were especially thrilled to see baby Anna Elena nursing and wiggling all her newly separated fingers. Her surgery turned out to be a relatively uncomplicated fix, and Nick and Tod were able to close the skin with absorbable sutures so the stitches would fall off as the skin healed around each finger.

"So, we're having cake and ice cream in the cafeteria?" Nick asked Buck, even though he already knew the answer. Maggie had whispered in his ear between cases that Buck had bought out the local bakery and market of all the sweets he could find. It was going to be a celebratory feast.

* * *

"Well, call me if you have any questions or if there are any complications."

Nick heard hesitation in Tod's voice about leaving the Hope Center. It was the following morning, and everyone stood beside the van that would take Tod and his family back to Guatemala City and the airport.

The children of the Hope Center had come to say their goodbyes. Tod's wife, Kim, and their daughters had hugged every one of them twice. "Okay, I'm getting in the van," Kim reluctantly announced. To Tod she said, "We're coming back." It was not a question. Their girls followed her.

"I guess we're coming back," Tod told Nick. He held out his hand one last time. "Thank you, my friend."

Nick grabbed it firmly, and they hugged. It was a bond shared by two warriors who had fought a great battle together, back-to-back and shoulder-to-shoulder.

Then Tod gave Buck a hug, "How much longer do you get to stay?"

"Looks like one more week. I sure miss my family, but someone needs to keep this guy in line." He gave Nick a playful shove.

"So you think you really are going to head to Tikal?" Tod asked both Nick and Buck.

They nodded and glanced at Maggie. They had not told her anything about it yet.

"Well, you be careful, you hear?" Tod said, getting into the van.

CHAPTER 36

NOAH INITIATIVE

"And your visit to Hoeryong?" Pak asked Kwon as they sat in Kwon's office, brightly lit with flickering fluorescent fixtures.

Kwon stared at Pak. The spymaster's cryptic orbs bored into his soul, but Kwon did not flinch. He did not dare to. He had not seen his wife or son; in fact, he had seen few actual prisoners. He instructed the prison's medical staff on delivery of the viral nasal dose and left the camp. He doubted he would ever see his family again.

Would I dare ask their fate if I am successful with the Noah Initiative?

It was Pak who suggested the name. He explained to Kwon, who knew little about the Bible, that the God of the Jews was angry at the condition of mankind and decided to wipe out the population and start all over. He spared Noah, leaving him and his family to repopulate the earth.

Pak hardly ever laughed with the professor, but Kwon remembered him chuckling about his name for the initiative. "How creatively ironic to use a story from the fascists' own history to name the destroyer that would befall them."

As if he was reading his mind, Pak asked Kwon, "And how do you feel that the Noah Initiative is progressing?"

"Very well indeed," Kwon spoke up. "I should have our vaccine within the week, and production of the virus is progressing well. Have you decided how many cities to release it in?"

"Based on the epidemiology models that you produced and the population demographics, I have chosen eleven. We have offices in each of these cities: Washington D.C., Los Angeles, Seoul, Rio de Janeiro, Beijing, Tokyo, London, Mumbai, Moscow, Johannesburg, and Tehran. My choice is based on widely used travel routes so the virus will spread like wildfire."

"Eleven," Kwon repeated. He stared at the ceiling, considering the numbers. "Based on what our men in Guatemala find on the effectiveness of aerosolization and the adequacy of the dose of the viral load…" Kwon did the math in his head, "we should be ready in three months."

"And what do your models show of the spread?" Pak asked.

"I suspect that sixty percent of the world population will have been exposed within the first month and eighty percent by the second. Of course, the virus will cause sterility within a couple of weeks of exposure, but it will have happened long before there is a drop in birth rate that will alarm the World Health Organization. By the time they pick up on the fact of the declining birth rates, it will be too late. The babies born in the next few months will be the last."

"Except for ours," Pak interrupted with a grin.

"Yes, except for ours. How do you think the world will respond?"

"I've played this out in my head a number of ways," Pak replied. "I think once the world finds out there has been a global castration, it will send the world economies into a tailspin very quickly. Fear does that. If you stop to think about the effects of the cessation of any population growth—no more babies being born—think of what that does to the medical systems alone, not to mention the industries surrounding childcare."

Pak took a handkerchief from his suit pocket, wiped his forehead, and continued.

"In twenty years, the youngest people alive will be of military age. You think any nation would want to send their young men and women to war? The world population will begin to severely retract after that. All the super powers will evaporate. Fifty years down the road, the world will be in such chaos that the New Order of Korea will have the upper hand and everything we want." Pak's voice raised a decibel as he thrust a fist in the air.

Kwon watched Pak try to keep his emotions in check.

They sat in silence until a fluorescent ceiling light snapped and flickered out.

"My only sadness, my friend, is that you and I will not be here to enjoy the fruits of our labors. It will be for the glory of our children and children's children. The people of North Korea will begin their rightful place in history. Pyongyang will begin its destiny as the center of the world. Just as the God of the Jews spared Noah, we will be spared. The God of the Jews caused the greatest ethnic cleansing in history by killing hundreds of thousands."

Pak was so excited, he jumped out of his chair. "The Noah Initiative, Professor, will be the greatest ethnic cleansing without killing one single person."

CHAPTER 37

SEOUL, SOUTH KOREA

From the corridor window of the 51st floor of the Seoul International Center, the evening sky was a kaleidoscope of color. From this height, the green dome of the National Assembly Building—illuminated by the setting sun—sparkled like an emerald set in white gold against a rosy abundance of blossoming cherry trees that surrounded the capital building and the Han River.

Two agents from the South Korean Anti-Terrorist Agency stood silently admiring the view as they awaited the elevator to take them to the lobby.

A marketing video describing the beautiful new Seoul International Finance Center looped on a large screen TV behind them.

Introducing the beautiful new…

The video began again. Even though the complex had been completed over a year ago, marketing couldn't stop regaling the center's advantages—its three towering office buildings, its five-star hotel, its underground mall, and its extraordinary sculpture garden and pavilion.

The IFC Seoul emerges as the heart of up and coming Yeouido, the video continued.

The agents knew they were at their country's seat of power and influence. South Korea's financial markets were housed in the same complex that included the LG Twin Towers, the Korean Broadcasting System, the Hyundai Capital Building, the Trump World Tower, and the National Assembly Building.

It was here on the 51st floor of the magnificent complex where they'd found The Friends of Children Organization. The opulence of its surroundings magnified the starkness of FOCO's nonprofit status and raised red flags: How could FOCO afford such accommodations?

The agents turned as the elevator arrived, and people exited. The agents were dressed alike, the man in an inexpensive black suit and the woman in a comparable dark business skirt and jacket. She deferred courteously for her senior partner to enter the elevator first. She bowed slightly when he did.

The marketing video continued to roll on the elevator monitor as the doors closed. It showed the Yeouido IFC transected by both the 5 Line and the 9 Line of the Seoul Subway System. It stated that 600,000 people passed through the complex each day.

The last graphic showed Seoul as the center of northeast Asia and its proximity to the major cities of the world. It stated that there were sixty-one cities with over one million people within a three-hour flight.

Introducing the beautiful new…

The agents heard the video begin again as they exited the elevator into the massive lobby.

The agents were disappointed they would have little to report to their supervisors. They had spent three weeks at FOCO and gone over every detail and document. The CEO of the nonprofit had been very helpful and transparent and almost apologetic for the organization's success. He had explained that most of FOCO's support came from China from a wealthy philanthropist who cared about childhood issues.

The agents would report that FOCO's list of projects around the world was impressive. But the Chinese funding was concerning and difficult to track. There was one program, however, that particularly concerned the agents. It was a small outreach in Guatemala. The agents were concerned that no financials had ever been produced. They would suggest further review and investigation.

CHAPTER 38

THE JOURNAL

It had been five days since Tod and his family left the Hope Center and Nick still had not told Maggie that he and Buck planned to go to Tikal.

Fortunately, the days were filled with a whirlwind of activity and he didn't have time or energy to spare thinking about it. Besides, he was having second thoughts about going. Two more nights in the past week he had been harassed by the same dream—John begging him to take refuge amongst the boulders.

Sitting in John's office, Nick glanced at the calligraphy above the door.

What are you trying to tell me, John?

Whatever it was, it seemed like a warning, which made the thought of going to Tikal more and more daunting. If not for Buck's encouragement, he would blow off the trip. But he also realized that if he did that, he would return home with a chapter of his life unresolved.

Suddenly, Nick's soul surged with nostalgia, and his heart ached for Montana and his parents. He longed for simpler days and the long, warm nights under the Big Sky. After a moment's hesitation, he pulled his phone from his pocket and called his parents. He was surprised when his father answered.

"Son."

"Hey, Dad."

"Everything okay, son?"

Nick hardly knew where to start in relaying his experiences of the past two weeks. "It's all really great," he began, warming to the task. He talked about the Hope Center and the orphanage and some of the patients and the cases he'd done so far. His father listened intently and asked questions about the clubfeet surgery. They talked for over thirty minutes, very unusual as his father was always quick to get off the phone. It was the first time Nick could remember that they spoke like friends and colleagues; he was surprised at his father's interest in what he was doing.

"Mom okay?" Nick finally asked, surprised that she was not on the phone.

"Your mom is at a women's meeting thing. How is Maggie?"

"She's good. Still pretty raw, but she is so amazingly strong."

There was a long pause. They ran out of things to say, but neither wanted the call to end. Nick heard his father sniff and wondered if he was crying.

"You know, Nicklaus, your mom and I are really proud of you."

"I love you too, Dad."

Nick hung up and stretched back in John's chair. He was flooded with emotion. This may have been the first time he heard his father say that. He wiped his tears and felt a stirring and a shifting of his own heart.

He looked around John's office and didn't know what to think. He hated that his time in Guatemala was almost over.

All the children with clubfeet correction were recovering nicely, and he'd sent all but Isabella home. Re-splinting her feet was easy after Carmen slipped her a little narcotic cocktail. As she slept, Nick straightened her feet another twenty-five degrees or so. He hoped that he could do it again before leaving.

The surgical team had operated on other patients, mostly neglected traumas, Nick's surgical specialty. He was glad to have Anna's help; she had become an excellent assistant.

She is such a quick learner. I've got to remember to write her a letter of recommendation when I get home.

He was also glad he was able to keep his lustful thoughts at bay and regarded her more like a little sister than a potential conquest.

Nick glanced at John's journal that sat open on the desk. Maggie had given him her blessing to read it. It had been a torturous read for Nick, but, strangely, also a source of comfort.

When he had found the journal in the top drawer of the desk, he had not opened it. After a couple of days, he decided to open it, randomly flip to a page, and read the first thing he came to. Whatever it was would be a sign to continue or not.

The random page read: *Dear John—my beloved son. How much I love you. I hear the cries of your heart and I know the needs you have. Be strong and courageous for I have given you a heart of a warrior.*

It went on for several paragraphs—all in John's handwriting. Nick had continued to read. It seemed like a love letter from a father to a son. Nick couldn't imagine Pops writing it. Then it occurred to him: Could the father be God? It would certainly go along with everything Maggie had been telling him and the calligraphy above John's door. He read more. Sure enough, it was as though John and his Heavenly Father wrote notes back and forth—notes of encouragement, notes of praise, notes of instruction. Nick had asked Maggie about these notes. Without batting an eye, she'd told him that they both wrote down things they felt their Father spoke to them. She told him matter-of-factly, as if hearing from God were the most natural thing in the world.

I'm not sure I would even know if God spoke to me, never mind write it down.

At times, John journaled the depths of his heart, confessing things done and left undone. Every struggle and every triumph was there in black and white. Nick had been sure John wouldn't mind his best friend delving into the depths of his heart. As he perused the volume, he found solace in the fact that John had his struggles. But he was surprised to be envious of the relationship between John and his Creator, His God, His Friend.

Father, can I know you like this?

Nick was holding the journal and flipping the pages when he asked himself the question. Suddenly he heard a faint voice in his head. He closed his eyes and strained to hear. In his mind's eye, he saw himself sitting in the dimly lit corner of the chancel, in the recess near the altar of the church. He wore the red acolyte robe and was trying to stay awake as the Priest labored on and on through another boring sermon.

There was the voice again.

He closed his eyes tighter and concentrated on hearing more. *"Nicklaus."*

The voice came quickly and vanished. It had been an exhausting week at the Hope Center, physically and emotionally. He thought his mind was probably playing tricks on him.

Could God really be calling me?

Nick leafed through the journal again. It was full of these love letters between John and the Father and John's day-to-day thoughts and notes to himself. When he read a note reminding John to get Maggie an anniversary present, he teared up.

He turned to the last few pages in the journal where John described his trips to villages in the northern part of Guatemala and listed his concerns—*No new pregnancies or births. El Naranjo, 6mos. Cruce Dos Aguadas, 5mos. El Chilar, 6mos. El Zapote, 5mos. No new clues from my last visit. Heavy use of pesticides in agriculture around villages. Have asked the farmers to get me the names of the chemicals they use. Villagers appear to be healthy otherwise. There seems to be less parasite load in children after getting new wells. No recent births. Ran into the Koreans from FOCO again today. NOT very friendly fellows for doing such good works.*

Nick swatted at a buzzing mosquito and looked at the map on the back on John's office door. "FOCO," he said out loud and looked at the stick-on dots that John had placed, indicating where FOCO had drilled water wells.

He turned the page of the journal and saw he was reading John's final words:

Labs came back today from El Zapote village. All normal, except evidence of recent viral load. Leave tomorrow to go back to villages.

CHAPTER 39

PURE EVIL

Suk could no longer stomach the screams of the young woman in the next room. He grabbed the keys to the FOCO SUV, slammed the door and left the house.

Her screams reminded him of the screams of the doctor when Hwang cut out his heart. *Why did I let Hwang talk me into the sacrificial killing?* They should have stuck with the plan to shoot him and dump the body. Hwang had convinced them that there was power in the ancient sacrifice, and Suk had relented.

But all it had seemed to accomplish was to make his two cohorts more violent and unpredictable. For Suk, it had filled his mind with unshakable images that obsessed his thoughts and dreams.

Sitting in the SUV, Suk shuddered involuntarily when another scream came from the house and thought about a recurring night terror that haunted him—being chased by a dark, disfigured creature.

They better not kill her! That is all we need—the local police coming to the house for a visit.

Cho and Hwang were drunk on beer and lust. Stepping into stop the mayhem might get him killed. As their time of completion in Guatemala approached, those two became more and more out of control to the point that Suk considered eliminating them. Poisoning them would be an easy task, but lifting their dead bodies to dispose of them would be difficult.

As he reached for the door handle of the vehicle, his hands trembled. It was a good thing their house in San Benito was secluded and no one else could hear the poor girl cry in pain.

She'd come from the local brothel. At fourteen, she was kidnapped in Honduras, smuggled across the border, and forced into prostitution. Now she was forced to be with Cho and Hwang who were brutalizing her. The brothel boss was handsomely paid in cash and always looked the other way when the girls returned with bruises and rope burns.

CHAPTER 40

COMING CLEAN

It was now or never, Nick knew. Then again, it had been such a pleasant evening so far. His news would ruin the mood.

Nick, Buck, Maggie, and Anna sat at a small wooden table underneath the thatched portico of the restaurant. It was a night of celebration and appreciation for Anna's hard work and for Maggie's…everything. The aroma of the fried fish, homemade French fries, and local salsa lingered in the night air. The waitress removed their empty plates and asked if they wanted coffee. A large macaw parrot on a perch in the corner made them laugh every time it spouted off colorful language.

A light rain cooled the night, and Maggie pulled a sweater over her shoulders.

"Thank you, guys, so much for dinner," she said, dabbing her mouth with a napkin and putting it down in front of her.

"Yes, thanks so much," Anna echoed.

"I hope you know how much we appreciate what you're doing down here, Maggie," Buck said. "This tough old soldier has shed more tears this week than he can remember. Of course I remember shedding a few when Jeremiah got his temporary legs. Oh, Nick. Where did the time go? I've been meaning to show you a picture." Buck grabbed his cell phone from his pocket, pulled up a photo, and showed it around the table—Jeremiah and Buck standing together on their prosthetic legs. Buck shed another tear. "Come to think about it, I guess I'm just a big cry baby."

They all laughed.

Nick was conflicted seeing his young patient in Memphis. He dreaded going back to the grind, but knew there were good works to be done at the MED. "Man, that's great. Thanks so much, Buck, for helping see to it that he was fitted."

The waitress set down a coffee in front of each of them. An old-fashioned jukebox played Latin love songs.

"You're being awfully quiet, Nick. You okay?" Maggie asked.

Nick looked at Buck and knew it was time. He swallowed. "Well, it's just that Buck and I are thinking of going to Tikal."

The color drained from Maggie's face as she leaned back in her chair.

"I don't know, Maggie," Nick was quick to interject, "there are still so many unanswered questions for me about John. I think I'm supposed to go to Tikal. I don't know how to explain it."

They sat in uncomfortable silence.

Maggie processed the news. "And if I tell you no?"

Nick looked at Buck. "Then we won't go," Nick said, almost hoping that was her answer.

"What good do you think it will do?"

Nick and Buck had decided they would tell her nothing about the map or the villages or FOCO. Maybe they were making too much of all of it.

"You can blame it on me, Maggie," Buck offered. "I encouraged Nick to do this."

Maggie smiled at Buck, but saw right through him.

"What are you thinking, Maggie?" Nick asked.

"I'm wondering if I could ever go with you."

"You are absolutely welcome. I hope you know that."

"I know that, Nick," Maggie smiled. "I just don't know *if* I could go. I know John is in heaven, probably stirring up some sort of ruckus as we speak," she said, trying to break the tension. "I've already thought about this whole thing. I know there is nothing I can do to bring him back to me. It's just that I couldn't stand it if something happened to either of you two."

"I promise I'll take care of him." Buck put his arm over Nick's shoulders.

Maggie shook her head. "I'm telling both of you to be

careful." She pointed a finger at each of them, almost daring them to disobey her.

They saw the resolve in her eyes.

"When would you go? Aren't you both leaving Sunday?"

"Uh…tomorrow?" Nick said tentatively.

"Oh, you guys." Maggie picked up her napkin, crumpled it, and threw it at Nick. "Nothing like giving a gal a little time to think."

"I'm sorry, Maggie. I know this is hard, but we won't go without your blessing."

Maggie sat in silence.

They knew she was praying.

Finally, she said, "Okay, but you guys have to promise to be careful. I think you should go, but I'm just not ready to go along."

Nick and Buck smiled without joy but satisfied with the decision.

Anna hadn't spoken during the entire conversation. Now that it had been decided, she said. "I'll go with you."

"No!" all three said in unison.

Anna's face turned red, but she continued, "Look, you guys speak about ten words of Spanish between you. A lot of good that's going to do you."

There was another long silence.

"Your whole team is headed to Antigua tomorrow for a week of shopping. You don't want to miss out on that, do you?" Maggie asked.

Anna leaned back in her chair, crossed her arms, and dug in her heels. "I know I'm going to be a whole lot more useful to ya'll."

Nick looked at Buck. They both shrugged. She was right. They looked at Maggie.

"All right, but I'm not feeling very good about any of this."

CHAPTER 41

THE ISLAND OF FLORES

"Come on, man, we're going to miss the plane," Buck hollered from the van.

It would have been a relief to Nick if they had. Buck made the arrangements that included flying. It never crossed Nick's mind that the plane wouldn't be a jet. But when Buck had showed him a picture of the six-seater plane they'd be taking, Nick was ready to call the whole thing off. Out of the trio, he was the only one who was anxious, although he tried not to look like a wimp in front of Anna.

I can't believe she is excited to fly in that puddle jumper.

He heard Buck call him again. He had almost forgotten that he wanted to look up FOCO before they left and quickly typed in the acronym on John's computer.

Scrolling through the list of Google results, Nick found FOCO—The Friends of Children Organization. He clicked the link and up sprung a colorful web page of smiling children.

FOCO's slogan—*Bettering the lives of children around the world*—scrolled across the screen. Nick noted that the main office was in Seoul, South Korea, but he was surprised to find offices in Washington, D.C., as well as Los Angeles, Rio de Janeiro, Beijing, Tokyo, London, Mumbai, Moscow, Johannesburg, and Tehran.

Geez, these guys must be pretty well funded. But there's nothing about Guatemala.

Buck resorted to blowing the van's horn.

"Okay, okay, I'm coming," Nick shouted and shut down the computer.

* * *

Nick examined the small plane as they began their taxi to the Quetzaltenango runway. Much of the vinyl covering on the ceiling was peeling or gone. Buck and Anna sat in front of him, and the pilot and co-pilot in front of them. Their grungy appearance made Nick wonder how often the plane was used to transport tourists and how often it was used to traffic drugs. He wished Maggie had come along so the six-seater would have been properly balanced, and he had someone to hold on to.

Anna's Spanish and her moxie came in handy when the pilots tried to jack up the price. She flatly told them no and encouraged Buck and Nick to walk away with her. The pilots gave up and agreed to the original price. Nick wasn't so sure it was a good idea to argue with the pair that held their lives in their hands. He would have paid double to stay on the ground. He stared at the mountains at the end of the runway. It wasn't simply the mountains and the condition of the plane that frightened him, it was the dark clouds gathered in the sky.

A loud squeal from under the plane was unnerving, and Nick imagined one of the wheels falling off as they approached the runway. He watched a state-of-the-art helicopter land at the airport and wondered what drug cartel owned such an expensive piece of equipment. He wished they had such rich friends in low places at this point.

Buck turned to him and shouted over the roar of the engine, "Not too late to change your mind."

Nick gave his friend a frosty stare, and Buck erupted with laughter.

* * *

The forty-minute plane ride was everything Nick imagined and worse. Not long after takeoff, they climbed into the storm. The small plane was buffeted by strong winds. He saw Buck reach up and steady himself against the flaking ceiling of the plane.

As they bumped through the clouds, Nick's imagination flashed images of them falling through the clouds, only to crash into the side of the mountain, and end in a fiery finale. But the most unnerving part of the flight was when he saw the pilots frantically searching for the airport below them, and Nick realized they were flying totally blind. As the plane circled in a stormy sea of impenetrable clouds, Nick wondered if this was how his life would end. Just when he thought his nerves couldn't take another minute, he saw the co-pilot pointing enthusiastically at the ground. The plane entered a steep nosedive; Nick feared they wouldn't recover.

He braced for impact as the plane leveled out in the very last moment, hit the runway with a loud thud, bounced three times, and settled on the pavement at the Mundo Maya International Airport. The pilot and co-pilot high-fived. Anna turned to see if Nick was okay.

He was shaking his head. "That was enough to make a guy pray."

She smiled at him.

* * *

Buck had made reservations at the Hotel Casona de La Isla. For fifty-two dollars a night, Nick wasn't sure what to expect as their taxi rumbled over the bridge to the small island of Flores on the outskirts of the main cities of San Elena and San Benito. The travel agent in Quetzaltenango told Buck that it would be a snap to find a local tour guide to take them to the Tikal ruins. He'd advised them to be careful of scams and people off the street claiming to be guides.

Anna asked the taxi driver where they could get something to eat. He suggested either Capitan Tortuga or Jalapenos near the hotel. Neither sounded good to Nick's churning stomach.

The taxi turned right from *Calle Sur* to *Calle 30 de Junio*. The driver explained that Guatemala gained independence from Spain in 1821, but the "Liberal Revolution" took place on June 30, 1871. The nearly ten-by-ten block island was easy to walk, and they would find all the streets marked by special dates in history.

Nick looked out the window at the brightly painted, neatly kept buildings and realized this was a tourist town. The taxi driver warned Anna not to wander alone; a pretty, blond woman would not be safe. She thanked him and asked about the signs that hung on every wall and billboard.

"We have government elections this month. Those are all campaign signs. There is always violence during this time, so it is best to be careful. The communists are trying to find control once again." He looked through the rearview mirror at Buck and Nick. "We always have people from your State Department that come here this time of year. You guys from the CIA?" He eyed them suspiciously, then cracked a broad smile and laughed.

Buck laughed and looked at Nick. "No, just tourist-O's," he said, affecting a Spanish accent, which made Anna laugh. With his military background, Buck understood the CIA and U.S. military were frequent and unpublished visitors to Central America.

The taxi pulled up to the Hotel Casona de La Isla, a yellow building with bright blue railings on the balconies of each room. Inside, the lobby was decorated in the colorful Maya weavings of bright blues, yellows, and greens.

A young woman at the desk greeted them warmly and gave them keys to their rooms. Buck and Nick shared a room, and Anna had her own. After the taxi driver's warning, Buck was relieved their rooms were adjacent.

"You guys want to meet up in ten?" Buck asked. "I'll find someone to run us up to Tikal, and we can go next door for lunch before we go."

"Okay." Nick sniffed at his shirt. "I don't mind changing my shirt after that plane ride."

"Tikal is about eighty klicks from here."

Anna looked puzzled. "Klicks?"

"Oh, sorry. Old habits die hard. Kilometers. Eighty kilometers."

Nick saw the take-charge personality of an alert drill sergeant coming out in Buck. He was glad Buck was with him.

CHAPTER 42

MODERN SLAVERY

Suk was angry. He was glad to see the girl was alive, but Hwang and Cho had gone too far this time. Her left eye was swollen shut and her black hair was matted and tangled. Suk gave the girl one of his T-shirts to replace her torn clothing.

He grabbed a large wad of cash to silence the brothel boss and helped the girl walk to the SUV. Cho and Hwang were passed out on the floor. It was everything he could do to restrain himself from slitting their throats.

The brothel was across the bridge in Flores in the center of the tourist area. Suk pulled to the front of the club where two girls in miniskirts stood smoking. He reached across the young girl and pushed her door open. Slowly, supporting her weight on the door, she lowered herself off the seat to the pavement. Without making eye contact, she turned and put out her hand for payment. The beating she had taken was minor compared to the one her boss would inflict if she returned without cash.

Suk handed her the stack of bills. "I'm sorry."

He watched her pull herself up the stairway railing and disappear into the dark club. The smoking girls who did nothing to help their workmate tried to entice him. He shook his head and pulled away from the curb. He drove a block away and stopped in front of the yellow and red DHL storefront. He had received e-mail confirmation that morning that the package had arrived, and he hoped for good news.

The man behind the international shipping counter gave him the envelope, and Suk ripped it open before reaching the door.

It was good news indeed. The one-page note smuggled through Seoul informed him that Kwon had received the vial, and the initiative was progressing well.

He sat in the SUV and read the line over and over again about the rewards awaiting him and wondered if the rewards would ever happen. He longed for a different life. Before he had sent the vial, he'd thought about asking for an advance, but didn't because such brazenness could be a death sentence. North Korea took great pride in infiltrating all countries with agents, and the agents spied on other agents. Any sign of disobedience would be met with doom.

He dreamed of living the rest of his life on a peaceful, tropical island somewhere. He'd even be happy to stay in Guatemala. Living outside of North Korea was infinitely better than living in his mother country.

CHAPTER 43

TIKAL

Miguel, their tour guide, turned out to be the cousin of the receptionist at the front desk. He was polite and spoke excellent English. His small van was spotless, and he drove carefully enough, allowing them to enjoy the scenery.

With his dark Latino looks and relaxed personality, Miguel appeared to be a few years older than Anna, and the two hit it off well. A bit too well for Buck's comfort, so when Miguel asked Anna to sit in front with him, Buck suggested otherwise and sat himself down in the front passenger seat next to the guide. He gave Miguel a protective father's nod.

"Where did you learn your English?" Nick asked.

"My father and mother divorced, and my father moved to Texas. I lived with him in Houston for three years. I moved back to Guatemala last year to help my mother. She has breast cancer and not sure she has much time left." His voice caught.

"I'm sorry to hear that. Anything we can do?"

"No, but thank you."

Nick liked Miguel already. He was smart and sincere.

As they passed the east end of Lake Petén Itzá, Nick admired the emerald-green water. He glanced in the rearview mirror and caught Miguel watching him.

"Lago Petén Itzá is twenty miles long, three miles wide, and about 500 feet deep," the tour guide said. "A dive team was here last year and found many Maya relics along the northern shoreline. You will see some of them in the museum at Tikal."

Nick recognized the name of the small town they passed

through at the far end of the lake, El Remate, and it hit him how real this had become. This was the impoverished area where Maria and little Danilo came from.

Miguel looked at his watch. "We will be to Tikal in about twenty minutes. That gives us a bit over four hours before the National Park closes. Is there anything specific you want to see during your time? How much do you know about the Maya?"

"I know very little, but Anna knows quite a bit."

Miguel looked at Anna in the rearview mirror and smiled. Buck cleared his throat to remind him to focus on the road.

"We are proud of the archaeological discoveries of Tikal, or Yax Mutal, as it was originally thought to be called," Miguel said.

"Yak Mutal?" Anna asked.

"The first Mutal. No one is sure what it means," he said. "Tikal was the name it was given after it was discovered in the mid-1800s. Tikal means *the place of the voices.*" He smiled at her in the mirror and, seeing her interest, continued.

"Tikal was the capital to the most powerful kingdoms of the ancient Maya spanning the period between 400 BC to 900 AD."

"How many people lived here during that time?"

Miguel shrugged his shoulders. "Hard to know for sure, maybe up to 90,000. What you'll see today is just a fraction of the original city. The archaeologists have mapped it out and it covers sixteen square kilometers and has something like 3000 structures—most are still under dirt."

Nick sensed Miguel's glances at him in the mirror were requests for him to comment, to prove he wasn't bored. Nick tried to look interested in the facts about Tikal, but he wasn't sure what or how much to say about the real reason for their visit. When Miguel continued to look to him for comment, Nick decided there was nothing to do but say it. He cleared his throat and began, "We're here for kind of a difficult reason."

He paused before asking, "Do you know about the American doctor that was killed here a while back?"

Miguel looked at Nick long enough to make Buck nervous.

"Yes, of course. That was very tragic. We are all so sick of the violence here in our country. It affects all of us."

"What do you know about it?" Nick asked cautiously.

"We are a small country, Dr. Hart, so everyone hears whispers. Death is common here, but we don't like to talk about it."

There was a long, uncomfortable silence.

Finally, Anna asked, "Can you tell us what you know?"

Miguel looked at his passengers. "Are you police or something? Did you know the man?"

"This man…His name was John, and he was my best friend. I guess I'm here to try to understand a little more about what happened. To pay my respects, you might say."

Miguel was relieved. "Well, let me first tell you about the Maya. Many people come here thinking that the Maya were some sort of murderous savages that sacrificed people all the time. That is not the case. The Aztecs of the north were much more warlike, and history shows they did a lot of human sacrifice to appease their gods. The Maya, on the other hand, did more animal and bloodletting sacrifice. Even the historical Jewish people believed that blood could purify them." Miguel was clearly on the side of his Maya ancestors.

"However," he continued, "it is an undeniable fact that occasionally the Maya did do human sacrifices, and, unfortunately, that is where many people focus their attention. I will point out to you in the museum one Maya vessel that was found depicting a small boy being sacrificed. The historians believe that this was only done in extreme cases, like to battle a great pestilence or culture-changing event. Much of the blood letting concerned fertility. This is kind of gross." He looked in the mirror at Anna to warn her. "They would pierce the genitals of men and women and run something like barbed wire through the area to draw blood. They believed that this particular blood was essential for regeneration of the culture." Miguel grimaced at Anna.

"Thank you for the history lesson," Buck said, eager to end talk of gory sacrifice, "but what does that have to do with the doctor's murder?"

"That's the thing. The only people in Maya history who were sacrificed like that were prisoners."

"Why is that strange?"

"Well," Miguel paused. "I know the tour guide that was with him. I mean *knew*. His name was Danilo, and he was a good man.

I probably saw him every day." Miguel stumbled over his words. "Danilo was found down the river…with his throat slashed. He was wearing a backpack, with the doctor's heart inside." His final word was barely audible.

After a moment, Miguel regained his composure. "Even the police don't think Danilo did it. But if the drug cartels did it, they have not admitted it. They usually fess up because they don't care about anything and think they can get away with everything. See, here's the thing: if it was a local gang killing, they would have just shot him and left him. It was like an ancient evil raised itself up out of the ground and killed them both—no one really knows."

Nick thought the young man was being dramatic to impress Anna, but when he looked at Miguel's face, he saw real fear.

* * *

As the road climbed out of the farmland surrounding the lake, they entered a very different world. The flatland gave way to rolling hills of dense jungle, so thick that it appeared to swallow the road ahead.

With the van windows open, the hot, arid air turned steamy, and a strong, earthy smell filled their nostrils. The jungle canopy covered the roadway and darkened the sky.

"Oh, Buck," Nick announced, sniffing the air. "I meant to tell you that I looked up FOCO right before we left. You remember, the notation that was on the map about the wells?"

"Oh yeah, we talked about doing that."

"The acronym stands for The Friends of Children Organization. It's an organization based out of South Korea. Looks pretty legit. Must be well-funded because FOCO has branches all over the world. I didn't see any mention of Guatemala though, but someone had ants in his pants and I didn't have more time to investigate the website." Nick snickered at Buck. "But from the home page pictures, it looks like they do a lot of good things around the world. Hard to know if there is any connection, but we should keep an eye out for them. Maybe they know something or talked with John."

Buck leaned toward Miguel. "You ever heard of FOCO?"

"I've seen their SUV around. It has a big orange star on the side that says FOCO. I thought it always stood for focus—*foco* in Spanish is focus."

"Ever talk with them?"

"No," he shrugged. "They are real loners and maybe not very nice people. But I hate to say anything bad about them because I hear they are doing good things for the villages here in the north."

"Why do you say *not nice*?" Nick asked.

"I have a cousin, who is…" He looked in the mirror at Nick, then Anna. "She's, uh, a working girl." He winked at Nick. "You hear things."

"What things?"

He looked at Anna again. "Maybe I can tell you later?" He smiled tentatively at Nick.

"You know where their office is or where they live?" Buck asked.

"No, I don't. But I can ask around."

They sat in silence. As they drove deeper into the jungle, Nick's mood darkened, opening wounds in his soul. This would be difficult and had the urge to turn back.

Sensing his uneasiness, Anna put her hand on his arm. "Can I pray for you?"

Nick sighed and nodded.

"Father, be with us today. I pray for strength and grace and peace. Jesus, I thank You that You, who is in us, is greater than the devil who is in the world. Protect us from evil, Father. Protect our hearts and minds. Amen."

Buck echoed the Amen, and Miguel made the sign of the cross. Nick smiled at Anna; she was always so kind.

Miguel pulled into a small, dirt parking lot next to a thatched-roof building with a sign that read, Museo Sylvanus G. Morley. There were only a few other cars in the lot.

"Sylvanus G. Morley was an American archaeologist who assisted with much of the excavation of this site," Miguel told them. "Do you want to go into the museum?"

Buck saw that Nick was in no state to make a decision and took charge. "I tell you what, son, I'm not sure we're up for sightseeing. Can you take us to the ruins, and we'll go from there? What we want to do is pay our last respects."

"You bet. It's about a mile and a half walk through the jungle to the site."

Buck saw the tour guide pull a large machete from under his seat. Miguel saw him watching. "Uh…it's the jungle. A jaguar has been seen in the area lately. Better safe than sorry," he said, holding up the large blade.

Miguel led the way. They walked single file in silence along the dirt pathway, occasionally stepping over large, fan-like roots of kapok trees. Vines of different shapes and sizes hung from mammoth trees, some with dangerously sharp spines.

A huge, iridescent blue butterfly floated above them. Miguel stopped and turned back to them. "That is the Blue Morpho butterfly. See how it seems to flash as it flies? Its topside is brilliant blue, and its bottom side is a dull brown. That one is probably a female because the males are even bigger. Their wing spans can get up to eight inches across."

Nick thought of the Monarch butterfly he had talked to at the Hope Center. *Perhaps it was a good sign for their visit.*

They watched as the Blue Morpho fluttered into the jungle canopy. With their attention turned to the treetops, Miguel pointed to a small group of spider monkeys who had been silently following them. The monkeys seemed to know they'd been spotted and began a chorus of high-pitched screeches. The largest male barked loudly, and the troop vanished into the thicket.

"Spider monkeys are very curious, but also quite timid. I don't know if we will see the howler monkeys today, but be careful. They can be very aggressive." He smiled at Anna and patted his machete to encourage her to stay close to his side.

A thunder clap made them all jump. "It looks like we may get a bit of a storm. I know a shelter. Follow me." Miguel quickened his pace, turning off the main trail onto a secondary path. The air-cooled a few degrees, the tree tops swayed, and the dense jungle grew darker. As the first drops of rain fell, Miguel led them to the mouth of a large cave.

"We will be safe in here."

Like a good soldier protecting his troops, Buck brought up the rear, herding them into the shelter just as the heavens opened and torrents of rain poured, followed by lightning and thunder.

"I thought you said a bit of a storm," Buck retorted.

"Now you know why it's so green here," Miguel smiled. "Hopefully, it will pass as fast at it came."

Water poured off the lip of the cave entrance, forcing them deeper into the sanctuary. When a bat flew over their heads into the storm, Anna screamed and took refuge on a nearby rock. Nick and Buck laughed nervously.

"Um, you may not want to sit there." Miguel offered his hand to Anna and pulled her up. He took a small flashlight from his pants pocket and illuminated the base of the rock she had been sitting on. A large, hairy tarantula scurried into its hole.

Anna squealed and leaned into Buck. "Okay," she announced. "I'm done with cave dwelling. I'll take the rain any time."

As the words left her mouth, the storm went from torrential downpour to steady rain.

"I think God heard your prayers," Miguel smiled at her. "These storms really come and go, but they can be pretty dangerous."

"Well, I don't know about you guys, but I'm not afraid of the rain. Bats and spiders are another thing. I'm out of here," she said, marching into the rain.

The three men looked at each other, shrugged, and followed her.

As the rain slowed, the jungle turned a fluorescent green, and the already impossible humidity increased a few more degrees. Their shirts were soaked inside and out as Miguel continued to lead them down the trail.

"We're almost there. Everyone okay?"

Another 200 yards on the muddy trail, they broke from the dense jungle to a wide-open expanse from a time, long ago. As if on cue, the sun broke through the clouds and illuminated the courtyard of the Maya empire, and the visitors stepped onto emerald-green lawns surrounding the ancient ruins.

They stood in awe at the magnificence—giant, stone structures rising from the earth, symbols of a great civilization.

"Welcome to Tikal," Miguel announced, spreading his arms with pride. "You are facing Temple III and the Bat Palace. The lost World Complex sits behind that. On either side are Temples IV and II—the Temple of the Grand Jaguar and the Temple of the Masks." He pointed to the pyramid-like structures with stairs leading to the top of the ancient architecture nearly fifteen stories tall.

"Unbelievable," Buck said.

"And to think they did this all by hand over 1500 years ago," Miguel added.

They looked at Nick, ready to take his lead on what to do next. He had not said a word. He stood with his arms crossed and his chin resting on one hand.

"What are you thinking, pal?" Buck urged.

"I honestly don't know what to think. It looks so peaceful. It's hard to imagine. I guess I thought it would be darker, like that storm. I just don't know—it's so beautiful here."

"Darkness to light," Anna murmured.

It was loud enough for Nick to hear, and he turned to look at her.

"Sorry. I didn't realize I said that out loud."

Nick continued to look at her, waiting for an explanation.

"I don't know," she said. "I don't want to sound too mystical. This feels like what I know about God. Always bringing things from darkness to light. Always wanting to bring life and beauty. Even in death, He brings us into new life, from glory to glory to glory. That's what the scriptures say."

Nick's heart was buffeted by the storms of emotion—from anger to peace, back to anger. Memories overflowed the erected walls of his psyche's protection and tears welled in his eyes. His legs buckled, and he stumbled down to sit on a large rock next to the trail—his shoulders quaked, followed by uncontrolled sobs.

"I don't understand," Nick shouted through spittle mixed with tears.

Pictures of John's face flashed on the screen in Nick's mind—John's look of serenity when he was focused on a problem and then, with a twinkle of guilt, when he was about to play a practical joke on a friend.

"John, why did you let this happen to you…God, why did you let this happen?" Nick cried out.

Nick was aware of a consoling hand on his shoulder. The catharsis of emotion was involuntary and at this point he didn't care.

Will I never see my friend again?

More tears poured out.

"I don't get it." Nick looked up at Buck who had his hand on his shoulder and then at Anna. He saw they were grieving with him.

His torrent of emotion eased as the last drops from the rain storm pattered against large foliage next to them.

A final image of John filtered through Nick's mind. It was a fleeting image, but it was as clear and real as the temples of Tikal, the rock he was sitting on, the disappearing rain, and the re-emerging sun—John was smiling at him.

"It's going to be okay."

Nick looked at Buck and Anna and even Miguel to see who'd said that.

"I'm sorry, you guys," Nick said, feeling embarrassed by his outburst.

"No, no, no," Anna and Buck reassured him.

"Welcome to the human race," Buck added and squeezed his shoulder.

Nick chuckled and tried to make light, "So that's what that feels like. I think I'll go back to my robot surgeon self."

But in truth, his heart was inexplicably changing. It was fuller, maybe even softer, and one thing for sure—more open.

Nick stood and received long hugs from Buck and Anna and didn't even begin to pull away.

"Man, what would I do without you guys?"

Buck held him by the shoulder. "The one thing I do know is that it's all going to be okay."

"Yeah, didn't you just say that?" Nick asked.

"Huh?" Buck responded.

Heat rose up Nick's neck. "Never mind. Thought someone said that a minute ago."

They looked at each other in bewilderment.

"Ah, the place of the voices," Miguel added, having watched the scene a step behind them all.

"You going to be okay?" Buck asked, ignoring Miguel's assessment.

Nick sighed and nodded.

"Maybe God is talking to you?" Buck said.

Nick did not know how to answer. Standing there staring at the place where his best friend lost his life, he realized there was way more to God than he ever thought—a goodness, a beauty, a closeness he had never known before. "I was really nervous to come here," he said, "but I'm so glad we did."

"Dr. Hart, do you want to go into the plaza?"

Nick thought a moment. "Does anyone know where exactly John was killed?"

"I have overheard people talk about it."

"Are you sure you want to know?" Buck interrupted.

Nick nodded. "Yeah, I really think I do."

Miguel pointed to the base of the Temple of the Grand Jaguar. "They found your friend's body there."

Before Miguel could finish his sentence, Nick walked in that direction. The others followed. When they got to the base of the great pyramid, Nick stopped in front of a large, round stone.

"It was here, wasn't it?"

"Yes, this is where they found his body," Miguel said.

Nick twisted from side to side, seeing the emerald jungle framing the manicured plaza of the ancient Maya. He shielded his eyes from the sun as he followed the grey stone steps up the temple to the crowning structure and single opening. In his imagination, he could see a Maya king standing in his colorful regalia, his arms stretched out over his people.

He returned his gaze to the round stone before him and bent to feel the smooth, flat surface. Any signs of horror—ancient or recent—had long vanished.

Nick's recent dreams of John calling him to the shelter of the rocks flashed in his mind. He could not make any sense of it as he looked from the round stone to the tall sculpted stone shaft standing guard over the stone altar.

"What is that stone?" Nick asked Miguel, pointing to the

stone monument.

"It's called a *stelae*," Miguel answered. "Often the huge slabs were carved with messages. It's how we know some of the history of the people. The *stelae* are all about announcing the king...or uh, *realenza dinina*." He looked at Anna to help him out.

She looked puzzled for a moment, then said, "*realenza dinina*—divine kingship, I guess."

"Yes, that is correct. The people thought of their leaders as gods," Miguel said.

"The only divine King I know is Jesus," Anna declared.

"Amen to that," Buck said.

Nick sighed.

Buck put a hand on Nick's shoulder and squeezed. Anna reached into her handbag, slung over her shoulder, and pulled out a damp cloth from which she carefully unwrapped a pink orchid. "Maggie cut this for me before we left and asked me to put it out for John." She gave the orchid to Nick. "I think you should do it."

Nick took the flower and put it on the stone. *If Maggie were here, she'd say a prayer.* He almost wished he could pray. Mostly, he was glad he'd come to see where John had drawn his last breath. His grief was allayed, and his heart was filled with peace.

But it didn't last. Horror destroyed his harmony and forced him to think of the torture John had endured. A storm of anger raged in his brain. Anger that he no longer had his best friend. Anger that the killer had not been brought to justice. Anger that evil lurked in the world.

His emotions were frazzled. His face turned red. He turned on his heels and stormed back to the van.

CHAPTER 44

CELEBRATION

The only emotion Pak and Kwon displayed was disappointment as they read the report from their associate in West Africa and looked at the horrific photographs. The swollen corpse lay in the fetal position with bloodstains around the nose and mouth—a result of painful hemorrhagic death and total organ failure.

Since the North Korean biological division had released the Ebola virus for testing in Guinea and Liberia, there had been a sharp rise in cases and in mortality. Health workers who cared for the patients accounted for many of the deaths. The World Health Organization's genetic analysis of this virus confirmed that it was related to the 2009 Ebola virus reported in the Congo. Pak and Kwon were not surprised since they had released that virus as well.

The two noted that the WHO report claimed the fruit of the garcinia monkey tree appeared to have the ability to stop the virus replication. But Pak and Kwon were not worried; the garcinia tree was close to extinction due to habitat destruction.

"I am pleased with the fatality rate," Pak said, "but why we are not seeing a wider distribution of the disease, I do not understand."

"Yes, that is disappointing," Kwon responded, without looking up from the report. Despite all his success, that one failure could send him straight to the gulag.

"The fruit bat is the natural host of the virus. That was where we found it. The WHO has educated West Africans about contact with bats. That has left human-to-human spread," Kwon explained, defending his program. "The problem is that human-to-human transmission can occur only by direct contact with broken skin or mucous membranes. We have been unable to supercharge this particular virus with the H1N1 influenza virus, as we have with mumps. I can promise you that the M2H1 is much more virulent."

"For our sake, I hope you're right." Pak clamped his hand on Kwon's shoulder.

* * *

The hostess at Capitan Tortuga seated them on the patio at a lakeside table. The view of Lake Petén Itzá from the restaurant was spectacular. With the storms passed, the lake glimmered with the lights of San Benito across the bay. A near full moon rose in the east.

"There are going to be lots of babies born tonight," Dr. Hart diagnosed.

"Is that really true?" Anna asked.

"It really is."

"Maybe it has to do with the gravitational pull," Buck laughed.

"I tell you what, not only does the full moon bring more babies, it also brings out craziness. Our ERs are always busier during a full moon. I hate being on call on those nights."

Because every table at the restaurant was full, it was taking a while for the waiter to bring their drinks. But no one seemed to mind. After a silent ride back to the village, Nick's anger had cooled, and when they saw his mood improve, Buck and Anna suggested they celebrate John's life with a margarita toast. Nick decided John wouldn't object.

"You doing okay?" Buck asked Nick.

"Yeah, I guess. I have to admit it was tough. I really miss him."

The waiter brought their margaritas, served in mason jars.

Buck lifted his glass. "I think it is appropriate that we have an empty place at the table."

Buck acknowledged the vacant seat at their table. "One of my Canadian comrades taught me a toast for fallen warriors. It goes like this: *You may have noticed the empty setting for one that is off on his own—it is reserved to honor our fallen comrades in arms. It symbolizes that they are with us, here in spirit. We should never forget the brave men and women who answered our nation's call to serve and served the cause of freedom in a special way. We are ever mindful that the sweetness of enduring peace has always been tainted by the bitterness of personal sacrifice. We are compelled to never forget that while we enjoy our daily pleasures, there are others who have endured the agonies of pain, deprivation and death.* So here's to John Russell, our fallen comrade."

Buck, Nick, and Anna clinked glasses and sipped their drinks.

Nick blotted a tear with his napkin. "Thank you, guys. I'm sure glad you're here with me."

They sat in silence as the buzz of the crowd around them mixed with soft music from a guitar player at the bar inside.

Buck broke the silence. "I told Miguel to pick us up at eight in the morning, if that's okay with everyone?"

"Fine," Nick said. "I really want to go to one of the villages John wrote about in his journal. Buck, did you figure out where they are?"

Buck pulled a map from his pocket and unfolded it on the table. He took the small glass bowl with a burning candle on their table and moved it to a corner of the map. "So this is where we are on the Island of Flores." He pointed to the south end of the lake. "The four villages that John wrote about are here." He pointed to four different places on the map. "El Naranjo is way out west here, El Chilar and Cruse Dos Aquadas are north, and El Zapote is east. I would suggest we start with El Zapote since it's probably the closest and easiest to get to. The others are pretty isolated and remote. That sound good to you?"

Nick nodded, but Anna asked uncharacteristically, "You think we are in any danger?"

"I asked your young suitor that myself today," Buck replied. "He seemed a bit hesitant to go to the other villages, but he thought El Zapote was close enough to the main trail that we would be okay."

Nick looked at Anna, trying to read her thoughts. "You okay?"

Anna picked her words carefully. "Yeah, I think so. Since we have been here…I don't know…a bit of oppression is what it feels like. I know that Christ is in us…" She paused, looking back and forth between the men. "I know this because, as we go into dark places, He changes the spiritual atmosphere. Light always pushes out darkness. I'm just not sure I have experienced this kind of…pressure. I guess that's how I would describe it."

"Just be glad your Uncle Buck is here to protect you." Buck clamped his big hand on her tiny shoulder.

Anna's mood lightened. She shrugged him off and smiled, addressing Nick. "You should have seen Miguel's face this afternoon. He'd asked me to dinner tonight, and before I could reply, Uncle Buck answered for me." She looked at Buck and laughed. "I can still see you towering over him, looking him in the eyes, and barking, *No way, Jose.* I kind of felt sorry for Miguel."

They all laughed.

* * *

At their house in San Benito, Suk, Hwang, and Cho sat on the back deck overlooking the Island of Flores, drinking beer. Hwang smoked a large cigar. They had reason to celebrate. Returning from La Libertad, their mood was jubilant. La Libertad was the first village where they used the mosquito sprayer to spread the virus, and it was an overwhelming success.

Even Suk was surprised by the people's lack of natural immunity when they could not find one person in the small village who wasn't suffering from mild cold symptoms. *It must be such a new virus that no one carries antibodies to it and it spreads rapidly between people.*

People who had not been infected during the spraying quickly came down with it after being exposed to those who had.

"Here's to you, Boss," Hwang raised his beer to Suk.

Suk raised his glass back.

And here's to getting rid of you soon.

"Cho, I wish you wouldn't clean your guns when you're drinking," Suk reprimanded.

"Are you afraid I'll shoot you?" Cho laughed, chambered the .45mm pistol, aimed it at Suk, and pulled the trigger.

Suk turned ashen. Cho and Hwang burst into laughter.

"Cho, you are an idiot!" Suk scolded, as his color returned.

"So, what's the plan for tomorrow?" Cho asked.

"I want to spray one more village for statistical significance."

"What's that?" Cho looked confused.

"To confirm it works—scientifically."

"Okay. Where are we going?"

"I have decided the last village we will spray is Melchor de Mencos. It's right on the border with Belize, just beyond El Zapote.

* * *

At the restaurant, the evening was winding down. Nick, Buck, and Anna relaxed as the waiter brought coffee. The dinner had been delicious, and as the crowded restaurant emptied, the friends listened to a flock of American coots singing on the nearby lake, their haunting warble echoing off the distant shore.

"So, Buck, you missing your family?" Anna asked.

Buck dropped his jaw before speaking, "How did you know I was just thinking about them? I wish they could have come down with me to meet you all. Maybe next time."

"You have three sons?"

"Yes, my pride and my joy, for sure. The boys are what got me through this mess." He lifted a leg and rapped his knuckles against his metal prosthesis. "Them and of course my wife, Katy. She's the true hero."

"And?" Nick patted himself on his shoulder.

"Oh yeah. This guy. I even survived this guy's care."

Buck slapped Nick hard on the chest, making him cough and they all laughed.

"Has Buck showed you a picture of his sons?" Nick caught his breath. "They're all handsome boys. Chips off the old blockhead."

"For sure. Anna, I'd like to introduce you to them," Buck winked at her.

"They'd like that too," Nick added.

A waiter dropped a plate in the restaurant. Nick turned to the commotion and noticed a couple at a table inside. When he looked at them, they appeared to avert their eyes. They were middle-aged and Asian. Nick keyed in on the woman. Even though the patio lighting was dim, he could tell she was stunningly beautiful. He tried to not stare, especially because he figured they were a couple, but he sensed that she was looking at him as well.

I wonder, Japanese or Korean? If I had to, I'd bet Korean.

Every time he looked in their direction, they turned away.

Strange. He thought about the conversation they had with their taxi driver about the upcoming elections. He stole one more glance at the couple and then went back to conversing with his friends.

CHAPTER 45

EL ZAPOTE

Miguel smiled with a mouthful of white, glistening teeth and waved to Anna, ignoring Buck's glower.

The three friends were enjoying breakfast, and it was a real treat—handmade tortillas, eggs and beans topped with cream. The hotel's small dining room was packed with weekend tourists. All the freshly squeezed papaya and pineapple juice were consumed quickly.

"Man, I still can't believe you won't try the granadia fruit," Buck ribbed Nick.

"I don't eat anything that looks like brains," Nick teased back.

"I think it must be similar to passion fruit, but it's tasty. The girl at the front desk told me they call it *booger fruit* because of the mucus-like texture," Buck laughed.

"Even more reason not to try it."

The meal finished, they piled into Miguel's van, and much to their guide's chagrin, Buck claimed the front passenger seat again.

"Our pilots pick us up at four this afternoon," Buck said. "I figure that gives us plenty of time to look around, but keeps us from flying at night."

"I think I'd rather walk back," Nick said as he looked at the cloudless sky. "Let's hope it stays like this."

"So then it's home tomorrow, Dr. Hart?" Anna asked without enthusiasm.

"I feel the same way, Anna. I'm not sure I'm ready to head back to the ol' salt mine." He smiled at her.

"So, are we headed to El Zapote?" Miguel asked, starting up the van. "The zapote fruit is coming into season so maybe you can try one there."

"Just so they don't look like a body part," Nick put in.

Miguel looked at him curiously in the rearview mirror.

"They tried to get me to eat some slimy fruit today," Nick explained.

"I understand. The *fruta de mocos*, I bet."

They all laughed.

"Can I ask why you want to go to El Zapote?" Miguel asked. "There is not very much to see there, I could show you more ruins up north," he added enthusiastically. "I will even buy you a zapote here in town."

"Thanks, Miguel, but we want go to El Zapote. I have a long-lost cousin that I want to visit there." Buck told him.

"Really?" Miguel asked.

"Do I look Guatemalan?" Buck said sarcastically.

"Geez, Buck, give the boy a break. You remember being twenty-five, don't you?" Nick punched his shoulder.

I'm watching you. Making the universal sign, Buck put his fingers to his eyes and then pointed at Miguel, and they all laughed.

* * *

Suk and his comrades were getting a late start, and he was frustrated. Hwang and Cho had drunk themselves into a stupor again last night, and they took their own sweet time preparing the vehicle and trailer with the sprayer.

Suk glanced at his watch. Finally, Hwang and Cho, still reeking of alcohol, piled into the SUV. The drive to Melcho de Mencos was more than an hour. They would arrive by 9:15, plenty of time to spray and return to Flores before the DHL office closed at noon. The limited hours on Saturday were a hassle, but Suk could hardly wait to share the good news with Professor Kwon—the success of the aerosolization.

* * *

The El Zapote village chief was surprised to see the Americans. Very few ventured this far from the Maya ruins. The community reminded Nick of Isabella's village with a central well and gathering spot. Mud and thatched roof homes were scattered around.

The chief was even more surprised when he heard they were friends of Dr. John. Welcoming them to his village, he explained that the good doctor had visited them a number of times and had fixed his wife's nagging hernia at the Hope Center three years ago. They were both extremely grateful to Dr. John.

The village appeared to have no electricity, so when the man invited them into his home, their eyes took a moment to adjust from the bright sun outside.

The chief encouraged them to sit at a handmade wooden table in the center of the room. Anna interpreted for the group. She had thought ahead to stop at a local bakery and gifted the man with a large sack of bread.

The man handed the bag to his wife, who shuffled to a corner to slice the loaf. She returned quickly with a plate of sliced bread and a small jar of jelly. She also brought a pitcher of juice covered with a towel to keep the buzzing flies from the sweet nectar.

Nick saw there was no refrigeration and decided to skip the jelly, but it would be rude to refuse the juice.

"The chief thanks you for coming, but asks why you have come this far? He also asks about Dr. John," Anna translated.

"He doesn't know?" Nick looked at the toothless elder's smile and then at Anna.

"It doesn't look that way. A lot of these villages are pretty isolated."

When Nick looked into the old man's eyes, the elder's smile left as he read Nick's face. *The news was not good.* "I'm afraid Dr. John was killed," Nick said. "He is no longer with us." Nick hoped that Anna would help in the translation.

The old man made the sign of the cross over his face, and his wife gasped.

"I cannot believe this," the man said.

The woman cried.

Nick was glad Anna told them the story and he didn't have to repeat it.

Finally, the old man put his hand on top of Nick's. "I am so sorry for your loss."

Nick realized that Anna must have told the chief that he and John were best friends.

"*Gracias, gracias*," Nick replied. "I'm sorry that you had to hear this news from us. You had not heard anything about this?"

"No, no, we have not. Dr. John was a saint of a man, this I know. Whoever did this awful thing to him will rot in hell. That you can be assured."

"Thank you for your kindness, but I have to ask you a question."

"Certainly, anything."

"When we were going through Dr. John's things, we found a map and a journal. It said that a number of villages in the area were without recent births—that these villages have gone a number of months without any new pregnancies or babies. The journal entry was close to a year ago. I wanted to come out here to see for myself and to check if there is any possible connection to John's death."

As Anna translated, Nick could tell he had hit on a great sadness for both the chief and his wife. The woman wiped her tears.

The man took a small sip from his juice glass and cleared his throat. "I am afraid that you talk about a great shame that is over my village." He looked at his wife and back to Nick. "I do not like to talk about this." He lowered his voice. "But because you are friends with Dr. John, I will make an exception."

"I'm sorry to bring you more pain."

"We have known Dr. and Mrs. John for a number of years now. There had been no babies born to our young people for over six months. We tried everything. We went to the Priest in San Benito and even let the witchdoctor chant over us. It was like a powerful dark spirit had fallen over our village."

He glanced at his wife for confirmation. She nodded.

"We sent word to the Hope Center and were thrilled when Dr. John came all this way to see us. He examined all the young people and found nothing—everyone was perfectly healthy—something we have always prided ourselves on. He prayed with us over our village. He warned us not to see the witchdoctor again and told me about the spiritual world, the world of good and evil. He even reassured me that God loves us and does not hold any malice against us. He was so kind. We never heard anything more from him. Now I know why, and I'm afraid that God really is mad at us."

Nick could tell that Anna was reassuring him that this was not the case, that there must be some explanation. But Nick could also tell the man's heart was hardened to the truth. Nick had one more question. "I'm sorry to pry, but have there been any new pregnancies or children born in the village since then?"

The chief looked at his wife and back at Nick. "No, not one."

* * *

They stood outside their vehicle parked at the well, saying their goodbyes. Anna prayed over the village, and Nick promised they would look into this problem.

"Uh, before we go, I need to find the latrine." Miguel held his stomach, and the elder pointed down the hill to the outhouse. Miguel quickly trotted off.

"Woozy stomach," Buck elbowed Anna. "Must be because he ate zapote fruit."

"Give him a break, Buck. He's a pretty nice guy," Anna reproved him. "And no, I'm not interested," she said, more firmly than she meant.

Just then they were distracted by a white SUV pulling a trailer coming toward them.

The SUV slowed as its three Asian male passengers stared at Buck, Anna, and Nick. The only exit was around the well and back the way they'd come. The SUV turned, sped up, and took off, churning a storm of dust in its wake.

Nick was frozen in disbelief. He recognized the FOCO logo on the side of the SUV. The letters sat in the middle of a large orange star, just like the image he had seen the other day on their website. He tried to speak and move.

Buck didn't hesitate. He threw open the door of the van and jumped into the driver's seat. "Crap." He slammed his fist on the dashboard. "Miguel has the keys." He leaned out the door and shouted in the direction of the latrine. "Miguel, get your butt back up here."

But all they could do was wait.

CHAPTER 46

THE CROSSROADS

They could have been lost tourists, Suk rationalized. But he didn't like the way the big man stared at him. He ordered Hwang to get them out of there. Hwang swerved the FOCO SUV, turned it around, gunned the engine, and sped down the road. Suk grabbed the handle above the door to steady himself. He hoped the sprayer had not been damaged in the hasty exit.

El Zapote was a mile off the main road. As they hit the junction, Hwang didn't bother to stop. A chicken bus blasted its horn at them, barely slowing down as it missed the trailer by inches.

"You don't have to get us killed." Suk mopped his brow.

"Why did we have to stop there anyways?" Cho asked.

"I thought that since we are leaving soon, I would check to make sure there were no pregnancies in the village."

"Who do you think those people were?"

"Lost tourists I hope. But I don't want to take any chances."

* * *

Nick couldn't push Miguel any harder. The FOCO SUV was at least ten minutes ahead of them. Miguel's van was comfortable for shuttling tourists along paved roads to Tikal, but it was no good for four-wheeling.

There was a loud scrape under the car as Miguel dodged another large rut. "I'm sorry, Dr. Hart. I'm afraid something's going to come loose if I go much faster."

"You're doing fine, son."

The dust had long settled ahead of them.

"Certainly not friendly chaps," Buck reflected.

"Yeah, pretty strange. Obviously didn't want anything to do with us."

Miguel weaved around one last mud hole, hitting the main road, and pulled to a stop.

They saw tracks of the previous vehicle. It had turned left.

"Where does that go?" Buck asked.

"To Belize," Miguel replied.

Buck looked back at Nick who looked at his watch. "Your call, my brother."

"The plane leaves at four?" Nick frowned.

"Yeah."

"It sure would have been nice to talk to those guys. They may be headed into Belize," he said, thinking out loud. "Miguel, I guess you better get us home."

* * *

Buck relented and allowed Miguel to take Anna for a Coca-Cola next door to Jalapenos. Anna assured him she would be fine. With Miguel's van keys in his pocket, Buck felt only a little better. "I'm off to check the tourist shops to find some cool Maya stuff to bring home to my boys," he said. "You two have a good time. You coming with me, Nick?"

Nick declined. He wanted to stretch his legs with a walk around the island and work up the courage to get back on the plane. He checked his watch. It was a little over an hour before they had to leave for the airport. He set off on his walk.

At least it's a beautiful day.

He was glad he'd come, even though he still had many unanswered questions. As he neared the tip of the small island, he looked out across the lake where the horizon gave way to the jungle and the ancient Maya city.

He threw a flat stone over the lake. It skipped seven times. The stone's long walk on water made him think about the mysteries of God. He knew so little, and after these last two weeks, he understood even less. Still, it felt like his life was changing, like a cog had been adjusted into place, setting off a whole new direction. He wasn't at all sure what it meant.

He bent to pick up another stone when he saw the Asian couple from the restaurant the night before enter the Island of Flores Hotel, across the street. Besides the FOCO men, these were the only Asians he had seen in the area. *I wonder if they work for FOCO? Maybe their office is here?*

He waited for the traffic to pass before he crossed the road to the hotel. The lobby opened to a large courtyard that led to individual bungalows spread out in a large V-shape. Nick didn't see the couple. His throat was dry with a strange sense of desperation. *Did I miss the chance to talk with the FOCO people again?*

He had to make a decision—search the bungalows to the left or right. Since he was standing closer to the left side, he walked in that direction. A number of guests enjoyed a large swimming pool in the beautifully landscaped gardens of the central area. Nick walked on his tiptoes, looking over the shrubbery into the pool area and inching slowly down the row of bungalows. He tried peering into them without appearing obvious. A young toddler in a swimsuit waved at him from one of the doorways. A woman quickly pulled her inside and shut the door.

When he reached the final bungalow, he stood with his hands on his hips and scanned the area. Still no sign of them.

He turned to walk back to the lobby when he spotted them on the opposite side of the complex, exiting the last bungalow. Nick searched frantically for a route to take him directly across the courtyard. Unfortunately, it was blocked by the shrubbery and a large security fence.

Nick took off in a jog down the pathway to the lobby, hoping to meet them there. But when he arrived at the lobby, they were nowhere in sight. He trotted down the other arm of the complex to the bungalow they had exited.

He saw that the pathway continued to the other side of the building. His heart sank when he realized it led to the main road. A taxi startled him. Its driver honked and looked at him, wondering if he needed a ride.

Nick waved him on and frantically surveyed the area. *Shoot.* He walked back to the last bungalow and stood in front of it, trying to gather his thoughts. He looked at his watch. He had to meet Buck and Anna in forty-five minutes.

Nick looked around and saw no one on the pathway. He heard children laughing and playing at the pool. He turned to the bungalow door and knocked. He waited and looked at his watch again.

He was about to do something terribly wrong, but he was desperate. He grabbed the doorknob and twisted. To his surprise, it turned, and the door cracked open. He ignored the loud voices in his head shouting at him to shut the door and get out of there.

* * *

As expected, the spraying in Melcho de Mencos took less than an hour. Suk wasn't sure if it was because it was their last assignment or if he had actually grown fond of the people of Guatemala, but he felt some angst as they drove around the small town, watching the people go about their lives, unaware of the fate that had befallen them.

As the FOCO SUV bounced down the dirt road returning to El Zapote, he became uneasy about the whites he had seen at the village. *Would they still be here?*

As they rounded the last bend in the road, he was relieved to see the van and the visitors gone.

He saw the chief standing by his hut as the FOCO vehicle pulled up to the well and stopped. He looked relieved to see them and waved. Walking out with his cane, he welcomed the men warmly and asked if they would like some refreshments. "I am glad to see you, my friends. I was concerned when you did not stop earlier," the elder chief told Suk.

"I'm sorry," Suk responded. Suk spoke fluent Spanish. "We saw you were busy and didn't want to interrupt. I have scolded Hwang for tearing away so fast."

"Please, my friend, you have done so much for our village, you are always welcome here. Come and sit with us," he said, gesturing to his house.

"I'm afraid we cannot stay to visit. I must get back to town."

Suk looked around the small village. He observed people getting water from the well they had drilled, making the hand-dug well at the center of the community obsolete.

"I hope to hear news of any new pregnancies since we were here last," Suk said.

"I am afraid not. There are none. I don't know what will become of our village if this continues. Our young people are beginning to talk about moving away. They think this place is cursed. Maybe this other doctor will discover something?"

Suk's stomach churned. "What other doctor?"

Blood drained from Suk's face. "The one that was just here. I wished you had stopped so I could introduce you. They are from the Hope Center, where Dr. John worked." Suddenly the old man turned sullen. "They also told us terrible news that the good doctor was killed. Maybe this place is cursed."

* * *

Nick had no idea what he was looking for or what he was doing in the bungalow. He was obsessed to find any scrap of information about John before he left this place.

No one was inside. The sitting room and efficiency kitchen were tidy. A laptop sat on the table, left open to a beach scene, the screen saver. Nick hit the return key to wake it up from sleep mode. Its loud beep startled him, and the screen went black with a lock icon that scrolled across it. He decided to not disturb it any further.

The bungalow had two bedrooms. He stepped inside the first. A man's pair of dress shoes lay on the floor at the foot of the bed, and some toiletries sat on the small dresser. The bed was tightly made with two pillows at the head.

Nick opened the top dresser drawer and found a neatly folded pile of men's underwear and socks. It was creepy, snooping through another man's belongings, but Nick found nothing alarming. There was also nothing about FOCO. He shut the drawer and decided to check the other room and get out of there.

The other bedroom smelled of jasmine and had two silk

scarves hanging from the handle of the dresser that had a makeup kit on top. Obviously, this was the woman's room. It, too, was neatly organized and well kept.

This is weird. I guess they must not be a couple. But if they are, they sleep in separate rooms. It was creepier standing in the woman's room. *If someone finds me in here, they're going to think I'm some sort of pervert.*

He opened the top drawer of the dresser, but when he saw lacy underclothing, he shut it quickly. *I shouldn't be in here.*

Nick was about to leave when a book on the nightstand with loose paper sticking out of it caught his eye. He moved around the bed and picked up the leather-bound book. It reminded him of a Bible, but the lettering on the outside was blocky, oriental writing. He opened the book and flipped the pages. They were thin and lightweight like scripture pages. The book was well-worn and reminded him of the Bible Maggie carted around.

He removed the paper and discovered it was a folded map.

He heard people talking outside the bungalow and froze. He didn't move a muscle. Then the voices faded and went away. Nick's heart had been pounding ever since he entered the bungalow, but now it throbbed like the Blackfeet drum. He sat on the bed to steady his weakened knees and his nerves.

Then he unfolded the map. His adrenaline ran wild and his hands shook. The map was of Guatemala. A number of areas were circled and something was written next to each one. Unfortunately, the writing was Asian, and Nick had no idea what any of it meant.

There were large red circles around Flores, San Benito, Tikal, and other Maya sites, as well as a few of the surrounding villages. *Must be just a tourist map.*

Nick carefully folded the map back to the way he found it. He panicked when he realized he had no idea where in the book he had removed it from. *Don't think I would make a very good spy.*

He guessed where the map had been, slipped it in, and put the book back on the nightstand. When he pushed himself up from the bed, he saw something slide from underneath the pillow. It was a handgun with a black handle. He looked around the bedroom and listened for voices. Not hearing any, he carefully picked up the gun.

It was a Glock 26, a 9mm. His father had one, and he'd used it many times at the shooting range in Montana. But this was a smaller version, custom fit for a smaller hand.

Nick hit the clip release and inspected the bullets—hollow points, meant to kill. His head swirled. *Why would a tourist have a gun? How would they ever get it into the country?*

With a loud click, he snapped the clip back into place and started to slide the gun back under the pillow.

Suddenly the floor creaked, and Nick jerked to his feet with the gun still in his hand. He turned to the noise only to receive a crushing blow to his forearm and a foot to his face.

It was the last thing he remembered.

CHAPTER 47

THE SEARCH

Buck watched the time on his phone tick off another minute…4:21. He was outside the hotel with Anna and Miguel. They were worried. When a taxi slowed, their hopes raised and fell when it didn't stop.

"I don't know, guys, I'm not liking this," Buck said, sounding more alarmed than he'd intended. "He knew we had to leave at four o'clock, right?"

"We could split up and walk around to see if we can find him," Miguel suggested.

Buck looked at him like that was the dumbest thing he'd ever heard. "The problem is, Miguel, I don't think our pilots will wait for us for very long."

Buck called Nick's cell phone for the twentieth time, and for the twentieth time, it went straight to voicemail. Buck fretted. "Miguel, go tell your cousin at the front desk that we're going to drive around to look for Nick. If he shows up, tell him to stay put so I can come back and throttle him for scaring the heck out of us."

* * *

The DHL office was about to close, and Suk didn't want to take the time to type out a note. Standing at the desk, he asked for a pen and paper.

He scribbled a note: "Aerosolization works perfectly. No new pregnancies. Work completed. Please advise."

Suk slipped the note into an overnight envelope, scribbled

the address in Seoul, South Korea, he knew by heart, and handed it to the clerk.

* * *

Buck, Anna, and Miguel arrived at the airport an hour late to tell the pilots they wouldn't need their services that day. The pilots were not upset; they'd get paid anyway, and were enjoying a big fat joint. The lead pilot gave Buck his cell number and told him to call if things changed.

"Have you called Maggie yet?" Anna asked Buck.

It was a call Buck dreaded, but Maggie would have expected them to land at the airport already. With his cell phone out of his pocket, Buck dialed her number. She answered on the first ring. "Where are you guys?" There was concern in her voice.

"This is Buck. We're still in San Benito."

"And?"

"Well…I don't want to worry you, but we can't find Nick."

"What?"

"I'm sure there is a good explanation," Buck said, trying to calm her and himself. "We were all together a couple of hours ago. Nick decided to stretch his legs. He must have gotten lost."

"You want me to come there?"

Buck looked at the stoned pilots. "Uh, not right now. I promise to call you back in thirty minutes and give you an update, or sooner if we find out something."

They thanked the pilots again and climbed into the van.

"You think we ought to call the police?" Anna asked both Buck and Miguel.

This time Buck let Miguel answer. "I don't know. I don't think so. I think at this point it would be a waste of time. The police department is kind of a joke here."

"Agreed," Buck said. "Let's head back to the hotel. We can drive around San Benito, check the town street by street. I can't imagine Nick would have crossed the bridge. At this point, I don't know what else we can do."

As they drove through town, out of the tourist area, the neighborhoods became increasingly impoverished. The streets were lined with piles of trash, its stench apparent even with the windows rolled up.

"With the elections next week, the trash company is on strike. There's been no pickup for several weeks," Miguel explained. "It's getting pretty bad. I'm sorry."

Buck saw a blue and white building with a large Red Cross sign. "That your hospital?"

"Yes, sort of. There is another government hospital on the other side of town, but it is terrible. My uncle actually got bit by a rat when he was in the hospital for his diabetes. This is actually a mission hospital. It's called Hospital Shalom."

"I've heard Maggie talk about this place," Anna said. "It's kind of a counterpart to the Hope Center. I think they even share supplies sometimes."

"I guess we should check. Pull over to the curb," Buck directed Miguel.

Buck stepped out of the passenger side of the van and walked into the one-story building.

Miguel looked back over the seat at Anna and smiled. "I'm sorry that Dr. Hart is missing, but I'm glad you're still here."

Because his attention was distracted, Miguel missed the FOCO SUV drive through the intersection in front of them. Buck did not see it either, as he returned from the hospital with his eyes on the ground and got back into the van. "No gringos," he told Anna and Miguel. "Let's head back to the hotel."

CHAPTER 48

WAKING UP

Nick held his face to stop his pounding head. His brain was foggy, as he tried to remember what happened. Had somebody crashed his beloved Porsche and left him trapped in the mangled wreckage? His mind reeled through time and space. He was afraid to open his eyes.

He touched his swollen nose and eye socket. His medical training revived, and he palpated his nose to see whether it was just swollen or actually broken. Then his consciousness drifted away, and he went limp. His unconsciousness won the tug-of-war. Catalepsy, a seductive mistress, pulled him deeper into its well of nothingness. Floating in a void, he saw himself in his doctor scrubs examining a patient's face. Happy to be out of his body, feeling no pain, he beat the air and swam closer. There he was, examining the patient's face, only the face was his face.

* * *

A cold compress stunned his forehead, shocking him back to life like Lazarus rising from the dead. Bright light penetrated his eyelids, and loud noise drummed his ears. His head was aching. He wrapped his head and ears in his arms for safety. Slowly, his consciousness regained control. He lowered his arms and felt his body parts. He was lying flat on his back. His head still ached, and so did his neck and forearm.

"Dr. Hart?"

He heard a voice. His eyelids fluttered. He opened his right eye, but his left was swollen shut.

"Dr. Hart?"

That voice again. Calling Dr. Hart. He was Dr. Hart.

When he was able to focus, he could see kind, dark eyes, and a woman's face. It didn't make sense.

"Can you hear me, Dr. Hart?"

He listened and watched her lips mouth the words, his neurons trying to make a connection between sight and sound.

The woman adjusted the compress on his head. She put a hand against his cheek. "Would you like a sip of water?"

Nick tried to speak, but only moaned and nodded.

She slid her hand under his head and neck and lifted him high enough to sip from the glass. He noticed that she was a small woman, *petite*, that was the word. Out of the corner of his right eye, behind the woman, he saw a taciturn Asian man with a pistol in his hand. Nick's brain clicked. His heart pounded, and bells of danger tolled in his ears.

Recognizing the terror in his eyes, the woman calmed him, "I'm not going to harm you, Dr. Hart. At least not any more than I already have," she smiled.

The woman hurt me? But she's so tiny.

He studied her smile. It was a gentle smile, in stark contrast to the sudden wracking pain that ravaged his face and head.

"Are you the one who hit me?" he choked.

"I'm sorry, Dr. Hart. But you were in my bedroom, and you were holding my gun."

Still hazy, Nick scanned the room. It came back to him—where he was, what he was doing. His heart thumped. He tried to sit up, but with surprising force, woman pushed him back down.

"Please don't get up yet," the woman said firmly.

Nick's mind and body surrendered. He was in no condition to resist.

"What time is it?" he asked, his mind trying to find a lifeline to reality.

The women ignored his question. "What were you doing in our bungalow, Dr. Hart?"

"I'm sorry," he apologized. "I should not have come in here. I was…" He stopped, too tired to explain. "Wait," he started, "how do you know my name?"

"We have your wallet, Dr. Hart. My partner ran your name through our database. We need to know what an orthopedic surgeon from Memphis is doing in Guatemala snooping through our bungalow."

"Database? Who are you? Are you with FOCO?" He asked the last question without thinking, and even in his muddled mind, he saw the woman react to the acronym.

"No, Dr. Hart, we are not from FOCO. We are from the South Korean Anti-Terrorist Agency."

Nick didn't follow politics, but he was pretty sure South Korea was one of the good guys.

* * *

Buck, Anna, and Miguel sat at the lakeside table at Jalapenos. Not even the beautiful day could offset the fear that crept over them.

"I'm not sure I've felt this helpless in a long time," Buck said.

Anna understood what a profound statement that was from a man who had endured so much from combat blast wounds, both physically and mentally.

"Anyone have other ideas?" Buck sighed. "Sitting here doing nothing is killing me."

Anna and Miguel looked down and shook their heads.

The sun reflected off the lake as it started to slip into the horizon. The waiter asked again if they were sure they didn't want anything to eat or drink. Of course they didn't.

Buck's phone sat in the middle of the table and startled them all when it vibrated and rang.

"It's Maggie," Buck told them as he looked at the caller ID. He picked it up. "I'm sorry, Maggie, nothing yet." He didn't mince words. "Yes, we are beside ourselves, too. I think we just have to wait."

Anna heard Maggie's concern, even though she couldn't hear exactly what she was saying.

"Well, sure, we could use the moral support. We'll be there to pick you up." Buck ended the call. "She's joining us first thing in the morning."

* * *

Nick's head still pounded, and when he was able to sit up, he got some relief from the Advil the woman gave him. Something in her eyes made him trust her, that, and she reminded him of Maggie—she had jet black hair pulled in a tight bun, dark eyes filled with understanding, and a soft and beautiful complexion. She also had Maggie's strong spirit.

"Here. Drink some of this. The sugar will do you good," she said, handing him a can of soda from the minibar.

Nick sipped the soda. It tasted good and lubricated his tongue. He told the woman and the man all he knew about FOCO and why he was in her bedroom. The woman's partner remained silent; he sat erect on the other side of the room, his gun tucked in an under-arm holster.

"Again, I'm really sorry," Nick apologized. "I had no business coming into your room. But I was so desperate for answers." He smiled, trying to diffuse the situation. "And I'm sorry I got blood on you." He pointed to blood splattered on her linen pants. He was still trying to comprehend the fact that this bantam woman had knocked him out cold.

He swallowed some soda. "Would you at least tell me your names?"

"Is there anything more you need to tell us?" the woman asked, again, ignoring his question.

What does she want to know?

"What about your friends? We saw you with them at the restaurant. We thought you might be from the U.S. government with the elections here this coming week."

Nick laughed. "Funny, that's is what our taxi driver thought."

The woman did not smile.

"Can't your database tell you all this?" He didn't mean to sound exasperated although she had given him no choice. Then he realized he had not even thought of Buck and Anna until she'd mentioned his friends. They would be worried sick. "I'm sorry," he apologized for sounding rude. "I know this all sounds crazy to you, but Buck is a good friend who brought down stuff for surgery, and Anna is just a kid doing good work here in

Guatemala. Can we at least call them and let them know I'm okay?"

When she didn't respond, Nick took a deep breath and said, "Look, take my phone and look at the pictures of the last few days, and you will see what we've been doing."

Nick's iPhone was on the table next to the man. The woman turned to the man and nodded. The man picked it up and turned it on. When they had searched his pockets for identification and found the phone, they had turned it off. If he were from the CIA, they would instantly be tracked.

"The security number is three four five seven," Nick told him.

The man tapped the numbers and looked through the pictures. He paused at one and stared at it for a long time, trying to decipher what he saw. He turned it toward the woman. Nick caught a look at what they were staring at. It was Isabella standing beside him with her not-yet-corrected clubfeet.

"That's Isabella, one of the kids we fixed," Nick said. It felt like ages ago.

Fascinated by the pictures, the woman took the iPhone, scrolled through a few more, and handed it back to the man. She turned to Nick with her lips pursed, nodded slightly, sighed. "My name is Miss Kim, Katelyn Kim."

* * *

Buck's phone rang again. It was probably Maggie, but Anna and Miguel saw shock on his face when he looked at the phone.

"Oh, my God." Buck answered the phone. "Nick?"

Anna and Miguel shouted with jubilation, then shushed each other so they could hear the conversation.

"You okay? Where are you? Hang on. I'm going to put you on speaker."

Buck, Anna, and Miguel could tell something was not right. Nick's voice sounded hoarse and nasal.

"Guys, I'm okay," Nick insisted. "I just ran into a little problem."

"Where are you?" Buck demanded.

"Really. I'm okay. A little banged up, but okay. I'm at the

Island of Flores Hotel. Miguel, I'm sure you know where that is. We are in the last bungalow on the right…bungalow number…"

Buck heard a woman's voice fill in the blank. "Thirty."

"Did you get that? Bungalow thirty."

"Nick, who's with you? Do we need to call the police?"

"Buck, no police. Please. Really, it's all okay. You know me—I kind of bumbled into a situation. Please just come and get me."

CHAPTER 49

NORTH VERSUS SOUTH

Sergeant Buck did not wait to be invited in. He threw open the door of bungalow thirty with such force, it banged against the wall as he charged in. Katelyn squared off with him and blocked his pathway, totally disarming the big warrior.

Buck regained his composure when he saw Nick sitting in a chair beyond her with a bloodied face and swollen eye. "What the hell is going on here?" Buck shoved the woman out of his way.

"Stop." It was the first word that Nick had heard Katelyn's partner utter.

When Buck looked to his left, he saw a man with a pistol leveled at his head. He stopped in his tracks.

Nick saw the muscles in Buck's arms and shoulders coil like a trapped snake about to strike. He shouted, "Buck, no!"

As the words left Nick's mouth, Buck's hand smashed down on the man's hand and knocked the pistol to the floor. In the same instant, Buck grabbed the man's throat and lifted him up off the ground.

Buck felt something like a lightning bolt hit his throat and collapse his trachea—causing him to instantly release the man and drop to his knees. Katelyn Kim had struck Buck's adam's apple with a spear hand thrust, almost simultaneously grabbed the pistol, aimed it at Buck's head and yelled, "That's enough!"

In the doorway, Anna and Miguel stood in shock, their hands raised in surrender.

"Buck, stop." Nick yelled as he saw Buck's fists tighten again.

Buck and the Asian man glowered at each other. Buck, still on his knees, looked at the woman. She stood at eye level with him, and she backed out of his reach.

"Buck, really, it's okay," Nick persuaded.

"Well, you sure don't look okay!"

"Buck, this is Katelyn Kim and this is, uh…" Nick realized that he didn't know the man's name.

"Mr. Kim," Katelyn said. "No relationship."

"They are from the South Korean Anti-Terrorist Agency. The good guys. And I think they have information for us."

Buck looked warily at the two. "Well, someone help this ol' soldier up then. It's one thing that's hard to do with these worthless legs." He gestured to Anna and Miguel.

* * *

"Now tell me again how you got knocked out by a girl?" Buck hooted. They were all in a good mood after finding Nick.

"I will, only after you tell me how you were brought to your knees by the same," Nick retorted. They all laughed again, including Mr. Kim.

Both Nick and Buck admitted they had never been hit so hard by a woman in all their lives. Nick thought that Katelyn blushed. With her fine Korean features, she resembled a princess more than a warrior.

When the dust settled, the Kims had invited Nick and his team to dinner at the hotel. Nick was still woozy from his concussion, but a frozen pineapple, banana, and mango smoothie hit the spot.

Katelyn changed the subject. "We have been investigating FOCO for a couple of years now. In fact, we were in their office in Seoul last week," she said, poking at the fish on her plate with a fork. "There have been rumors that they are connected to North Korea, but we have never been able to find the connection. If there is one, we suspect that even the current leaders of FOCO in South Korea don't know. The FOCO people have been more than willing to cooperate. But the money trail always ends in Beijing, and the Chinese, of course, give us no further information."

She took a small bite of fish, dabbed her mouth, and continued.

"The problem is, FOCO has been doing many good works around the world, so no one is anxious about making accusations. We heard about North Korean activity here in Central America with some of the elections, and we knew that FOCO had a project here in Guatemala, so we were sent here last week to investigate. So far, we have found very little, except for this man we caught in my bedroom." She smiled at Nick.

"I'm afraid I have told you everything we know," Nick said. "I honestly don't know if there is any connection to the absence of pregnancies in the area and FOCO. We could take you out to one of the villages tomorrow, and you could see for yourselves. Buck, you still have that map?"

Buck pulled the rumpled map from his pants pocket, and Nick unfolded it on the table. He pointed to El Zapote. "We were here yesterday. Like I told you, this is where we saw three men in a FOCO vehicle, but didn't get a chance to talk with them."

He grimaced at Miguel who then looked at his shoes.

"There is another village over here called Cruce Dos Aguadas that we could all visit. I kind of wanted to see another one of the villages anyway," Nick continued.

"Oh, Nick, I meant to tell you," Buck put in. "Maggie is coming here tomorrow morning."

Nick shook his head "I don't think that's a good idea."

"I'll let you tell her that when we pick her up." Buck smiled.

"Miguel, would you be able to take us all?" Nick asked.

"I think so, Dr. Hart. Cruce Dos Aguadas is a little more isolated than El Zapote, but I will ask my uncle to make sure the road is not washed out."

* * *

Suk stirred the coals in the fire pit outside their rental. Large embers of burned paper rose to the sky. He had purged every correspondence, record, and receipt he could find. But he could not bring himself to burn his scientific notebook. He would keep it at least for now.

Someday, the world will know I helped Professor Kwon.

It would be the only thing left. It would be his legacy.

"Boss, you want a beer?" Hwang yelled from the back deck.

"No."

"What time we leaving tomorrow?"

"I want to get away by eight. You think you mongrels can drag yourselves out of bed that early? I want to sweep through all the other villages before we leave. We should get departure instructions any day."

"Cho and I are going into town. Wake us up when you're ready to go in the morning."

CHAPTER 50

LAST TRIP

Maggie was not happy when the team met her at the airport the next morning. She could hardly look at Nick's battered face. The purple bruising had spread around both his eyes and nose. She stood on tiptoes and kissed him on the cheek. "You look terrible. But I'm glad you're okay."

"I had to *adjust* my nose last night in the mirror. I thought I was going to pass out again. How does it look?"

"Like a dog pile," Buck said. "Does your face hurt?"

"Uh—"

"Well, it sure hurts me." Buck made everyone laugh.

The Kims stood off to the side as everyone hugged Maggie.

Greetings aside, Nick said, "Let me introduce you to my plastic surgeon." He pointed to Katelyn.

She bowed politely to Maggie and extended her hand. "I am sorry." She bowed again.

"From what I understand, he deserved it," Maggie replied, "and now I know I can count on you to keep him in line." She gave Katelyn a quick hug.

Katelyn turned to Mr. Kim. "This is my partner, Mr. Kim."

Nick wondered if he had a first name, but since the man had hardly spoken a word, he decided not to ask.

"The Kims want to see one of the villages we told you about last night on the phone, Cruce Dos Aguadas," Nick told Maggie.

"Sure you're up for a road trip?" she asked him.

Nick pulled a bottle of Advil from his pocket and shook it. "Let's go."

* * *

Miguel had borrowed his uncle's seven-passenger van. It was roomier than his and higher off the ground for a more comfortable ride. His uncle had told him the road was passable unless there was a lot of rain. But now, it was clear and sunny.

Buck, with approval from the others, offered Mr. Kim the front passenger seat. He and Nick sat in the middle bucket seats, while the women, whose legs were shorter, had offered to take the back.

"I love your sandals, Katelyn," Maggie told her as they climbed in the van.

"Thank you. I bought them before I left at the Itaewon, one of the main shopping districts in Seoul. You will need to come to Korea someday and go shopping with me."

Nick smiled to himself. *I knew these two were going to get along.*

Nick was glad the road was paved for at least half the two-hour drive to the village. He tried to relax and listen to Maggie and Katelyn talk.

"Forgive me for saying this, I'm just doing my job," Katelyn said. "Last night I looked you up and read about your ministry. I am sorry to hear about your husband, John. It is rare in our business to read about someone so well liked. I am truly sorry."

Nick saw Katelyn squeeze Maggie's hand.

"Thank you." Maggie patted her hand and quickly changed the subject.

"I have always wanted to go to Korea. One of my college friends went there as an exchange student and loved it." Pleasantries aside, Maggie got to the point. "You really think there's a connection to North Korea in this...mess?"

"We cannot be sure. I have been with the Anti-Terrorist Agency for fifteen years now, and we have chased leads all over the world. Sometimes they amount to something and other times not."

Nick tried to do the math in his tired head. He wondered how old Katelyn was. He figured she had to be in her late thirties at least, but with her beautiful complexion, he could not be sure.

"Are the North Koreans really involved in that much terrorism around the world?" Buck butted into their conversation.

"Well, unfortunately, yes. Counterfeiting, computer espionage, sex trafficking. The list goes on. There are indications that the Heartbleed computer virus that infected millions of computers may have originated in the North."

"You guys must hate them," Miguel added, joining the conversation.

"No, actually we don't. We fear some of their leaders, certainly, and dislike the ideology, but hate them, no. You must remember: North Koreans are still Koreans. They are our family. When the Korean War took place, families were often split apart. Many have not seen or heard from each other for many years. We don't hate them; we pray for them every day."

Miguel regretted his comment, but the rest of the crew pondered Katelyn's reply.

"Are you a Christian?" Maggie asked.

"Yes, I am a follower of Jesus."

"Are you from Seoul?"

"Actually, I grew up in Pusan. It's right on the tip of the peninsula. During the Korean War, the North invaded all the way to Pusan before the U.S. came to our aid and pushed them back. My grandfather was captured and taken to the north. My grandmother still lives with my parents in Pusan. We don't know if Grandfather is still alive. Grandmother lives her life as though he is. She is a very strong woman."

"Obviously a chip off the ol' block." Buck nudged Nick.

"My father was in the Korean war," Nick told Katelyn, "but he never wants to talk about it, and I've never really understood why it happened."

"The Forgotten War—that is how it is often referred to around the world, except by those of us who live in Korea. For us, the war is ever present," Katelyn explained. "Even to this day, schoolchildren practice weekly for the possibility of air raids or missiles. In reality, we are still at war; the fragile peace is threaded together with the Korean Armistice Agreement. You know the city of Seoul has almost ten million people and is only thirty-five miles from the DMZ? A handful of short-range missiles from the North could kill hundreds of thousands of people." She paused to gather her thoughts. "As far as why the war happened, that is a much harder question to answer."

A blasting air horn interrupted her speech. It came from a passing bus, packed with people, and forced their van onto the narrow shoulder. Katelyn grimaced at Maggie.

"Everyone all right?" Maggie scanned their faces to be sure. Then she turned to Katelyn. "Please go on. Tell us more."

Katelyn pulled herself together and continued. "Like many parts of the world, there was much conflict over our tiny peninsula. Someday in heaven, we will better understand the battles that rage in certain parts of the earth. The Christians in Korea believe that our home is holy ground, and there is a constant battle between good and evil."

Maggie nodded. "I'm glad that we know who wins."

"Yes, we have faith," Katelyn added, "but until that time, we must continue the good fight. You have to remember that Japan controlled our homeland in the first half of the 1900s. Korea was considered to be part of the Empire of Japan. Unfortunately, when this happened, many of our people were forced into labor in Japan—mineworkers, factories, any menial work and worse, I'm afraid."

She stopped talking when Miguel slowed the van to let a Maya family cross the road.

"Here is a statistic I'm sure many people do not realize," she went on. "When the U.S. dropped their nuclear bomb on Hiroshima, it's estimated that twenty-five percent of the people that died there were actually Korean because it was such an industrial city, and many of the workers were Korean."

"The world sure seems messed up," Nick added.

"During World War II, as the Soviet armies fought Japan and moved south, they invaded parts of China and came into North Korea," Katelyn continued. "You may remember that the ruthless leader of the Soviets at that time was Stalin. As World War II was ending, around 1945, Korea was divided at the 38th parallel, basically between the Soviets and the United States. Stalin installed Kim Il-sung as the leader of the North."

The van left the paved road, hit a large pothole, and bounced violently.

The passengers adjusted, and Katelyn went on. "Kim Il-sung was determined to create reunification with the South with the backing of Stalin's Soviets and Mao Zedong's China. He attempted this by force."

"Talk about an unholy trinity," Buck shook his head and grabbed a handhold to steady himself on the rough road. "Stalin, Mao Zedong and Kim Il-sung."

"Yes, and you can see where that has led us to today."

Everyone contemplated the history.

Finally, Maggie broke the silence. "And you still don't know if your grandfather is alive?"

"No. Even in my line of work, we haven't been able to find out any information."

"Do you have any brothers or sisters?"

"No. Like many Koreans, my parents only had one child. They started me in Tae Kwon Do when I was very young, probably out of fear that the North would invade again. They wanted me to be able to protect myself. I had my black belt by age twelve, and I was on the Korean National team by seventeen."

Mr. Kim spoke up for the first time. "Miss Kim would not tell you this, but she took gold medals in three consecutive World Championships, a true national hero." He said this with pride.

"I guess that makes me feel a little bit better." Nick touched his nose and looked at Buck.

"I was recruited by the National Intelligence Service, the NIS, shortly after that and then after five years transferred to the Anti-Terrorist Agency," she told them, deflecting her colleague's compliment.

Nick looked back at Katelyn and smiled. Still trying to do the math, he realized that she could be close to his age.

How unfair. She looks thirty at most, and I feel sixty.

With the pavement long behind them, the van climbed the steep mountain road. Miguel hugged the uphill side of the road while his passengers peered warily off the edge. At least the chicken bus's last stop had ended with the pavement, clearing the rough road of the possibility of a head-on crash with it. The passengers were relieved until their van met a truck, but Miguel and the driver were able to maneuver around each other. The back of the truck was noisy with people. The driver told Miguel they were villagers from Cruce Dos Aguadas going into town for their monthly shopping trip. Miguel told him they were headed to the village, and the driver said the chief was still there because he didn't like going into town.

* * *

Hwang, Cho and Suk were finally on the road to Cruce dos Aguados.

True to form, Hwang and Cho had come home late and drunk the night before, and Suk had had a difficult time rousing them for their last tour of the villages.

Hwang's erratic driving made for a harrowing trip, and Suk hung on for safety while Cho slept like a baby.

Fantasizing about eliminating Hwang and Cho helped Suk get through the day.

* * *

As Nick's van pulled into Cruce Dos Aguadas, he saw that the village was smaller and more isolated that El Zapote, but just as depressing.

The chief described in detail the lack of pregnancies and how the village was in despair because of it. The chief, a Christian, told them, "It is like satan has gained a foothold, and now the young people have begun to abuse alcohol and drugs. It is like God's design for our lives has been removed, and darkness has crept in."

"Can you tell us about the men from FOCO?" Katelyn asked.

"They have been the one bright spot in our lives, although we have not seen them for a while. The men have been very good to us. They drilled our new well." He pointed to the wellhead and hand pump off the central area. "Every time they came to our village, they would bring us food and supplies for our farm— shovels, hoes, and such. They would not ask anything in return."

"It sounds like they were very helpful," Katelyn responded. "Anything else you can tell us?"

The chief thought for a moment. "I guess the only thing that didn't work out so well was when they gave us a vaccination for the flu, and we all still got sick. Not bad sick, more like a cold. They told us it was probably a reaction to the vaccine. We are perfectly healthy now."

"Yeah, except for having infertility problems," Buck whispered to Nick.

Katelyn looked at Nick and back at the chief. "Anything else you want to tell us?"

"Please pray for my village. If our women don't get pregnant, our village will be no more."

CHAPTER 51

TERROR

"What do you think?" Nick asked Katelyn as they bounced down the mountain road away from Cruce dos Aguados.

"It's so hard to know. Something in my gut tells me that there is something up with FOCO. We located their house in San Benito, and Mr. Kim and I will go there today when we get back to see if we can talk with them."

"Will that be safe?" Maggie asked.

"It's our job," Katelyn reminded her. "Our government believes that the North has been involved in suspicious biological activities, but we have been unable to connect all the dots. Dr. Hart, do you think this history of the vaccination could be related to the infertility?"

"I have never heard of anything like it. People can get sick after a flu vaccination, so it's hard to tell."

"Do you know of any viral disease that causes infertility?"

"Ms. Kim, you are talking to a dumb bone doctor. I'm probably the wrong guy to ask. I've got a good friend back in Memphis who's an infectious disease doc. We could call him."

"Oh shoot," Miguel said, interrupting their conversation.

"What is it?"

He was agitated. "I just saw the glimpse of a car coming up the road." The jungle road curved around the mountain, and sometimes, if the light was right, you could catch sight of a vehicle through the foliage behind or in front. "I don't feel safe. I don't think they can get around us. I'm going back up into that wide spot a little ways back. Wait for them to pass."

Miguel backed up slowly, easing into the wide spot on the side of the road. His passengers held their breath, as well as their seats and armrests—as if that would do any good if the van tumbled off the fifty-foot drop at the edge of the wide spot into the dense jungle. It took only a few minutes to back into the safe spot, but it felt like an eternity.

"You okay, Nick?" Maggie asked. "You're looking a bit peaked."

"I guess I'm okay, but my head's starting to pound."

Miguel stopped the van. They could hear the car coming and waited. He rolled down his window, pulled in his side mirror, and watched, ready to wave the oncoming vehicle past. He glanced up and down his side of the van to make sure there was room to pass.

That was when a large SUV came around the curve in front of them. Nick had his eyes closed, and Buck was busy talking with the women. It was Miguel who recognized the vehicle.

"It's the FOCO Jeep."

Nick bolted upright. His head spun.

"This is going to get interesting," Buck said, sliding open the side door of the van. It was parked so close to the edge that, even in the wide spot, it was difficult to get a foothold on the ground to navigate to the front of the van, so he turned toward the rear. Buck was determined to prevent the men from getting away again. He worked his way to the back of the van and into the road, waving his arms frantically, commanding the SUV to stop.

Cho, in the front passenger seat of the SUV, recognized the big man. "Boss, it's those people who were snooping around El Zapote yesterday." The sun's reflection on the SUV's windshield blocked the North Koreans from seeing Mr. Kim in the van's passenger seat.

Hwang stopped short, staring at the man in the road and salivating like a rabid wolf. "What do you want me to do?"

Suk knew Hwang wanted to run the man down. "Pull up beside the van," he ordered. "Nothing else we can do, you idiot."

Hwang snorted and pulled the SUV alongside the van but didn't plan to stop. The vehicles were inches apart and inches from the edge of the mountain.

Without smiling, Hwang nodded to Miguel. Everyone heard the SUV dislodge a rock at the edge of the road, causing the vehicles to lurch closer. Hwang hit the brakes hard and the Jeep jarred to a stop. The vehicle drivers faced each other, window to window.

Miguel could smell the alcohol on Hwang's breath, but he did not see Cho pull the gun from between the seats.

Cho tensed, still hungover and queasy, his hand clutching the weapon. The gun shook when he saw Buck walking toward the SUV.

Cho's agitation escalated once he saw a Korean, sitting in the van next to Miguel, reach inside his jacket. He panicked, aimed the gun at Miguel's head, and pulled the trigger, showering blood and brain matter on Mr. Kim. Cho shot again, blasting Mr. Kim in his right shoulder before he could get to his own gun. Cho's third shot hit Mr. Kim in the throat.

Anna and Maggie screamed in terror. Katelyn took action, shoved them to the van floor, and sprawled on top of them. Nick dove out the side door Buck had already opened, stumbled, and barely caught himself from going over the edge of the road.

Hwang gunned the SUV forward, smashing into Buck with full force, throwing him off the side of the mountain. Cho continued to fire randomly at the van.

Katelyn kicked the van's side window with such power, it exploded the glass. She pulled her pistol from its holster, leaned out the open window, and fired at the back of the SUV. Anna and Maggie covered their ears to muffle the shots as Katelyn emptied her clip at the departing SUV.

Suk had already hit the floor of the SUV. One of Katelyn's bullets found its mark to the back of Cho's head, and another pierced Hwang's shoulder, shattering his collarbone, causing him to lose control of the vehicle. The Jeep grated against a rocky cutout in the road, bounced through a large rut and back onto the road.

Without thinking, Nick ran after the SUV. He jumped on the driver's side running board and grabbed at Hwang who managed to keep driving, even as Nick clawed at his face and ripped hair from his head.

Hwang steered the SUV into the overgrown brush alongside the road, trying desperately to scrape Nick off the vehicle. The thicket tore at Nick's side but he hung on, grabbing Hwang's thick neck.

The road curved suddenly. Hwang slammed on the brakes and shoved the door open, dislodging Nick's hold and throwing him into the road in front of the Jeep.

"Run him over, you fool!" Suk ordered.

But Hwang was out for blood. He leaped out of the SUV, pulling his huge hunting knife from the sheath on his back. Gripped with rage, he lunged at Nick, slamming him to the ground, knocking the wind out of him.

"I'm going to slice you open like I did your friend," Hwang bellowed.

Breathing hard, Nick's eyes locked on Hwang, watching him wave the knife, knowing it was coming for him. He mustered his strength and rolled to the side of the road.

No sooner than Hwang had leaped from the Jeep, Suk had climbed into the driver's seat. He gunned the SUV, pulled the door closed, stepped on the gas, slammed into Hwang, knocking him to the road just as he was about to lunge and impale Nick who saw the knife fly into the jungle like a missile. With no regard for Hwang, Suk took off up the road.

Hwang gathered his equilibrium and clawed at Nick who staggered to stand but couldn't escape Hwang's grip around his ankles. He desperately tried to kick the big man's hands away, but Hwang regained his strength and pulled Nick under him, grabbing his throat.

Nick gagged as Hwang squeezed his neck. Nick fought for his life, twisting and hammering at the man, using up all his strength. Hwang toyed with him, laughing like a house cat toying with a mouse.

"You American pigs don't know when to quit." Hwang cackled. He loosened his hands to let Nick float to consciousness. "I will let you die when I say so."

When Nick blinked, Hwang tightened his grip again. Nick couldn't breathe and darkness swallowed his vision. He was seconds from passing out. *Help me Jesus.* It was his last thought.

Hwang put a final squeeze on Nick's neck, and when he felt his victim go slack, he let go with satisfaction. Before he could stand and savor his victory, a bellowing cry made him turn to see a mad man coming for him. It was Buck, charging like a maimed jaguar aiming for a kill.

A gargantuan palm tree had broken Buck's fall off the mountain and saved his life. It had taken him a minute to remove his mangled prostheses and another to claw his way up the slope on his stumps. Now his stumps brought him barreling toward the Korean terrorist.

Buck tackled him with full force. He heard Hwang's spine snap. With the Korean writhing in pain, Buck seized a large rock and smashed it onto the side of Hwang's head. As it hit its mark, Hwang howled and blood spurted from his ear.

Buck rolled around and grabbed Nick, pulling his lifeless body to him. He put his mouth over Nick's, exhaled a large breath, and started CPR.

Buck took a breath. "Come on, Nick." He looked up. "Lord, I command life back to his body," he shouted and continued chest compressions.

Finally, Nick gasped, coughed, and threw up.

* * *

When all they could hear was jungle sounds, Katelyn eased the van back onto the road and backed up slowly in the direction the SUV had gone. She stopped when she came to Buck and Nick lying on the road. She got out of the van with her gun drawn, shouting, "Where is the other vehicle?"

"Gone," Buck called back.

Katelyn saw Hwang lying in the road and bent to feel for a pulse. He was dead.

Nick watched Buck stand on his stumps.

"I'd have two shattered tibias, if I still had tibias," Buck said. "This is about the only time in my life I'm glad I was wearing prosthetics."

Nick tried to sit up, still coughing violently.

"Help me get him into the van," Buck yelled. "We need to go after the SUV."

"I don't think so," Maggie said, standing beside the van. "Anna has been hit. She's bleeding pretty badly. We need to get her to a hospital."

CHAPTER 52

IN THE BALANCE

Buck helped Katelyn with the gruesome task of moving the bodies of Miguel and Mr. Kim to the back of the van. They put Nick in the van, and as adrenaline flowed into his cells, he became more and more alert.

He realized Maggie was tending to Anna, her hands covered in blood.

"Oh God, oh God, oh God!" Maggie wailed.

Her wailing in addition to the adrenaline increased his cognizance. He saw Anna sprawled on the van floor with a gunshot to her left upper abdomen. "Oh my God," he echoed Maggie.

Nick struggled to take off his shirt and knelt to help. He put pressure over the wound with his shirt.

Maggie moved to Anna's head and stroked her forehead. "Anna, are you still with us?"

Anna eyes fluttered open. "What happened?"

"Anna, lie still. You've been shot. We're going to get you to the hospital." Maggie looked frantically at Nick.

Katelyn started to help Buck into the van, but he brushed her aside and used his strong arms to pull himself into the front passenger seat. He told her to drive. "Afraid I can't reach the pedals like this," he said.

She climbed in behind the wheel.

"We need to get Anna to care. Urgently." Nick stated the obvious.

Katelyn put the vehicle in drive. "And the plan is?"

Nick looked at Maggie. "We've got to get her to a hospital with an OR. A trauma center would be the best."

Maggie looked frantic. "The closest trauma center is in Guatemala City, an hour to the airport and then an hour and a half plane ride, if we could get one."

"No way," Nick said, looking at Anna's pale face. "Give me another option."

"What about the hospital in San Benito? We saw it yesterday," Buck said.

Nick could tell Maggie was not happy while she considered the suggestion. "It does have a small operating room, but I don't know if they have a visiting surgical team there or not."

"Am I going to be okay?" Anna pleaded.

"We are not going to let anything happen to you," Maggie decreed.

"I'm not sure we have any other option," Nick said. He looked at the blood soaking his shirt and then at Maggie. "Katelyn, how fast can you get us there?"

"Everyone hang on, and we'll see."

* * *

Cho was dead. His corpse slumped against the dashboard. Suk had no idea of Hwang's fate or the people in the van.

"Stupid, stupid, idiot," he shouted at Cho's dead body.

He drove to where the road widened enough to turn around. There was nowhere else to go but back down the mountain. The road ahead dead-ended a kilometer past Cruce Dos Aguadas. Beyond that, the jungle was impenetrable. If he went to the village, the people might see the vehicle with blood splattered on the inside of the windshield and that would invite questions and alarm he preferred to avoid. There was only one way out and that was back from where he'd come.

He grabbed Cho's gun from the floor. His hands shook violently. He had no idea what he would find going back down the road—an enraged Hwang standing in the middle of the road over all the dead white bodies waiting for him, or the others with guns blazing to kill him.

With the pistol in one hand pressed against the steering wheel and the other tightly gripping the wheel, he decided to drive slowly down the road.

* * *

Fortunately, it was only fifteen minutes to pavement. Then, it was forty minutes to San Benito at normal speed. Katelyn aimed to shorten that as she floored the gas pedal and blared the horn to move traffic out of her way.

Nick felt Anna's thready pulse. She came in and out of consciousness, and he knew she may have lost half her blood volume.

Maggie kept checking her phone. "I've got one bar. Finally."

"See if you can get through to the MED," Nick rattled off the number.

Maggie punched the numbers and listened.

For a long moment, there was nothing, then, "It's ringing!"

"Tell them I need to speak with Dr. Carson Moore. STAT," Nick ordered.

"I have Dr. Hart here, and he needs to speak with Dr. Carson Moore right away."

There was a long pause.

"Then connect me to the OR," Maggie demanded.

"Put it on speaker," Nick suggested.

"OR. This is Vangie."

"Vangie, this is Dr. Hart. Put me through to Moore's room."

"Dr. Hart. Longtime no see. How are you?"

"Vangie, I'm afraid I don't have much time. Please put me through," he shouted into the phone.

The phone clicked a few times, and when Nick heard Van Halen playing, he knew he was in the right room. He could hear the sounds of the OR in the background.

"Dr. Hart, I have you on speaker. Dr. Moore is scrubbed in."

"Carson, this is Nick Hart."

"Nick, my friend. I heard you'd gone native. Where are you? You sound terrible."

"Hey, Carson, I hate to interrupt you in surgery." Nick tried to talk as loud as he could, but his voice was still raspy from nearly getting his windpipe crushed. "Sorry, I have no time to chit-chat. I really need your help." Alarm was easy to hear in his voice.

Maggie and Nick heard the OR quiet and the music's volume decrease.

"I'm just doing a boring gallbladder. What can I help you with?"

"I'm in Guatemala. A friend has been shot. Left upper quadrant. Lost tons of blood. We are about twenty minutes away from a hospital."

"Crap, Nick, you have gone native."

"Carson. Please."

"They're going to need a lap. Left upper quadrant? Abdomen or ribs?"

"The entry wound is through the last few ribs. Yes, on the left."

"You know how a bullet can bounce off the ribs and end up anywhere. You better call ahead to the hospital and tell the surgeon to prepare for emergency lap. They've got to open the belly."

Nick glanced at Katelyn who read his look, grabbed her phone, and gave it to Maggie to call Shalom Hospital.

"We're headed to a little mission hospital," he said. "I'm not sure they have a surgeon there."

"Shoot, Nick, how long has it been since you cracked someone's abdomen?"

"Since internship."

"Twenty minutes, you'll be there?"

"Yeah."

"I'm finishing up now. Call me back when you get there. You ready for some real surgery, you dang sawbones?"

* * *

Suk crept down the road. There was no sign of the other vehicle. He was getting close to where the encounter happened. He stopped to check the gun. He took the clip out and was shocked to see it empty. He pulled back the chamber—empty.

Frustrated, he threw the gun at what was left of Cho's head. The useless weapon clattered on the dash.

"You idiot," he yelled and smashed his fist on the steering wheel.

There was nothing else he could do but move forward.

I'll ram them off the road if I see them.

As he came around the curve, all that was left at the scene was a body lying in the dirt. It was Hwang. Suk stopped and got out of the car.

Cautiously looking around, he realized that he was alone, surrounded by jungle noises. He walked down the road a hundred yards to a curve and warily peered around. The other vehicle was gone. He looked over the edge at the place where he thought the large Caucasian man had gone over. Twenty feet down the steep slope he saw bright, shiny metal bars, dirty and bent. When he saw a shoe attached to one of the bars, he realized why the man survived the impact. *Prosthetic legs.*

The only other thing he saw were tracks in the dirt that looked like the man had crawled back up to the road.

As he walked back to his SUV, he decided to dump Cho and Hwang off the side of the mountain, and he realized something else. He was free.

CHAPTER 53

SHALOM

When they pulled up to the front of Shalom Hospital, Nick saw Dr. Becker standing at the door awaiting their arrival. Fortunately, the hospital had answered Maggie's call; unfortunately, there was no visiting surgical team. Maggie had told Nick that Dr. Becker, a retired anesthesiologist, and his wife, an OR nurse, ran the place. They invited surgical teams down for a week or two at a time to operate and minister to the local people.

Dr. Becker pushed a gurney up to the van, and his eyes widened at the sight of all the blood.

"We're in deep trouble here," Nick said, looking at Anna who was ashen and unconscious. There was no time for introductions.

"What's your plan?"

"We're going to have to open her belly. We've got to stop the bleeding if at all possible," Nick said, getting out of the van.

"My wife is preparing the OR. We've got to start some fluids now, or we won't even make it there."

Nick hoped that Dr. Becker, now in his seventies, had seen it all in the forty-plus years that he had administered anesthesiology.

"With her blood loss, her veins are going to be impossible to find. What about a central line?" Nick suggested.

"I've got a better idea." Taking large trauma shears, Dr. Becker cut off Anna's pants. All her clothing would eventually be cut off anyway. He swiped an area below her knee with alcohol and plunged a trocar deep within her proximal tibia; the pain made Anna moan.

Buck looked at Nick inquisitively.

"It's an intraoseous IV," Nick explained. "Smart. We dump a large volume of fluid into the bone, and it goes right to the vascular system. We've got to get her volume up, or her heart will stop with nothing to pump."

Nick looked up as Becker plugged in the IV fluid bag, and a steady stream flowed in.

"That will do for now. I'll try to slip in a central line when you guys are prepping her for surgery. I'm afraid it's just me and the Missus here today. You're going to need some help," he looked at Maggie, Katelyn, and Buck, who stood a little over four feet tall without his prostheses.

"Maggie's going to scrub with me. She used to help John in the OR."

The team wheeled Anna to the operating room. Nick handed Katelyn his phone and told her to call Carson Moore. He gave her the number. He heard her talking with Moore, telling him the situation.

The team lifted Anna onto the OR table. The jolt and the fluids brought her to consciousness. As Becker started a large-bore IV in her arm, Maggie held her and kissed her face. "Lord Jesus, protect this child."

Anna looked in Maggie's eyes. "I'm not afraid," she whispered.

"You guys better start rockin' and rollin'." Moore's voice came through the speakerphone. Nick could hear the frustration in his voice and knew he wished he was there.

"She's going to sleep now," Nick told him as Becker injected the anesthetic into the IV.

"Nick, I'm thinking that the bullet may have hit her spleen if she's losing that much blood," Moore said. "At least I'm hoping. If it turned north to her heart, this will be a very short operation," he said soberly. "So let's take a tour to her spleen first thing."

Nick and Maggie did not bother changing into scrubs and sprayed antiseptic foam on their hands for a prep. Becker slipped in an intratracheal tube and placed Anna on the ventilator, while his wife washed off Anna's chest and abdomen with betadine.

Nick and Maggie put on sterile gowns and gloves and hung a large lap drape over Anna.

"You guys there yet?" Moore yelled through the phone. "Your friend's not going to be very happy with the incision, but, Nick, just do a full-length laparotomy incision from her chest to her pubis. You're going to have to see everything."

Maggie handed Nick the scalpel. He took a deep breath. "Jesus, help us."

The scalpel plunged through Anna's delicate skin, exposing the thin, fat layer, and took the incision right down to the abdominal musculature. "I'm down to fascia," he called into the phone.

"Okay, Nick. Split through the linea alba, the fascia that runs up and down from the sternum to the pubis. Curve around the navel."

Nick followed the instructions, being careful to not go too deep and enter the bowel.

"You should see the greater omentum, the fat layer covering the bowels."

"Oh my God!" Maggie cried out.

"And?" he yelled.

"There's a ton of blood in here!" Nick cried, terrified.

"It's okay. Keep going."

"Her pressure is really dropping, guys," Becker hollered.

"Nick, reach up in the left upper quadrant right under the diaphragm. I want you to sweep your hand up and out. You should feel a softball-size organ as you go. Pull this right out into the wound. That's the spleen. Remember, its blood supply is a pedicle of vessels that feed into it. If the spleen is bleeding, pinch off those vessels. If not…I'm afraid…"

Nick reached up under the diaphragm—blood soaking through his gown sleeve—the pressure causing blood to splash onto the floor.

"Oh my God. Oh Jesus," Maggie cried in prayer.

Sweat poured from Nick's forehead.

"What do you see?" Moore shouted through the phone. "Nick?"

It seemed an eternity until Nick withdrew his hand, holding an angry-looking organ, blood pouring from part of it. Quickly, he pinched off the vessels running to it. The bleeding stopped immediately.

The room erupted with a cheer.

"Thank God," Moore said.

"I hate to rain on your parade, guys, but her blood pressure is eighty over nothing, and we need to hope that's the end of the bleeding or else we're going to lose her," Becker broke the joy. "Suck up as much of her blood as you can, and we'll give it back to her."

Nick looked up and realized the Beckers had wisely hooked a blood saver unit to the suction, and they could filter and return Anna's own blood to her.

Moore instructed Nick on how to clamp the vessels and tie them off with suture. Then Nick took Mayo scissors and cut the organ free. Fortunately, it was an organ she could live without. Maggie held out a surgical pan, and he dropped it in.

"Done," Nick pronounced.

"Okay, good deal, my friend. Well done," Moore said. "We may turn you into a real surgeon yet. Let's run the bowel now and look at the other organs to see if a fragment could have hit anything else."

Moore walked him through each quadrant and system. Besides sucking out large clots around the abdomen, Nick and Maggie could find no other damage.

"Carson, I don't see any other damage."

"Okay. That's awesome. Let's get her closed up and off that table."

Nick looked up at Becker. "Well?"

He shook his head. "I don't know. Her pressure is pretty low. She's hanging on by a thread."

Dr. Hart, the surgeon, had been running on high-octane adrenaline. Suddenly it occurred to Nick that it was his dear friend Anna whose life hung in the balance; it was Anna who had barely survived the surgery. It was personal, and he had no idea if her brain suffered damage from anoxia, or if their hasty surgery would cause her to die a horrible death from a raging abdominal infection. Worst of all, it was his fault for letting her come with them. With his head spinning, Dr. Hart ripped off his mask, and Nick puked into the garbage can behind him.

CHAPTER 54

BLOOD OF LIFE

"I hate seeing what I did to her," Nick said, looking at Anna's toned abdomen with an angry scar running its full length. After they had closed the large abdominal incision with surgical staples, Maggie cleaned the blood from Anna's body.

"She's alive," Maggie said.

"I'm trying to keep her pressure up as well as I can, but I'm afraid she's pumping more saline than blood cells," Becker added. "I will keep her in an induced coma for now. It will be easier on her heart. I'm sorry we don't have a respirator. I can support her breathing on the anesthesia machine for now, but we need to get her to a place that does."

"What do you think?" Nick asked Maggie.

Maggie wiped a smudge of dirt from Anna's forehead and sighed loudly. "Oh Lord, what have we done?" She used her shoulder to wipe a tear from her own eye. "I need to call her parents to let them know what happened. They need to know."

"Your friends are outside," Becker's wife said. "Let me cover her up and bring them in. We need to pray together," She placed a dressing over the wound and pulled a blanket over Anna's pale body. Then she called Buck and Katelyn into the OR.

Buck had found a wheelchair and rolled in anxiously. Katelyn followed.

When he saw Anna's ghostly face and the breathing tube down her throat, Buck burst into tears. He wheeled to the OR table and put his hand on her shoulder. "Oh, Anna, I am so sorry," he sobbed. "Please forgive me."

The team gathered around the bed and laid their hands on Anna.

"Jesus, help us," Maggie cried. "We need you, Father. Breathe life into Anna. Spare this child, Father."

"Yes, Father, we ask for your love and mercy to fall on her," Becker added.

Becker's wife stomped her foot, "We command the grip of death to let go of Anna, in the powerful name of Jesus."

Nick's mind swirled. He stumbled for the door. Thinking he was going to vomit again, he raced out the back door of the small hospital. Darkness filled his vision, and he fell to his knees in the courtyard. Severe pain in his knees kept him from passing out, and he rolled on his side, acutely aware of the crushing pain in his chest. It felt like every sorrow, every mistake, every regret crushed his chest. He couldn't breathe.

Was this how it was all going to end? Here in this stupid little hospital?

He knew loneness, but never like this. Emptiness and fear were swallowing him.

"Help me," he cried between gasps. He struggled to speak and clutched his chest.

Grief and shame tore at his mind.

What have I done? What have I not done? Things done, things left undone.

Deep sorrow inundated him as he gasped and sobbed. His body shook violently. He coughed, and the coughing nauseated him. His stomach heaved. He rolled on his other side and curled into a fetal position.

"Father, forgive me," he whispered, his lips quivering. "Of all the people I know, she does not deserve this. Oh God, let me take her place." He sobbed. "Lord, I offer my life for hers. Take me, Father, that she might live. Forgive me, Father, for my sins. Forgive me for living my own life and not realizing who you are. Please, Father, save her."

Nick broke into loud sobs.

Unbearable fear gripped his heart and visions of his recent dreams swamped his mind. The raging storm of his imagination and the inability to find John fueled Nick's desperation. "God, help me!"

As the words filled his mouth, he saw a vision of John calling to him to take shelter amongst the rocks. The scripture in John's office scrolled like a banner across his cerebellum: *'The Lord is my rock and my fortress and my deliverer; The God of my strength, in whom I will trust.'*

It was taking all his strength to fight it, to consciously ignore what he understood in his heart, what his analytical brain resisted. His mind reeled back to Tikal where he saw Anna standing by the large sacrificial rock where John had taken his last breath. He heard her say: *The only divine King I know is Jesus.*

He listened to his heart. "Jesus…save me," he said.

Nick surrendered.

The words lifted the pressure off his chest. His clenched fists and his legs relaxed.

Nick was no longer afraid. He realized that Maggie was sitting beside him with her hands on his head. Emotion welled inside him, and he struggled to think and to speak. She stroked his hair, and he wept.

Finally, when he was able to speak, he said, "Maggie, I am so lost. I feel like I have so blown it. I haven't lived up to anyone's expectations of me. I'm not John, I'm not a good enough surgeon, I'm not the perfect son, and I'm not a good friend. I don't know what to do." He looked into her eyes, pleading for answers. He saw compassion.

She pulled his head onto her lap and let him grieve.

His body continued to relax as she wiped tears from his face.

"You only have to be who God made you, nothing more," Maggie said, leaning over him and kissing his forehead.

* * *

The sun lay low on the horizon when Suk parked down the road from their rental. He had wondered if he would have visitors and was not surprised to find them. Two local police cars sat in front of the house, their lights flashing.

Suk hoped they would not be smart enough to decipher any of his scientific writings, even if they found the hidden research book.

He had to make a decision. Should he risk hiding out somewhere in town for the day and then go back to the house and get his book, or should he set off immediately and work his way out of the country? Mexico was close to the north, but the only legitimate road to Mexico was six hours to the west, and the border could be much more difficult to cross.

Belize was only an hour and a half drive. After seeing the city of Melcho de Mencos at the border, he imagined it would be simple enough to find someone to pay to take him across undetected.

He looked at his watch. The DHL office would be closed now. He was relieved. Would he even want to send a note to the professor telling him of Hwang and Cho's missteps? He was confident that nothing at the house would point to North Korea, especially if the bumbling, local police investigated it.

Looking through the trees surrounding the house, Suk knew it was time to go. He hoped someone would feed the ferrets.

* * *

Maggie wiped her eyes as she hung up the phone. Anna's parents had been shocked and afraid and livid almost simultaneously. Anna's father, a high-powered attorney in Alabama, had emptied both barrels of anger and frustration at Maggie.

"There will be hell to pay. Why in the world would you allow Anna to go to that part of Guatemala?" he had raged. He'd closed by telling Maggie they'd catch the first plane to Guatemala. She was unable to tell them if they would be retrieving Anna's body or bringing her home.

It was one of the most uncomfortable calls Maggie had ever had to make, but she understood. The team did, too.

Her next call was almost as uncomfortable. It was to the local drug cartel. Nick told her that if Anna was going to have any chance at surviving, they needed to get her out of San Benito. There was no way she would survive a five- or six-hour ambulance ride to Guatemala City or Quetzaltenango. Tikal was about equal distance between them. Guatemala City had more to offer as far as an Intensive Care Unit, but the Hope Center had a respirator, and they would have more control of her care.

Most ICUs crawl with antibiotic-resistant bacteria that kill patients more often than what sent them there. Because of that risk, the team decided it was best to take Anna to the Hope Center.

The fastest way back was by helicopter, and the drug cartel's helicopter was the fastest and the closest. Fortunately, a year ago, John had saved the life of the son of the cartel leader. The boy had had a ruptured appendix. It was time to call in that chip.

"They can be here in forty-five minutes," Maggie told the team as she hung up. "I told them what you said, Dr. Becker, to land on the street in front of the hospital."

"Great. I wish we had blood to give her. I'm afraid we don't keep it here. Do you happen to know her blood type?"

Maggie shook her head, "I'm afraid I don't."

Katelyn spoke up. "I am O negative. Doesn't that make me a universal donor?"

Becker looked at Nick. "It used to. Folks can still have a violent reaction to it. Nick, what are your thoughts?"

"We've really moved away from it at the trauma center. It's just so easy to give patients an exact match. It's risky, but it's always a balance between risk and reward, isn't it?"

"Her pressure is still really low, and her heart is pumping as fast as it possibly can. I think it is worth the risk," Becker said.

"I think so, too," Nick agreed.

Katelyn rolled up her sleeve. "Let's do this."

* * *

Suk was shocked at how simple it had been to get into Belize. The official border crossing was on the main road and was heavily guarded and difficult to cross. But ten blocks south, he was able to simply walk across the street and into Belize.

A man in the local cantina had been eager to help, and the FOCO SUV was more than enough payment. Suk was instructed to walk two miles down the dirt road to Benque Viejo Del Carmen where he would see a Pizza Hut on the main road.

He was to wait there for a man to pick him up and take him into Belize City. From there, he could go anywhere in the world. Cash would make any visa problems disappear.

CHAPTER 55

IT IS DONE

The dawn of a new era was upon them. Without firing a shot, Pyongyang would become the rightful center of society. Pak stared at the note from the courier. The aerosolization of the M2H1 virus was successful. Now all that was left was the release.

The courier stood at attention in front of Pak's desk, clueless as to how the world was about to change. Pak took a pad of paper from his desk and began a note. Professor Kwon had told him what equipment the offices should purchase. The Guardian 1500 mosquito sprayer was more than adequate. About the size of a small generator, it was portable, easy to use, and easier yet to conceal.

His note would instruct their man in Seoul to have each office purchase the sprayer. The offices would receive packages containing liquids for the sprayers in several weeks. Office workers would not be told what they were spraying; they would do as they were told. Sending the fine mist off the top of their respective office complexes would infect hundreds of thousands a day—millions by the end of the week. The world changing mist would waft through the air undetected and unnoticed.

Such a stark contrast to an atomic explosion!

Pak gave the note to the courier who snapped to attention, turned on his heels, and left the office.

The Noah Initiative had begun. Pak folded Suk's note and tucked it in his sports jacket pocket. Kwon would want to see the news first hand.

Pak leaned back in his chair. Now that the project was all but finished, he was sad as well as relieved. He could only guess at how long it would take for the virus to affect the world economy. It would have been faster to detonate a series of nuclear bombs around the globe. Spraying the virus was like dropping millions of microscopic blasts on the population. The Noah Initiative may not have been as fast, but it was cleaner and just as effective. All he could do was wait.

CHAPTER 56

DARKNESS

Darkness swallowed the night. They heard the thunderous thumping of the large helicopter, but didn't see it until it was directly overhead, and the pilot switched on a flood of landing lights.

Dirt and garbage swirled as the craft settled on the street. Once the rotors slowed, the team quickly moved Anna from the OR to the helicopter. There was enough room to squeeze her stretcher between the seats. Nick and Maggie sat near Anna's head to guard her airway and rhythmically squeeze the Ambu bag that breathed for her.

Katelyn helped Buck out of the wheelchair and into a seat.

Nick was shocked at what drug money could buy. The helicopter was accented with Birdseye maple, and all the seats were covered with soft Italian leather. Despite their arsenal of weapons, the drug men were helpful and polite.

The helicopter flew low over the treetops, something the drug men were probably accustomed to. It turned in a steep bank and soon landed at the front of the Hope Center. The cartel men helped carry Anna's stretcher into the hospital.

Anna was stable and showed no sign of a transfusion reaction. The blood helped bring her pressure up, but there was no way to assess her neurologic status until they woke her.

Carmen met them to manage her pulmonary care. As she hooked Anna to the respirator, she kept looking at Maggie and Nick.

"You don't look so good yourselves," she told them.

It was the first time Maggie really looked at Nick since the incident. His nose was a little crooked, and his face was swollen and bruised, as was his neck from Hwang's strangling claws. Somewhere along the way, the white of an eye had hemorrhaged.

Maggie hugged him. "We have done all we can for now," she told him. "Why don't you go take a shower and get some rest? I'll stay here with Anna, and we'll call you if anything changes. You really need to rest."

Nick was too exhausted to argue.

* * *

His respite was restless and short, but at least he had been able to sleep. He looked at his watch as he walked to the hospital: 3:33. A few short days ago, the clock in Miguel's van had read the same. It was Anna who had said she loved the number because it always reminded her of Jeremiah 3:33: *'Call to me and I will answer you and tell you great and unsearchable things you do not know.'*

Miguel was dead, and Anna's life hung in the balance.

How life can change in the blink of the eye.

It gave him little comfort, even though Anna was the one who loved reminding them of that very thing. It was the fragility and uncertainty of life, in part, that motivated her to share Jesus with people. She often used Jesus' own words from John 14:6: *'Jesus answered, "I am the way and the truth and the life. No one comes to the Father except through me.'"*

She was a beautiful, young woman who carried a confidence and knowledge of heaven, more than anyone he knew, except Maggie.

Father, let me know you like that.

Nick walked to the room where they had created their own ICU. Outside the door sat five of the older girls from the orphanage, wearing pajamas and wrapped in blankets. They looked up and smiled. He tried to return a smile and entered the room where he saw the whole team, including Buck and Katelyn, still gathered around Anna. Had he been the only one who had chosen to sleep? Guilt and shame swept over him.

The lights of the room had been dimmed, and Anna's regular heartbeat echoed from the heart monitor—the respirator rhythmically pushing air into her lungs. Maggie and Katelyn stood on each side of her bed, softly singing an old hymn. Carmen sat near the head of the bed watching the monitors, and Buck sat near the foot of the bed, bowing his head in prayer.

Anna was surrounded with love.

Buck looked terrible, his eyes were swollen and red. As the self-appointed protector for Anna, he had taken her injury extremely hard. He did not even look at Nick and continued to stare at the floor.

Both Maggie and Katelyn smiled at Nick as he came to Anna's bedside. He patted Maggie on the back. "How is she?"

She looked at Carmen and the monitors and back at Nick. "She has remained relatively stable. Thanks be to God."

Nick felt of Anna's forehead; it was warm and clammy.

Carmen spoke and Maggie translated. "I think there has been a slight reaction to the blood, but the worst is over, and the blood has allowed them to turn the respirator down. She's not requiring near as much oxygen as before."

"Carmen thinks we should start weaning her off the narcotics in the morning and see if she starts breathing on her own," Maggie said. "That will tell us volumes about her neurological status. She thinks the faster we can get her breathing tube out, the better."

Nick sighed with some relief. It was all good news, but it would be a miracle if she survived. "I see you have your young prayer warriors at work outside."

"Are they really?" Maggie asked.

"You didn't ask them?" Nick questioned.

She smiled like a proud mama. "It comes so naturally to them. It's just part of who they are."

"Why don't you guys get some rest? I'm feeling better. Let me take my shift."

Maggie smiled at him. "You look in a mirror yet? You still don't look so good."

"Yeah, thanks a lot. You should see the other guys." He smiled and looked at Katelyn.

"How about I go make some coffee?" Maggie said. "I don't think I could sleep anyway,"

"Me either," Katelyn added.

"Buck, you should at least go get some sleep," Nick told him.

Buck just shook his head.

CHAPTER 57

REGRET

Suk's hands trembled as he lit a cigarette. His half-eaten breakfast sat cold in front of him. He glanced nervously around the restaurant. No one seemed to pay him any mind. A young couple in beachwear and flip-flops sat near him, oblivious to the world around them. Two couples sat at a four-top behind them, drinking coffee and casually chatting in the morning sun.

"*¿Si Quieres más café?*" The waitress startled Suk as she came up behind him to pour steaming coffee into his cup.

"No," Suk snapped at her, loud enough that one of the tourists glared at him.

The waitress shrugged, murmured something, and moved to the next table to fill cups.

Suk fumbled for his sunglasses, pulling them down from the top of his head and sliding them over his eyes. He looked over the water. The Caribbean Sea extended endlessly before him, emptying into the great Atlantic.

Like the vast ocean, his future stretched out before him. But instead of feeling liberated, he felt trapped by foreboding anxiety.

Why do I feel this way?

Suk shook his head to clear it.

I have done my job well. Professor Kwon must be proud of our accomplishments.

He took a long drag from his cigarette. He exhaled a large cloud of smoke and sniffed at the air.

What is that smell? He sniffed the air again and closed his eyes.

He saw Hwang standing over the doctor's body with the bloodied knife in one hand and the still-beating heart in the other. The musky smell of blood and the dankness of the jungle filled his nostrils. A hint of sulfur seemed to burn his nose.

Screams from the man and the howler monkeys resounded in his ears. His eyes frantically searched the restaurant. *Why are people looking at me?*

Panic assaulted Suk's brain. He jumped to his feet, tipping over the chair, and ran from the restaurant.

CHAPTER 58

THE BATTLE

Buck and Katelyn watched the pilot of the corporate jet do a flyby over the small landing strip at the Quetzaltenango airport. Seemingly satisfied, he made the jet fly a wide arc over the mountains and swooped down onto the runway, the engines roaring in reverse thrust to stop.

As a senior partner, Anna's father had the firm's jet at his disposal. The firm's satellite office in Washington, D.C. woke the ambassador to Guatemala in the middle of the night, and the clearance to fly into Guatemala came early that morning.

Katelyn wheeled Buck to the plane as it rolled to a stop. The door lifted open and the stairs swung down. Anna's father, formally dressed in a navy blue business suit, marched down defiantly. Anna's mother appeared at the door, clutching a tissue to her nose. Except for the fact that she looked like she had been crying, she could have been Anna's sister.

Buck put his hand out to the man. "Sir, I'm Buck Hansen. I'm—"

"Take me to our daughter," he demanded, walking past the wheelchair and ignoring Buck's hand.

* * *

Anna's mother had not stopped crying since they got to Anna's bedside. Anna's father sat next to the bed holding Anna's hand. No amount of power or money could ease the pain of seeing their child fighting for her life. The Guatemalan heat had forced him to remove his jacket and loosen his tie, and he sat red-faced, staring at the floor.

Anna looked terrible, and her vital signs reflected the danger she was in. One of an ICU patient's enemies had come—edema—and it was everywhere. Her face was so engorged—her eyes swollen completely shut. Fluid bubbled out from around her breathing tube. It was a constant struggle to keep her breathing tube free of the fluid leaking from her lungs. If edema caused her brain to swell, she would be dead soon.

Nick wondered if they had missed something. *Could a bullet or rib fragment have penetrated the diaphragm and entered the heart or lungs?*

He listened again to the different quadrants of her chest while checking the monitors at the head of her bed.

Blood pressure 78/59

Pulse 135

Oxygen Saturation 89 percent

All terrible and it was worse that they were trending downward.

Nick was not an intensivist, someone trained in the care of the very sick in ICU, but he knew she was in trouble. Consulting with Dr. Moore throughout the evening and even with Anna's father's own cardiologist, airlifting her out of the Hope Center was out of the question. There was no way she would survive the flight.

The other doctors suggested an IV drip of Levophed, a type of norepinephrine, to keep her pressures up. It was fortunate that Carmen was able to secure some from the local hospital. Anna's blood pressure leveled off, and her brain and vital organs were getting blood flow. But it was at the expense of blood flow to her arms and legs. Nick recalled more than one patient losing a finger, toe, or worse from the medication. But at this point, it was a necessary risk.

He looked at the Foley bag that collected her urine from a catheter. The urine was dark, and the volume was low; her kidneys were shutting down.

Nick looked at Anna's father and then at her mother. She must have recognized the signs in Nick's eyes. She cried sharply, startling her husband.

"Maggie will have the chest x-ray developed shortly. Maybe that will give us some answers," Nick tried to reassure them.

Anna's father's head drooped with a nod, and her mother dabbed Anna's forehead with a damp cloth.

Nick knew anyone who has cared for a family member or a friend in ICU understands that it becomes a place of anxiety and fear. A place of great loneliness and hopelessness, seeing their loved one strapped to the bed with tubes coming out of every orifice, lying motionless with their chest rising and falling with only the aid of the respirator. There are few other places that produce such a great sense of helplessness—blood pressure and pulse rates rise and fall, one step forward, two backward, and monitors constantly go on and off, reminiscent of the great battle.

Nick had treated many patients who barely remembered recovering. They often woke up in a room weeks later wondering what had happened to them, not knowing their family had spent sleepless nights and agonizing days at the bedside, watching the moment-to-moment battle unfold.

This was no different.

Nick patted Anna's arm. *Fight, Anna, fight. If only there was more I could do.*

Nick smiled at Anna's mother and walked toward the door.

He was almost through the door when he heard it. He jerked around and saw that Carmen heard it, too. She stood looking at the heart monitor. Anna's heart rhythm had changed from a constant sinus rhythm to an irregular beat. With all the fluid she was losing into her tissues, her electrolyte balance was tipping.

"Get Maggie," Nick yelled out the door.

Nick rushed to Anna's side and looked frantically at Carmen as Anna's heart flipped into ventricular fibrillation. Her heart quaked in her chest, pumping no blood.

Both Carmen and Nick recognized it immediately. No translation was necessary. Carmen ripped the cardio version paddles from their cradle on the anesthesia machine and thrust them into Nick's hands. She pulled the blanket off Anna, exposing her bare chest, and then she quickly squirted lube onto the paddles Nick held.

"Everyone, take a step backward and let go of Anna and the bed!" Nick yelled.

Carmen nodded at Nick, but he recognized the sound of a fully charged defibrillator. He pressed the paddles onto Anna's chest and pushed the buttons.

There was an audible thump as Anna's body spasmed and jumped from the shock.

"Oh my God!" Maggie screamed as she raced into the room.

Nick and Carmen's eyes were locked on the monitor, trying to will the erratic line to become a normal heartbeat.

No change.

Nick dropped the paddles on the bed and began chest compressions.

"Tell me when I have done two minutes," he yelled at Maggie.

Nick saw Anna's mom fall to her knees.

"Two minutes," Maggie shouted.

Nick stopped, and they all stared at the monitor.

No change.

He grabbed the paddles as Carmen reset the charge.

"Stand back," he ordered everyone and pressed the button. Anna's body flailed and a large plug of mucus rose up in her breathing tube. Carmen suctioned it out and immediately turned back to the monitor.

No change.

Nick restarted chest compressions. "Come on, Anna."

He was about to tell Carmen to give her a milligram of epinephrine, but she was already drawing up a syringe. "Epinephrine?"

She nodded and injected the medication into the IV.

"Two minutes," Maggie told him without being asked.

Nick did a few more compressions to make sure the medicine had been circulated. Then he grabbed for the cardio version paddles.

No change. Anna was dying.

Nick placed the paddles on her chest. Everyone stepped back without being told, and he discharged the voltage.

No change.

He continued chest compressions and saw Carmen digging

in her medicine drawer, searching for another medication. "Amiodarone?" he asked.

She shook her head. "Lidocaine. Amiodarone…no." She waved her finger, suggesting they did not have the medication.

Lidocaine would have to do.

They were losing the battle.

"Epinephrine?" Nick asked Carmen. She looked down at her watch, quickly calculating the time. She nodded and reached for the syringe.

Nick continued chest compressions, and even though his arms ached, there was no way he was going to give up. His mind scanned through the algorithm for treating v-fib. They were running out of options.

"Two minutes," Maggie told him, but it was almost irrelevant. At this point, blood flowing to Anna's brain was running low. As long as the monitor showed any activity, he decided he would continue to shock. He continued compressions for five more cycles.

The lube on the paddles was gone, and he held them out to Carmen to replenish it.

He turned back and placed the electrodes on Anna's chest and almost pushed the buttons without thinking. He saw Maggie run to the foot of the table. Then he saw a small tuft of hair at Anna's feet. In the chaos, one of the orphans had wandered in and managed to press her face up against the bottom of Anna's pale foot.

Protecting the child from electrocution from the shock, Nick pulled the paddles off Anna, and Maggie swept the child into her arms. "Oh, mija, you should not be in here."

Nick replaced the paddles and was about to yell clear.

That is when he heard it. They all heard it. The beautiful, rhythmic beating of Anna's heart. Carmen squeezed Nick's hand, and they all turned to the monitor.

Normal sinus rhythm.

CHAPTER 59

MIRACLE

Nick sat on the floor, exhausted, and Maggie held the orphan, now asleep. It was clear—the child had ushered in the presence of God and a miracle.

"Miracles are funny things," Maggie whispered. "There's no way to wrap your head around them or explain them. They just are. It's like catching a glimpse of something, only to have it disappear when you try to look for it."

Nick's medically trained mind wasn't so sure, but the evidence was staring him in the face. The urine collection bag hanging from the side of Anna's bed was quickly filling. Her kidneys were working. He heard her regular heartbeat bleeping from the monitor. He looked again and saw that her blood pressure was solid at 124/68 and her pulse was steady at 85.

Could it have been the mucus plug that was dislodged during resuscitation? The medication? Something else?

Anna's mother hugged everyone she could get hold of. Anna's father pressed his face against Anna's and kissed her forehead over and over. Tears streamed down his corporate face.

Why am I having such a hard time understanding this?

Nick's mind swirled. He looked at the clock on the wall. Thirty minutes ago, he was doing chest compressions. His analytical mind ran through the *what ifs* and wondered what landmines lay ahead. His tired body was bound to the floor, but his buoyant heart leapt with joy.

* * *

The morning wore on in a blur of exhaustion and relief. Everyone was too tired to leave the room, but it was clear Anna's life was spared. As her narcotics wore off, she opened her eyes, shifted her body, and tried to speak around her breathing tube. Relieved as they were, it was terrible to stand at her bedside to watch. Her lungs were not quite ready to work on their own; in the haze of narcotics and trauma, her face filled with anxiety, and she pleaded with her eyes to understand what was happening.

Carmen humanely titrated her narcotics, adjusting them so Anna could sleep and allow her body to rest.

By afternoon, Maggie took charge. She ordered everyone out of the room to eat and rest. But Carmen and Anna's mother refused, and Maggie was smart enough not to push.

CHAPTER 60

RECOVERY

The following morning before breakfast, Maggie rose to bless their meal. The team and Anna's parents were still unbalanced from exhaustion. Their giddiness was fueled by Anna's continued improvement and lots of coffee.

All the orphans and the team gathered in the cafeteria, except for Carmen who was starting to wean Anna off the narcotics.

"We have so much to be grateful for this morning," Maggie said. Her voice cracking with tears. "Anna is getting better," she told the children. "God is so good." Maggie put her hand on her heart.

The children erupted with cheer and shouts of praise to God.

Not realizing how famished they were, everyone dove into the meal, including Nick, even though his throat was still sore when he swallowed.

When everyone was chewing in silent content, Katelyn spoke. "I hate to break this joy, but I need to tell you that I am headed back to Tikal today. I have been communicating with the authorities and the local police about the men in the FOCO SUV. The police found two of them dead on the road to the village. The third is missing. The police searched the house they were apparently renting and found very little information. There is much we don't yet understand."

She took a sip of water. "The Beckers were kind enough to make arrangements with the funeral home in San Benito, but I…" she lowered her voice so the children could not hear. "But I need to make arrangements for Mr. Kim to get home."

As joyful and hungry as Nick was, the reminder of what they had left behind hit him hard, and he lost his appetite. The thought of Miguel's mother, who was fighting end-stage cancer and had now lost her son, was unbearable. He had been so focused on Anna that he had pushed everything else from his mind.

Katelyn was right. There was still so much to do.

"I am so sorry about Mr. Kim," Nick told Katelyn.

"Yes, he was a very honorable man, a good man. He has left a wife and a young daughter behind."

The table went quiet as they contemplated this.

"I am so sorry," Maggie said and put her arm around Katelyn's waist.

"Is your Agency sending help? You can't go alone," Nick insisted.

"They are. They will be here in a few days. But I'm afraid our investigation can't wait."

"One of those..." Nick was going to swear, but saw the children looking at him. "One of those bad guys is still out there. I am not going to let you go by yourself."

"I can take care of myself."

"Yes, I know that. But if we can get Anna's breathing tube out this morning, I'm going with you," he said firmly.

"I should be going with you also," Buck said. He put down his fork. "But a lot of help I am." He turned his wheelchair away from the table and headed for the door.

Nick got up from the table. "I'm going after him." Before he left, he pointed his finger at Katelyn, "But you're not going anywhere alone."

* * *

Nick caught up to Buck in their room. He put his hand on the big man's shoulder. Buck's shoulders quaked, and his chest heaved. "We should have never allowed her to go," he cried through his tears. "I promised to protect her."

Nick let him grieve. He grabbed a chair and sat down next to his friend.

"I tell you, I read the cries of David in the Psalms when things were not going well, and he's like, where are you God?" Buck said between sobs. "Then I hit a point like this, and I find myself asking the same thing. It's so easy to question God. Maybe that's why people are so fast to blame Him."

Buck wiped his tears with his hands. "This life is no cakewalk. I'm glad I have my faith and the promise of heaven. How do you get through this life otherwise?"

Buck's sobs subsided.

Nick put his hand on Buck's immense forearm. "Buck...I uh...I pray that I can become half the man you are—your faith, how much your wife and family mean to you, how you treat other people, your integrity and courage. Maybe, I never told you this back when I was caring for you, but being around you...I guess it makes me want to be a better person. Everyone talked about you at the hospital, how you treated the nurses and the rest of the staff, even when you were in all that pain. You are truly one of the most Christ-like people I know." Nick paused. "Buck, I consider you one of my best friends, and now I owe you my life. You knocked that monster off of me. I know I was down for the count. I don't even remember what happened next. I only remember coming to in the van."

Buck looked Nick in the eyes and smiled. "Well, nothing that a little mouth-to-mouth and a few chest compressions couldn't solve."

Nick opened his eyes wide, realizing what Buck had done for him, and then he cracked up. "I've been wondering why my sternum is so sore. And why I've had this overwhelming urge to brush my teeth over and over."

They both chuckled.

Nick stretched his arm and hugged Buck's neck. "Thank you, you big lug. Thank you for saving my life."

Buck pulled away slightly so he could look Nick in the eyes. "You understand, don't you, that Jesus was the one who really paid the price for your life?"

Nick saw Buck's sincerity. "Yes. Yes, I really do," he declared. "After Anna's surgery..." Nick struggled finding the words. "I am not sure how to describe this...but I feel like God touched me. I'm not sure what this means, but I gave my life to Him."

Buck's eyes widened. "Then the pain I'm going through is worth it," he acknowledged. "I have a great sense, my friend, that your life is about to change in really big ways."

CHAPTER 61

REST IN PEACE

Nick called Maggie from San Benito and was reassured with the news. "Thank God." He turned to Katelyn, "Anna's awake and talking," and back to Maggie, "Call me if you see any problems. Otherwise, I'll call in an hour or so. Yeah, love you too. We will. I promise."

"Maggie tells us to be careful," he told Katelyn who was driving the rental car to the funeral home. They had waited until Anna's breathing tube was removed and she was stable before they took the plane back to Tikal. Nick preferred the fancy helicopter, but Maggie advised against becoming too friendly with the cartel.

"So, Anna is doing well?"

"It sure seems that way. What a miracle. Must be that good blood she received," he smiled at Katelyn.

"I think having a good surgeon helped," she smiled back at him.

Katelyn's complexion was paler than usual from donating the two units of blood, but it highlighted her black hair, pulled back in a tight bun, and her red lipstick. If she felt drained from being low on blood, she did not let on to it.

* * *

Suk sat in his room in the small hotel in Belize City. He felt quite alone. As much as he hated Hwang and Cho, at least they were company and fellow countrymen. For one of the first times in his life, he longed to be back in North Korea with the professor. It took all the strength he could muster not to call Professor Kwon and ask for advice.

He was a fugitive. He thought that once he had gotten rid of his two companions, he would be free. But now he was a prisoner, or might as well have been. He needed to get a fake passport and a new identity, but he was too exhausted to make the effort. He stretched out on the bed and pulled the blanket over his head.

* * *

Maggie wiped Anna's forehead with a cool washcloth. She had finally convinced Anna's parents to take a break, get some fresh air, and walk around the compound.

Maggie gazed at Anna. "I'm so thankful to God for your life, my dear child."

Anna frowned as she struggled to shift in the bed. "You get the license plate of that truck?" she said hoarsely, her throat still sore from the tube. When she tried to laugh, it made her cough.

Maggie put a pillow on Anna's abdomen. "Here, hold on to this if you need to cough. It will help support your belly. Dr. Hart wants you to breathe deeply and cough. It's good for your lungs."

"Where is he?"

"I'll tell you the whole story when you get your strength up."

Anna's brows wrinkled with concern.

"He's fine, Anna. He'll be back in a few days."

"I want to thank him for saving my life." Her voice was groggy from the pain medication. She touched the tube running out of her nose.

Maggie gently pulled her hand away from the nasal-gastric tube. "Dr. Hart told me that you will need to have that down in your stomach for a few days until your bowels wake up from the trauma."

Anna nodded. "My throat is so dry."

"I know it is, my dear, but try to sleep. You need your rest."

Anna's eyelids shut, then fluttered open, and she smiled.

"Maggie. It's all true. I was there!" Then her eyes closed and she fell asleep.

* * *

The funeral home was modest, but the undertaker was kind; he actually knew Miguel. The bodies were embalmed and lay in homemade pine caskets.

The undertaker asked if they would identify the bodies for legal reasons. He told them he did not have much to work with on Miguel. Nick fought back nausea as he looked at the young man; his soul was filled with an overwhelming sadness for Miguel whose life had been extinguished too soon. Anna would take it hard.

After she looked at Mr. Kim, Katelyn nodded to the undertaker. "I know I won't be home in time for his funeral. Do you mind if I sing over Mr. Kim? He was a good man and an excellent partner."

"I think that would be nice for both of them," the undertaker said.

Katelyn began whispering a prayer in Korean. Then she sang a haunting Korean song. Nick had never heard anything so lovely in all his life. It was as if the angels were singing harmony. At the end of the song, she laid her hand over Mr. Kim's heart and then Miguel's.

Nick wiped tears from his eyes. "Katelyn, that was the most beautiful thing I've ever heard."

"It's a lullaby my grandmother taught me. It was something her mother sang to her and her mother, sang to her. It's about resting in God's great love with His arms wrapped around you when nothing can hurt you."

Even the undertaker was moved and wiped tears from his eyes. He made the sign of the cross over them all.

In broken English he said, "God bless you for that. It brought life into this place of death. It brought life to this old man." He gave them both hugs.

Nick was equally moved when Katelyn offered to cover the cost of the arrangements for both Mr. Kim and Miguel. When

Nick protested, she waved him away. "Please, Dr. Hart, Miguel gave his life for us. It is the least I can do."

They told the man they would be back in the morning to accompany Mr. Kim's casket to the airport. The undertaker promised he would ask Miguel's family about plans for his burial.

CHAPTER 62

YERTLE THE TURTLE

Sitting in the run-down police station, Nick and Katelyn realized why Miguel disparaged the local force. The two officers spoke very little English. The older sweated profusely, and his uniform was unbuttoned to expose a big beer belly. Both seemed edgy and intimidated, possibly because of Katelyn's impressive credentials. But Katelyn was patient and kinder than Nick. Through broken English and a little Spanish, Katelyn and Nick managed to understand that the two officers had been to the scene of the shooting and to the house FOCO rented, and they had found nothing.

The fat officer talked with his hands and his mouth about some town and then about Belize. When Nick and Katelyn looked puzzled, he pushed his weight out of the creaking chair and led them to a map on the wall. He pointed to the town on the border with Belize.

"FOCO auto." He mimicked driving a car with an imaginary steering wheel. Then he pointed to the town of Melchor de Mencos. "Here."

He waved his arm from left to right. "Belize." Then he held up his hands and shrugged.

Katelyn understood and bowed. She turned to Nick, "Sounds like they found the FOCO SUV in Melchor de Mencos, and they think the man has gone to Belize."

He nodded. He missed Anna's translating skill.

Katelyn and Nick thanked the policemen and turned to walk out of the station.

"Excuse me," the younger policeman said and reached behind his desk. He brought up two mangled prosthetic legs. Nick could tell the older officer was angry with his subordinate for revealing the treasure so easily.

As Nick gathered the mangled legs, one foot fell to the ground. The younger man picked it up and balanced it on the pile of metal in Nick's arms.

The fat man straightened up and buttoned his uniform. He held out his hand palm up and said something in Spanish.

"I think your friend wants a tip," Katelyn told Nick.

Nick faced him squarely and glared. "I'll give you a tip all right. Get out of the business."

Katelyn interceded and stepped between them. She shook the man's hand, thanked him, and grabbed Nick by the arm. "Let's go, Dr. Hart. No need to make enemies here."

Nick turned to see the policeman inspect the hundred-dollar bill Katelyn had slipped him. As they left the building, he said more sharply than he intended, "I can't believe you paid off that jerk."

"Sometimes, Dr. Hart, it is wisdom to know which battles to fight." She kept her hand firmly on his arm and led him to their car.

* * *

Katelyn and Nick enjoyed a tranquil lunch by the lake—each relaxed in the company of the other. The day had warmed, the sunshine had melted some of their worries, allowing them to share personal anecdotes of their lives.

After lunch, Katelyn asked Nick to drive. As soon as he put the car in gear, she was on the phone speaking in Korean. Nick tried to drive and decipher the crude map Katelyn convinced the policeman to draw for her.

When she terminated her call, she told Nick she had notified her agency about the man in Belize. "They have contacted your Homeland Security. I doubt that he will be on the run for long. Your Agency is sending officers down to meet with me tomorrow, others will rendezvous with my team in Belize."

"My agency?" Nick mumbled.

"Pardon?"

Nick didn't realize he'd spoken out loud. "Oh, I was thinking how funny that sounded. *Your agency.* I think we live in different worlds, you and I. The only thing I know about Homeland Security is all the folks in blue uniforms at the airport."

Katelyn smiled at him.

"I get this feeling I live in a very sheltered world," Nick frowned. "I've never even been to Korea, and here I am with a South Korean spy chasing North Korean bad guys. It's a little bizarre, don't you think?"

Katelyn laughed hard. "That's funny. I'm not a spy."

"A few weeks ago, I'm sitting pretty in Memphis, minding my own business, making a good living, feeling like *Yertle the Turtle*, king of the pond, and now…I just don't know."

"*Yertle the Turtle*?" Katelyn raised an eyebrow.

"I guess you didn't grow up on Dr. Seuss."

She shook her head.

"Dr. Seuss wrote children's books. I grew up on them. My mother read them to me all the time," he said. "Ol' Yertle thought he was something. You know, *king of the pond.*"

Katelyn put her hand over her mouth and giggled.

"Yertle wanted to be more, so he stood on the backs of all the other turtles to be higher than the moon." Nick explained the story. "The bottom turtle burped and caused the whole lot of them to fall. Yertle took a great tumble into the mud. I'm kind of feeling like ol' Yertle right now."

Katelyn stomped her foot and laughed out loud. "You are *Yertle the Turtle*. You are so funny, Dr. Hart."

Nick had to laugh at her Korean pronunciation of *Yertle the Turtle*.

"The turtle that drives a blue Porsche Boxster," she added, hardly able to control herself.

Nick almost braked. "Wait a minute. How in the world do you know that? You really are a spy."

Katelyn laughed even harder. "My dear Dr. Hart, I know practically everything about you." Her dark eyes examined him, and she turned serious.

"Well, that's not fair," he shot back.

"But I'm really not a spy."

Nick glanced at her. She was a riddle of mystery and admiration.

She looked straight ahead, the colorful silk scarf around her neck flying in the breeze.

Well, if you are a spy, you are the most beautiful spy I know.

He saw her glance at him and was embarrassed that he may have held his gaze too long. Without thinking he said, "I still have a hard time believing I was knocked out by such a tiny, beautiful woman."

His comment made her pale cheeks blush. "You're not going to let me forget that, are you?"

"That you're beautiful or that you knocked me out?"

She gave him a funny look but said nothing. Nick was not sure if she was offended or complimented, but she intrigued him. There was something about her that he rarely saw in a woman.

Nick pressed his chest, trying to push away the encroaching loneliness, the ubiquitous companion of his singular life. He thought about something Maggie had told him: *We are made to love and be loved.* Here were two women that caused his heart to leap—one widowed, but her heart belonging to John, and the other single, but married to her job and living a continent away.

Perhaps it was a mutually embarrassed silence that came over them as they drove down the Boulevard Manuel Balizón looking for the turn to Avenida Real. They passed the Shalom Mission Hospital where trash was still scattered from the helicopter rotors.

Katelyn touched his arm gently. "You okay?"

He shut off his emotions and changed the subject. "That nightmare seems like a million light years ago. Like a bad dream," he nodded toward the hospital.

"Your ability to save Anna was quite something," she smiled at him. "And by the way, Maggie introduced me to Isabella this morning. I remember the picture you showed us. What a transformation." She squeezed his forearm. "God has given you quite a gift, Dr. Hart."

"Thank you. But, Ms. Kim," he continued, exaggerating her surname, "would you please stop being so formal? Nick will do."

CHAPTER 63

PLEA

Professor Kwon was not surprised to see Pak approaching. Kwon needed a respite, but was rarely allowed quiet time on his own. He enjoyed Moranbong Park in the shadow of Kim Il-sung Stadium and hadn't visited for over a year. But with the Noah Initiative coming to completion, there was nothing more for him to do in the lab. His assistants were busy assembling the vials for distribution to their destinations around the world. It had seemed like a good time to take a break.

The clean air of Pyongyang made for a brilliant blue sky, and the sun warmed the morning enough for Kwon to remove his overcoat as he sat on a bench overlooking the Taedong River.

The flock of pigeons gathered around Kwon scattered as Pak stopped in front of him.

"A beautiful day, Professor."

"Indeed."

"And it has become even more beautiful." Pak reached into his jacket pocket and pulled out the note from Guatemala.

Kwon read the note without emotion and handed it back to Pak who folded it and put it back in his pocket.

"You don't seem overjoyed with the news?"

"I'm sorry, Song-ju. I am. But I was confident that the aerosolization would go well."

"You have done a good job, Professor."

Kwon didn't look at him.

Pak was concerned. "Is there something I could do for you, my friend?"

Kwon suspected Pak knew what he was thinking.

"I...I would hope," Kwon looked at Pak's dark, emotionless eyes. "I would like to see my wife and son before my life is over."

Pak's eyes bore into Kwon's. For a moment, his gaze was stony. Then a smirk spread across his face. "I will see what I can do."

With that, Pak turned on his heels and walked away.

Kwon watched the arrogant man stroll away, and suddenly he felt a chill shake his body. He pulled his overcoat over his shoulders.

Huddling on the bench, Kwon imagined the flight of his virus. It would be almost anticlimactic. There would be no explosions, no large-scale panic. At least not at first. For a time, there would be no media coverage, no notoriety, and no fame. The offices would silently release the virus mist over the people and that would be that. The virility of the virus would do the rest.

Kwon sighed. He wished he could study the transmission rates and monitor the spread as people went about their normal routines—boarding trains, sitting in board rooms, flying on planes, going to parties and sporting events, and every other possible place the virus would disseminate itself. It would make for a world-renowned epidemiological study. It would be so fascinating if he could do the study. But it was not to be. Probably that was reason he was so melancholy today. That's what he told himself.

CHAPTER 64

FERRETS

Katelyn covered her nose and mouth with her scarf.

"Phew. That's terrible," she made a face.

As soon as they walked into the living room of FOCO's rental, they saw the source of the stench, and the minute the ferrets saw Nick and Katelyn, they protested loudly.

"What the heck?" Nick said, pulling his shirt collar over his nose. They stood in front of the wall of cages. "FOCO likes ferrets?"

The animals stood in their cages and screamed at the pair.

"Looks like they're all out of food," Nick yelled above the racket. He saw a food container and began filling their food dishes. One by one, they stopped bawling and ate.

"Well, that helps with the noise," Katelyn said. "I guess there's nothing we can do about the smell, unless you want to clean the cages, too," she teased.

He exaggerated a fake laugh at her.

They soon discovered that the police had searched the house top to bottom—they'd dumped every drawer on the floor and overturned every piece of furniture or shoved it out of place.

"So much for a crime scene," Katelyn said. "I imagine that anything of value is in the pockets of the lunatic police." She was angry.

Nick slid the back door open to let in some fresh air. He saw empty beer cans and cigar stubs on the picnic table on the deck. He stepped onto the deck and looked over the lake. A light breeze rippled its surface.

As he looked back at the picnic table and across the lake, Nick realized that the view from the house was of Flores Island and the hotel where he, Buck, and Anna had stayed. It was unnerving to think that these guys could have been on their radar, and vice versa. He regretted coming to San Benito in the first place. He looked over the edge of the deck and saw a fire pit next to the lake.

"Hey, Katelyn, you might want to check this out."

He pointed to the fire pit that was full of ash and burnt paper. Finding the stairs, they made their way down to the edge of the lake to get a good look at the fire pit. Katelyn found a stick and poked at the ashes. As carefully as she prodded, the ashes collapsed into powder.

"Looks like anything of importance was burned," she said. "I'll have my men go over it all with a fine-tooth comb: fingerprints, DNA, even these ashes. But I was hoping we would find something that would give us a hint at what they were doing here."

Two ducks flew overhead, calling to their companions on the shore.

"Does any of this make sense to you?" Nick asked.

"They were obviously up to no good, but it's not the usual MO that we see. No sign of drug manufacturing. No counterfeiting equipment. If they were doing human trafficking, we would have found girls instead of ferrets."

"Yeah. What are we going to do with all those animals? I kind of feel sorry for them."

"I'll have my people see what they can do," Katelyn said as they went back into the house when she immediately covered her nose to block the smell. "Sure you don't want to take them home for pets?"

As they walked by the cages, one ferret chirped at them. Nick stopped and looked at the animal. It made an affectionate rub on the cage door, then somersaulted a number of times. Nick laughed. "You still hungry, boy?"

He grabbed the food container and dumped a little more food into the dish through the door. The ferret rubbed his back against the cage, and Nick stuck his finger through the wire to pet the animal. But just before he touched it, the ferret hissed loudly and bared its teeth.

Nick jumped back. "You little creep!" Startled, he smacked the cage with the food container. This sent the ferret retreating to the back of its cage and the other ferrets screeching in chaos.

Nick's heart pounded. That's when he saw it. He recognized it from his college chemistry days—a laboratory notebook wedged between the cages. He plucked it out as fast as he could to escape the hissing ferrets' teeth.

Katelyn was already at the front door. "You done fighting with your friends?" she called.

"Uh, I think you need to see this."

CHAPTER 65

THE SPY'S SPY

The rumble of the hot water pipes in the building complemented the sounds of her husband's snoring. He always snored when he had been drinking. At least she had been able to calm the girls. From the bedroll next to theirs, she heard an occasional whimper.

It took all her willpower not to touch her eye to check the swelling or rub her tender scalp, both consequences of his actions. Earlier, Pak had dragged his wife by her hair and slammed her against the wall. Right now, she lay perfectly still.

She smelled the alcohol on his breath, even with her back turned from him. She wasn't concerned by the fragrance of another woman's perfume; the more his needs were satisfied by another, the better for her. Just thinking of such physical contact with him repulsed her.

She wasn't sure why he had come home so enraged, but she thought about what her mother had told her—those with a bad conscience have a difficult time fighting off demons. She could withstand the beatings, but she was concerned for her daughters' feelings. They watched every time he beat her. It was impossible not to see in their small apartment.

She waited until she was sure that he would not awaken from his alcoholic stupor. When she was positive she would not disturb him, she rolled off the bedroll onto the floor. As she pushed herself up, she grimaced and realized her wrist must have been cracked when he attacked her. But she pushed through the pain and on toward her goal.

Apart from getting beaten, she looked forward to these nights when Pak came home drunk and passed out. They were the only times she dared to look through his belongings. It was her job; that and her daughters gave her reason to live. She had already withstood many years of beatings, when one day a woman approached her outside the market. It did not take her long to accept the woman's offer to pay her to spy on her husband. The hope that one day these people would rescue her and her daughters and help them escape to the South sealed the deal.

She quickly and quietly rifled through his pants pockets and was disappointed to find nothing. She found a matchbook in one pocket of his suit jacket. She carefully opened it and found nothing except matches. It was probably from one of his nightclubs.

She jumped back when Pak snorted and turned over. She froze in place, wondering if she should continue her search or crawl back onto the bedroll.

His rhythmic breathing resumed, and she continued her search. In the front breast pocket of his jacket, she found a piece of paper, pulled it out, and unfolded it. She held it to the light coming through the hallway door and read: **Aerosolization works perfectly. No new pregnancies. Work completed. Please advise.**

She had no idea what it meant, but let the writing and the words burn into her memory so she could reproduce them exactly for her handler in the morning.

CHAPTER 66

ON THE TRAIL

Nick found it strange to sit at the same table at Capitan Tortuga restaurant where he, Buck, and Anna had sat a few days before when they'd toasted John's life. He hung up his phone. He'd just checked with Maggie and watched Katelyn talk with her associates on her phone.

He held up his coffee cup and waved to the waiter for a refill. He was exhausted, and caffeine was the only thing that kept him on life support.

Anna's fever was up slightly, but Maggie reassured him that her belly was neither distended nor tenderer than it had been and, therefore, unlikely to develop peritonitis.

Nick told Maggie that post-operative fevers often come from atelectasis in the lungs. Small areas of the lungs collapse after surgery and release high levels of fever-producing hormones. It was best to encourage Anna to take deep breaths and cough to fully re-expand her lungs.

Otherwise, Anna was in good spirits and told everyone about a near-death experience and "visit to heaven." She couldn't wait to tell Nick all about it in person.

Maggie promised to continue to encourage her to rest.

Katelyn had asked Nick not to tell Maggie anything about the laboratory notebook he found or what they discovered. There was no reason to incite panic, no matter how innocently it was phrased. The notebook was entirely in Korean, except for some mathematical equations and calculations. All that Katelyn told him thus far was the fear of a biological catastrophe.

Nick watched Katelyn talk; her Korean had a rhythmic exquisiteness to it. He had no idea what was being said, but she scribbled notes in Korean quickly on a pad of paper next to the laboratory notebook.

"*Ye, Ye,*" she said over and over.

She set her phone down and watched the waiter pour Nick's coffee. She waved off a refill. She leaned back in her chair and waited for the waiter to leave. She looked over the lake; the evening was turning to night. Nick could tell her mind was racing, but decided against interrupting her thoughts. She would tell him eventually. He bided his time.

Finally, she spoke, "This place is about to be swarmed with different security agencies from around the world. I'm not sure you understand the hornet's nest that you have uncovered, and my superiors have ordered me to tell you nothing."

They sat in silence for a long time. He really liked Katelyn; she was smart, athletic, and one of the most striking women he knew, but he was hurt by her silence. *John gave his life for this.*

She seemed to know what he was thinking and interrupted his brooding. "In my culture, going against one's superior is rarely done. I've never done it myself." She slipped her notepad into the laboratory book. "What I am about to tell you, you have to promise to keep to yourself for now. I feel like I owe you... we owe your friend, John, for his ultimate sacrifice. I know I can trust you. After what I saw you do for Anna, I would trust you with my life." She looked at him and smiled.

Even though there were only a few other occupied tables in the restaurant, she leaned toward Nick and lowered her voice.

"Our countries, along with the rest of the G8, are appointing a special task force. The seriousness of this cannot be overstated. Your government is negotiating with Russia to bring the Chinese on board. It is only because of the fight on terrorism that has allowed such cooperation. They are treating this as a highest-level threat. Our Agency is in FOCO's Seoul office as we speak. They continue to be cooperative. It appears they never had direct contact with the men here, and it was a bit of a shell game. We have not had the chance to talk with all the offices because of the time differences, but the offices we have questioned thought that a different office was managing the project."

"Crazy. So, they knew there was philanthropic work going on here, but no one was aware of who supervised the project?"

"Exactly. And since their funding, as far as we can see, wasn't coming out of any of their budgets, no one ever asked."

"So who was footing the bill?"

"That, right there, my dear Dr. Hart…Nick…is the million-dollar question. That is why it is so important that we get the Chinese involved. It appears that the money was coming from Beijing. But even they may not know the source."

"And you think these men were working on a biologic weapon…a virus…that causes infertility?"

She looked at him very seriously and scanned the restaurant to make sure no one was listening. "Yes. I am having a difficult time deciphering what much of this journal means," she said, patting the notebook, "but we will translate it and get it into the hands of the world's leading virologists to make heads or tails out of it. It has to be top priority. We have no certainty who is behind this, except to suspect the North Koreans. You have to remember, China would have much to gain in this scenario, or Iran, or one of the many other enemies of western culture."

She lowered her voice another notch. "And at this point, we have no idea what they are planning to do with the virus."

"Release it?"

"Possibly. Even the threat of release can change world politics."

They sat in silence as Nick tried to absorb the magnitude of the situation.

"Geez, pretty scary stuff. What will we do next?"

Katelyn looked away for the first time. "My team arrives here tomorrow, along with Homeland Security. I," she put the emphasis on the singular pronoun, "will be meeting with them and showing them what we found." She looked Nick in the eyes. "And you." It was more of a statement than a question.

It was Nick's turn to look away, but she was right. He was stepping into water too deep for him. "I guess I'll head back to the Hope Center."

He leaned into her and lowered his voice. "But honestly, Katelyn, if the world as we know it is coming to an end, I'd rather stay here with you." He smiled, still unable to fully comprehend the weight of the crisis.

"You are sweet, Nick," she smiled back and squeezed his hand. It was a lovely gesture, but he knew he would be on his way to the Hope Center tomorrow and then home to Memphis. He wasn't sure if he still had a job when he got there or if he really cared.

CHAPTER 67

TORMENT

Suk wore a path on the grungy hotel carpet, pacing obsessively. His hair was disheveled and greasy from a week without a shower, his eyes bloodshot and wild. He had ventured out of the hotel only three times. The first was to meet a man that was rumored to be able to help him with a fake passport and visa. He met him at the cantina next door. When the man continued to raise the price, Suk became irate and was tossed out by the bouncer. The other two trips from the hotel were simply to buy whiskey and cigarettes.

The demon of paranoia sat at Suk's right hand and filled his mind with fear. The mixture of alcohol and the lack of sleep caused the neurons in his brain to misfire—unraveling his mind.

"What am I going to do? Professor, help me," he murmured again and again.

A lit cigarette hung from his lips, and a large ember dropped on his shirt and then onto the floor, creating another burn mark on the carpet. He stumbled through the whiskey bottles that littered the floor, found one that still had liquid at the bottom. He lifted it to his mouth and drained it. A disfigured shadow stood staring at him across the room, and Suk threw the bottle at it. It hit a large mirror on the wall, shattering with an ear-splitting crash.

Suk sunk to his knees. "Professor, help me."

He figured he would be discovered by the authorities and could see the police storming through the door at anytime. *All I've ever wanted to do is be a good person. Just to please you, Professor.*

His mother had called him her tender child that day he'd brought home an injured bird from school and nursed it back to health.

"Mother, forgive me."

The note he'd scribbled yesterday lay on the floor next to him. There was no way to undue the evil that he had unleashed. All he could do was to apologize and to ask that they forgive him for being weak.

Another dark figure laughed at him from the corner. Suk hurled a second whiskey bottle at the creature that tortured his mind. The bottle hit the wall and ricocheted off the night stand, sending the phone clanking to the floor. He crawled to the phone on all fours. He recalled the Professor's number by heart. There were only a handful of numbers in North Korea that could accept international calls, and Kwon's was not one of them.

It was improper, but he dialed the international operator service. *If I can just speak to the Professor, he will know what to do.*

A young man with an Indian accent answered the phone. Suk's hand shook so badly he could hardly hold the receiver to his face. He asked the boy to connect him to a number in North Korea.

"Please hold."

Suk's heart pounded in his ears and he slumped over on his side. The phone made a series of hopeful clicks. What would he say to the man who was like a father to him? Would he be angry that he called?

"Hello?" Suk said into the phone. He heard only continued clicking. *What is taking so long?*

"Hello?" he asked again. The phone clicked again and then went dead.

Suk let the phone drop onto his chest. He slowed his breathing.

In a moment of clarity, he knew what he had to do. He had thought about it all week, but he had no gun, no pills. He reached down to the top of his pants and pulled his belt from its loops.

CHAPTER 68

GOODBYES

Nick figured one more week wouldn't make much difference, considering the trouble he was already in with the MED. Anna's father promised that his firm would help with any legal issues if the need arose.

The corporate jet roared to life and quickly lifted off from the Quetzaltenango runway with Anna and her parents. Nick and Maggie waved at the aircraft from outside the old hangar, well aware that the passengers probably couldn't see them.

Nick shielded his eyes from the sun and watched as the jet climbed toward the mountains and took a sharp turn to the left. He was worried something was wrong when the plane continued to arc. But as the jet rumbled past them, it wagged its wings in farewell before turning and heading north.

"That Anna." Maggie shook her head and smiled. "I can just hear her talking her dad into that one."

Nick laughed. "I know a dad who would do anything for his baby girl."

Nick and Maggie stood in silence, watching the plane disappear. The roar of the engines gave way to a pair of cooing doves perched on a nearby telephone pole.

Anna would be taken to Hope Memorial in Birmingham, but, in all reality, she could really go home. Anna's father had insisted she be checked out, and Nick didn't bother to argue. All her tubes were out, including her IV. They had switched her from IV to oral antibiotics three days ago when her abdominal wound quit draining. For days they had all been concerned about the incision. *Thank God for antibiotics.*

Nick hated all the goodbyes, but the most painful one was yet to happen. Buck had left five days ago, anxious to return to his family. All the California kids were gone as well.

Maggie would be taking him to Guatemala City first thing in the morning. It was hard to imagine leaving, standing there looking out over the green of the mountains with the sun reflecting off a small cloud captured by the top of the volcano.

I wonder about staying.

For lots of reasons, he knew he couldn't. For one, it was too complicated with Maggie. He loved her, but she was committed to John. Rightfully so.

Maggie turned to him, looking serious. "A horse walks into a bar and the bartender asks, *Why the long face?*"

Nick smirked, shook his head, and looked toward the mountains.

She poked him in the ribs, making him flinch.

"God, you're annoying." He pushed her hand away.

"I bet you're looking forward to being back in Memphis."

"Yeah, I was just thinking that…like a dang root canal."

They stood waiting for the other to make a move to leave. Neither wanted to.

"You going to be okay…without…" he stopped himself. It sounded too narcissistic.

She smiled at him. "Nick, thank you so much for being here. For helping our kids. Yeah, I'm good. You know, people to see, places to go."

"I don't understand where your energy comes from, this crazy joy." He realized that he really was annoyed. If he had lost the love of his life he would be stuck at the bottom of a whiskey bottle of self-pity. After watching her for the last few weeks, Nick knew she returned to her life without John for the children's sake, he also saw more than that in her easy smile. "Where does your strength come from?"

She looped her arm through his and kissed him on the shoulder. "You really still wonder that, after being here all these weeks?"

"I know, I know. I'm just a thick-headed bone doctor."

He thought about one of the banners that the children had

made for Isabella before her surgery. *The joy of the Lord is my strength.*

"I don't seem to be made out of the same faith fabric as you, or Anna, or even Buck, for that matter. That night we operated on Anna, I told God that I believe. I believe in Jesus. I gave everything to him."

"And?" Maggie asked.

"Well, of course I still believe all that. I'm just not sure I feel any different," he said, feeling flustered.

Maggie had learned to let Nick process and said nothing.

"I thought after I confessed to God, I would be, I don't know, different." Nick was not about to tell Maggie he had admired the derrière of the nurse that flew in with the jet.

"Ah. You mean like magic. *Bibbidi-Bobbidi-Boo.*" Maggie waved an imaginary wand over Nick. "Okay, you're different."

"Stop," he scolded her.

Maggie squeezed his arm in hers. "Oh, Nick, you *are* different. But once we turn to God, we have to keep walking out our faith." She thought for a moment. "Sometimes I have to choose to turn to Him day by day. Sometimes, hour by hour." She paused. "Even sometimes, moment to moment. But the one thing I know, Nicklaus, is that He is always faithful."

CHAPTER 69

RELEASE – ONE MONTH LATER

Nick scanned the lead article of the USA Today newspaper as he sipped a soda in the surgical lounge of the MED.

He read that it took the virologists three weeks to identify the M2H1 virus from blood samples of the ferrets and some of the villagers. Typically, it took three months or longer to sequence a complete viral genetic code, but thanks to a new process and many sleepless nights, the virologists did it in weeks instead of months.

Last time he talked with Katelyn, they had chatted about the progress of the international team and decided that understanding as much as they could about the virus in such a short time was light years away from deciphering the intentions of the people behind it. Could they mass produce it? What were their plans for it? And would they truly ever use it? The one thing the Centers for Disease Control understood was that the clock was ticking.

Starting from *the seed* of original virus to an FDA-approved vaccine could take months or even years. At least South Korea, China, and the United States had agreed on a cooperative agreement to work together on the vaccine.

Nick took another swig from the soda can. His cell phone rang. It was Katelyn.

"I was just thinking about you," Nick said.

"Hello, Nick."

"Katelyn, I'm so glad to hear from you."

"You as well, Dr. Hart." She had returned to her formality. He wanted to correct her, but thought better of it. She sounded tired and depressed.

"Where are you?"

"I'm in Tokyo."

"You get to have all the fun," he said, trying to lighten her up.

"Dr. Hart, they have released the virus."

Nick was stunned. Stunned that they would actually release it. Stunned that she would tell him. He didn't know what to say. He looked around the room at the other doctors and nurses enjoying their break and realized the world was about to change.

"Can you even be telling me this?" He didn't know what else to say. "Do you think it was the North Koreans."

"Presidents of various countries will announce the news tomorrow. I wouldn't be surprised if the news leaked somewhere sooner. And yes, it was the North Koreans."

"Where was it released?"

"We have confirmed two cities for sure. FOCO has offices in eleven major cities, so I think we have to assume that there may be others. The FOCO offices around the world each have one missing employee. Every one of them turned out to be Korean. They had been hired with South Korean credentials, but we suspect they are assets from the North. A worldwide manhunt is underway for these people."

Putting on his analytical hat, Nick asked. "Are you certain they released it?"

"Fairly certain. In both offices we found foggers like they use for spraying mosquitos with traces of the virus in them."

Nick thought about the trucks he had seen in Guatemala driving up and down the streets billowing huge clouds of pesticides. "And you're sure it's the North Koreans?"

Katelyn paused. He could tell the wheels in her head were spinning.

"Look, Dr. Hart...Nick. The world may get a bit crazy when the news hits. I have been called to testify to the Subcommittee of National Security of your Congress in a few weeks. I would not be surprised if you're called to testify as well. You were there."

"Great, just what I need."

"That and a little notoriety. I'm just warning you, the news sharks will descend on you. At least I have the protection of my badge. Please do not repeat what I'm about to tell you," she said firmly. "The Chinese dragged their feet and, only after the virus was released, admitted that the funding had come from North Korea, and when a note about the release of the virus surfaced out of the North, it led us to Pak Song-ju, North Korea's Minister of Cabinet General Intelligence."

"Never heard of the guy," Nick said.

"We know him well. He is the equivalent of your CIA director. We suspect that Professor Kwon, North Korea's leading microbiologist, had his fingerprints all over the project. And the third man in the van was a Korean with the last name Suk, he was one of Kwon's colleagues."

"Did you find the man?"

"Yes. At least we found his body. A week after you left San Benito, Suk was found in Belize City. He had hung himself. He left a note indicating his remorse for development of the virus."

"A lot of good that does. How did you find him?"

"The FBI raided his room when the NSA traced a call that had been made to North Korea from a hotel in Belize."

"The long arm of justice I guess," Nick said. "I guess he got what he deserved."

"Yes, I guess. I think he was a pawn in whatever evil drove this. It kind of reminds me of Judas Iscariot and his suicide after his betrayal of Jesus."

CHAPTER 70

THREE MONTHS LATER

Nick's breath fogged the airplane window, and he wondered if the lights below were New Orleans. Just as Katelyn had warned, his world was getting turned upside down. The announcement was made as scheduled and it consumed the media. Nick had done a handful of interviews for the major news channels, trying to adhere to the briefing the State Department fed him.

Katelyn had kept Nick informed about much of what was happening that was kept from the general public. It was not clear whether or not Kim Jong-un was involved. The only ones they knew about for sure were from the top leadership: Pak, Kwon, and Suk.

It took weeks to verify their worst fears—the M2H1 virus was released in all eleven major cities from FOCO facilities. The virus had spread quickly, as its instigators had expected. It caused a mild upper respiratory illness that lasted as long as a typical cold. In fact, it was difficult to tell the difference. When measured against a regular, run-of-the-mill summer cold, epidemiologists found the virus almost impossible to track.

The global population had only begun to wrap their heads around the possibility of a future without babies. Waiting on his plane, Nick read the news on his smart phone that a successful vaccine was still months away, and no date of dissemination was announced. No one knew if it was too late to contain the virus.

There were preliminary reports of scattered infertility, but not enough to send the markets crashing. Nick remembered the villages they'd visited and concluded that much of the world was in denial. The shock wave would eventually hit.

He'd taken precautions and told his financial planner to sell every bit of stock he owned and put his money in gold. Its worth had already doubled. But Nick wasn't sure gold would matter in the long run. He was reminded of a scripture Buck taught him from the Book of Matthew: *'Do not store up for yourselves treasures on earth, where moth and rust destroy, and where thieves break in and steal. But store up for yourselves treasures in heaven, where neither moth nor rust destroys, and where thieves do not break in or steal. For where your treasure is, there your heart will be also.'*

The flight attendant interrupted his thoughts, and he declined another soda and snack. He turned back to stare through the fogged window.

The last time he spoke to Katelyn, she sounded discouraged. There had been no way to stop the release of the virus. Buck and Nick had been hailed as heroes, but Katelyn and her team had not fared as well. There was always a scapegoat, and her agency was it.

Nick would travel to Washington, D.C. next week to testify before Congress about the release of the M2H1 virus. He would face many members of Congress who had already called for sanctions against North Korea.

A lot of good that would do now that the virus was out there.

He hated the thought of a full day of testimony, but Katelyn would be there, and he looked forward to having dinner with her. It would be the first time he had seen her since leaving San Benito.

Some turbulence startled Nick, and the pilot turned the seatbelt sign on. Nick checked his watch. They would land in Memphis in another hour. He still hated to fly.

Since his return, Nick's partners at the MED had been happy to let him catch up on his share of the call, and it seemed like all he did was work. On the bright side, Anita Roe was finally off his back. Even she regarded Nick as somewhat of a celebrity because she recognized it was good for the hospital's image.

Buck was scheduled to pick him up at the airport. He and Buck had become best friends; Nick found he spent more time at Buck's house than in his lonely apartment. He hoped the ER call tomorrow night at the MED wouldn't interrupt their weekly

Bible study. Nick was learning to pray without feeling self-conscious, and he was learning to believe in something besides medicine and science.

Nick reached into his front pocket, pulled out his phone, and scrolled to a picture of himself and Isabella standing in front of the Hope Center. Maggie had taken it just before he'd left. It had been the third time he returned to the Hope Center, and each time he had dreaded leaving. When he was there, no one from the press bugged him, and he liked it that way.

He was thankful his patients were doing well, especially the children with corrected clubfeet. Their pins had been removed, and they wore their splints faithfully. There had been only two minor infections, one in an adult and one in a child, but both responded well to antibiotics and were healing.

Isabella was still at the Hope Center where she had blossomed, making friends with the other children and becoming a real chatterbox. When some of the skin around her incisions died and sloughed off, the team had put her on a regular wound care program that helped her healing. To send her home to dirt floors was not an option. Besides, at the Hope Center, she was one very happy little girl. In any case, Nick thought she would be able to return home in another couple months. But at that time, she would be wearing shoes.

He had promised Anna to send pictures of the kids; he hoped he'd remember. Anna was fully recovered and had been accepted to medical school at five different programs. She would have been accepted on her own merit, but the glowing letters of recommendation from Nick and Maggie helped seal the deal. She could take her pick, and she decided on Emory in Atlanta because of its outreach to the poor.

Her parents had long forgiven them all and became huge supporters of the Hope Center. They had already planned an outreach to the center with their church. Anna told Nick that when she showed her father around the orphanage, it was the first time she had ever seen him cry. Nick knew what it was like to receive a redeemed heart.

He scrolled over a few pictures to one he took of Maggie singing with the children. He chuckled to himself when he thought of Maggie's answer to a question that had been in his heart for months. One quiet night when they were sitting on their bench at the Hope Center, he had asked the burning question: *You ever think about remarrying?* He had asked plainly without suggestion or innuendo, but the question had made her cry.

When she'd worked through her tears, she said, "You think I could find someone willing to adopt seventy-three kids?"

They chuckled until she turned serious. "You know, I miss John about every second of every day. I ache to have him hold me. But you know, in my mind, he is still alive."

She swirled the ring still on her finger. *Forever Yours* was engraved inside as well as on her heart.

They sat in silence for a long time. Finally, Nick turned to her and said, "I want you to know that I am always here for you, and if you ever need anything…ever…all you have to do is ask."

"Anything?" she teased him.

He blushed. "You know what I mean," he said, trying to take his foot out of his mouth.

"I love you, Nicklaus Hart, and I know John loves you for caring for me, but I'm doing okay. I feel stronger day by day, and I know that I will be with John again one day."

EPILOGUE

GOOD NEWS

Eight Months Later

"Dr. Hart! Dr. Hart!" Isabella yelled. She practically ran to him and threw her arms around his waist. She still limped, but it was good to see her upright. She'd grown several inches over the last eight months, a result of good nutrition and a lifted spirit.

Nick tenderly kissed the top of the head.

"Hi, *mija*," he said. It meant *my daughter* in Spanish. It was how Nick felt about her. Nick had learned some Spanish, leaving *cucaracha* in the dust, and he liked to practice it.

With the world economy in a slump, it was difficult to get to Guatemala, but Nick had refused to miss this occasion. Isabella's wounds had finally healed, and she was going home today.

He knelt beside her and she wrapped her arms around his neck. "I get to go home today, Dr. Hart," she said in English.

"Isabella, your English has gotten so good."

She pulled away, looked at Maggie, and beamed. She looked back at Nick and said very seriously, "I am going to work very hard in school. I have decided to become a doctor like you."

"I have no doubt you'll be a good one," he told her, marveling at her transformation. "Maybe this will help you." He gave her a brightly colored backpack.

When she took it, she made a funny face, exaggerating the weight of it. Everyone around them laughed. Isabella was very smart and had a quick wit; Nick thought she'd make a wonderful doctor—if not a talented actress.

Using both hands, Isabella put the backpack on a nearby chair and opened it. She rolled her eyes and grinned. "That is why it is so heavy," she exclaimed. Nick had filled the backpack to the brim with school supplies, including a calculator and a new watch. Isabella grinned from ear to ear and threw her arms around him again.

"God bless you, *mija*," Nick said, fighting back tears.

Isabella's parents thanked Maggie and Nick over and over again. Her mother held Isabella's sister, Elsa, whose clubfeet had corrected perfectly. But Elsa was not happy to see the doctor and buried her face into her mother's neck.

Nick patted her back. "God bless you too, Elsa."

When the time came for the family to return to their village, Maggie and Nick said their goodbyes. She put her arm around Nick's waist as they waved to the family.

"She practically wet her pants waiting for you," Maggie told him. "Hope you feel pretty good about helping that family." She hugged him tightly.

"So should you," he put his arm around her shoulder and hugged her back.

"How long do you get to stay?"

"I'm afraid I have to turn around and go back tomorrow. It's kind of crazy out there. They're talking about shutting down the MED. I'm not sure we understood how fragile the economy really was. The pregnancy rate has dropped fifty percent in the last three months alone. It's all the cable news channels report, and the more they talk about it, the greater the fear grows, and the bleaker things get. I even find myself growing into despair."

He looked at Maggie and was surprised she was smiling.

"I have someone else to show you," she said and pulled him toward the clinic.

When they entered the clinic door, they found a young mother standing in the exam room holding a bundle wrapped in blankets.

"Another clubfoot, huh?"

"You'll see," Maggie said. She held out her arms to the mother who smiled and handed her the bundle. Maggie carefully unwrapped the blankets to reveal a baby in its diaper. She put the newborn in Nick's arms.

The baby whimpered slightly from exposure to the air. Nick cradled it in one arm and examined it, starting at the feet. He was surprised to find two perfectly shaped feet and straight legs. Moving up, he checked both hands and inspected the fingers.

He was confused.

"She looks perfectly healthy. What am I missing?" He was about to ask more questions when he noticed an elderly couple sitting on the other side of the room. The man was vaguely familiar.

He smiled at them and looked at the baby. Then he looked at the baby's mother and at Maggie. His brain worked to connect the dots. Maggie grinned at him, as if willing him to make the connection.

Then he remembered where he had seen the old man. It was the chief and his wife from El Zapote.

Nick's jaw dropped. "Are you saying—?" He looked at the baby again.

Maggie's smile expanded, and she nodded enthusiastically, announcing, "This baby is from El Zapote!"

Nick was astonished. "Are you sure? Were both her mother and father exposed?"

"Absolutely. Both her mother and father were there at the time of exposure, and both came down with the symptoms."

Nick looked down at the baby, at this hope for the village and for the world. "How could it be?"

"Is it possible the effects of the virus wore off?" Maggie asked. "I believe God restored their fertility."

Nick nodded. "This is incredible. This is awesome news," he exclaimed, letting his tears fall freely. "God bringing redemption to the world through a baby. That is good news!"

* * *

POSTSCRIPT

NORTH KOREA

The two officials from the State Department who briefed him were dead serious. He'd spent time with them since the release of the virus and even considered them friends. He had never seen them so serious.

"Why me?" Nick asked.

"Who knows." The taller one answered. "You're the man on the Wheaties box right now. Kim Jong-un probably watches Fox News, like the rest of us."

Nick never saw a hint of a smile, but he did detect anxiety and curiosity.

"The decision is strictly up to you; we know there is considerable risk." The older official said. "Rarely does any request come through official channels for a visitation to North Korea. The North Korean diplomat in New York delivered it to us himself. Even the diplomat seemed puzzled, but he reassured us that the invitation had come from the highest level of his government."

"Look, this may be one of our best shots for learning more about this elusive country." The other official took his turn. "The North Korean government denied the release of the virus up until two months ago. But recently, it issued a statement of apology, saying that the people behind the incident had been punished."

"Of course, it had been the prudent thing to do, considering the world's outcry and the Chinese cutting off funding to their country," the first official added. "Otherwise, nothing has changed; North Korea is moving ahead with another nuclear test."

"North Korea—forever the enigma," the other added.

"So the bottom line is, we do not know what to make of the request and cannot guarantee your safety." The more serious of the two leaned into Nick. "You could end up in one of the infamous prison camps, and there would be nothing the United States could do."

* * *

As Nick sat in the presidential palace of Pyongyang, North Korea, he was reminded that Katelyn was the one who had convinced him to accept the invitation.

The warnings from the State Department continued to ring in Nick's ears as he waited in an ornate outer office of Kim Jong-un's official residence. Nick had been waiting for over an hour. Sweat dripped down his back under his suit. The rush of adrenaline coursing through his body was almost unbearable.

When the double doors swung open, Nick sprang to his feet to face a legion of large, robotic men surrounding a heavyset young man in a black suit with a North Korean flag pinned on its chest pocket. It was déjà vu—the exact representation, complete with the identical suit in the photograph of Kim Jong-un that the State Department officials had shown him.

As he had been told, Nick bowed to the young man. Although he had already gone through a metal detector and endured a hearty pat down, Kim Jong-un stood a safe distance from him with two burly security men between them.

Nick tried not to lock his knees and worried that he would pass out. The Leader stared at Nick, looking him up and down.

Finally, Kim Jong-un gave a simple command, and his security men parted. A smile crossed Kim's face. "Dr. Hart, welcome to North Korea. Won't you please come into my office?" He spoke in perfect English.

Kim Jong-un turned on his heels and went into his massive office. His security detail escorted Nick inside and pointed to the seat where he should sit. Kim Jong-un sat in a large ornate chair across from him.

Kim said something to the security detail which did not please them, and a short, curt discussion in Korean ensued. Kim emerged the winner, and the security detail left the room, leaving Nick alone with one of the most feared men in the world.

Without speaking, Kim continued to stare at Nick. Nick was getting even more nervous.

Finally, Kim crossed his arms and said, "Dr. Hart, you have saved my country from a great embarrassment. The release of the M2H1 virus should have never happened. The men responsible have been dealt with." He paused so Nick could digest his words. "You must wonder why I brought you here."

"Yes. Thank you for your invitation."

"I will not waste your time," Kim said, getting down to business. "Dr. Hart, I am unsure how much you know about our history."

"Some," Nick replied courteously.

"And about our religious history?"

"I'm afraid I know nothing of that."

"You see, Dr. Hart, I know you are a Christian." Kim paused. Nick had no idea where this conversation was headed.

"My great-grandmother was also a Christian."

The information surprised Nick.

"A number of months ago, I…" Kim stopped and stared at Nick, sizing him up as if trying to decide whether or not to continue.

"I'm not sure how to describe this," Kim began, uncrossing his arms, leaning forward, and lowering his voice. "In a dream, a man appeared to me. He glowed like a bright light. He told me his name was Jesus, and he said: *Why do you persecute me?* And then he was gone. Dr. Hart, could you please tell me about this Jesus?"

The story does not end here…
Nick Hart is off on another globe-trotting
adventure, in the sequel…

THE TREE OF LIFE

3 CHAPTER PREVIEW

A crisis of Biblical proportions has just struck modern Turkey. A devastating earthquake threatens to destroy one of the most ancient of lands and cultures.

At the same time, across the world, Dr. Nick Hart finds himself spiraling down in spiritual crisis, which threatens to undo all he learned and gained from his Christian conversion and the miracles he witnessed in ministry to impoverished Guatemalans.

THE TREE OF LIFE, the sequel to the mystery thriller, *MAYA HOPE,* sends Nick off on another international adventure, where he is caught up in a quest to aid a devastated population and recapture meaning for himself.

In so doing, he puts himself in mortal danger, falling prey to ISIS and crossing paths with Russians on a quest, themselves, for the fabled Tree of Life.

Will he survive, and will he find Life beyond mere survival?

the **TREE** of
LIFE

A
MEDICAL
THRILLER

A Dr. Nicklaus Hart Novel

TIMOTHY BROWNE, MD

PROLOGUE

SHAKEN

Ibrahim stood at his bedroom window, wiggled into his jeans and pulled his T-shirt over his head. He scrunched his feet into his shoes, not bothering to tie the laces. His friends had started the game without him and he flew down the staircase and through the living room to the front door.

"Ibrahim," his mother yelled.

His mother's plea stopped him at the open doorway of the family apartment, long enough to gulp down the fresh air and stretch for the sun like a prisoner released from his cell. After being confined inside for two tortuous days, he was free.

His mother had tried her best to entertain him during that time, but he'd been restless and refused to be comforted. She'd given him games, and cards, and books, but the games were stupid and he hated to read. His father, for the most part, was silent, parked in his corner chair reading old newspapers, and his bratty little sister irritated him like a buzzing mosquito he couldn't swat. Worst of all, there was no television to watch. Their set had broken a year ago, and his father wouldn't get it fix. But now he was free and couldn't wait to be with his friends. He took the apartments steps down to the street two at a time, as his mother appeared at the doorway.

"Ibrahim, Ibrahim," his mother called, "tie your shoes, and please do not wander too far."

He crossed the street, paused on the sidewalk to fix his laces and closed his eyes. Sunshine hugged his shoulders. He was alive. His other senses woke up to his freedom. His nostrils flared with the aroma of fresh bread wafting from the corner bakery. His ears tuned to the everyday sounds of his neighborhood springing back to life—steel gates rattled as shops opened for business, a taxi parked at the curb honked for its passenger, and men and women chatted and bustled on their way to work.

His friends call to him to play, and he heard his mother holler again, louder this time.

"Ibrahim, please answer your mother."

He ignored her. Like many seven-year-old boys, he craved his mother's attention, but not now. He had waited long enough and his friends were watching. It was time to enjoy his freedom. He meant no offense; he loved her very much, and he knew both she and his father loved him. One reason he knew that was because he was their only son and they'd given him one of the most significant names in Turkish history. The great Ibrahim was the father of the world's great religions—not only Islam, but Judaism and Christianity as well, where he was called Abraham. Ibrahim's parents reminded him often that he, too, would grow to become a great man.

"Ibrahim!" His mother's voice grew tense.

He opened his eyes, and waved to his mother. She stood in the doorway of their small apartment complex across the street. Her long black hair, uncharacteristically uncovered by a scarf, fell around her shoulders. She looked pretty with her hair down.

"Ibrahim, please stay where I can see you."

His mother glanced nervously up and down the street. She had good reason to be concerned. Rumors had flooded the city that the militants were nearby. No one seemed to know for sure, but his father said the newspapers were filled with reports of ISIS taking over northern Iraq and Syria. He had listened intently to his parents discuss the group's goal of establishing an Islamic State in the ancient area of Mesopotamia, which included the region of eastern Turkey…their home. That morning at breakfast, his father murmured something about politics to his mother, but nevertheless appeared happy to return to his job at the bank.

The entire population of Ibrahim's city of Van had taken shelter for the last two days. Only a few people had dared to venture outside their homes. Everyone waited for violence, but the only sign of war had been a battalion of their own army rolling through the city, headed to the border between Turkey and Iraq to provide security. All was quiet. The rumors had turned out to be false.

"I'll be back for lunch, Mama," he shouted over the sound of a large diesel truck rumbling down the street.

She blew him a kiss. He wanted to blow one back, but not in front of his friends, who rolled a soccer ball to him. He skillfully footed the ball, bounced it onto one knee, then the other, and sent it back to his friend.

He couldn't help glancing at his mother to make sure she had seen his performance. She shook her head, and smiled. When he flashed her a grin and a thumbs up, she waved at him to go on and play.

He had taken three steps toward his friends when it struck.

Everyone froze in terror, turned to each other, and then scattered in every direction. One man dropped his grocery bags, spilling vegetables all over the sidewalk. Men and women screamed, but their cries were silenced by a horrific, thunderous roar, unlike anything Ibrahim had ever heard. Was it a bomb? Instinctively, his head snapped in the direction of the passing truck, expecting it to be obliterated, replaced by a huge crater in the middle of the street.

The truck was intact, but the terrible sound increased, louder and louder, deafening: roaring, grinding, exploding. The air was choked with thick dust and heavy with fear. Ibrahim could no longer focus his vision.

Instinctively, his attention snapped back to his apartment and his mother. Maybe the rumors were true, and the militants had just attacked with a rocket.

The cataclysmic roar intensified as the street heaved upwards and split in two. His nostrils burned with the rancid smell of natural gas. His world was shaking so violently it could be only one thing—

Earthquake!

Disoriented, Ibrahim saw his mother fall down the steps, and then he realized, he too was flat on the asphalt. Life reeled in slow motion. He crawled toward his mother. He could see her shaking, trying to pick herself up. He heard her scream, but he couldn't hear the words.

He glanced back at his friends in time to see a huge concrete slab teeter from a building and slam to the ground. They disappeared in a cloud of dust.

Ibrahim pushed himself up only to be knocked down again by the earth's seismic waves under his feet. Screeching steel overhead forced him to cover his head. The sign advertising cigarettes crashed onto the car parked beside him, smashing its windshield and piercing his skin with shards of glass. Waves of thick, swirling dust saturated the sky.

"Mama!" Ibrahim yelled, but he couldn't hear his own voice.

His throat burned with the acidic powder forcing him to gag and cough hard.

He willed himself to stand, but the street shuddered so violently that it became impossible. Dripping blood, he pushed himself to his hands and knees in time to watch with horror as the three-story apartment building next to his began to crumble and implode.

His mother's eyes were ablaze with terror as she forced herself to her feet and screamed at him. He strained to hear, but no words were audible. She kept her center of gravity low and her arms stretched out for balance, only to be knocked back to the pavement. She would not give up. She pawed at the ground, pulled herself up, tumbled, and regained her balance, forcing herself off her knees.

A large power pole slammed to the concrete, landing just feet from her and its transformer exploded into a shower of sparks. The severed natural gas line lit like an acetylene torch and roared to life, the heat scalding his face.

Paralyzed with fear, he cried to her, "Mama, Mama."

Determination filled his mother's eyes as she stood at the edge of the large fissure that ripped the road. She squared her frame to leap.

He screamed to her that their apartment complex was collapsing behind her—his sister was still inside. The front of the building split off and fell toward them.

His mother was in mid-air when the wall hit, slamming her to the ground and crushing her body. She landed only inches from him, but he could not move closer to her. Blood flowed from a split in her scalp and with a glimmer of hope, he saw her eyes were open.

"Mama!" He reached for her. "Mama, please." Her eyes went dark and absent.

He tried to pull himself to her, but it was impossible, he couldn't budge.

"Mama," he called, fighting to move, clawing the ground and stretching his body. Searing pain gripped his legs and he screamed in agony. His legs were trapped, clamped to the asphalt with unforgiving debris. Ignoring his pain, he lunged toward her. He forced his body forward, reaching for her, grasping, but he was only able to touch her long, beautiful hair.

"Mama."

He gasped for breath. The air was thick with dust and smoke and death.

His world dimmed. He knew no sound, no air, no pain… he knew nothing except his mother's hair clutched in his fingers.

"Mama."

CHAPTER 1

AN ACCIDENT
MIDNIGHT – THURSDAY

Blood dripped from the operating table onto the floor and Dr. Nicklaus Hart winced at the bloody mess in Trauma 2 at the Regional Medical Center of Memphis, the MED.

"He fell off the back of the speedboat," explained Dr. Ali Hassan, Nick's Trauma Fellow.

Nick cringed. The eighteen-year-old would never be the same. It was a miracle that he had survived.

"The rest of the boys were badly shaken up, but from what I understand, the driver panicked as the boat was swept by the current and threw it into reverse. I guess the propeller hit him like this…" Ali demonstrated with both arms and one leg pushed out in front of his body.

Nick adjusted his surgical cap as he stared at the mangled flesh that used to be arms and at the ripped open knee, exposing a shattered patella. He shook his head and sighed. "We better cover him with every antibiotic known to man. God only knows what is growing in that water." He wrinkled his nose at the mixture of blood and skanky water.

The anesthesiologist painted the boy's skin around the clavicle with sticky brown betadine and expertly slipped a large-bore subclavian line into the vein running under the collarbone to pour in much needed fluid, blood, and medication. The team had done a masterful job in resuscitating the young man who had arrived at the Emergency Department in full code with no pulse and minimal blood in his system.

"What in the world were they doing on the Mississippi at ten o'clock at night?" Nick asked and cursed the heavy mist that had fallen over Memphis, obscuring landmarks and making the air disagreeably damp and chilly. "How did they ever find him in the river?"

"They were waterskiing and just hanging out, I guess... drinking and smoking weed. Not a bad thing I suppose, because their lighters were handy to find this guy in the dark. One of them knew enough to throw tourniquets on his arms when they got him back in the boat."

The team of three anesthesiology Residents adjusted dials on the respirator, injected medications into the IV, and changed out one bag of blood for another. It was a blessing at the MED, a teaching hospital: there were plenty of hands for situations like this when Trauma 2 hummed with activity.

Two separate scrub teams set up sterile tables of surgical instruments, and several nurses performed their duties with precision—slipping a catheter into the boy's bladder, making sure he was positioned carefully on the table, fetching last-minute instruments and medications, and helping the Resident doctors get into their sterile gowns.

"You able to talk with his parents?" Nick asked looking at the mangled hands and arms. The left hand was barely recognizable with only the thumb remaining on the palm. Dead-looking mounds of muscle replaced a healthy forearm. The right side was even more unnerving with a near perfect, uninjured pulseless hand attached to the rest of the arm by shiny white tendons, stripped of their muscles. Shredded skin covered what was left of the elbow.

"They're all from Mississippi. And yes, they know it's bad. I talked with his step-mom. His dad was too upset to talk. The family should be here by the time we're done."

"Show me the x-rays and tell me your plan."

They walked to the large bank of lighted panels. Ali had already placed the most relevant films on the view box for his Attending.

"I was kind of surprised to see the spiral fracture of the right humerus." Ali pointed to the upper arm bone film. "I guess the propeller twisted the arm all the way up. The skin flap was pulled up to here." He indicated on his arm above the elbow. "I could put a finger into the fracture. The elbow is trashed, but I think we should try to keep as much length in his arm as we can, so I thought we could put external fixation on the humerus after we debride all that we need to. I want to save as much skin as we can for coverage."

Ali didn't have to mention amputation, that was a given. Nick saw shards of bone in what was once the forearm. There was nothing to repair.

As he studied the x-rays, nurse Jasmine turned on the stereo, and music from AC/DC filled the room. He frowned. "You mind finding something a little more soothing?" he hollered above the organized chaos. She rolled her eyes and changed the music, and he heard James Taylor singing "Fire and Rain."

He turned back to Ali. "And your plan of attack?"

"When I explored the wound in the ER, the patella was split. We'll do the amputations, wash the heck out of everything, put the ex-fix on the upper right arm, and place wound-vacs on everything. Of course, we'll be coming back to the OR every day for a while until it's all clean, and then we can fix the patella and humerus," Ali said.

Nick squeezed his Fellow's shoulder. "You did well, Ali." He couldn't help but notice the large scar that ran from the corner of Ali's mouth to his ear. Ali had told him it was from a tree branch, but when he wouldn't make eye contact, he figured there was more to the story. He shrugged it off. Probably none of his business anyways.

Jasmine interrupted the doctors and thrust a clipboard of papers to be signed in front of Ali. He smiled warmly at her and accepted his assignment gracefully. Jasmine frowned at Nick causing his eyes to move from her shapely figure, back to his Fellow.

Nick liked the man. With the stress and bedlam of the MED it was easy to be unkind, but he rarely saw Ali get rattled. Ali was only a few years younger than himself, and he often felt conflicted as to whether he should consider him an equal or a surgeon-in-training. He was becoming confident in Ali's ability to make good decisions and leaned toward the former, but it was his responsibility to remain the teacher.

Ali had completed his orthopedic residency in Seattle, at Harborview, Nick's alma mater. Ali interviewed at many medical centers for a trauma fellowship, but when he didn't secure a spot, one of his professors, who happened to be a close friend and colleague of Nick's, called and asked for a personal favor to pick him up as a Fellow for the MED. The professor told Nick that Ali was a bit older than most candidates because he had done a five-year general surgery residency before changing to orthopedics and that was possibly why other programs had overlooked him. It was unusual to have someone trained in both specialties, but Nick had a growing sense of gratefulness to have him as his Trauma Fellow for the year. Ali had been at the MED for two months and was adjusting well. He was competent, but not overly so, and he understood his limitations; this was something Nick appreciated.

Ali handed the clipboard back to Jasmine and smiled at Nick.

"Sounds like you saved this young man," he complimented Ali.

"Thanks, Dr. Hart, but it was really the EMTs and the folks in the ER who did that. I just hate seeing what that propeller did to this kid. It's going to be difficult for him to wipe his own nose." Ali shook his head.

"Hey, Turk, you mind helping out here?" One of the Residents washing the mangled arms with betadine called to Ali.

Ali looked at Nick inquisitively, waiting to be excused from his mentor. Nick thought the other Residents called him Turk because he was originally from Turkey, but wondered if the nickname bugged him. He looked into Ali's dark eyes for a clue. If it did, it didn't register in his face. Ali was consistently polite and friendly to the entire staff.

He speculated that the other reason Ali might have been turned down for a fellowship at the other medical centers was because of his religion. But being a Muslim in a predominantly Christian area like Memphis did not seem difficult for Ali.

Nick nodded toward the OR table. "I need to go scrub," he said to Ali. "Good job, man!"

As he exited Trauma 2, he glanced at the clock on the wall. Midnight.

James Taylor was still belting out about fire and rain and lonely times. It seemed so fitting.

It's gonna be a long night.

* * *

Beep, beep, beep. That sound. What is it? Beep, beep, beep. Where am I? Beep, beep, beep. Nick took a swipe in the direction of the annoyance and sent the contents of the nightstand crashing to the floor. The breaking of glass was enough to arouse his consciousness from a fretful slumber.

He peered over the bed and the nightlight revealed a broken lamp. He rolled back on the small twin bed, rubbed his head, and wondered what time it was. Beep, beep, beep, his pager rang out again.

His head cleared enough to remember where he was. Crap. Oh, yeah, the call room.

The beeping wouldn't stop on its own and he reached over the side of the bed and searched for the scourge of his life—the umbilical cord to the Residents and the ER. He pushed the button by feel and the message lit up. It was the ER and it was 4:45 in the morning, only two hours after they had finished with the boy from the speedboat accident.

Two hours of restless sleep. The worst part was he had a packed day of patients in the clinic ahead of him. He pushed on his chest and sighed, remembering his nightmare, one that he often had. He was in the operating room; the case was going horribly wrong and when he looked down, he discovered he had forgotten to put on his surgical gloves. The medical staff would crucify him.

Nick startled when the house phone buzzed, indicating that it had been knocked off its receiver and onto the floor. He fished for the phone and dialed the ER.

"Emergency Department," an unfamiliar voice on the other end declared.

"Hart," was all he could croak out. He thought it strange that Conner, the informal, always chipper, front-desk clerk, hadn't answered the call.

"Hold one," the voice said.

Nick waited until the phone clicked. "Dr. Hart. Sorry to wake you. This is Ali. I'm afraid there has been a most unfortunate incident in the Emergency Department. A meth-head came in and shot up the place. Connor, the front desk worker, and Riley, one of the triage nurses, have been killed. Security was able to stop the man before he got any further."

"What? Seriously? Riley...and Connor?" He asked trying to clear the fog in his head. He sat up on the side of the bed and rubbed his face. He hated the ER, but his co-workers made it more tolerable. Riley was one of his favorites. She always worked nights, always quick with a smile, and always kind, even to the worst of humanity that came through the doors after midnight. His friends in the Emergency Department were the closest thing to family that he had in Memphis.

"I'm sorry, Dr. Hart, to break the news to you."

"What a screwed-up world," he said, glancing at his bloodied scrubs on the floor. "I'll head down."

"You should wait. The ER is on lock down and it's a real zoo down here. Besides, the shooter was shot multiple times by security and he is still alive. We are on our way to the OR with him."

His heart sank. What a perfect way to spend the rest of the night. Treat a guy that is most likely wacked out on meth, HIV positive, and has absolutely no resources to pay his bills. The jerk would probably sue him or the hospital for whatever reason and walk away with a few million dollars in his pocket.

Nick thumped his chest trying to beat the sarcasm from his heart. "What's he have?" he asked.

"Gunshot wounds to the left shoulder and left arm, and one through and through to the leg that just needs to be washed out. The bullet to the arm shattered his humerus. We'll irrigate and debride the wounds and put an ex-fix on the arm to stabilize it temporarily," Ali said and added, "We've got this, Dr. Hart. I only wanted to give you a heads up."

Nick thought for a moment. He was critical of the Attendings that didn't get their butts out of bed to help the Residents, but he was exhausted and laid his head back on his pillow. "All right, but call me if you need me," he said. "Or let him die for all I care."

CHAPTER 2

ATTACK

FRIDAY

Nick walked into the clinic wearing his white coat over his scrubs, but when he caught his reflection in the window, he saw that nothing could camouflage the dark circles under his eyes and his pale, unshaven face. He headed straight for the coffee machine. The older he got, the more his body ached like the flu after a night of call.

He thought he'd fallen back to sleep after the early morning page and conversation with Ali, but his head didn't feel like it. He woke up wondering how the case had gone. He intended to walk through the ER, but after hitting the snooze on his phone alarm a few extra times, he didn't have time before his morning clinic started. He would go check on the crew during his lunch hour. The ER personnel were well acquainted with tragedy, but this was different. It was unbelievable that Connor and Riley were dead. Guilt hit him that he knew little about their personal lives. He thought they were both unmarried, but wasn't sure.

He stirred three packets of sugar into his coffee and took a sip.

"Dr. Hart."

He turned to see Antonio Scott standing behind him, wearing a crisply pressed white coat over an expensive looking blue shirt and gold tie. Antonio was a hand surgeon and, like many he knew, was fastidious and wound tight to the point of being prissy.

"Hey, Antonio," Nick said trying to sound chipper. Because Scott was a colleague, he had tried considering him a friend, but ended up holding him at arm's length. Nick had witnessed the man almost getting into a fist fight with another surgeon who dared park in his parking spot. But Scott was the top moneymaker for the group and the newly elected Chief of Staff for the MED. Most likely, the money and the promotion went hand in hand.

"You get your rest?" Antonio said sharply.

"Uh…" Nick looked at the man, whose face was already turning crimson, highlighting his ginger hair. He was of Irish descent and stood a full foot shorter than Nick. His sharp attire couldn't hide his barrel stature. "Call…you know," Nick shrugged, sensing a brewing storm and sipped more coffee.

"Well, I sure in the hell didn't. You hear about your patient?"

Which patient? Nick's mind searched his files. The kid from the boating accident last night or one of the twenty or so patients he currently had in the hospital? His brow furled trying to understand the man's cryptic anger.

"I've been up since six a.m. dealing with your crap. You know about the shooting early this morning in the Emergency Department?"

Nick was not surprised that they had called the Chief of Staff about the incident. "Yes, I heard. What a…"

"Then the OR called me and told me that your patient was dead. I asked to speak to you, but they said you weren't there… that you were sleeping."

"The meth-head? I thought the guys…"

"That meth-head happens to be the mayor's son," Scott cut him off again. "I just got off the phone with their attorney. Crap, Hart, why weren't you in there?"

Nick's mind raced. He thought of all sorts of things to say to his accuser. Scott was one of the worst Resident abusers and rarely left his multi-million-dollar home in the middle of the night to get in his three-hundred-thousand-dollar Bentley to come help the team. The Residents told Nick that the first thing Scott would ask about a patient was their insurance status. Scott probably thought call was easy, but only because the Residents stopped calling him if the injured was uninsured.

Nick's cell phone rang, and he pulled it out of his pocket. He saw it was Ali. He had already missed three calls from him. He must have knocked the phone to silent or missed them as he tried reviving himself in the shower.

"Ali?" He answered the phone.

"Dr. Hart, thank goodness. I have been trying to reach you. I'm afraid I have bad news about the shooter from this morning. We got him to surgery and when the anesthesiologist induced him, he went into full code. I guess he had so much meth on board that the anesthesia made his pressure drop out and they couldn't ever get him back. I wanted you to know before anyone else told you the news," Ali said.

Nick looked at Scott whose face was nearly turning purple. He wasn't sure why the man seemed to dislike him so much. He suspected it was jealousy, especially after the attention that he had received after his service in Guatemala. Scott was one of those people that thrived in the spotlight and wanted it all for himself.

"I'll call you back Ali, thanks."

"The mayor's attorney is already accusing us of letting his kid die for shooting up the ER."

"And?" he asked sarcastically.

"Hart, you know how these things work," Scott said flashing his anger. "Someone is going to have to take the bullet, and it's not going to be me."

"That's an appropriate metaphor," he said. He was in no mood to take any grief from the man.

"These are the kinds of stupid antics with which you seem to like to acquaint yourself." Scott raised his voice and stepped closer to Nick who didn't budge. "They're also the sort of thing that can bring a stain on your reputation, let alone mine."

"I'm sure you are very concerned about that," he challenged.

"Look, Hart...I know who you are. I am the head elder of my church and we deal with your kind all the time."

"My kind?" Their voices were echoing down the hallway.

The man shot daggers from his eyes. "I've heard about your philandering...your...sin." His anger made him stumble over his words. "And you call yourself a Christian?" His spittle hit his scrub top.

One of the clinic nurses stood in the doorway and cleared her throat. She put her hands on her hips, gave them both a disgusted look, and pulled the door to the breakroom shut.

"I'm suspending your hospital privileges for the day. You need to go home." Scott said.

"You can't do that."

"You bet your ass I can. You want to leave on your own, or shall I call security?"

"I have full day of clinic."

"We have that covered," Scott said. "You have today and tomorrow to get yourself together. You're back on the call rotation on Sunday." He turned on his heels and left the room.

* * *

Nick slept hard and woke with a stiff neck and raw attitude after being sent home by the Chief of Staff. He rarely had an opportunity to sleep during the day, so he woke up feeling drugged. He was angry at Scott for judging him and acting like a pious buffoon. He knew many of Antonio's secrets as well. He was not going to stand by and let the guy throw him or Ali under the bus. He had done nothing wrong; the Residents perform surgeries all the time under the watchful eye of the Fellow or fifth-year Resident, with or without the Attending's supervision. It is part of the training to help grow their confidence to be out on their own. He did regret joking with Ali about letting the patient die. Unfortunate words. But he hoped that Ali understood that he was joking.

Nick pulled up to the front of the Madison Hotel in downtown Memphis. If he was forced to have the night off, he was going to make the most of it. After a long, hot shower, he had donned his pressed white shirt, blue jeans, favorite pair of cowboy boots, and a layer of Axe cologne. He didn't bother to shave.

"Be careful with her," he said when he handed the keys to the young valet, who licked his lips at his shiny new, aqua-blue Porsche 911 Carrera.

"Yes, sir," the boy said and enthusiastically jumped behind the wheel.

"You do have your driver's license, right?"

The boy gave him a sideways glance and sped off.

He watched his car turn a corner. The car was extravagant, but it was the one perk he enjoyed. Even the short drives from his apartment to the hospital seemed more joyful. He could have even walked from his apartment to the Madison, but with the gun and knife club in full swing after sunset, it was just another good reason to enjoy his expensive toy.

Nick strolled through the posh lobby and into the elevator. He was headed up to the Twilight Sky Bar on the roof of the Madison.

He stepped off the elevator and into the festive night air. The music and social scene were already hopping as he made his way to the bar. "Tito's and tonic." He nodded to the bartender and leaned on one arm against the stainless-steel bar top, surveying the crowd. It was too early for people to be dancing, but the lubrication was well underway.

Nick pushed back a wave of his sandy-blond hair, tossed by a breeze off the Mississippi. Two women in tight-fitting miniskirts put some extra swing into their steps as they passed him and smiled. The beauties, balancing on high heels and showing off their assets, left a trace of sweet perfume.

The taller of the pair slowed, raised her hands, wiggled her hips and sang, "It's all about the bass, about the bass..."

Her friend joined in, flashing Nick a mischievous smile and finishing the song, "...no treble." The pair giggled and continued trolling the bar.

He looked back at the bartender who was smiling at him.

* * *

Nick lost track of how many Tito's Sonics he drank—enough to numb his run-in with Scott and too many to drive himself home. The girls invited him to continue the party at their place and were annoying the Uber driver with their boisterous laughter after Nick told them a joke.

He sat sandwiched between the pair in the back seat when his phone rang.

He pulled it from his front pocket and looked at the caller

ID…it was Maggie. The phone was already on its third ring. He wanted to talk with her, more than anything. But he would sound stupid drunk…and there were the girls.

Fourth ring.

God, how I miss her.

Fifth ring.

I just can't. Nick let her call go to voice mail and hated himself for it.

"Maggie?" one of the girls said, looking at his phone. She must have read the conflict in his body language.

He nodded and put the phone back in his pocket.

"If I find you sneaking around on me I'm gonna whoop your butt," she said highlighting her threat with a wagging finger. She broke out in a boisterous laugh that jiggled her large breasts.

AUTHOR'S NOTE

REDEMPTION

I have written *Maya Hope* out of obedience and a spirit of prophecy. As every author will tell you, truth is mixed with fiction. This is a novel; however, it is important to know that the historical, geographic, and political issues are based on truth. Likewise, the stories of the children of Central America are based on truth. Their names have been changed, but I want you to meet the real Isabella, and I have included some photos on the next page.

In all my travels around the world, including North Korea, I know our God as a God of restoration and redemption—a God of goodness and loving kindness.

Please join with me in prayer for those peoples around the world that do not receive adequate medical care, including those in our own country. And pray for the beautiful countries of North and South Korea, that they will be unified in the name of Jesus.

I pray for you, dear reader, that you find restoration for your own life. Many blessings to you!

Timothy

For more information about the author
visit: www.AgapeOrthopaedics.com

MINISTRIES

There are many wonderful organizations throughout the world helping the poor, the broken and the destitute. They can use your help in reaching the world. Here are some of my favorites that I have personal experience with:

Mercy Ships
    https://www.mercyships.org

Hope Force International
    http://hopeforce.org

YWAM Ships
    https://ywamships.net

SIGN Fracture Care International
    https://signfracturecare.org

Samaritan's Purse
    https://www.samaritanspurse.org

Wounded Warrior Project
    https://www.woundedwarriorproject.org

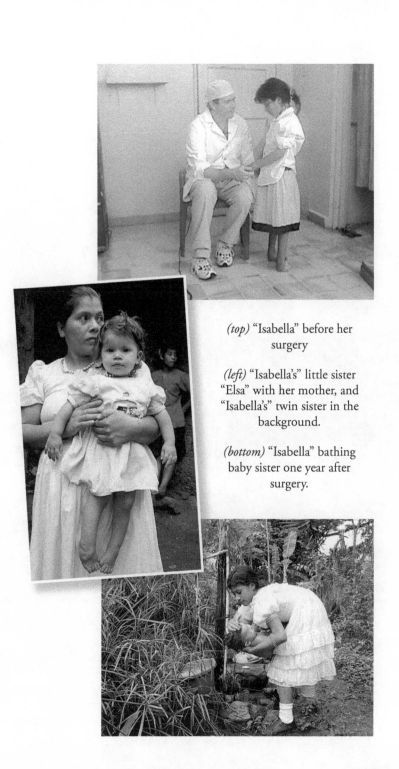

(top) "Isabella" before her surgery

(left) "Isabella's" little sister "Elsa" with her mother, and "Isabella's" twin sister in the background.

(bottom) "Isabella" bathing baby sister one year after surgery.

CPSIA information can be obtained
at www.ICGtesting.com
Printed in the USA
LVHW111726150720
660781LV00004B/677

9 781947 545007